PENGUIN METRO READS

WHEN I AM WITH YOU

Durjoy Datta was born in New Delhi and completed a degree in engineering and business management before embarking on a writing career. His first book, *Of Course I Love You . . .*, was published when he was twenty-one years old and was an instant bestseller. His successive novels—*Till the Last Breath, Hold My Hand, When Only Love Remains, World's Best Boyfriend, The Girl of My Dreams, The Boy Who Loved, The Boy with a Broken Heart* and *The Perfect Us*—have also found prominence on various bestseller lists, making him one of the highest-selling authors in India. Durjoy also has to his credit eleven television shows, for which he has written over 1000 episodes. For more updates, you can follow him on Instagram (www.instagram.com/durjoydatta).

ALSO BY THE SAME AUTHOR

When I Am with You

BESTSELLING AUTHOR

DURJOY DATTA

Penguin
metro reads

An imprint of Penguin Random House

PENGUIN METRO READS

USA | Canada | UK | Ireland | Australia
New Zealand | India | South Africa | China | Singapore

Penguin Metro Reads is part of the Penguin Random House group of companies
whose addresses can be found at global.penguinrandomhouse.com

Published by Penguin Random House India Pvt. Ltd
4th Floor, Capital Tower 1, MG Road,
Gurugram 122 002, Haryana, India

Penguin
Random House
India

First published in Penguin Metro Reads by Penguin Random House India 2022

Copyright © Durjoy Datta 2022

10 9 8 7 6 5 4 3

This is a work of fiction. Names, characters, places and incidents are either the
product of the author's imagination or are used fictitiously, and any resemblance
to any actual person, living or dead, events or locales is entirely coincidental.

ISBN 9780143448358

Typeset in Bembo STD by Manipal Digital Systems, Manipal
Printed at Thomson Press India Ltd, New Delhi

www.penguin.co.in

To the two cute buttons in my life

1.

Kamlesh Ahuja

Kamlesh Ahuja of No. 1 Property Dwarka Wale watches impatiently as Dhiren Das stands on the balcony of the first floor apartment inspecting the untended, weed-infested garden on the ground floor.

'Kamlesh ji, 10 per cent extra. I will transfer the deposit right now. Give me the ground floor too.'

Kamlesh shakes his head. 'Dhiren ji, Sector 23 area is mixed-use. See the *kothi* [bungalow] in front of us; gym on the ground floor, a family lives on the first. It will be the same here. There might be a boutique, a gym, maybe a bank. I am still talking to people,' informs Kamlesh. 'So unless you can rent it for three years . . .'

'Sir ji, *kal ka nahi pata* [we don't know about tomorrow] and you're talking about a year.' After a pause, he adds, 'Kamlesh ji, your one-year rent will be paid in advance.'

Only criminals pay a year's rent in advance, and it's his job to look at tenants with humiliating suspicion, so Kamlesh asks, 'What do you do, Dhiren ji?'

Dhiren's tall, over 5'10" by Kamlesh's estimation, clean-cut, mid-twenties, engineer-type. But he still could be a fraud. The biggest frauds in the world wear business suits and the robes of god.

'I'm in cryptocurrency.'

'What currency?'

'Sir ji, it's a blockchain-based decentralized currency system.'

'Software?'

'*Wahi samajh lo* [You can think of it like that].'

'*To yeh bolo naa* [Say that then],' says Kamlesh irritably. 'Dhiren ji, did you get your Aadhaar card?'

Dhiren takes it out of his back pocket and hands it to Kamlesh. 'It's new,' notes Kamlesh, turning it around and adding with a laugh, '*Asli hai naa* [It's real, right]?'

'I changed my name, didn't like what my parents gave me. Do you like your name, Kamlesh ji? Or would you rather be Amitabh? Or Rajesh?'

Kamlesh scowls. 'Your *pita ji* [father] must have given it a lot of thought before naming you.'

'My father never thinks of me,' says Dhiren. 'Anyway, you said the landlord had some questions for me? *Poochhiye* [Ask away].'

'Do you eat non-veg? Chicken? Mutton? Pork?'

'I know what non-veg means, Kamlesh ji. How frequently does the landlord drop in to check?'

'He—'

'Is only eating banned or even cooking? What if I cook biryani for my friends but I don't eat it myself?'

'Dhiren ji, these are the rules. They are strict about non-veg and alcohol.'

'And Muslims, you told me.'

'And Muslims. Their house, their rules,' asserts Kamlesh irately.

'Kamlesh ji, you should try my biryani. Keep the leg pieces aside and eat the rice. Trust me, you will give me your entire *jaidad* [inheritance]. And Kamlesh ji, *waise bhi* [you know] they won't come all the way from Pitampura to check what's in my kadai.'

'They live in South Delhi, not Pitampura,' corrects Kamlesh immediately.

'*Kyun jhooth bol rahe ho* [Why are you lying]? A five-storey house, J.D. Market, right next to the metro,' corrects Dhiren. 'It's on the Internet, Kamlesh ji. Everything is on the Internet these days. The owner's son has put this house up on Magicbricks, even shared his number to contact him directly.'

Kamlesh always suspected the owner's elder son to be a know-it-all *gaandu* [asshole]. He composes himself. 'Dhiren ji, if you have to eat chicken–mutton, then I will have to show you other properties.'

Dhiren smiles slyly. 'Kamlesh ji, on the days when you're with your friends, with a few pegs of Royal Stag sloshing in your stomach, and everyone's singing Rafi songs, tell me, on those days, are you a vegetarian? Or are chicken lollipops allowed?'

Kamlesh's face burns as if he has been slapped. He touches both ears and whispers God's name. 'I'm pure veg. My wife's a Jain so I don't even eat pyaaz [onions] and lassan [garlic] on Tuesdays and Saturdays.'

Kamlesh finds a rising admiration in Dhiren's eyes, which are large, black and surprisingly expressive for a guy.

'You're unlike the others, Kamlesh ji,' says Dhiren, approvingly. 'Sharma ji from Best Properties told me I can eat whatever as long as no one gets to know, but you have integrity. I was joking about the biryani. I'm a vegan.'

'You're a what?'

'Vegan, the purest of the pure.'

'There's nothing like that.'

'Kamlesh ji, *main batata hoon* [I will tell you]. *Dekho* [See], the worst humans are the Chinese who eat everything. Who will look at anything moving and eat it. Snakes, bats, even earthworms.'

Kamlesh grimaces. 'I have heard some people from the North-east also eat all of that.'

'Slightly better are the ones who eat beef, pork, chicken or fish. They will all go to *narak* [hell] and burn for a thousand years,' declares Dhiren.

Kamlesh touches his ears and mumbles a soft apology for the innocent cows killed for meat.

Dhiren continues. 'Over them are people like you. You call yourself pure vegetarians, but Kamlesh ji, no offence, there's nothing pure about you people.'

Kamlesh straightens up. He's a Brahmin! Generations after generations haven't touched their own shit. How dare he call him impure?

Dhiren says, 'And over the pure vegetarians, the purest of them all is us. The vegans.'

'What do you people eat?'

'We don't eat dairy. Or eggs. Or paneer. Anything that comes from milk, we don't even touch it. Ghee is poison. So are most sweets.'

This is taking religion too far, Kamlesh thinks. *Everyone must be allowed to interpret religion in their own way. Why would these vegan people be purer just because they don't eat paneer and drink milk? Even Lord Krishna had butter. This hierarchy didn't make sense. Was he really inferior? He would have to ask Pandit ji. But Pandit ji himself serves sweets made of milk.*

'No honey. Or butter. What's left to eat then?' Kamlesh asks.

Dhiren makes a face as if saying those words are polluting his pureness. 'You tell me, how would we feel if our wives were tied up, forced to produce babies, and then had their breasts milked? That's exactly what we do to cows for their milk.' Dhiren takes a deep breath and continues. 'So what does the landlord do? I'm guessing he's vegetarian, but what else?'

'Import–export mainly, Dhiren ji. They have a lot of businesses.'

'Do they steal from this country? Do they pay their taxes? I want to live in an honest man's house. I can tolerate living in an impure vegetarian's house, but a thief's house? I'll tell you what, send me their income tax returns for the last three years. I will check.'

'Dhiren ji, I can't ask—'

'I don't want to pollute myself,' insists Dhiren. 'And Kamlesh ji, neither should you pollute yourself any more than you already have by participating in the torture of cows.'

When he says this, Kamlesh finally sees a crack. Kamlesh finally recognizes what's happening here. Property dealing is about reading people, but today he realizes he has walked straight into a trap—Dhiren's playing him. He wants Dhiren to leave, but he remembers the listing on Magicbricks from the owner's gaandu son.

Kamlesh is sure Dhiren will eat butter chicken, guzzle down barrels of Old Monk, have sex with girlfriends, play loud music and masturbate all over the walls.

'*Beta, bade haraami ho* [Son, you are an asshole].'

'Kamlesh ji—'

'*Haan, Dhiren ji, aapke saamne sab chor hai. Aapse pure to koi nahi hai* [all of us are thieves in front of you. No one is more pure than you],' says Kamlesh, his patience breaking. 'I will need the deposit today, in cash. Girls are not allowed here.'

2.

Kamlesh Ahuja

'*Beti* [daughter], we will paint the entire floor before giving it to you. It will be as good as new,' claims Kamlesh.

Aishwarya Mohan had called him at eight that morning to view the rental property for the fourth time in four days. A finicky customer is a good customer; it shows intent and will. Which is something Kamlesh hadn't expected of Aishwarya when she had come for the first viewing.

She is puny, a few inches over five feet, and dressed like she is about to meet the boy her parents have selected for her. Her words are little melodious squeals, strung together in harmony; it's like she's singing them. Her eyes are large, as if she's constantly surprised. Every time he has met her, she's been courteous; so soft-spoken, her voice was barely audible. She's dusky, the colour of his afternoon tea when just the right amount of milk is in it. Today, she's wearing what seems like the same pair of jeans and kurti she wore the last time. Kamlesh has learnt to never like prospective clients, but he has a good feeling about her.

Aishwarya walks around the property, pulling open the creaky doors, making mental notes about electric boards, tapping on the cracked plaster.

'*Agar aap final kar rahe ho aaj* [If you are finalizing today], you should have got your father along. We would have been introduced as well,' says Kamlesh.

'What's this smell?'

'Don't worry about it. Close a house for three days and pigeons will trickle in and shit all over the place. We will clean this up.'

'*Main pagal thodi hoon* [I'm not mad]. It's not the pigeons. It's the walls, the seepage. The entire house smells.'

'Beti, the house . . .'

Aishwarya ties a handkerchief around her nose and mouth. 'The *malik* [owner] should have taken care of it. Did you get a plumber to check the drainage pipes or not?'

Kamlesh wonders if Aishwarya is having a bad day. That time of the month?

'Beti, we will fix everything. It will hardly take a couple of days.'

'The children of my class can build better houses, Uncle.'

'Beti, let me order some tea and let's—'

Aishwarya rolls her eyes and interrupts, 'How soon can you send me the electricity and gas bills? Just send me pictures over WhatsApp.'

'Trust me, beti, it's all paid in full.'

'Uncle, why would I trust you? I saw your ad in a newspaper, I don't know you. If it's all paid, just show me the papers. Why are we talking about this? *Paper dikhao* and we will move on.'

'*Arre*? *Kaisi baat kar rahi ho* [What are you saying]? Where are we running away, madam? I'm in the business for twenty years. People ask, where do you get the best golgappas in Dwarka? It's the one outside No. 1 Property Dwarka Wale's shop. And you're talking to me like this.'

'Then you know that electricity, gas and tax papers are important, hai naa? Send me the documents, Uncle.'

Kamlesh has heard this tone before. It's the way his daughter's friends call him Uncle—in a derisive, mocking tone. As if they won't ever get old and become aunties.

'I don't have a lot of time, Uncle, I have to go to work also. Hai naa documents [You have the documents]?'

How dare she talk to him like that, this foetus of a girl? One slap and she would be splat against the wall. If this was his village, Patparganj, he would have taught her a lesson she would never forget.

'This is how business happens here. You're new to this field. You will learn.'

'Achcha? Is this how business happens? Then I will give you the deposit also a month later. *Main kaha bhaagi jaa rahi hoon* [Where am I running off to]?'

Kamlesh bristles. 'Madam, now you're talking as though we are frauds. We won't run away for two or four paise. We do everything here professionally. We wouldn't be showing you this property four times otherwise. That's why I asked if your father wanted to see it. Property is a man's—'

'Papa loves his retirement. He says if people still have to work after they're fifty, they have failed.'

Kamlesh is fifty-two.

'Madam, you will have to tell me quickly if you want this property. We don't have time to come here every day. The first floor is already rented and that boy took just one viewing . . .'

The girl now meets his eyes. 'Who did you rent it out to?'

'It's a young *ladka* [boy], does things with computers, nice boy, quiet, doesn't talk much, came here with his parents to look at the floor. He's a vegetarian, *dharmic* [religious], homely boy.'

Aishwarya raises her hand. 'Okay, Uncle, enough. I'm not getting married to him. Does he know that there will be a nursery below?'

'Madam, you didn't confirm, so I didn't tell him. You're opening a playschool, what's the big deal? *Bataiye ji* [Tell me], do you want it or not?'

'Uncle, not at the price you're offering. I will have to get drainage and electricity work done from my pocket. I will text you my price. You can reply to it with documents if you agree. Also, send me the Aadhaar card of the person living on the first floor.'

'As I told you, *achcha ladka hai* [he's a good boy], his name is Dhiren Das.'

'Why don't we let the police decide if he's an achcha ladka or not? I can't have someone random living right upstairs from the kids,' Aishwarya points to the first-floor balcony. '*Theek hai*, I will text you, Uncle.'

Before Kamlesh can say anything, Aishwarya is already on her way out.

'*Randi saali* [Whore],' Kamlesh mutters under his breath.

He watches as she waves down a rickshaw and boards without negotiating. A few minutes later, the property dealer receives a

WhatsApp message. The price the girl sends is on the lower side but acceptable.

3.

Aishwarya Mohan

Aishwarya thinks of herself as a nice person, even though her friends call her a people-pleaser. She doesn't see a problem with being nice. Why not be nice when you can? She can be assertive and stern when she has to, and she's effective at that. She's a teacher who has successfully disciplined hundreds of little kids, the hardest humans to control. But she's never rude. Except with her parents and her brother. Now she's added another name to the list—Kamlesh.

Her head bursts, the scar on her hand that runs from her elbow to her palm heats up. All because she was rude to him. The conversation with him filled her with negative energy.

But she knows it was necessary for her to be rude in order to bring Kamlesh down to the price she was ready to pay. For her dream, she would do anything. Even if it meant not being the nicest, most agreeable person in the room.

Her phone beeps, breaking her train of thought. It's a document from Kamlesh: Dhiren Das's Aadhaar card. For an Aadhaar card picture, it's surprisingly sharp. And then she realizes it's not the picture that's sharp. The guy's features are screaming for attention. Even in the pixelated fuzziness, the sharpness of his jaw, the pointedness of his nose and the thick hair parted on the side are conspicuous. His face is that of an athlete, but it's not weather-beaten, so maybe someone who's into indoor sports: squash, boxing, basketball? He's good-looking in the way boys are when they are on the cusp of turning into men. She checks the date of birth and calculates: twenty-seven years. Aishwarya types the name 'Dhiren Das' into her Internet browser. It's an odd name, so there aren't many hits. But none of them look like *him*. She makes a mental note about actually following through with the police verification.

The rickshaw stops two blocks past the traffic signal. Aishwarya pays the driver and gets into the back seat of a parked car. She scoots next to the two babies who are strapped on to their car seats. Just looking at them soothes her.

'How—'

Aishwarya cuts the two girls in the front seats. 'Shut up, and let me calm down a little.'

She turns to Vihaan and Amritanshu, both two-year-olds, who start to wiggle in their seats and reach out for Aishwarya's face as if it's made of candy.

'Aw, look at both of you, cutu buttons. You missed Maasi, didn't you? Didn't you? *My pyaara shonas, meri pyaari jaan, mera sab kuchh, mere chhote chhote se cutu puppies* [My love, my life, my all, my cute little puppies]. You want to come to Maasi? Of course you do, because Maasi is the best, and you love Maasi. Come, come,' says Aishwarya in a sweet, baby voice, and unsnaps them from their car seats. 'Some day I'm going to pour chocolate on you and eat you like little marshmallows.'

Both boys are now giggling as they sit on Aishwarya's lap while she pretend-nibbles their hands. The mothers on the front seats pretend they aren't happy with Aishwarya's abundant love for their children.

'You're spoiling Vihaan,' complains Vinny Shahi. Vinny had conceived Vihaan on the very night of her wedding. She and her new husband, Varun, were drunk, had sex, found each other naked when they woke up, but had no memory of having had sex.

'Amritanshu will now keep screaming, "Where's Maasi, where's Maasi" all night,' adds Smriti Gupta. Smriti had planned

Amritanshu with military precision. She took folic acid and vitamins for three months and then put her husband, Amit, on a strict schedule of routine sex.

Aishwarya continues nuzzling into their chubby neck rolls. 'Did you have a goodu-goodu day? Of course you did. Is your tummy full now? What did you eat? Tell me everything!'

Vinny turns to Smriti, 'Had I gone, I would have put that Kamlesh in his place and forced him to agree to my price.'

'Vinny, it's not about getting our price, it's about getting what's fair given the area and the property he's offering,' says Smriti.

Aishwarya looks at both of them. 'Sorry, but I wanted to crack it on my own. The nursery is my thing. I will do this my way.'

Smriti can't believe Aishwarya. After all, she's a CA with her own practice in Janakpuri with her husband Amit—Gupta CAs. She says, 'What's the point of having Baniya friends when you can't exploit our centuries-old intra-caste fucking that's led to our twisted genes and expertise in numbers?'

Vinny, whose sari showroom, the one she inherited from her husband's side, is a four-storey landmark building that has forty-four running cases on it at the Tis Hazari court. She knows exactly how to survive in the shark tank of doing business in Delhi. Both Varun and Vinny carry hockey sticks in the boot of their cars. Vinny says, '*Behen* [Sister], you have to be a little haraami if you want to run a business or you will be chewed raw.'

Aishwarya shows them the text from Kamlesh with the offer price. It immediately shuts them both up. The price is lower than what they had in mind.

There is silence in the car.

The dreams we see as young people are seldom the ones we chase after as we grow older. But Aishwarya, she has never wavered. Everything she has done in life has been to get closer to this moment.

Vinny breaks the silence. 'You're resigning today, then?'

Aishwarya nods. After today, there's no looking back.

'Don't forget to settle your PF with them. Send me the forms and I will fill them up for you,' advises Smriti.

'I will drop you to your school. Mondays are slow at the shop,' adds Vinny in a soft voice.

'Mondays are busy,' says Smriti, 'but nothing Amit can't handle.'

'Thank you, guys,' says Aishwarya. 'It was showing surge pricing, you know. 600 bucks for thirteen kilometres, it's daylight robbery.'

Both Smriti and Vinny roll their eyes because they know Aishwarya rarely uses the cab-hailing app on her phone. She would have changed two metros, three buses and walked a few kilometres to save a hundred rupees. This why Vinny and Smriti know the money they have loaned her for her nursery is safe. She's magical with kids and thrifty with money—there's no way she's going to fail.

*

In the head of the nursery's room at Bal Bharat Public School, Paschim Vihar, Amarjeet Kaur, Aishwarya's mentor of eight years, asks her with downcast eyes and a voice tinged with sadness, 'Are you finally leaving us then?'

'Sorry, ma'am,' Aishwarya says in a small voice.

'You're breaking the hearts of a lot of young boys. Many of your students want to marry you. Now, what will I say to them?'

'Being a four-year-old is never easy, ma'am. I will come to visit you from time to time.'

'Aishwarya beta, I wouldn't have to wait if only you married my son. He has a great future ahead of him and he doesn't have a single vice.'

'Bunty is six years younger than me and still in college. He used to call me Aunty until last year.'

'Always marry a younger man, Aishwarya. They will always respect you and even be a little scared of you.'

'I'm not getting married any time soon, ma'am, you know that.'

Amarjeet frowns. 'You're still going to raise a child alone?'

'Most women raise their children alone.'

Amarjeet doesn't argue because it's as true as death, but that doesn't mean she agrees with Aishwarya. 'Aishwarya, husband and wife come together to give birth to a child. I might have raised my son alone, but my husband is the father. That's how it's always been.'

'Ma'am, you're encouraging me to borrow money, chase this dream of opening Cute Buttons, but you're saying I can't get pregnant without having a boy in my life?'

'You can't tell a child their father was a laboratory. It's just not right, beta. It's not how things are done. You have to get married.'

'Would you put all your money in a scheme where you could lose all of your money, emotions and love? Ma'am, getting married looks to me like an expensive fiscal and emotional gamble.'

'Marriage is not a scheme or a gamble, it's a custom, beta. And shouldn't you at least wait till your business is stable? There is a loan you have taken from friends, a new business, and you want to add a baby without a father to that?' asks Amarjeet worriedly.

'That would mean starting my business with hypocrisy.'

'So, in the middle of starting a business, you will get pregnant with some man who won't even be in the child's life.'

'That's what Cute Buttons is about, ma'am. To give parents, mostly women, the freedom to keep doing whatever they want to during motherhood and after. If I hesitate, put this off till another time, then what message am I sending? I should be able to carry a child, deliver it and raise it without thinking what would happen to my career,' declares Aishwarya, her words filling her with renewed passion and belief in her idea.

'People lie when they say there's no age to start a business,' concedes Amarjeet.

'You have to be young?'

'To be stupid, you have to be young. And you're both.'

4.

Dhiren Das

Dhiren Das sits at the Starbucks across the road from the psychologist's office in Nehru Place. Dhiren stalks the therapist's Instagram profile from his own private Instagram account, which has 248 posts, zero followers, 345 following.

His own Instagram account is barren. No one has found this account. He only follows handles that post pictures of food—the only things worth following on Instagram.

Dhiren knows what the founders of the app intended to do with it. Instagram first burst on to the scene when phone cameras weren't as competent as they are today. The app sought to hide the imperfections by adding filters: by making our breakfasts, the autumn sky, the new Honda City, the polluted cityscape look more *aesthetic*. We soon added those filters to our faces and our bodies to conceal our imperfections, our oddities, stuff that made us unique. Soon, in the window display of Instagram, we all became mannequins with orange-teal skin, doe eyes, sharper noses and something to sell. This aesthetic, this alternate world of blemishless-ness is now our residence of choice. Instagram's now a country, managed beauty its passport, relevance its traded currency.

As he's crossing the road, he looks to his left, then to his right. Honking cars zip in front of him. One misstep and he will be a splotch on the road.

Dhiren looks at the path of the oncoming truck. He will not do it, he knows that. He's terrified of failing and ending up maimed, because losing a leg is worse than dying. He tells himself he needs to see a therapist because he thinks disabled people are better off dead. He wants to know how people like him—assholes—live with themselves. Because he's not doing a good job at it. He drags his dark past with him, and it fills him with anxiety and burning self-hatred. He wants to get rid of it, be a new person or whatever.

'Look who's here!' says the smiling receptionist in the waiting room, rubbing his hands in delight, pupils dilated.

'Wow, you're happy.'

'We are happy to help you, Mr . . .' The receptionist looks into his notebook. 'Dhiren Das, we are happy that you decided to work towards your mental health. It's an ongoing journey, and we will be with you at every step. Cash or card?'

Dhiren takes out a bunch of grubby notes from his pocket. The receptionist counts them and stuffs them into a drawer. He sanitizes his hands and says, 'Wait for five minutes.'

Dhiren plonks down on the sofa and starts to sift through the magazines. There are year-old editions of *Architectural Digest*, *Caravan*, *India Today* . . . and that's when he sees it: a two-year-old copy of *Forbes* magazine.

That *fucking* magazine.

His breathing becomes shallow. He looks up and the receptionist is looking at him. *Does he know? Of course he knows. Was this some kind of a joke? Did they google him?*

He had thought that being in therapy excluded you from judgement.

But who wouldn't judge him? Of course the therapist would! What was he even thinking? You can't just wash off your past as you'd do with a stain.

On the top right corner of the magazine is the headline that's kept Dhiren up at night for years: **FROM TRAILBLAZING ENTREPRENEUR DUO TO THIEVES**

Inside the magazine, he knows there's a two-page spread with his pictures, testimonies from his victims and reports of attempted suicide. There's also a lone comment from him, which the magazine chose to print in bold: **IT'S NOT MY FAULT, IT'S THEIRS, SAYS FOUNDER OF CRYPTO CRICKET**

'You're up,' says the receptionist.

Dhiren rolls up the magazine and dumps it into the small dustbin before getting up. Dhiren's therapist is in his late forties. He had picked an older one to make sure the therapist had treated people worse than him.

'Why are you here today?' the man asks, sitting in an office straight out of an IKEA catalogue.

He is dressed in an old, white polo T-shirt and crumpled beige trousers. He's not fat or thin, just medium everything, like a thermodynamics professor or a bank teller.

'If you see eight patients a day, that's 30K a day. Multiply it by twenty-six days, and it comes to . . . 7.8 lakh a month? This is legalized robbery for listening to gossip.'

'Is it important to you how much I earn?'

'It's like having a friend who charges you money every time you meet him. How long do you think it will be before an AI-powered app replaces you? All you will do is sit here and ask pre-determined questions.'

'What made you decide to talk to me and not a friend?'

'This is glorified customer care.'

'And yet you didn't speak to a friend.'

A wave of shame hits Dhiren.

'Dhiren, is there someone you would have talked to about this?'

Dhiren wants to give this process an honest try, so he says, 'Neeraj.'

'Then why didn't you talk to Neeraj?'

'Because he's as fucked up as I am,' snaps Dhiren. 'This entire thing is a fucking cliché. You're trying to find hot buttons to make me feel something. That's what you sell—making people feel something, like terror at a horror movie, or hunger at a McDonald's.'

'In the past few minutes, I've been a robber, worse than an AI-powered app, as good as customer care, a movie hall and a fast-food restaurant. But we still don't know anything about you, except that you don't have anyone to talk to. You don't have friends, but I want to tell you that's understandable.'

'It's not,' counters Dhiren. 'Autistic kids, dictators, war criminals, small crooks, rapists, virtue-signalling leftists, ignorant right-wingers, feminists, pseudo-feminists, men's rights activists, vegans, everyone has friends. Even two-year-olds have friends. Everyone but me.'

'Is there a reason behind that?'

'There is. You know what I'm thinking right now? I'm thinking, if you irritate me, I can go to Google reviews, drop in a one-star review, and write that you prescribed me some medication that I overdosed on and almost died. I can also add a neat little subtext claiming you touched me inappropriately. I'm thinking how easy it is for me to do that, and you wouldn't be able to tell which patient because of doctor–patient confidentiality. I'm not going to do that, of course, but I could. That's what I am, the biggest haraami you will ever meet.'

'Are you, Dhiren?'

'Without a doubt.'

'When you searched for a therapist on the app, you typed in the keywords . . .' the therapist says, consulting his pad, 'therapist . . . anxiety . . . letting go of the past . . . to be happier.'

'I had to fill something so . . .'

'Because you had to fill anything, you wrote "to be happier"?'

'Yeah, so?'

'If you could have filled anything, you could have written that you wanted a cure for your . . . what did you call it . . . haraaminess? So, what I want to ask is, is that something in the past? You're no longer a haraami?'

5.

Aishwarya Menon

Aishwarya stands outside her newly rented property—her new home, her business and her lifelong dream, Cute Buttons. The terror paralyses her. In the moments that matter, the advice from the fast-talking, hand-gesturing, wide-eyed motivational speakers, who promise their one-minute video will change the viewer's life, is dirt. The quotes about courage, the inspirational interviews, the anecdotes of uphill battles are worth nothing. She offloads her suitcases and pays the cab driver.

You're doing this, she tells herself and tries to calm her thrumming heart.

The two-storey kothi in Sector 22, Dwarka, is solidly built. It's a corner property, as a nursery should ideally be for safety reasons, but what sold her on the house was the first floor, which gave her the possibility of expansion. If everything goes as per plan, she could rent the first floor, too, from the guy she knows nothing about yet, Dhiren Das, and eventually buy it. Dhiren's private entrance is on the other side and there's a car parked there. It's a modest but well-maintained Hyundai Accent, which tells her that the guy is not a spendthrift and is probably hygienic. But no matter what kind of guy he is, Vinny and Smriti have begged her to maintain a strict, rude, irritable persona in front of him.

'He should want to move out,' Vinny had said.

Smriti had added, 'Make sure you're unlikeable. You will want to treat him well, but don't give in to your impulses. Don't be nice.'

She will worry about these things later.

For now, she pastes the cute cardboard signage she had crafted with flowers, quills and sparkle pens just above the nameplate— *The Cute Buttons Nursery*. The ungreased hinges groan as she pushes open the heavily rusted gates. Setting the suitcases on the side, she opens all the doors and windows, letting out the sharp odour.

She looks at the date on her watch; she has exactly six months until the admissions open.

For the next five hours, Aishwarya vacuums, scrubs and cleans, emptying out three big bottles of phenyl. In the garden outside, she collects a heap of garbage to be thrown out. She changes the light bulbs and tube lights, fixes the regulator of the fan, unrolls a mattress in the corner of the big living room and makes her bed. She clears out the three bedrooms and is surprised at how big they are without the broken furniture. On her phone, she makes a small list of things that need to be replaced—windows, door frames, tiles, curtain rods. It's evening by the time it's done. The house is still in a shambles, but it's clean and well-lit and looks spacious. Then, she adds more entries to her to-do list:

Fix the walls.

Find a father.

Flooring.

Furniture hunting.

Plumbing.

Do paedophile check on first-floor boy.

Miscellaneous.

She stares at the penultimate entry. Two days ago, she had visited the Dwarka Police Station and met with the incharge, Vishwas Bothra. She had told him about Cute Buttons, the nursery she planned to set up, and that she would need a clearance certificate of the tenant because the man, Dhiren Das, would be in close proximity to the children.

When her phone rings, for a moment she thinks it's the police station, but it's her father.

'Hello, Papa.'

'I have made lauki, boondi-wala raita, bharta [savoury curds and brinjal mash] and pulao. I was going to cut a salad, but I thought I would check with you first.'

'Papa, don't entice me with food. If I come there, I will have to leave very early tomorrow and if I get late, I will get stuck in traffic and waste the entire day.'

'One day won't make a difference,' he mutters.

'You will say the same thing tomorrow.'

'I will wake you up at sharp five in the morning, and I will drop you also.'

'I don't want you to see the place yet, Papa. Let me make some progress.'

'Beta, what sense does that make?'

It makes perfect sense to her. If Papa comes and doesn't get Yatin and Maa along, she will feel ignored by Maa, as she has felt her entire life. And if he does bring them, Yatin and Maa will look at the crumbling walls, the broken flooring, the blocked sinks and tell her that she will never be successful.

'Where's Yatin?'

'Your Maa and he have gone to the mall. He said that he needs another pair of formal shoes. I don't know what he's doing. His baggage is already over forty kgs,' her Papa says and adds after a pause, 'The flight's on Monday. Will you come to the airport?'

'Is Maa going with him?'

'Yes, I sent you the tickets. He needs the extra baggage—'

'I didn't open them,' she says, masking her anger. 'He's not a child. Maa doesn't need to go with him. He will be living with the guys from his office. It's Bangalore, not a village.'

'But, beta, the baggage—'

'Maa's return ticket is after a month,' she interrupts.

'You opened the tickets.'

'Of course I did.'

'He has never lived alone. And he doesn't know how to cook,' mumbles Papa.

'Why is Maa going then? If he only needed the extra baggage and to fly with a cook, he should have taken you.'

'Aishwarya . . .'

'Why are you lying to me? I know he's Maa's favourite. I don't care. Let him be a baby,' she says, reconciling again with the fact that her mother would never like her.

Earlier this morning, when she had sent her mother a picture of the Cute Buttons plaque, all her mother had sent was a message, 'Okay'. She hadn't called her, or offered to help her set up her home. She hadn't needed her mother's help but an offer would have been nice. She was 65 km away from her family's apartment in Faridabad, moving into a crumbling kothi, and her mother hadn't blinked an eyelid. Instead, she was going with her grown-up brother to Bangalore for an entire month to make sure he adjusted well in a furnished apartment with four other grown boys.

'Papa, I will call you later,' she says. 'Bye, there's someone at the door.'

'Who—'

Click.

She looks at the wallpaper. It's a picture of her family. They are all smiling in the picture, a rarity—clicked on the day

Yatin cleared his entrance exam. If only her life was that picture stretched over decades. What wouldn't she give for that—to be loved, and to love with all her heart. She knows love in families is tricky and has the power to hurt immensely.

The bell rings again.

She switches to the CCTV app and sees a grocery delivery guy on his scooter poking at the bell.

'Can you use the other door? This is not the entrance,' she tells the guy who has kept the paper bag on the floor and is backing out.

'Next time!' the delivery guy shouts and drives away.

Aishwarya picks up the bag. Her eyes flit to the other entrance. It's blocked by a huge, black-filmed SUV. This means Dhiren Das has obnoxious, insensitive friends, who could come over during nursery timings. *Shit.*

Just then, the bottom of the bag gives way. Ugh! She gathers everything up and goes inside. From her suitcase, she pulls out another bag and puts the groceries Dhiren had ordered inside it—rice, a bunch of mint leaves, cloves, onions, chicken, saffron, cardamom, bay leaves . . . wait a minute . . . kewra water. Is Dhiren going to cook biryani? That reminds her she has to buy a cooking stove from Amazon, or order food from Swiggy for tonight.

Or, in return of the favour she will be doing him by delivering his groceries, Dhiren can offer her some biryani. She can straight-up save a couple of hundred rupees.

But then, she remembers the SUV. Dhiren probably has a college friend over with whom he would finish a bottle of Royal Stag, sing Punjabi songs and vomit half-digested biryani into her garden from the first-floor balcony.

Instinctively, she opens the CCTV app, which receives images from the cameras she had got installed on the day she signed the lease. She scrolls back on the timeline to when Dhiren moved in.

The footage is from two days ago.

Dhiren is at the gate with a suitcase and a backpack. The footage is 4K quality—she had insisted on it—and so she realizes that the Aadhaar card picture hasn't done justice to the boy. What the picture missed were his broad shoulders, which were conspicuous even under the loose T-shirt, his ramrod straight back and the confidence in his walk. The entrance gate to the first floor is jammed. He kicks it twice. When it doesn't budge, he throws his suitcase and backpack over it, and then jumps over in one smooth motion. He opens the gate from the inside. Then he stops for a moment, spots the camera and looks straight up at it. He's as still as a statue. And though the footage is old, Aishwarya feels a chill run down her spine. It's as if he's gazing at her right now. There's a certain roughness in his features. Or is it anger? He then looks away and disappears inside the house. A little later, he emerges with two huge garbage bags and carries them all the way to the dumpster on the other side of the road. This time he's wearing a hoodie, but Aishwarya can spot the outlines of his body—a curious mix of muscularity and languidness. On his way back, he scrapes and oils the hinges of the gate till they are smooth. She waits for him to look at the CCTV camera again, but he doesn't.

A little later, a truck with the logo of a furniture rental company parks behind his car. There is very little in the name of furniture—a bed, a couch, a stove, a table and two chairs. For the next day and a half, the boy doesn't leave the house. And today, an SUV is parked right in front of the entrance. A man in a Delhi Police uniform steps out. When he comes into focus, she recognizes him immediately: IPS Vishwas Bothra.

6.

Dhiren Das

Dhiren's making tea for the twenty-eight-year-old Vishwas Bothra, and from the window he can see the government-issued SUV is parked blocking the road outside. The last thing Dhiren wants his neighbours to see is the police hanging around his house, and yet, here is Vishwas, parading his government-issued licence to terrorize. *Chutiya saala* [Bloody bastard].

'Imagine my surprise when the girl gave me your Aadhaar card and asked me to verify you,' says Vishwas, chuckling. 'I wanted to say that this *bhaisahab* [brother] is a colleague, I know *everything* about him, but I didn't. You should say thank you.'

All Dhiren wants to do his punch his toad-like face.

'If you tell her anything and I lose my deposit, I will take a cut from what you guys get,' warns Dhiren. He slices a few pieces of ginger and puts them into the tea.

'Good house,' points out Vishwas.

'That *madarchod* [motherfucker] Kamlesh pulled a fast one. The girl's opening a nursery downstairs. He told me there would be a gym or a bank.'

'*Batao* [Look], the tables have turned. Never would I have thought someone would cheat Dhiren! But what's it to you? The deposit is a drop in the kind of money you're sitting on.'

'Why are you here in your uniform?'

'It's nice, isn't it?' says Vishwas, running his hands over his chest, fixing his nametag and smiling.

'Do you look at yourself in your uniform and jerk off in front of the mirror?'

Vishwas flinches. 'Dhiren bhai, *paise lete hai aapse* [we take money from you] doesn't mean you will talk to us like this. I would have got late, so I came straight from office. Anyway, they will think I'm your friend.'

'Since we are such good friends, I am thinking I will stop paying you people.'

'Dhiren bhai, I work for the government. There's a hierarchy and there are seniors, and I am answerable to them. It's not like your old start-up *ki kuchh bhi kar liya* [that you do anything you please].'

Dhiren pours tea for both of them. Of all the policemen Dhiren has had to deal with, Vishwas might be the ugliest, but he was the least annoying. He wants to but doesn't spit in his tea.

'So, you were saying you have seniors,' says Dhiren.

'They are strict,' points out Vishwas. 'Nice tea, Dhiren bhai. You have magic in your hands.'

'Tell me something, Vishwas. I have heard that all the young IPS officers like you have to line up to lick their seniors' assholes thoroughly each morning, before the seniors line up to give blow jobs to the politicians. Is that true? I'm sorry if I'm coming across as stupid, but I really don't know how hierarchy in the government works.'

'*Kaise baat karte ho yaar aap*? [How can you talk to us like that?] You're lucky that you have money, Dhiren bhai, *warna* [otherwise] . . .'

'That's what I am asking. What will you do if I stop paying you guys?'

'Don't ask me that, Dhiren bhai.'

'When you first met me, you were just like Akshay Kumar in his movies, so righteous, so uncomfortable with this bribe, and look at you now. You are like a seasoned stripper, absolutely at home with me stuffing notes down your underwear.'

'Are the people who stuff the money any better than those who take it, Dhiren bhai?'

'So what happens to me?'

Vishwas sighs. 'Light custodial torture. No sexual stuff, apart from some lathis inside your anus, might rip off some nails, we will leave your testicles alone. But our seniors now ask for videos. Trust me, I won't enjoy it. But, you know, occupational hazard. It's a government job, after all.'

'*Satyamev jayate* [Truth always triumphs], bhai,' says Dhiren and does a small salute. He gets up and says, 'Shall we start? Let me start stuffing the money down your panties.'

Dhiren walks to his computer desk where a gaming laptop glows angrily in RGB lights. As his fingers glide over the keyboard with intent and speed, he can feel Vishwas breathing down his neck, trying to make sense of the code and the numbers.

'Dhiren bhai, exactly how much money do you have? There are people in the office who say you have over 1000 crore or more. How much is it *exactly*?'

'Tell your guy not to get carried away and buy a car or something instead,' warns Dhiren.

Vishwas takes out his phone and opens a voice recorder.

'What's this for?'

'To tell my seniors how all this cryptocurrency thing works, how they can access their money. You know none of us understand this bitcoin stuff.'

'What do they teach you at the academy? To deep-throat politicians better?'

'Dhiren—'

'Grab a tissue, I can see tufts of pubic hair in your mouth. It must be hard for you to speak with your mouth dripping with ball-sweat, saliva and pre-cum. The country is proud of your service to the police and the state. Now swallow, and listen.'

Dhiren records his instructions for the senior police officers on how to access their crypto wallets, which websites they can use to spend it and other details.

'Who would have thought that one day, money would be a string of zeros and ones?' asks Vishwas.

'There's still time, invest in bitcoin. Or next time, I can throw the money on the floor for you guys to pick up with your ass cracks.'

Just as Dhiren finishes the transaction, the bell rings.

'That must be the grocery guy. Do you like biryani, Vishwas?'

Vishwas's eyes light up. 'I won't say no to anything you cook, Dhiren.'

Dhiren opens the door. He immediately recognizes the girl from the ground floor.

Aishwarya Mohan.

She's . . . little. The big bag she's carrying, he assumes that it's his delivery, looks odd in her hands. For a moment, she stands there without saying anything. Which is good, because Dhiren gets a good look at her face. She's not young, he can tell by the little crow's feet on the side of her eyes, but it's remarkable that she still has the face of someone young. But now, he thinks, it's not her face but the brightness in her massive, anime-like eyes that makes her look younger than she is. Or maybe it's the Disney character-themed pyjama set that she is ten years too old to wear. What makes her look even more petite is the sharpness of her diamond-shaped face outlined by her razor-sharp jaw. It's like she was drawn with a ruler. She has a complexion he has often heard himself being described as—desert.

'Thank you,' he says.

The girl is distracted. 'Huh?'

'For the delivery,' says Dhiren and takes the bag from her hands.

'Namaste,' says Vishwas from behind Dhiren. Seeing Aishwarya trying to place him, he adds, 'We met at the police station. You came for the police verification, remember, for

Dhiren bhai. I thought I would come and let you know that Dhiren bhai is a friend.'

'You're opening a nursery,' says Dhiren. 'Kamlesh didn't tell me about that. He should have made that clear.'

The girl finally seems to snap back to the present. 'Do you have a problem with children?' she asks in a stern voice that's incongruous with how petite and cute she looks.

'Well, they are children.'

'You were a child once, Dhiren,' she says.

Dhiren watches as she tilts her face and stares at him. For a moment, the stare feels familiar—it simultaneously shames him and comforts him. And then he realizes what it is. It's the typical grave, disciplinary look of a teacher. Suddenly, it feels like she's a giant and he's a toddler; she a teacher, him a student.

Aishwarya turns to Vishwas. 'I can't have big cars in this corner. I expected better out of you, but don't make the same mistake again. That's very bad behaviour.'

Dhiren looks on as Vishwas shrinks in size, the smile on his face vanishes, and he stares down at his shoes.

'Okay,' Vishwas mumbles.

Dhiren enjoys this moment. All his curses didn't affect Vishwas as much as the mild scolding from Aishwarya did.

'I'm sorry,' she says, turning back to Dhiren. 'But there are going to be a lot of children here.'

'You don't have to apologize. It's Kamlesh's fault,' says Dhiren.

'When did I apologize?'

'You started your sentence with "I'm sorry", but—'

'Old habit,' she says with a small smile, easing up. 'I will go now.' She's about to turn but stops. 'Sorry, one question if you don't mind.'

'Did you apologize again?'

'Are you cooking biryani? Sorry, I peeked into your—'

'I will send some over,' says Dhiren. 'If Vishwas here leaves anything for you. He's a dog, throw him a bone and he wants everything.'

A couple of hours later, IPS Vishwas Bothra takes biryani to Aishwarya with a small message: Dhiren's a nice guy, and she has nothing to worry about.

7.

Vinny Shahi

'I can't believe we are *actually* watching a movie,' whispers Vinny into Varun's ear.

Varun pops the last of the popcorn into his mouth. 'Young Vinny–Varun would be disappointed in us.'

Vinny pushes her head into Varun's chest. 'I love you, but I'm tired. I'm always tired.'

Three years ago, Varun and Vinny had been on adjacent seats—on one of their early dates—and Vinny, in a desperate bid to impress Varun, had taken his dick all the way inside her mouth. Varun had returned the favour by licking her out.

Two weeks before that first date, Varun and Vinny's parents had found each other on Shaadi.com and thought that it would be best if the kids exchanged numbers and went out for a coffee. Vinny had found Varun to be just like the pictures she was shown—he was slightly taller, clean-cut, wore polos and dark-coloured trousers, and was a solid type 8. Vinny thought of herself as an 8 too—she was 5'9", thin and had breasts she was proud of. Years of squats and a short-lived college athlete's career had given her a muscular butt and a strong core.

In those early days, Vinny always thought of Varun as a prop to elevate her own beauty, like a handbag or a clutch. Their flaws complemented each other, she had thought at the time.

He was too fair, like a boiled egg, and she found her face too chubby and her eyes too narrow. This is what arranged marriages are: a detailed report card of caste, looks, income potential and desperation. As instructed by their parents, they exchanged numbers, the coffee turned to vodka, and soon their dates ended in the same corner of the movie hall—their popcorn untouched, but the tissues used up.

But things have shifted now. The last two years have been tough. With Vihaan turning two, they are beginning to find each other's bodies again.

'You think Vihaan's okay?' whispers Varun.

'Aishwarya is more responsible than both of us combined.'

'Is she still going ahead with the plan?'

'It's going to be amazing, just wait. She has paid the deposit too. It's a big house—'

'Not Cute Buttons, the pregnancy.'

'Let her do what she wants to. What's it to you?' asks Vinny. 'And you know Aishwarya's child will be perfect. She's a better parent to Vihaan than we are!'

'Yeah, you're right.'

After the movie ends, Vinny and Varun drive back to their two-storey house in Punjabi Bagh. They find Vihaan sleeping calmly in his crib and Aishwarya waiting for them like an eager puppy, her eyes lit up. 'How was the movie?'

'We watched it. Ask us anything. It wasn't even that good. Wasted our time, to be honest,' says Vinny. She has no stories to tell about stolen blow jobs, or movie-hall-seat sex.

Aishwarya is disappointed. 'The point of Friday nights with Maasi is so you guys can do something crazy! You didn't do anything?'

Vinny is surprised at how quickly Aishwarya shifts from being a loving, patient, mother-type figure to a girl who talks as if she's sixteen.

Vinny shakes her head. 'Going out with Varun and having him alone, just for me, in itself is doing something crazy. The only time we spend together is when Vihaan's diaper leaks and changing it becomes a two-person job.'

'Things will be better once Cute Buttons is up and running. Then you can get a lot of time together,' says Aishwarya. 'I had made khichdi for Vihaan. Do you guys want some? It has carrots, beans, asparagus, potato and broccoli.'

'Baby, can you warm some for us?' Vinny asks Varun.

As Varun leaves, Vinny mumbles a soft 'thank you' under her breath. Aishwarya rolls her eyes.

Vinny knows she would have had a nervous breakdown trying to raise Vihaan had Aishwarya not been her friend. When Vinny accidentally conceived Vihaan, both Varun and she had wanted an abortion. They weren't ready for a kid. But Vinny's mother found the pregnancy stick, and then Varun's mother knew, so an abortion was out of the question. In those long, scary nine months, Aishwarya kept assuring Varun and Vinny that she would be there for them. But Vinny hadn't known how serious Aishwarya was till the time she birthed Vihaan.

Vinny picks Vihaan up from his crib and kisses him softly on his forehead. It brings tears to her eyes to feel how much she loves Vihaan.

'Aishwarya, I love him so much, it pains me. But sometimes I just . . . I feel we are bad at this.'

'I know, I understand that. That doesn't make you bad parents.'

And Aishwarya does it again. Vinny notices how quickly she shifts back to her role as mother and teacher figure from her friend who just a few moments ago wanted to know if she gave Varun a blow job.

'I don't know how you do this, Aishwarya. I can die for Vihaan, I really can. But you ask me to raise him alone, I can't. I . . . just can't.'

'Vinny, I won't die for him. That's why you're the mother and I'm not. But I will do everything else for him. We all have our roles.'

For the last two years, Aishwarya has spent every minute of her free time taking care of Vihaan, and has done it with a happiness that's so complete, it looks fake. It is she who has potty-trained Vihaan, taught him Hindi and how to eat on his own.

Aishwarya has always been good with kids—and with adults. She has boundless patience and love for everyone. Vinny had once told Varun, 'We need a person in our lives to keep treating us as a child long after we have reached adulthood. We like to pretend that we are strong enough to deal with pain, loss, grief and disappointment, but the truth is, we would still like to roll around on the floor and throw a big tantrum; we would like to cry, break things, shout and scream, and yet be loved for who we are. We need to be seen as children and be forgiven for it. Aishwarya is that person for me. Aishwarya can see that people are still little children inside, and she takes care of them.'

For Vinny, it was love and comfort at first sight with Aishwarya. She was in her first year of college, a fresher, and had just moved into a paying guest (PG) accommodation. Aishwarya had walked into the PG with her father to inspect the flat. Vinny was in the bathroom, shoving fingers down her throat and vomiting the baingan bharta she had eaten an hour ago. Vinny was stick-thin—she knew that, everyone knew that—but during that phase of her life, the fear of gaining weight had consumed her. When she was done and came out, Vinny saw Aishwarya hunched over, peering into the creaking, smelly fridge.

'It's what the property dealer gave us. It stinks. By the way, I'm Vinny, first year, Hindu College.'

'I'm Aishwarya. I will defrost it, clean it and keep three bowls with vinegar, lemon and baking soda in it. The smell will go away.'

'That sounds like black magic.'

'Were you crying, Vinny?'

Vinny flinched. 'My family has a long history of alcoholism, so all of us have eyes like these.'

Vinny had used this pretext before. People bought it all the time.

'There's some . . . stuff on your T-shirt,' said Aishwarya. Her eyes are large and kind again. Like Bambi's. 'You were vomiting.'

Vinny hurriedly wiped it off. 'It's boy trouble. The boy hates me. So I can't eat well.'

'I don't think any boy can hate you. You're . . . kind of hot.'

'Hot people can be hated.'

'Only if they are evil, and you're not evil. You're too young to be evil.'

Vinny sighed. The truth bubbled out of her involuntarily. 'The boy is me. I hate myself. So, this . . .' she pointed to the stain on her T-shirt '. . . is because of that.'

What was it about Aishwarya that had made Vinny spill out her most well-guarded secret? It was her eyes—those were the real black magic.

Aishwarya came forward and hugged Vinny as though she meant it. The kind of hug that's not a single word like 'goodbye' or 'hello' but the kind that tells a story, a confession, a declaration.

The next day, Aishwarya moved in. She cleaned the refrigerator, cooked a simple meal and they ate together. Aishwarya breathlessly told Vinny about her college—Hansraj, sports quota, her obsession with cricket and about her dream: Cute Buttons.

'I have a superpower,' confessed Aishwarya. 'I'm a baby whisperer. You give me a crying child and I will turn it into a sleeping one.'

'That's chloroform, not a power,' said Vinny. After a pause, she added, 'I have one too. I can run. Athletics team, Hindu.'

By the end of the week, Vinny felt she had been Aishwarya's friend since forever, and by the end of the month, they were inseparable.

These days, Aishwarya often calms down a crying Vihaan, but the first child she calmed wasn't Vihaan. It was Vinny.

'This shouldn't taste good,' says Vinny, eating the vegetable-heavy khichdi.

'Look at this,' says Aishwarya and gives Vinny the phone with the CCTV app open. 'Dhiren, the boy who lives upstairs, he's measuring the terrace. Do you see him?'

'You have a CCTV camera on the terrace?'

'Is that not part of Cute Buttons?' asks Aishwarya sternly. 'What do you think he's making? A shed-type gym?'

'What if he is?'

'Then his friends will be coming over for group dead lift things. That will be terrible. I can't let that happen.'

'And I'm assuming you have already thought of something.'

She nods. 'The terrace is going to be Cute Buttons's from tomorrow. I'm not going to let a boy take it away from me for some nonsense benches and squat racks.'

8.

Dhiren Das

Ramesh and Raju, brothers and managers at Satija Sporting Goods warehouse, reach the godown to find a fuming Dhiren at the door.

Dhiren bows in front of them and says mockingly, 'Arre sir ji, sir ji, why did you come now also? Don't worry, go and sleep some more, I will wait here. Just complete your beauty sleep and come after lunch. I will just stay here the entire day.'

'Bhaisahab, sorry, sorry, last night we drank a little bit. It was Chhotu's birthday. He just turned twenty,' says Ramesh and opens the shutter. The godown is a fire hazard, a death trap packed to the ceiling with cricket bats. 'Here, *maal ready hai* [the consignment is ready],' says Ramesh, pointing to a far corner of the room. 'Straight from England. She has seen a lot in her time. She's fast. Virat threw a bat at her because she frustrated him so much. Smith, Sonali, Mandhana, Root, everyone's had her. It's a steal at 5.5 lakh rupees. You need to be a fan to buy this.'

Dhiren's not a fan; he's obsessed with cricket. He can trace his unhealthy obsession back to the summer of fifth grade. Papa had bought a 45-inch television just so he could call his office friends over to watch cricket matches on Sundays—his only day off in the week. Dhiren loathed the game, and the TV.

Cricket had snatched his father away from him.

But then he saw an opportunity. If he could be an expert on cricket, Papa would not need to call any of his friends over to discuss matches with. For a month that summer, Dhiren obsessively watched highlights of old matches and interviews, and forged himself into a cricket fan—just to get a few hours with his father.

Dhiren pays in cash for the bowling machine, his fingers trembling with anticipation. Ramesh and Raju load it on to the pickup Dhiren has hired for the day. As Raju and Dhiren cover it with tarpaulin, Raju's face falls. The prized possession of Satija Sporting Goods is no longer theirs.

'*Aise lag raha hai dulhan lekar jaa rahe ho* [It feels as if you're taking the bride away],' says Raju.

'Unload, let's play,' says Dhiren, uncovering the bowling machine. 'Two overs, your birthday gift.'

Raju grins and runs inside to pad up—pads, helmet, thigh guards, elbow guards, chest guard, wrist guards—leaving nothing to chance. Dhiren and Ramesh set up the bowling machine. Raju takes the stance, Dhiren sets it for 100 miles per hour, the bowling machine whirrs and lets one rip. Before Raju can even bring his bat down, his stump's shattered. Raju plays four overs, gets bowled nine times, misses a bunch, nicks a few.

'Thank you, bhaiya,' says Raju once they finish loading.

On his way home, Dhiren picks up a cricket bat, a cage and nets for the terrace set-up. He had picked his house partly because of its large, unobstructed terrace, shaped like a big square, the perfect size to set up a cricket net—and he's excited.

Just as he walks up the stairs to his floor, a nasty, nauseating smell strikes him. The odour's so strong that it makes him gag. *Fuck.* He closes his mouth with his hand to not vomit. He enters his apartment fearing the worst but realizes quickly it's coming from the terrace. He wonders if the septic tank has burst. He double masks and makes his way upstairs. The smell's so pungent that he feels he will faint. Fucking Kamlesh.

He pushes open the door and steps out.

'*Behenchod* [Sister fucker]!'

He looks down and his foot is buried ankle-deep in brown, slimy sludge. He pulls it out, brown goo dripping from it.

'Careful!'

He looks up and it's . . . Aishwarya(?) in a makeshift hazmat suit, with handkerchiefs tied around her nose and mouth.

'How did this happen?' shouts Dhiren from under his masks. 'CALL KAMLESH! WE HAVE TO CALL THAT . . .' Dhiren screams and frantically takes out his phone to call the property dealer.

Aishwarya shouts, 'THE SMELL WILL GO!'

That's when Dhiren notices the shovel in Aishwarya's hands.

'It's going to be beautiful!' she exclaims like a madwoman, taking off her handkerchiefs. Tiny flecks of foul-smelling grime are stuck to the side of her face. 'We are going to have shimla mirch and baingan, even matar [capsicum and brinjal, even peas]. Is there something you want? We can plant that too.'

'What are you saying?'

'It's going to be an amazing vegetable garden! Just imagine! The kids are going to love it! Do you like cucumbers? Or lilies? I'm sure you love lilies.'

It takes a few seconds to register. All of this is Aishwarya's doing.

Dhiren feels his face burn with anger. He charges at Aishwarya, plodding through the ankle-deep manure, shouting, 'Are you out of your mind? A vegetable garden? HERE?! ARE YOU FUCKING STUPID? This is not your terrace!'

As he steps forward, Aishwarya flinches, tries to move away and stumbles. Seeing her stumble, Dhiren reaches out for her and finds his own feet stuck in the muck. They both tumble into fresh animal dung.

'FUCK!' shouts Dhiren, extracting himself from the muck, spitting it out of his mouth.

Aishwarya wipes her face calmly and says, 'I'm sorry, but trust me, Dhiren, you will like it.'

೩.

Kamlesh Ahuja

Kamlesh Ahuja has always been a cricket fan, but his family hates it.

They are always busy on their own screens. Kamlesh knows this is the root of all evil in Indian society. Families are falling apart because they are staring at different screens. Earlier, families used to like the same dinner-time TV shows, news anchors, *antakshari* [a singing game] programmes, and used to think in similar ways. Generation after generation voted for the same party, knew which religion, caste, *gotra* [lineage] is superior, and followed the same traditions. Now even siblings fight over politics, religion, clothing, sports, food, television shows. Once a quiet, obedient herd led by the patriarch controlling the TV remote, they are now spiders, each entangled in their unique web of screens, each with their own mind. Terrible.

*

'Why can't she grow her potatoes in the front lawn outside the house? The terrace is mine, the lawn is hers,' asserts Dhiren.

Kamlesh turns to Aishwarya because Dhiren is right.

'Sorry, Uncle, but a vegetable garden and a flower garden are two entirely different things,' argues Aishwarya. 'Dhiren, please understand. We are talking about little children here.'

'If you need to farm, I suggest you take the highway out of Delhi, find a patch of land, hook a plough on to the kids and make them grow cucumbers there.'

'Uncle, a flower garden is different from a vegetable garden,' explains Aishwarya in a soft, firm voice. 'The children grow up in the city with no idea about the food they eat. They need to be taught this from a young age. This is how they will grow attached to this soil, to nature. Dhiren, you can play cricket anywhere.'

'Beti, you're right. Kids these days . . .'

'What do you mean they won't know the difference between a flower garden and a vegetable garden? What kind of children are these who would pluck a flower and eat it?' asks Dhiren. He turns to Kamlesh. 'Kamlesh, which IPL team does your son support?'

'He has no interest in cricket,' answers Kamlesh sadly.

'What about the *seelan* [dampness]?' asks Dhiren.

'What about it?' asks Aishwarya.

'Photosynthesis is not a perfect process, if you haven't noticed. Some of the water is going to drip down and rot the walls. How do you think the landlord will like it, Kamlesh?'

Kamlesh can already hear the ranting landlord screaming at him.

Aishwarya waves her hand like it's nothing. 'Uncle, I have coated the floor with waterproofing. You can check if you want. A cloud can burst, and nothing will happen.'

'That place is for my bowling machine, Kamlesh,' insists Dhiren.

'Sorry, Dhiren, but a terrace is no place for a bowling machine. What if you hit the ball and it breaks the neighbours' windows?'

'That's what nets are for. No ball is leaving the terrace.'

Aishwarya turns to Kamlesh. 'Wouldn't you like some fresh vegetables every week, Uncle? *Bhindi chahiye to bhindi milegi, nimbu chahiye to nimbu milega* [You will get lady's fingers if you want, lemons if you want them], anything you like. Wouldn't you, Dhiren?'

'I have ten apps on my phone that will deliver organic vegetables in less than ten minutes,' argues Dhiren.

'Dhiren, yaar . . .' says Aishwarya.

'Not your yaar,' snaps Dhiren.

Kamlesh raises his hand. '*Dono chup* [Both of you, quiet].'

A few seconds of silence pass. Kamlesh makes up his mind. It's an easy choice for him to make—an obvious opportunity to impress his wife with fresh vegetables. He turns to Dhiren.

'Dhiren ji, cricket is a team sport. There's a park just three minutes away by car. You're new to the area. You will make friends, hai naa?'

'That's what I was telling him,' says Aishwarya. 'I offered to take the bowling machine to the park with him.'

Kamlesh turns to Aishwarya. 'But if I see seepage, I will lock the terrace forever and the repairs will come out of your deposit.'

Dhiren throws up his hands. 'This is incredible!'

'Sorry, Dhiren,' says Aishwarya. 'It's the best for all of us. Look at the bright side. Fresh vegetables for your vegetable biryani!'

Dhiren says, 'There's no such thing as a vegetable biryani.'

He storms out. Kamlesh notices Aishwarya's eyes following Dhiren as he leaves the room.

'Uncle, *aap chai peeyoge* [will you have tea]?'

'*Kam cheeni* [With less sugar],' he answers sharply.

Over the years, he has been trained to spot any untoward signs between renters of the opposite sex. He realizes he has been wrong about both of them from the beginning. Dhiren had fooled him in their meeting. And Aishwarya had conned him into believing that she was a nice, homely, polite girl before turning into a clever *lafangi* [wastrel] when it came to negotiating the price.

He's not naïve. These two are fighting, for sure, but he can see the way they look at each other, especially Aishwarya.

As Aishwarya leaves for the kitchen, Kamlesh gets up to inspect what she has done with the house. There are no structural changes yet. All the old furniture is missing. The tubes and bulbs are new. He's shuffling through the house when he notices the little brown packet on the table. He tips it over slightly to check what's in it. A strip of Flexon, two strips of Brufen and . . . *what*? . . . two unused pregnancy strips and a cup of some sort in a box on which there's an illustrated vagina. There's another box of syringes on which there's a picture of a man clasping his arms around a woman's stomach.

He knew it.

He knew the girl was a raging slut.

'Uncle, chai?'

10.

Aishwarya Mohan

Aishwarya needs at least two cups of tea every morning to be fully awake. But for the past week, waking up has been easier. The new house, the new stove she makes tea on, the list of chores and her new vegetable garden make her spring out of her makeshift bed.

Like every morning, she makes herself strong tea and puts on her jacket to check on her week-old vegetable garden. She unlocks the enormous padlock she has put to keep Dhiren out. For the past week, she has had nightmares of him wrecking the garden with his bat.

The vegetable garden is still *there*.

To make up for Kamlesh's decision, she had made papri chaat and kept it outside his door. The next day, he had returned the Tupperware box with kheer in it (she had heated a small portion to eat, but after the first bite, she had finished the entire box cold).

She wants to apologize to him in person, but he seldom leaves the house. Not that she goes out often. She has spent the last week working eighteen hours a day on designing the rough layout of Cute Buttons.

She touches the soil to check if it's wet enough. She sprinkles water on the small offshoots that she can see. *Like babies!* she thinks.

She leans against the wall and sips her tea, her body flushed with the satisfaction of working on her childhood dream. She feels fortunate to be within touching distance of her goal.

She looks over to see if Dhiren's in his balcony. He's not, but there are a few utensils drying, his cricket kit and the bowling machine. There's also an empty coffee mug. Despite not seeing him for the past week, she finds herself thinking about him, the way his face dropped—like a child's—when Kamlesh sided with her. She feels as though there's a certain sadness surrounding him; something inside her makes her want to reach out and talk to him. There have been times in the week when she has stared at the balcony hoping he would be there. And times when she has gone right up to his door and but never knocked. And sometimes, she checks the CCTV app to see if he ever leaves the house. He wakes up even earlier than she does. For half an hour every morning, he does some kind of calisthenics on the bars he had installed in his balcony. He glistens with sweat, his muscles straining, and she forwards through it because she feels embarrassed at wanting to watch all thirty minutes of it. She wonders if his side-hustle is being an MMA fighter, because that's what he's built like. Sometimes, he picks up his bat and shadow-bats for a while. And then he disappears inside and never emerges. He gets grocery deliveries, and she can smell a variety of dishes—palak paneer, saag, mutton, different types of daal and it makes her hungry. And then sometimes she finds herself craving for the biryani he had made, and the kheer—the guy has some sort of magic in his hands.

She finishes her tea, locks the terrace and makes her way back.

The chart on her work desk tells her today's the last date for her to finish the layout and send it to the *thekedar* [contractor] she has hired for the job. She switches off her phone, puts on her favourite playlist and fires up SketchUp, the interior design software she has taught herself. For the next ten hours, she toils hard, taking minimal breaks. By the time she's done, it's seven in the evening. She leans back in her chair and admires the rendition of Cute Buttons the software shows her.

Satisfied, she settles on a couch and switches on her phone. She's greeted by a barrage of texts from Vinny and Smriti.

Shit. Shit. Shit. Shit. Shit.

It strikes her immediately. She runs to the bathroom and hurriedly takes a shower. A little later, with half-dried hair, haphazardly done make-up, wearing a red dress, she looks at herself in the mirror. *Cute*, she thinks. She calls Vinny and Smriti, pretending she hasn't forgotten. She's fixing her make-up when they receive the call.

'You had forgotten about today, hadn't you?' asks Vinny.

'Take this as a sign, Aishwarya,' warns Smriti. 'Maybe this is not the best path for you to take.'

Aishwarya knows what's going to happen now—Vinny and Smriti are going to start bickering with each other. She knows to step out of the conversation and let the kids fight.

'Don't listen to her, Aishwarya, go get that baby,' snaps Vinny.

'Aishwarya, *sun meri baat* [listen to me]. If you think Akshay is good enough for you to have his child, you guys can start dating again. You two were perfect, just *perfect*,' begs Smriti.

'They broke up, you missed that part, behen. She wants the unconditional love of a child, not the conditional love of a husband. Is it too hard to understand?' asks Vinny.

Smriti bristles. 'The two of you are right and the entire world is wrong. We don't know anything, only you guys know. Don't be so stupid. Sensibly *soch* [think], children from families . . .'

Smriti checks her words at the last moment.

Aishwarya smiles for she has heard this before from others, and she understands where Smriti is coming from. Smriti is from a family where family is what family's supposed to be. A devoted father, a loving mother, a sibling—just like it's shown in government advertisements.

'I will complete your sentence, Smriti. Children from broken families are damaged. Is that what you wanted to say? Maybe that's true. Children are impressionable, they do get affected. But I will be there for my child, helping him or her through every one of those issues. I will love my child with all my heart and hope that he or she grows up well-adjusted.'

Smriti doesn't contest Aishwarya. 'I'm just . . . concerned.'

'I know that, babu,' says Aishwarya kindly. 'You're my best friend.'

'Excuse me?' asks Vinny.

'You too,' says Aishwarya with a smile. 'But I need to go now.'

11.

Aishwarya Mohan

Aishwarya's last date, which was two years ago, was with Akshay. The date had ended with them deciding to break up. The decision was mutual. They wanted different things in life, and they needed those things more than they needed each other. Clarity in break-ups brings closure. But even with clarity, you can't escape a broken heart. They nursed themselves by being friends, something only a few lovers can claim to have done. Akshay had moved to Bangalore, which meant it was easier to heal for both of them. They always knew they were the lucky ones who might have lost in love but had come out with a friendship. When Aishwarya had told him about wanting him to be a sperm donor, Akshay had said it was the least he could do as a friend.

*

He's already at the restaurant when she gets there.

'Are you my date?' she asks, tapping him on his shoulder.

Akshay turns around and smiles widely. 'How is it that every time I see you, you become hotter?'

He's 5'10", lean with only a beginning of a small paunch, still boyish at twenty-nine. Akshay flips his long hair like a Disney prince. There was a time she saw him as a boyfriend, a lover and a possible life partner. Now she just wonders, what parts of him does she want in her child? She thinks of him as a friend with some brilliant strands of DNA.

She sits opposite Akshay. 'I was so nervous about this. And now that I see you, I'm like why was I nervous? It's you!'

'Remember how fidgety you were on our first date? Like you were at an interview or something?'

'But dates are like that.'

'Like interviews?'

'Exactly. They are life-changing, double-sided interviews. You're both the interviewer and the interviewee. You're putting yourself out for a job of a potential partner while evaluating for the same. That's why you lather, shave, dress up, charm and lie.'

'What's the cost-to-company of a successful date then?'

Aishwarya thinks for a while. 'A relationship, a cure for loneliness. Those who don't date, who remain single, are entrepreneurs. They value freedom over stability. Like you.'

'And like you too,' says Akshay with a laugh. 'Shall we order? I have been sitting here with water for a while and the waiter is giving me strange looks.'

They both place their orders. Akshay slows down the waiter when he takes a lot of time in picking a wine.

'Fancy, wine-shine, haan?' she jokes once he's done ordering. 'There was a time you would have had Old Monk neat from the bottle in peak summer. Where's the Akshay I dated?'

'Arre, don't make fun of me. It's an occupational hazard. I go to these meetings and everyone knows what they are drinking. I can't go like, hey, give me Haywards 5000.'

'How's the beta testing coming along?'

Akshay smiles. *Perfectly aligned white teeth. How lucky would the child be to get his teeth? And his perfect brain?*

'Good, but there are bugs in the app . . . a lot of bugs. But we have more money now. So we are throwing money and engineers at the problem. How's Cute Buttons going?'

Akshay and Aishwarya had met four years ago at a start-up boot camp. Aishwarya had pitched her idea for Cute Buttons.

After the boot camp was over, Akshay had come up to tell her that she deserved to win. And starting then, they'd dated for two years.

An hour passes by; the wine bottle is empty, Akshay has ordered another and they are giggling like teenagers on a first date. Aishwarya didn't want to get drunk. And having not had any alcohol for a year or two, she didn't know one glass could get her tipsy.

'Logically, the break-up was the best thing to do,' muses Akshay, his eyes glassed over.

'No one believes that it was mutual. They think either you cheated on me or I cheated on you. Mostly, it's you who cheated on me.'

'*Hadh hai* [This is the limit]. Why am I the culprit?'

'You're too fair. Fair boys are not trustworthy,' answers Aishwarya. And then she adds after a pause, 'Actually, brown boys aren't trustworthy either.'

For a moment, her mind flashes to Dhiren. *What must he be doing tonight? Is he on a date? In a black shirt, a pair of blue jeans, maybe? What's the girl like? Will he bring her home? Why is she thinking about him?*

Akshay breaks her train of thought. 'The beta would have never been ready had I spent my entire time obsessing over you.'

'Look who's hitting on me,' chuckles Aishwarya. 'That's good! You seem drunk enough to impregnate me.'

'You make it sound so unromantic.'

Over the last couple of months of them discussing this, Aishwarya has made sure there's no romance in the equation. She likes him, he's genetically sound, and she would rather have him as a sperm donor than someone else.

'Akshay Gambhir, start-up whiz kid, now a squirting dildo,' says Aishwarya with a chuckle.

'Wow. Once you called me your *jaan* [life]!'

'You prefer baby facilitator? Sperm manufacturer? A sentient piece of tissue that squirts life force?'

'You're such a charmer,' says Akshay.

Then he suddenly falls silent.

Aishwarya notices the furrowed eyebrows. It's something she doesn't want her child to inherit from Akshay—his tendency to worry about the littlest of things.

She lowers her voice and explains, 'We don't need to do it today. I told you about the other option, right? There's a Lifecell in Bangalore too. You go there, you drop off your sperm, they will ship it to me and I will take care of the rest.'

'You told me.'

'Or if that's uncomfortable, you can do what we decided. Come home with me. I have an assortment of porn you can choose from, ejaculate in a cup, I will suck it up in a syringe and push it down . . . you know,' she says. 'Coming home will be more fun because Smriti and Vinny think we are going to have sex.'

'Why would we have sex?'

'When I told them you're going to help me out, they assumed we'd be having sex,' says Aishwarya. 'I didn't correct them. It's funny that two mothers think that's the only way.'

'In their defence, before you told me, I didn't know about . . . what's it called? This injecting sperm thing?'

'Intrauterine insemination.'

'Yes, that.' With downcast eyes, he runs his fingers around the edges of his plate.

'Is something wrong?'

He looks up. 'It's complicated, Aishwarya. I have said this before—'

'And I have told you before that it's no big deal. I just need your cum.'

'Words every guy wants to hear.'

Aishwarya reaches out for Akshay's hand. After a moment, Akshay retracts his hand. 'I can't.'

Aishwarya frowns. '"I can't" as in? Not today or not ever? Look, we can talk about—'

'I like someone.'

'So what?' says Aishwarya before the words register. 'Excuse me?'

'She works with me. She's actually an investor, so if anything—'

'Akshay yaar,' says Aishwarya, trying not to be angry. 'You dating someone has got nothing to do with me. All I want is—'

'I can't do it,' says Akshay firmly.

'You don't have to tell her. It's just . . . as if you're an anonymous sperm donor. It's like that.'

'But I'm not anonymous. I can't hide that I got a girl pregnant.'

'You're not getting anyone pregnant! I'm just borrowing your genes. Look at it like that. You're just coming home and ejaculating in a cup!'

'Can you stop being so loud?'

Aishwarya takes a deep breath. 'Okay, listen to me.'

'No.'

'What kind of girl is this who would have a problem with you masturbating? What about men's rights?'

The couple at the next table turns to look at them.

'Aishwarya, I won't do it.'

Aishwarya leans back in her chair.

'I'm sorry, Aishwarya.'

'You could have texted me that, Akshay,' says Aishwarya and gets up. 'Why didn't you tell me this when you were in Bangalore?'

'I wanted to do this in person. I care—'

'No, you don't. If you cared, you would have known how important this is for me,' says Aishwarya, seconds away from breaking down. 'I'm not paying for dinner.'

'Aishwarya, don't leave.'

'I need to find someone who doesn't have his dick locked in a chastity cage.'

Aishwarya leaves the restaurant, feeling suffocated in her tiny dress.

12.

Dhiren Das

Dhiren paces about his room, checking his phone every thirty seconds. His groceries should have been here an hour ago, and his anxiety is getting worse.

Neither meditation nor colouring fucking mandalas nor listening to calming music helps temper his anxiety. The only activity that works is cooking. Every time he's anxious, he picks out the most elaborate recipes and tries to replicate them as perfectly as he can. The concentration required in cooking and the pleasure of eating sedates his brain—a sort of food coma. These days, he can't even point out why he's so anxious all the fucking time. Lately, his life's been boring, just the way he likes it, and yet his mind latches on to something seemingly harmless. And then, he spirals into an anxiety loop fed liberally by overthinking. His heart starts to beat faster for no reason, making him angry, which gets him more stressed and off he goes on a roller coaster on the way down.

Sometimes, he knows the trigger—a strange look from someone in the street, an article about a start-up founder going to jail, a phone call from an unknown number. Sometimes, he fails to find a reason.

Today, his anxiety started for the strangest reason ever. He's not even sure if it's the reason because it makes no sense. He was in the balcony reading some mails. It was a calm evening until he saw Aishwarya getting into an Uber. She looked gorgeous in a red dress that hugged her body snugly and slid dangerously up her sculpted thigh when she sat in the car. Her hair was still wet. Even from far, he could see her eyes, framed by a winged eyeliner so bold it seemed it could take off. The brown of her skin was so smooth it felt unnatural. He had never set eyes on someone that amazing, that gorgeous.

These were no reasons to be anxious.

Or were they?

Did her presence, the exchange of the Tupperware box, give him a false hope of normality? A hope for a friendship? But what friendship? His friendships are bound to be doomed. There have been plenty of opportunities for him to talk to Aishwarya. He has noticed she doesn't cook. She spends all her time cooped up, working. And she orders her food from outside—that can't be good. He can share his food and start a conversation. But he knows better. And then, there have been times he has noticed her looking up at his window. It's mostly after he cooks something expansive—like a rich mutton curry or a sarson ka saag. It brings Aishwarya to the garden like a cute little puppy, sniffing and hungry.

Where are the damn vegetables?

He opens the delivery app. It says the order's already been delivered. Dhiren goes out to the balcony to see if the delivery guy is lost. He picks up his bat that's kept in the corner out of habit and starts to shadow-bat while looking for the guy. Cricket's another thing that helps soothe his anxiety. When he has a bat in hand and faces a bowling machine, his mind's at rest. But even then, he shouldn't have made a big deal out of it by calling

Kamlesh. He broke his only rule: *to hide from the world*. Because that's what he fucking deserves. That, and his vegetables on time.

That's when he sees where his food is. Aishwarya is in her garden, sitting on a broken chair. Around her are the grocery packets, delivered as the app said. And, from what he can make out, she's munching on a carrot. He feels his breathing slow down. He should be angry, and yet he finds his heart settle.

He jumps from the balcony to the parapet. Then on to the side ledge, and then to the garden.

'Look! Spiderman!' squeals Aishwarya when she spots him.

'Hey,' he says, angrily pointing to his groceries.

'Here, there's some left,' she slurs, barely able to form words. 'Promise I will pay for the carrots.'

Dhiren sees the dried streaks of tears, the dishevelled hair of a runaway bride, the drunk eyes. And despite looking like she hasn't showered in days, she is beautiful.

'What were you about to make today? By the way, that kheer? Total *tabahi* [destruction]. Licked the bowl clean. What do you keep making up there? The entire house smells like . . . wow! I'm gaining calories just by smelling your food.'

Dhiren says, 'You're drunk. And you're supposed to be a role model for the kids.'

'And look at you, you're like a male model with all your muscles and stuff,' she smiles.

'What?'

'It's the weekend, Dhiren. People my age drink A LOT. So what if one day I drink a lot? It's not like I'm pregnant or anything. Hey? Do you know, Dhiren, that there's no conclusive evidence that alcohol is bad for unborn children? Like, nothing. Not that I would drink or anything, but just saying.'

'I have to go,' says Dhiren, picking up the grocery bags. 'Go and sleep.'

'Are you a chef, Dhiren? But Kamlesh Uncle said you were in software. Haw? Did you lie to him? Or is it like a passion? Software by day, but always wanted to open a dhaba?'

He's walking away when he hears a chuckle. He turns to look at her. 'What now?'

'You're shadow-batting even with grocery bags.'

'I was—'

'I have seen you shadow-bat in your balcony. I'm sorry, but you're not very good.'

'Bye.'

'Let's see how good you are with a real ball,' says Aishwarya, scrambling up. She's swaying. 'Get a ball. I will bowl a few.'

'Why do you drink if you can't handle it? You should go to bed.'

Aishwarya giggles. 'Oh, we are saying obvious things now? What's next? *Achche ghar ki ladkiyan bahar nahi jaateen* [Girls from good families don't go out]? Are you scared of facing a girl's bowling?'

'No . . .'

'Okay, so here's the bet—'

'There's no bet.'

'Two balls, you just have to touch the ball once. If I beat you, you make me a . . . khichdi. And not like a dal khichdi, but one with all the vegetables you have ordered. That's what you were about to cook, right?'

Dhiren turns and leaves. But five minutes later, he returns with a Kookaburra ball. Partly because he doesn't want to leave her drunk in the garden, and partly because he's curious as to how this will end.

'Look who's back! Bulky Spiderman!' she says. 'Let's think, what do you get if you win the bet? Oh, yes. The terrace. You win, you can set up the bowling machine on the terrace.'

'Are you sure?'

'Of course I'm sure!'

Dhiren's not going to take away the garden from her because of a drunk bet. But he's surprised at how a big part of him is okay with taking it away from her. He's still surprised at how big a chunk of him is still an asshole.

Aishwarya flings off her heels. She points to the far end of the garden. 'There. You can see there are old scratches of a wicket there. Go, stand there . . .'

'I'm not going that far for underarm bowling.'

'Go naa, Uncle. Just go. It's going to be leg spin.'

Aishwarya is now at the other end of the garden, thirty yards away, swirling the ball between her tiny, split fingers, still smiling stupidly. Dhiren reminds himself to look at the ball and not at her. It's easier said than done. In the soft glow of street lights, she looks dazzling.

Aishwarya takes three hops, her arm comes down in a tight loop. Dhiren's bat is out there to meet the ball, but it flies miles away from the bat. He's so far out of the crease that he stumbles to the ground.

'It must have hit a rock or something,' protests Dhiren as he staggers back up.

'You're so cute, Dhiren. Like a little, fluffy toy dog. But like a hot toy dog. Try again.'

Aishwarya takes position again. She wipes the ball against her dress and strides into action. Dhiren swings, the ball spins the other way. It gets Dhiren right in the crotch. The pain takes a few seconds to register. And when it does, Dhiren's clutching his balls. The pain radiates outwards from his penis to his stomach. He doubles over. He can hear her laugh and laugh and laugh.

'Do I lose?' she asks. 'Because you did touch the ball! With your balls, lol, lol, lol, lol.'

13.

Dhiren Das

Aishwarya emerges from the bathroom in a Team India jersey with Sonali Raj's—the Indian women's team captain—name on the back and loose pyjamas. Dhiren has seen the jerseys drying out in the garden, but he had never thought of her as a leg-spinning genius. She looked athletic with distractingly strong thighs, her back a little too wide for her small frame and pinched shoulders, built like a gymnast, but he hadn't guessed cricket. He has to look away every few seconds to not stare at her body, the soft outlines of her breasts and her shapely legs.

Dhiren points at the jersey and says, 'Yes, yes, I get it, you play well.'

Aishwarya looks down and is immediately apologetic. 'No, no, I just wore this because . . . I have three of these, so. And sorry, I didn't mean to laugh earlier.'

As she comes close, Dhiren notices that the make-up is gone. She has washed her face and her skin is slick with moisturizer. Her sharp nose is shining under the kitchen's downlight. She's beautiful in a way that's comforting, like a painting or an ASMR video. Just looking at her makes Dhiren relax.

'You don't have to make khichdi. I was a little . . . out,' she says.

He slips a glass of lemonade in front of her. 'Why's your kitchen such a mess?' he asks, chopping the vegetables for the khichdi.

'I . . .'

'Don't apologize,' he says, sensing there would be another sentence starting with an apology. 'It's not going to take long.' He puts a pan on the stove, adds cumin seeds, bay leaves, cinnamon, cloves, green cardamoms and lets the spices crackle. 'So you played in college?'

'Almost made it to the Ranji team as a bowler,' says Aishwarya. She pulls down the sleeve of her jersey to expose her right shoulder. 'You see this? My right shoulder is bigger than the left. One summer, my coach made me bowl with a heavier ball to develop speed and strength. I have been lopsided ever since. You should see me in an off-the-shoulder dress.'

Dhiren would like to see her in an off-the-shoulder dress. *Or without.* She pulls her jersey back up.

'Guys take a lot of offence when they can't hit me for sixes. You didn't,' she says with a smile.

'The pain was blinding, couldn't think.' Dhiren sautés the chopped onions and adds garlic paste, tomato and chilli to it. 'We are living in the age of taking offence.'

'Sorry, but no,' Aishwarya shakes her head. 'We are living in an age of politeness. Earlier, one could say anything hurtful and get away with it. Now we are setting rules of what's acceptable. Why be hurtful when you can be kind?'

Dhiren wants her to keep talking, her voice a soothing balm. 'You're a Sonali Raj fan.'

'I worship her,' she says. 'Also, she's the best cricketer who has ever lived.'

'Ever? Bradman? Sachin? Kohli? Muralitharan?'

'Cricket is a girl's sport, Dhiren.'

'Now that's offensive,' Dhiren frowns.

'No sport in the world has as much complexity as cricket. Football? Men trying to kick a ball into a net. Tennis? Smash a ball across a net. Rugby? Grab and claim a ball to be theirs.'

'And cricket?'

'Dhiren, *aap socho naa ek baar* [think about it],' she says, leaning forward, catching his gaze. 'Cricket has elegance. You dress up in bright white clothes, put on sunscreen and carefully hang a small towel on your waist to clean the ball. It's a game that demands to be overthought. You're constantly thinking what will happen on the field five days later, how the soil will behave, will the grass die, what do those clouds on the horizon mean, will the ball be too rough, what part of the ball needs to shine like it's new, should we appeal to the good side of an umpire to give a favourable decision. It's a game of soft touches, deft fingers, impeccable timing, rather than brute force. It's played only after a leisurely breakfast, and even then we break for lunch, have drinks in the middle, and then sit around and have tea for a bit. Who does that better than us? The women. Do you see it?'

In a few short sentences, Aishwarya has made Dhiren reimagine the game.

'I see it,' he says.

It wasn't the sound logic, it was the way she looked into his eyes and made him picture a game at Lord's—Sonali Raj and her team sipping tea in spotless whites, discussing the state of the grass on the pitch, deconstructing the weather and wondering whether the opposition batsmen are troubled by their footwork.

Dhiren locks the pressure cooker. 'Three whistles and a bit more.'

'You really didn't have to do this. I'm sorry,' she says.

'I had to make some for myself anyway, so . . .' says Dhiren. 'You didn't eat at the date?'

Aishwarya's smile dies out. 'Ex-boyfriend.'

'A second chance?'

'It wasn't a romantic meeting. I just wanted his cum inside me.'

'Wait, what? What did you want?'

'Oh,' she slaps her forehead and laughs. 'I'm not a cum enthusiast. I want to be pregnant, Akshay was supposed to be the donor. We were about to go the artificial insemination route. But he said no.'

'For a teacher, your communication skills are sub-par.'

'I'm going to blame it on the alcohol.'

'But aren't you like, nineteen? Why would you want to be a mother so young?'

'There's nothing more I have wanted in life.'

'Okay, hypothetical question. What would you choose? Playing for India or having a baby?'

'Eleven babies; six girls, five boys,' she answers. 'But why should I have to choose? So, eleven kids and playing for India.'

'A bit much. And you will raise these children alone? That sounds rough,' he says, still struggling to wrap his head around it. *She's starting a new business. Why would she want to be a mother at the same time?*

'You have seen little girls who play with baby dolls? I never got over that phase. Also, I just think having a guy in the picture is a complication. I want my child to have all my attention, and men don't usually help a lot.'

'You're making men redundant,' says Dhiren.

Dhiren can feel it coming. Just like she did with cricket, she's going to launch into some zany but cute explanation. And he's hoping she does. She's smiling, but she stays quiet.

'You want to say something so badly, don't you?'

'Sorry, but I do!' she squeals. 'I have had this conversation SO MANY TIMES that I have a theory.'

He chuckles. 'Please enlighten me.'

And so she begins, her eyes lighting up.

'Men, in the strictest evolutionary sense, are of limited use. Women needed them in the past when bands of men used to hunt down megafauna like the sabre-toothed tigers or giant sloths or mammoths, or fight wars that hinged on strength, heavy chain mail and sturdy swords, or row tirelessly across oceans and tread the Silk Route deserts to establish trade relationships. Do we need so many men now? If the goal of any species is to breed the best, why not get a few of the strongest, smartest men to impregnate all women? Keep the best of men locked up in gilded cages, keep them well-fed and milk them for their sperm. Natural selection suggests we get rid of the rest.'

Dhiren is completely absorbed by how animatedly she is laying out her theory. Not just with her words, but also her eyes, her hands, her body, like she's doing a puppet show with characters, voices, songs. She becomes a sabre-toothed tiger by flashing her canines and a giant sloth by lumbering on the table menacingly. When she mentions wars, she swings her hand around and grunts as if she's a medieval warrior, and looks around scared when she's on the Silk Route.

She can go on the entire night and he will be right here, listening, bewitched by this gorgeous storytelling gypsy who knows everything.

'You're suggesting genocide. But if that's so obvious, why didn't it happen till now?'

'Men are clever. They realized their need would be limited in the future. So, the ancient ones—kings, nobles, religious men, traders—all the powerful men came together, worried, scared, and in a moment of brilliance, they invented the rules of monogamy. One man, one woman. Suddenly, all men were needed. Every single man was important. Legends of love were told, romantic books were written, movies were made, Hallmark cards were printed, weddings were celebrated, pregnancies were made important, and women were told that they should *want* these things—love, wedding, romance, families. But it's the men who need these. If you're genetically ungifted, the only way to survive is romance. Without romance, only the strong, the disease-resistant, the tall will survive.'

Her storytelling is wizardry. She can move her large pupils around and put a man into a hypnotic trance. Dhiren hangs on to every word of hers. He feels he has to agree with what she's saying. How can her eyes lie? Dhiren wonders if this is how a religion comes into being—a ravishing person with a great story.

'Romance is a conspiracy?' asks Dhiren.

'Romance, once strictly optional, was now mandatory. Romantic love didn't make women whole, it saved men from oblivion and extinction. Children were now meant to be god's gift, brought into the world after the blissful union of a man and a woman. But it's all a lie concocted by ancient rishis, priests and prophets—all men! Think about it, why not get children off the assembly line? Why not make sure they get the best of genes from a man and mix them up with a little bit of the woman who carries them and raises them as truly their own?'

'I mean . . .' Dhiren can't finish the sentence.

She continues. 'Think climate-wise too. We waste precious food in sustaining bigger bodies of men, with higher metabolism rates for the same contribution to society. How much can we save by not having so many men? We already do that with cattle, thirty cows to one bull. We only keep the best bull.'

The three whistles and two minutes on low flame are up.

'Wow,' mumbles Dhiren.

She breaks out of her own train of thought. 'Sorry, I'm talking too much, no?'

'I mean . . . you did call me a bull and most men useless cattle, worthy of slaughter, and keeping the good ones in a cage.'

Aishwarya giggles. Dhiren unlocks the pressure cooker. He serves them on two plates with raita and pickle. They move to the sofa.

'When did you make the raita?' asks Aishwarya.

'You were talking at length. I had time.'

Aishwarya lifts the plate to her nose, takes in a deep breath like a coke addict and asks, 'Do you want a review?'

'I'm sure it's great, MasterChef Aishwarya.'

Aishwarya takes a bite and closes her eyes. 'Your overconfidence is not misplaced. It's like my tongue's wrapped in flavours. It's amazing. Let's be quiet and eat this. I have been smelling all kinds of tasty things you make. Today's finally the day! By the way, please don't remind me about all of this tomorrow.'

'I have been thinking about what you said,' says Dhiren, putting a spoonful of khichdi in his mouth. 'What if?'

'What if what?'

'What if monogamy was invented by women?' offers Dhiren.

'How?' she asks, ghee dripping from the sides of her mouth.

'What were the ancient men and women doing?' he begins. 'They have a lot of time on their hands. So, naturally, they have orgies so wild, the widest lenses from the Pornhub team can't capture them. After every orgy, a few women get pregnant, but have no idea whose child they carried. The men leave for their hunts. Women are left behind with the babies. With time, the women get tired of washing cave-baby bums. One day, they decide they don't want to do it alone. And so they spend the next thousands of days scheming to avoid raising children alone.' He stops to have a spoonful of khichdi.

'Why did you stop? I'm listening, but this khichdi is so good. Continue!'

'They use the insecurity of men to start the cult of monogamy. Women start picking a single man and brainwashing him—you're mine and I'm yours; if you find me in some other man's cave, maybe you're not a man; and yes, this baby's yours, it's your legacy. They teach men to be possessive, jealous, protective.'

'Are you going to finish your khichdi or can I take some?' asks Aishwarya. 'I will take some.' She scoops three spoonfuls from his plate.

'The agenda continues today. Women want men to have paternity leave so they are at home with their child through the shitting and crying. Women have worked hard to get men away from the trenches of the world and into the trenches of the household quite successfully.'

Aishwarya's eyes are half-closed.

'Hey?'

'. . .'

'Aishwarya?'

'. . .'

He snaps his fingers in front of her eyes.

She mumbles, 'Good night,' and in one smooth motion, keeps the plate aside, pulls the rug over herself and goes out like a light.

Dhiren takes the plates to the kitchen, and as silently as he can, washes up, dries the utensils and puts them back in the cabinets. He feels irritated seeing the haphazard arrangement of pots and pans, spices and grains, and so he quickly rearranges them. Satisfied, he leaves, and for the first time in months, he doesn't have to lull his senses to sleep by watching a movie. He gets into bed and falls asleep almost instantly.

14.

Aishwarya Mohan

It feels like the light in the room is searing her retinas. Aishwarya wakes and reaches out for her phone. Her head is threatening to burst open. Squinting, she checks her WhatsApp. Vinny and Smriti are screaming 'PLAN B' in the group. She wants to crawl back into a blanket fort and sleep till the sun burns itself out. The next moment, she jerks herself awake and sits up straight so quickly that her head spins.

Her phone's still blowing up.

Plan B.

Plan B!

Excuse me, Plan B? Should I talk to the fertility clinic?

She drags herself to the kitchen. She heats up water in the microwave and mixes in two spoonfuls of coffee. The bitterness of the coffee jolts her. The haze clears. The memory of being turned down by Akshay comes to her in pieces. How stupid of her to think she could bury the rejection with alcohol! There's a sharp pain in her right shoulder. Her back muscles feel like someone doused them with kerosene and torched them.

Khichdi.

The memories of last night now rush in.

No.

Did Dhiren cook? Oh yes, he cooked. Of course, he was cooking, he was right here. We talked, didn't we? About what? About women? Monogamy something? She buries her head in her palms. *No. What were you even saying? What was he saying?* She looks down. *Did you wear this jersey . . . to show you're better than him at cricket? Wow, Aishwarya, just wow. The bet? Oh shit, the bet! Are you stupid? You bet the terrace? What must he be thinking about you? You drunk, drunk stupid person. Oh my god! Did you tell him everything?* Buddhu hai kya *[Are you stupid]? But he did cook, so maybe he didn't think too badly of you? But you were sitting drunk with his groceries in the garden. What were you thinking? You're impossible, Aishwarya. How pagal can you be? Who asked you to drink, you dumb, stupid girl?*

She looks around—the kitchen looks different. Clean. Organized. Did she get drunk and clean the kitchen? She spots stickers on the cabinets. *Big utensils. Chai utensils. China. Steel Plates.* It's not her handwriting, not her stickers. *No!*

Did I ask him to clean the kitchen? No. No. Of course I didn't. But he did. Or maybe I did ask him?

She opens the fridge—similarly organized—and finds khichdi in the small Tupperware box. Did he do it without being asked?

Her train of thought is broken by the loud honks of a truck outside followed by the ringing of her doorbell.

'AA RAHI HOON! I'm coming!' she shouts and runs outside.

The thekedar and two workers are waiting at the door. Seeing them sends a rush of joy through her body. The hangover vanishes. Cute Buttons will finally come into being. Today, the work will start and this ramshackle house will be transformed!

'Madam,' the thekedar angrily raises his hands in the air. '*Kahan ho aap* [Where have you been]? We came in the morning also. You didn't open the door only.'

'Sorry, sorry, I had fever last night. Shall we go inside?'

'Madam, first let's talk about the rate here,' he says gruffly.

'I will make chai for you—'

'No, no, no need, let's discuss here only,' he cuts her off.

When Aishwarya first met him and finalized him, he was kind, called himself a partner, said Aishwarya was like his beti. He promised *bhagwan kasam* [swore on god that] he would give special rates and top quality, five-star work. He seems to have changed.

'Madam, we checked your plans, *nahi ho payega* [this can't be done].'

'What do you mean "nahi ho payega", Uncle? We talked, we settled on the price. Let's keep our word and start the work. Call your men inside.'

The thekedar waves her off. 'Labour won't touch anything till we talk about the price. Firstly, we need 40 per cent advance. And what you want done will cost *kam se kam* [at least] 20 per cent more. You changed all the designs.'

'Uncle, I'm like your daughter and you're doing this to me. I was counting on you,' she says, trying to compose herself.

'Beti, rate is rate. I called you beti but that doesn't mean I will work on loss. Go to the market and check it. Extra *toh lagega* [will be needed].'

'Uncle ji, please, let's just start work. You can't change the pricing at the last moment. It's been months we have been talking about this.'

'Madam, you're wasting our time. *Apne bachhe ki kasam* [I swear on my child], I said I will think about the discount and now you're holding a gun to my head. Either we work at my rate or I will leave. *Jaldi batao* [Tell me quickly], what are we doing?'

The thekedar throws a look at his two labourers who nod and get back into his truck.

'Call your papa and ask him if it's acceptable,' says the thekedar.

'Arre, why would I call my papa? This is my business, not his. I talked to you, nahi?'

'Yes, but you're not understanding only. We can't work on the old prices.'

'But why? You promised!'

'Again, we are going round and round. This is work, madam. What promise? Did we sign something? You're holding my neck only, that do work at the old price when I have told you we can't.'

'I can't pay you any more than what we decided. I don't have the money.'

'Madam, this you had to think before you called us. If you didn't have the capability, you shouldn't have come into this only. What can we do if you don't have money? We also work, we have children, we need to feed them. We can't be working for free.'

'Sir, I'm paying you the old price, what we decided!'

'*Phir wahi baat*! Again you're saying the same thing!'

'Uncle—'

'Madam, *aap khud hi kar lo phir* [you can do it yourself then],' says the thekedar. He turns away without a word and walks towards the truck. 'Don't waste our time, madam.'

Aishwarya follows him. 'Uncle, Uncle, Uncle . . .'

'Call me if you want to rework the price.' He gets into the truck and slams the door. 'You have my number.'

'Uncle, let's talk . . .'

The thekedar drives off. Aishwarya keeps standing there for a few seconds, stunned. She plods back inside the house, heart thumping, fingers trembling. *Keep it together, Aishwarya.* She sits at her desk and stares at the Excel file on her screen. A 20 per cent increase would have been just the start. This is what thekedars do, Vinny had warned her, but Aishwarya had insisted she had found a nice man.

It's late evening and she has called every thekedar on the list in her diary. She has reworked the calculations, and it's clear that she will fall short of money.

The thekedar's words ring in her ears. *If you didn't have the capability, you shouldn't have come into this only.* How dare he say that? Capability? Does he even know who he's talking to? She can mother a chimpanzee cub and turn it into a fully-functional human adult. If that thekedar as a child had access to what Cute Buttons would be, he wouldn't have been such an obnoxious man.

Madam, aap khud hi kar lo phir . . .

Why not? she thinks. *Why not? I will show him what I can do. How difficult can it be?* She types 'flooring' into the YouTube search bar. And stumbles into the strange, unexplored world of DIY. There are DIY girls with YouTube channels who have turned their parents' rickety bedrooms, crumbling bathrooms and old living rooms into beautiful, paradisiacal, Instagram-viral-worthy spaces. They paint, they tile, they fix—all the while being on camera. All that's needed is patience, the right information and the right clothes. Aishwarya has all of these now. In the next hour, she fills up her diary with notes, types of flooring, cement mixes, glue types.

She crosses out the thekedar list in her diary and overwrites: *Screw the thekedar. DIY.*

*

At Counter 12 of Ace Hardware, Dwarka, the only customer, a bright-eyed Aishwarya, is feverishly cross-checking her list one last time to see if she's got everything. In the four carts filled to the brim, there are three types of laminate flooring, paints, a collapsible ladder, stools, paintbrushes, worker's belts, adhesives and the like. The flashing total on the calculator screen puts a wide smile on Aishwarya's face. Just on raw materials, she's saving 25 per cent of what the swindling thekedar was asking for. And unlike what he had advised, which was to redo the *entire* flooring, she knows now that she can paint over tiles, use stick-on tiles, and for the wooden flooring, she can use click-on versions that don't require hammering and breaking old tiles. She can save a fortune!

The cashier bills it. The van she's booked is already waiting outside. She can't wait to get cracking. In her mind, she can see Cute Buttons coming into being. Once outside, she helps the driver load up the van. They are almost finished when an edge of the collapsible ladder cuts open a small gash on her hand. She hurriedly wraps her handkerchief around it to staunch the bleeding. The excitement overwhelms any pain. But her excitement meets a rude end when the van reaches Cute Buttons.

Vinny and Smriti's cars are parked outside and the gate's open. Vinny marches out, eyebrows knitted, arms crossed in front of her, furious. Smriti follows closely behind, disappointment and concern in her eyes. Aishwarya knows her friends—they will make a big deal out of this.

'When were you going to tell us about the thekedar?' interrogates Vinny.

'And were you going to do everything yourself? *Pagal ho gayi hai*, are you mad?' butts in Smriti.

Aishwarya shrugs. 'I have seen a few YouTube videos. It's absolutely doable, it's not a big deal. Also, it makes perfect economic sense.'

Vinny notices the bloodied handkerchief around Aishwarya's hand.

'This *bewakoof ladki* [stupid girl],' grumbles Vinny. 'Smriti, bandage this, I will unload the material.'

'Hey, I'm fine. There's no need to overreact. It's a scratch.'

Smriti holds Aishwarya by the arm and takes her inside. The gash is small but deep. Smriti wraps the wound with her bony, angry fingers. Vinny marches into the room and sits in front of her.

Before the girls start to bicker and complain, Aishwarya puts on her assertive teacher voice and says, 'Listen to me, both of you. I know you guys can give me more money for a new thekedar. But I'm going to send back any money you send to me. I can do this. I really can, and I will do this. And both of you have to support me on this because you know I can. Look at me, and listen to me. I will show you.'

She gets her laptop and shows them the playlist of twenty-three videos she has compiled that she needs to emulate to redo the place.

'Watch just a few carefully. It's not that *hard*. These girls are doing it all by themselves. Look at this. Look at what her living room was and what she did with it. And if she can do it, I can too.'

Vinny and Smriti nod like obedient children.

'What about your pregnancy, behen?' asks Vinny. 'You can't be doing heavy lifting while you're pregnant, *gadhi* [idiot].'

'First of all, there's hardly any lifting. And secondly, Akshay's out so . . . I don't know where I'm at. Maybe he will come around. Right now, I need to start work as soon as possible. I can't afford to lose any more time.'

The girls nod. When Aishwarya talks in that tone, there's no refusing her. It's like they are puppies and she their trainer.

For the next half hour, the three of them scrub through the YouTube videos Aishwarya has bookmarked. Both of them agree that if anyone can do it, it's her.

'Can you smell that?' asks Smriti, sniffing.

'Is that mutton?' asks Vinny.

'That's Dhiren upstairs. He cooks well,' says Aishwarya. And then something inside of her lights up at the prospect of seeing Dhiren again. A warm, bubbly feeling. It's the perfect pretext. She can thank him for the khichdi and the organization of her kitchen, and she can apologize for being an embarrassment. She asks them, 'Do you guys want some? I can ask him if he has some left over.'

'Are you guys friends now?' asks Vinny, possessive as she always is.

Aishwarya has conveniently skipped the drunk-khichdi incident from last night because she knows the girls will throw a fit. She has no intention of telling the two of them about it too. They might be grown mothers, but when it comes to boys in her life, they still behave like teenagers.

'We are cordial neighbours,' she answers.

*

Aishwarya is at Dhiren's door, her head muddled with the amazing aroma of mutton that's in the air and the anticipation of seeing him again.

He opens the door in a black Under Armour tank top and shorts and immediately takes her breath away. His unnaturally sculpted body's covered and yet it feels to her like he's naked, bare. *Look away, just look away.* But there's a lot of distracting skin, sinewy muscles and veins in her view, and she wants him to wear a jacket so she can tear her eyes off him. Her eyes fix on the thick vein on his bicep, which snakes down to his forearm and splits into a bunch of meandering veins. She feels an overwhelming need to touch his forearm. Though what he's wearing is loose, she can make out the rough outline of his chest. She tells herself to snap out of it.

'Hey,' she says. She feels her insides soften, and a smile creeps up on his face. 'Thank you for last night. I'm sorry if I embarrassed myself.'

'It's safe to say we both embarrassed ourselves,' says Dhiren and mimics how he got beaten in cricket.

'Sorry for calling your batting terrible. You're . . . maybe just a little out of touch.'

He nods as if he knows she's lying.

She continues. 'I have a very strange request.'

'Surprise me.'

'Ummm . . . do you have some mutton left over? My friends, they smelled it and . . .'

'I will get you a casserole,' he says without a second thought. He turns away and then stops. 'Do you guys have rice? Or wait, I have some atta left over. Give me five and I can make a few lacchha paranthas. Come inside.'

Aishwarya steps inside. Dhiren leads her to the kitchen.

There, he sprinkles a fistful of water into a bowl of dough and kneads it. His fingers are deft and quick. Aishwarya watches the dense muscle fibres of his arm separate and pulse with the effort as if they have a life of their own. She's surprised by how much attention she's paying to his arm, a beautiful, rugged arm, but just an arm nonetheless.

With considerable effort, she looks away.

The living room is dimly lit—there are no overhead tube lights—only small lamps in the corners bathing the wall in warm white light. The room's practically bare, she notices, but he has made some adjustments. He has changed the flooring—she knows now from the YouTube videos she has watched. It's the wooden click-on tiles. She can smell the paranthas now, but she can also smell agarbatti and a smell she recognizes as his. There's a large couch, but no TV. In a corner, there's a big desktop computer on a table and stacks of books on both sides. But other than that, the room's empty. He has painted the walls white, but she doesn't remember any workers coming in or going out in the time since he moved in. From the little that she can see of the bedroom, there's only a low bed, a plant by its side, another tottering tower of books.

'Here,' says Dhiren handing over a bag with the casserole and paranthas.

'Thanks,' she says, breathing him in. 'I should go.'

And she walks away, a slight shiver running down her spine, thinking of his eyes on her, thinking of his low bed, of his arms, of him, of his half-droopy eyes, of his stubbled face.

Back downstairs, all three of them ravenously polish off the food.

'I think I should get a dabba from him every day,' jokes Aishwarya when they are done.

She wonders when she will see him again, what other pretext she can find. And then she forces herself to snap back to reality. She can't let a boy derail her focus. Cute Buttons needs her, now more than ever.

15.

Dhiren Das

Bookmark Dhiren has made it through a week without seeing Aishwarya again. He can continue that streak. But he's not doing it for himself, it's for her, he tells himself. Last week, he had heard the thekedar arguing with Aishwarya and had guessed she had taken it on herself to renovate Cute Buttons. And for the last week, he has witnessed her toil from dawn till dusk, sometimes late into the night.

It's been seven days and there have been over twenty food deliveries from joints as bad as Arora Chinese Hut. She has forgotten to water the vegetable garden thrice. Of the times he has seen her in the garden cutting through tiles and mixing paint, she has looked tired, bloated, sunken. He has wanted to offer help, but he hasn't because that is the smart thing to do. It is none of his business. He had moved into this neighbourhood to hide. Not to go about making friends and accidentally exposing himself. If he starts helping Aishwarya, how long before her friends want to meet him? What if they recognize who he really is? And so, for the past week, he has put his head down, stayed in his apartment and avoided any meetings with her. But how can he not help her?

Not after today.

This afternoon, she was sawing through a piece of stubborn wood when the saw slipped and slashed her left palm—precisely where she got hurt the last time.

Dhiren checks the sambhar. When he tastes it, his taste buds singe, and that's just how he likes it. He hopes *she* likes it too. He packs the food and makes his way down. He finds her in the kitchen, putting noodles on to a plate from a thin polythene bag. She looks up, her face slick with sweat. She's already thinner, bony, cheeks sunken.

'You don't have to eat that,' he says.

'I smell sambhar,' she says with a grin so wide it's reflecting in her eyes. 'I hope you have enough for you because I can eat a city right now.'

Dhiren sits next to her. The past seven days felt as though he had held his breath, and now that he sees her, it feels like he can finally breathe. He fixes two plates. She says nothing and digs in, shovelling spoonfuls into her mouth. He watches her ears go warm from the spices. She likes it because every couple of minutes, he ladles a little bit of the curd, sambhar and rice on to her plate, and she wipes that clean.

'There's more upstairs,' he says when he notices Aishwarya stealing glances at the casserole.

'If I eat any more, I will have to take a year-long nap.'

'Naps are great, a nap never hurt anyone.'

'Where have you been?' she asks. 'I saw the lights on every day, but you never came down, so I thought . . .'

'I was . . . a little busy.'

'Were you ignoring me? I came up twice, rang the bell. No answer.'

'I don't spend the *entire* day at home.'

'No, no,' says Aishwarya. 'You were home. I could smell everything. It was bhindi one night, and some kind of fish the other night. So I thought maybe you have had enough of me.'

He was there. He had wanted to open the door. But his mind had taken him on a wild, horrid ride. It had shown him a future where they were friends and she finally found out who he really was. That couldn't end well. So he didn't open the door.

'I . . .'

'It's okay. People get bored of me. I talk a little too much about kids and Cute Buttons,' says Aishwarya, still eating, only expending half of her mind on the conversation.

She pushes the plate away. It has been licked clean. 'Wow,' she says. 'I ate like a refugee, didn't I?' She laughs. 'Thank you so much for cooking for me.'

'Presumptuous of you to think that I cooked for you,' he says. 'I cooked for myself and there was some left.'

She leans back and taps her tummy. 'Look at this. So round,' she says with a laugh. 'Thank you for being nice to me.'

He wants to tell her that no one's nice, and that her niceness seems almost unreal. Absolute niceness is actually a pretence. Most times, we are nice to manipulate others into accepting us. We are nice in fragments and pieces, but no one's nice as a whole. Parts of us are broken, damaged, vengeful, jealous, angry, hurt, unloved, hated. Cruelty is always honest, but niceness isn't. He's not being nice to her; being here is a selfish pursuit. Being with her, talking to her, is the only way he can stop his overworked brain, dull his anxiety and think of happiness as a possibility.

Dhiren says exactly what he decided not to say. 'Aishwarya, I can help you with the flooring. I have done this before.'

'No. I can't . . .'

'You look tired and I have free time. Let me lend you a hand.'

'I would need both hands if you're to help me,' she says and laughs.

'Wow, good thing you only interact with children.'

'I can't let you help,' she says firmly.

For a brief moment, he sees why she will make a great teacher. She can be cheery with her expressive Kathakali eyes, but one look and she can make you sit down and obey.

She continues. 'I can't let you do this. I have nothing to offer you. I'm broke and running on fumes here.'

'That's not true,' he says. 'In return, you can bowl to me from time to time, train me a little.'

'That's nonsense, Dhiren. I can do that anyway.'

'And I can work for you anyway.'

Dhiren wants to shut up, retract his words, but he has no control over it any more.

'Tell me something, Dhiren,' she says, still in her strict-teacher persona. 'Is cryptocurrency worth so much that you can just while away your time like this? Because this feels like I'm taking advantage of you. I can't do that.'

Dhiren breaks into a laugh. 'Take advantage of me? Aishwarya, that has never happened to me and will never happen either. I'm going to wash these plates, change and you're going to tell me exactly what needs to be done. Okay?'

He turns away from her.

Fuck.

16.

Aishwarya Mohan

Aishwarya was opening the packet of noodles when Dhiren had walked in carrying sambhar, which she smelt way before she saw him. She could have shot out questions like an assault rifle. *Why didn't you open the door, not once, but twice? And if you were home, why didn't you come to see me? Did I cross some line? Did I accidentally flirt with you and put you off? Why did you water the garden if I had put you off?* She wanted to know what she had done wrong. And yet she forgets everything when she smells that sambhar.

Now, they are working on the flooring of the sleeping room of the Cute Buttons nursery. But she's curious as to why he didn't open the door. On both days, she waited for fifteen minutes. She had wondered if there was a girl inside. And then, like a creep, she had checked the CCTV cameras—no girls. She knew she had no right to feel angry about the imaginary girl, but she did.

For the entire last week, she had worked like a dog. But as she wrapped up every day, her body crying for rest, sleep and food, she had wanted to see him, watch him cook, talk to him and turn her insides to jelly like he did that drunk night and the next morning. There were times during the last week when she slipped into day-dreaming about him, of where that drunk night could have taken them. She wished for him to come down with food, scold her for making a mess in the kitchen again, set it all right and listen to her speak without thinking it's odd.

Aishwarya's eyes dart towards Dhiren. He's lifting his T-shirt to wipe the sweat off his brow. She has to ask him not to do it because his sweaty, taut abdominal muscles are distracting. *For someone with a sedentary job and a knack for cooking, he's fit*, thinks Aishwarya. She feels irritated for relentlessly thinking about him.

Block it out. Yes, in fact, his abs are like blocks. Shut up. She gets back to work.

A little later, Aishwarya's phone rings. It's her father. 'Dhiren?' she calls out. "Don't say anything, not a word, not a breath. He shouldn't know you're here.'

Dhiren nods. The call lasts for ten minutes. It sounds like a safety check. *Lock the doors. Yes. Did you hear there was a robbery in Dwarka? Yes. I hope you're eating well. Yes. Don't let strangers in. Yes. Don't put your phone on mute. Yes.*

Click.

'Sorry about that,' she says. 'Papa thinks I am a perfect victim for a kidnapping, murder, robbery, accident, malnutrition.'

'I know how they can get. It's hard to grow up if you don't learn to lie to them.'

'Do you remember your first lie to your parents?'

Dhiren shakes his head. But Aishwarya can sense he's hiding something. It's one of the things Aishwarya noticed about Dhiren when she first met him. His eyes were always shifty, nervous, not at ease, looking to run away. She has wanted to ask him at times but has checked herself thinking it would mean crossing a line. Now, as she asks the question, it's clear to Aishwarya that Dhiren is used to masking whatever pain he's carrying with food, with his casualness, with the occasional frowns and anger. She has seen her fair share of children, and the way children and adults hide their pain isn't all that different. The only way to make them share their pain is to tell them your own pain, to be vulnerable. If it would take Aishwarya sharing her own pain about her family to make him share his, she will do just that.

'I remember my first lie like it was yesterday,' says Aishwarya. 'I was eight. I was at a clinic in the neighbourhood. Maa told the doctor, "She fell down while playing." I repeated the lie. I was taught to repeat the lie.'

'What had happened?' asks Dhiren.

'An hour ago, Maa had slapped me so hard that I had stumbled and hit my head on the table. What had I done? I had picked my one-year-old brother up from his crib to show him a pair of mynahs that had come to the window. Maa said I could have dropped him, he could have got hurt.'

The wound had healed in a week. But she never forgot how her mother had looked at her when she hit her. It wasn't anger, it wasn't concern for Yatin, it was hate. Pure, unbridled hate.

She looks up at Dhiren whose eyes have clouded over.

'I'm sorry,' he says.

'It was a long time ago.'

Aishwarya expects him to share too. And for a few moments, while he's looking at her, it feels as though he will.

'Shall we get back to work?' he asks.

Aishwarya shakes off the painful memory. 'For someone who hates kids, you're in a hurry to get children here.'

'I didn't say I hated them,' says Dhiren. There's a long pause, after which he says in a voice that's a lot softer, 'Do you have siblings?'

'Yatin,' says Aishwarya. 'He's younger. You?'

'Dead.'

Aishwarya feels breathless, like someone has sucked the air out of the room. Her mouth goes dry. There are times people around her discuss their worst fears. For some it's losing all their money, reputation, health, their own death, loss of parents, or some combination of these. For Aishwarya, it has always been as clear as day what her biggest fear is. It is losing a child. Every time she reads in the news about parents losing their children in accidents, to suicides, to crimes, she knows what she would have done if she was in their position. She would have ended her life too. It's the kind of pain she knows she can't bear. She's surprised to see people growing old after their child's death. It seems impossible to her. The death of a child is the end of the world. When older people die, the grief's tempered. They could have lived longer, but they *have* lived. When young children, innocent of heart and mind, so capable of being happy and spreading it around, perish, it's grossly unfair. Aishwarya's heart sinks.

'I'm so sorry,' says Aishwarya. 'Was it long ago?'

'I was six,' he says.

'I'm sorry if I'm intruding,' she says, her heart in pieces. She wants to reach out and hug Dhiren. She wants to make the pain in his eyes go away.

'Abortion,' says Dhiren. 'My parents killed her.'

'Dhiren?'

Dhiren's eyes glass over. 'Maa was four months pregnant. They didn't want the child. They . . .' His voice falters, his fingers tremble, a tear peeks out from the corner of his eye. '. . . I was there, in the nursing home, sitting right outside where they did it. They went in, and they came out. Just like that. Like it was nothing. Absolutely nothing.'

'But . . .'

Aishwarya wants to tell Dhiren that bringing a child into a house that can't take care of it is worse than an abortion. But she knows this is not the time.

Dhiren wipes his tears and stares down at his hands. 'I heard them talk in the car, you know. What did they think? A six-year-old wouldn't understand these things? Of course I did. You know what they said?'

'Dhiren.'

'They said their projects and office work wouldn't leave enough time for a child.'

Aishwarya watches him look at her, trying to contain what's inside of him.

'And that was it. I was alone,' he says. '. . . again. So, to answer your question, my parents weren't around a lot to listen to my lies. For them, everything was more important than their children.'

'I'm sorry, Dhiren.'

'The child would have been almost Yatin's age. Can you believe that? If only they hadn't killed her,' says Dhiren. He looks up to meet her eyes. The pain crushes Aishwarya's heart. He continues. 'I could have taken care of her, you know. How difficult could it have been? And then there are nurseries, right? When I would have been in school she could have been in a place like . . . this . . .' He looks around at the half-renovated Cute Buttons. '. . . and then I could have taken her home.'

'It must have been hard on you.'

Dhiren chuckles sadly, shrugs and says, 'And I made it hard for them. I made sure they suffered like I did. They deserved it.'

'What did you do?'

'I told everyone what they did. Classmates, teachers, my dada-dadi, family friends. Everyone I knew. I made it my opening line. "*I have a dead sister, they killed her*", I used to say.'

Aishwarya watches his eyes burn with anger.

'I did that for years actually,' he said.

'They . . .'

'Fuck them,' he grunts. He falls silent, and slowly the air around them seems to become thick and weigh down on them. He looks up, 'Shall we take a break?'

He walks out before Aishwarya can string together a response.

17.

Dhiren Das

Dhiren and Aishwarya are at the dingy, foul-smelling Swastik Pure Veg restaurant, sipping tea and tapping away furiously on their laptops.

'They do have the best tea,' says Aishwarya, looking up from her laptop.

Dhiren nods and gets back to doling out cryptocurrency advice to business people who often seek him out for a quick return on their money. Sometimes, Dhiren can't believe how easy it is. Bankers and traders around the world are so set in their ways, they refuse to learn the market.

Every now and then, Dhiren watches Aishwarya gobble the complimentary digestive biscuits quicker than the waiter can serve them and knows it's the most beautiful thing he has ever seen. Every few minutes, her glasses slip down her nose, and she lets them slide till they are at the tip before pulling them back up. Although she barely speaks a word, Dhiren feels drained. His senses are exhausted by taking in everything Aishwarya's doing: how her fingers float over the keyboard, how she wrinkles her nose every time she forgets something, how she slumps into the chair slowly, how pretty she looks.

Dhiren thought his last week's overshare about his parents would have made things weird. But Aishwarya has let the moment pass as if it was *nothing*. Instead she just said to him, 'Parents are tricky; they screw us up in unique ways.' That little sentence, and the look of understanding in her eyes, felt like balm on the festering, septic wound he had been carrying for years now. Even now, after an entire week, he keeps going back to that moment to feel calm and at rest.

And then, sometimes he wonders in what unique ways her parents screwed her up. He has known her for over a month and he has yet to see her talk to her mother. This, despite the fact that her father calls her *very* frequently. But he guesses things can't be that bad between her mother and her because her parents are visiting Cute Buttons today. Dhiren can't be there while they are.

Aishwarya's phone alarm rings.

'It's time,' she says. 'My parents won't stay for more than a couple of hours. So you can come back then. I'm so sorry. But if Papa sees you, I will have to answer all kinds of questions.'

'Take your time,' he says.

And thankfully, she leaves, because the three college boys from the other table haven't looked away from him for the better part of an hour. He recognizes the look—the look of wanting revenge. Dhiren knows something will go down. He's glad Aishwarya's not there to watch it. He slowly places his laptop in his bag. Below the table, he rotates his wrists. When he gets up, so do the three boys.

Dhiren's just outside the shop when the biggest of the boys calls out, 'Hey!'

He turns and the boys are in his face, within punching distance.

'Look, guys, if you're here to fight . . .'

And then, it happens in a split second.

'MADARCHOD!' screams the littlest guy.

Dhiren notes the dank, sour smell before darkness takes over. His upper body is now in a wet rice sack. At DTU, *bori mein daal kar maarenge* [we will put him in a sack and beat him] is the preferred mode of campus ambushes for errant juniors, egomaniacal professors and boys who text taken girls. The sack's effective. Dhiren can't flail his arms around. He is now a stationary, large target for the boys' kicks. The first kicks land straight into his ribs. *Stay in the game, stay in the game, you have done this before*, he tells himself.

The trick of getting away cheap from a sack-beating is to freak out the attackers by being unresponsive and making them believe they have caused serious injury—a cracked skull, a concussion, a broken neck. 'Fraud *bhosdi ka* [fucker],' says one, panting. Dhiren senses a window of opportunity and rolls away from them. The boys struggle to keep the sack steady, but they are too tired. Dhiren pulls off the sack with ease and steps up and away from them. He had overestimated the frazzled boys in front of him. They are no fighters, they are front-benchers he can slap around in his sleep.

'I don't want to hurt you guys,' says Dhiren, reaching into his pocket. He grasps his bunch of keys, the pointed bits extending from his clenched fist. It's not Dhiren's first fight. 'I have to get one punch right and one of you will lose an eye.'

The boys from DTU seem to know his college history because they take a tentative step backwards.

The tall, gangly boy in the Metallica T-shirt with sickly thin arms, sparse facial hair and long, well-shampooed flowing hair growls, 'I am going to eat your heart! Fry it in hot oil and eat it!'

'That's a very unambiguous fantasy,' says Dhiren.

'TU MAREGA AAJ [YOU WILL DIE TODAY],' shouts the big guy, who is built like an old, well-fed Labrador, barely catching his breath.

Dhiren rolls his eyes. 'Bhai, you're just fat, no strength. Three minutes and you're panting.'

'*Betichod, ladki ghuma raha tha hamare paise se* [Bastard, you are taking girls around with our money]!' says the small guy, who could pass off as an eighth grader if he wore a school uniform.

'For your size, you swear a lot,' says Dhiren. 'How much money did you guys lose?'

'It's not just us,' says the big guy, sweating and panting.

'We will cut you apart, drink your blood,' says the Metallica guy, baring his misshapen teeth.

Dhiren says kindly, 'Calm down, bhai, get yourself a girlfriend and listen to Arijit Singh.'

'I HATE ARIJIT!'

'Listen, Metallica, your anger is an expression of your repressed sexual urges. I'm telling you, man. Calm down.'

The small guy screams, '*Lund ukhaad denge* [I will cut off your dick]!'

Dhiren scowls. 'What are you guys watching at the hostel?'

That's when Dhiren notices the flock of motorcycles and Activas at the red light. The DTU juniors aren't kidding around.

'Sorry guys, I didn't mean to do this to my juniors,' says Dhiren and steps forward. 'This is going to hurt.'

The Metallica boy doesn't take the threat seriously and raises his frail arms. Seconds later, he's on the ground writhing and squealing like a dying puppy. The other two miscalculate and charge naïvely into Dhiren. They fall to the ground in quick succession, clutching their abdomens, howling for help.

In the distance, the red light turns green. Dhiren weighs his options. He can wrest the keys from one of the squirming boys and make away with their motorcycle, but a chase on the busy Dwarka roads isn't ideal. And his car's parked too far away.

Just then, a roaring car screeches to a halt in front of him. 'Bhai! *Idhar* [Here],' says Neeraj and throws open the door. '*Aajao* bhai [Come, brother].'

Dhiren hasn't seen Neeraj in a long time. But he's out of options. Dhiren runs and gets into the car. Neeraj floors the accelerator. The swarm of DTU motorcycles gives chase, but they are no match for the beastly eight-cylinder Volvo Neeraj is driving. They leave the bikes in the dust.

Once they are clear, Neeraj turns to Dhiren. 'Bhai, where's the party for the new start-up?'

'I don't know what you're talking about.'

'Never thought I would say these words to you. You, owner of a day-care centre. Who would have imagined? By the way, what should I call you? Because your old name—'

'Dhiren,' he answers. 'Take a right here.'

'What's the catch? Are you going to pivot it to an edtech thing?'

'Turn towards Gurgaon.'

'Bhai, do you realize it's a strictly brick-and-mortar business? It's a lot of investment over a lot of years.'

'Take the highway, the first U-turn, and stop the car on the side.'

'If I hadn't come in time, you would have been lying half-dead in the gutter, bhai. At least talk to me.'

'Stop the car,' says Dhiren. 'Don't make me pull the handbrake.' Dhiren does it anyway because he knows Neeraj won't listen.

The car swerves violently before coming to an abrupt stop in the middle of the road. Dhiren throws open the door and jogs to the pavement, leaving Neeraj to deal with the cursing hordes of Haryanvi drivers.

And yet, when Dhiren goes back to pick up his car, Neeraj is waiting near it. This time, Neeraj isn't smiling; Dhiren recognizes the cut-throat haraaminess he was once proud of. 'Either I go to Aishwarya and tell her exactly what you're hiding, or we share a chicken sweet-and-sour one by two like the good friends we are . . .'

18.

Neeraj Kothari

Four years ago, a bright-eyed, freshly minted graduate, Neeraj Kothari, had walked into Gamer Inc., a new heavily funded gaming company based in Gurgaon. Of the many promising games in development, one was a heavily backed cricket game to rival the likes of the FIFA and NBA console games. Neeraj's desk was right next to the workstation of the twenty-four-year-old game designer, Dhiren Das. Just a couple of years older than Neeraj, he was said to have been the reason this game was getting made. Dhiren Das's workstation was wire-management heaven. There were seven monitors of different sizes, and yet Neeraj couldn't spot a single spare wire lying about. And no Dhiren. Not that day, or in the days that followed.

Neeraj met Dhiren for the first time at the monthly meeting. It was a serious meeting where employees were being crucified for being late, lazy, inefficient, untalented. But Dhiren rocked back and forth in his chair during the entire meeting and no mention of his absence was made. This leniency towards Dhiren rankled Neeraj, who was always the first one in the office and the last to leave.

'I sit here,' said Neeraj, pointing to his desk. Dhiren was at his desk, reading a news site. 'I'm Neeraj by the way.'

Dhiren nodded. 'Dhiren.'

'I didn't see you last week. Holiday?'

Dhiren shook his head. 'Work from home. I'm a hypochondriac. It's serious. So if someone sneezes in office, I have to spend a week in the hospital.'

'That's . . . not right.'

'The HR allows it.'

'No, I mean, you're not a hypochondriac. You're lying to everyone.'

Dhiren swivelled towards him and looked right at him for the first time. Neeraj's stomach churned. Even though Dhiren was leaning back in his chair, Neeraj felt he could pounce and smack him in one fluid motion.

'Who told you that?' he asked. His voice was a sharp rasp, lips a cross between a snarl and a smirk. Neeraj couldn't figure out whether Dhiren was angry or sniggering.

No one told him Dhiren was lying about his hypochondria. But the biometrics guy did warn him that Dhiren was a haraami of the top order. A guy from the graphics department called Dhiren exceptional and brilliant but with a habit of asking for raises by threatening to quit the company. And then, a girl in the insurance claims department told Neeraj that Dhiren had rarely used his office-issued medical insurance. What kind of a hypochondriac hadn't figured out medical insurance?

'There are no sanitizers on your desk, no wet wipes, no paracetamol in your drawers or Dolos,' answered Neeraj. 'There are no tabs of WebMD or Mayo Clinic or searches for symptoms. And the HR knows you're not a hypochondriac. Why don't they stop you?'

Dhiren lowered his voice to a whisper and said conspiratorially, 'Mental health issues. No one fucks with mental health issues these days. Everyone's scared of an unhappy employee with a Twitter account. But madarchod, why did you get into my system?'

'I didn't have a choice,' confessed Neeraj. 'The office people said you are the entire reason why the cricket game is being made. That it's your game design document that sold Gamers Inc. on it, blah-blah. They said you're the most important, irreplaceable cog of the team. It made me furious. You have no background in software, game development, design. You aren't even a gamer. You're just some garden-variety civil engineer who loves cricket.'

Neeraj had never been second-important in any project he had undertaken. If he was to be in the team, he had to be at the centre of it all. He had to be the most brilliant, smartest guy in his team. His brilliance was not the only reason Neeraj hated Dhiren. The people in Dhiren's team might have called him a bastard, but the girls also blinked just that little bit more while talking about him. It's just genetics that makes him look as perfect as he does, you stupid people, he wanted to scream in their faces. The girls would never talk about Neeraj the way they talked about Dhiren. Neeraj stood at 5'6", and always had an admirable paunch. Even his fingers were well-rounded and pudgy. He tended to sweat after an hour of coding. But he thought of himself as cute, and both his ex-girlfriends used to tell him they liked his face—like a little child's.

'They were right about your game design,' admitted Neeraj. 'It's brilliant.'

'I have been waiting for this day, Neeraj.'

'What day?'

'Today. The day a guy in his first week on the job walks up to me and tells me that my game is good. Thanks, Neeraj. I needed this. Thank you. You have brought tears to my eyes.'

It takes a few seconds for Neeraj to realize he was being sarcastic.

'I have a few sugges—'

'Fuck off, please.'

Despite the snub, that night Dhiren found out where Neeraj lived and called him out for a drive. He listened to everything Neeraj had to say over sweet-and-sour soup at Arora Chinese Hut. Dhiren alternated between looking distracted and smirking. He made Neeraj feel he was talking out of his ass. Neeraj had never felt so stupid.

When he was done, Dhiren leaned back in his chair, stared at Neeraj's paunch and said, 'Get a standing desk, Neeraj. If you keep moving, you won't have a heart attack at thirty. Skip office tomorrow, come home.'

Neeraj did as asked.

Dhiren's house was jam-packed with screens, cricket equipment, gaming accessories and books. He was serious about the game.

'You want to watch the test match or work?' he asked.

'We can do both,' answered Neeraj.

It seemed like the right answer because, for the first time, he saw Dhiren smile as though he meant it.

Within the first month, Neeraj and Dhiren put in eighteen-hour workdays and overhauled the game; Neeraj lost 8 kilos while eating more.

Neeraj slowly saw what Dhiren truly was. Dhiren wasn't any worse than anyone else around. He was rough, sure, and always put himself before anyone else. But that didn't make him a haraami, just honest.

All his life, Neeraj had been constantly worried about how others might see him. Dhiren, on the other hand, didn't give a fuck. Neeraj wanted to be like him, *exactly* like him. He desperately wanted to give no fucks. He thought Dhiren's lack of care was liberating. And so, he started to model himself on Dhiren. Learning not to care about others is difficult, but once you are there, it's a weight off your shoulders. They worked together for a year, mostly from Dhiren's home where he lived alone.

At first, Dhiren mostly shut Neeraj out of his personal life. It was clear to Neeraj that Dhiren was damaged in some sort of way. And he guessed there was something about his parents because Neeraj had *never* seen him talk to them. At first, Dhiren would lie and move on to the next topic.

'Yeah, we text sometimes,' he would tell Neeraj.

And later, he would brush it away.

'We had a fight.'

And slowly, the better friends they became, the less inclined Dhiren was to lie.

'We don't like each other.'

And then one day, Dhiren told Neeraj that he had almost cut himself off from his parents.

'I think my parents had me because they wanted to shut up their parents about grandkids,' said Dhiren. 'And after me, they believed they had had enough. The funny part is . . .'

'Is there a funny part to this?'

'. . . before I was ten, all my grandparents were dead. But I came with no return policy. I'm sure if I did, they would have returned me.'

'Dhiren bro, but if you came with a return policy, how could we have become friends?' Neeraj said to break the tension.

'Fuck you, Neeraj.'

'Fuck you too, bhai.'

Then one day, Dhiren, drunk as they often got on the weekends, told him about the abortion. And how he weaponized that information and humiliated his parents for years.

'My parents once told me they couldn't afford another child. They would have to give up their careers and sacrifice a better future for me to raise another one. They told me they were working so hard for me. So I could be successful, have everything they didn't and all that bullshit.'

'What did you say?'

'I asked them if they killed my sister because they wanted me to have better clothes, better schooling, a better future.'

Neeraj knew what was going to come.

Dhiren continued, 'I apologized to them. Because of me, they had to kill that baby. I was the murderer. Not because they wanted more professional success, but because they wanted enough money to feed me kiwis and Oreo biscuits. So last year, I returned to them all the money they had spent on me. With, of course, the prospectus of an IVF facility. They could have another baby with me out of the picture.'

Neeraj poured Dhiren another drink and promised himself he would always be there for his friend.

During that time, Neeraj thought those days would never end. They would make this game, and then another one, keep getting rich off doing something they loved.

But their careers were in for a rude shock.

Out of nowhere, Gamer Inc. filed for bankruptcy. For weeks after the announcement, Neeraj groaned and grunted with the hurt of wasted effort, the opportunity of being appreciated taken away.

Meanwhile, Dhiren found a shady buyer in Qatar for the raw data of player mechanisms, game worlds and the infrastructure. He recruited a reluctant but sufficiently angry Neeraj. Together, they stole everything from Gamer Inc. Their payment was in Bitcoin, Ethereum, Solana and Dogecoin—untraceable to them.

'I called the guy in Qatar. He tried to get engineers to make the game for him and failed. He wants us to make the game for him, you and me. Even split the revenue,' said Dhiren.

And so, Dhiren and Neeraj started working on their own game. A six-player online cricket game, three on each side, where players played for money and spectators could put their money on them. With every win, the players levelled up. The only money people could use was cryptocurrency, which was mostly untraceable. Straight away, they knew this was illegal.

Within three months, the game, Crypto Cricket, now registered in Dubai, took off. Hundreds of thousands of college boys got hooked. The gameplay and the mechanics were far superior to any cricket game they had ever played. Many liked the game, but far more liked the gambling part of it. Reddit communities came alive looking for the people who had made the game. It wasn't long before the identities of Neeraj and Dhiren were revealed. They, of course, vehemently denied that the game was theirs. The game was registered in the name of a Dubai-based company and they had no part in it.

By the time they completed the first six months, the game had a million downloads. Though games like Ludo King and Real Cricket 20 had over ten times the downloads, Crypto Cricket pulled in way more money—more from the betting spectators than from the players themselves. A few early players, KillerKirti20 and DhaasuD23, became legends and obscene amounts of money were bet on their games. Despite their denials, Dhiren and Neeraj became recognizable as the gaming gods who had built an empire out of nothing.

There were times Neeraj would suggest they reveal that they were the game designers. After all, people loved the game and loved them!

'If anything goes wrong, they will crucify us in a second,' Dhiren warned Neeraj and reminded him that, on the whole, people are assholes.

And so, Dhiren and Neeraj quietly kept working twenty-hour days to keep the game running.

As it became a household name among the young, most didn't withdraw the cryptocurrency, coins, etc., from the game servers—making it a repository of crores of rupees in the form of various cryptocurrencies. College students would have tens of thousands on the game, just lying there.

Then came the government crackdown.

One fine day, the Securities and Exchange Board of India [SEBI] had had enough and cryptocurrency usage was outlawed. Only crypto-exchanges were allowed to keep the currencies. A mad rush ensued to withdraw money from Crypto Cricket. But the servers crumbled under the traffic. Neeraj tried his best to get them back online, but that couldn't be done before the ban came into effect. The game was taken off and was inaccessible.

This left Dhiren and Neeraj with the money of a million-plus users on their platform. That was an obscene amount of money. Young kids had lost thousands, men had lost lakhs. There was no way they could have returned the money without admitting to wrongdoing and answering questions: Is this your game? Did you pay taxes? Where's the registration? They weren't going to jail for returning the money to the gamers.

The more it became clear that the money wouldn't come back, the more famous Dhiren and Neeraj came to be. Not heroes any more, they were now frauds. They had stolen first from Gamers Inc., and then from millions of people.

The police didn't have the proof or the technical know-how to pursue them. What they did have though was custodial torture. To avoid that, an iron-clad system of bribes was set up between the police and them. They would never have a case against them, and the police would get their due.

The first six months were the hardest. Young boys everywhere would spot Neeraj and a swift beating would follow. Later on, he hired a couple of private security guys to follow him around, but it was too awkward. So he started hiding in top-of-the-line hotel suites.

Neeraj waited for things to cool down. In the meanwhile, he got himself a Bollywood physical trainer, lost 23 kilos, put on some muscle, cut his hair in a crop and became unrecognizable. After a year, he moved out of the hotels and rented himself a place.

Now, sitting in front of Dhiren at Arora Chinese Hut, the sense of what he has lost bears heavy on him. He might have more money than he would ever need, but he has lost his best friend—Dhiren.

19.

Dhiren Das

At Arora Chinese Hut, Dhiren orders the sweet-and-sour soup and the honey chilli potatoes with extra chilli just like they used to. The past few days have been outstanding. His anxiety has stayed away. But right now, sitting with Neeraj in open view, it's back with a vengeance. The air seems to close up on him, threatening to crush him. Nothing's going to happen, he tells himself and breathes. It doesn't help.

'I hate this,' says Dhiren, stirring his soup.

'And you used to hate children too, bhai. So Cute Buttons—'

'Shut up and eat, Neeraj. We eat, I go back and then I never see you again.'

Neeraj smiles. 'Give me a week and I will send you a few app mock-ups if you're thinking of testing out an online nursery model. I am on board with whatever you decide to do.'

What the fuck is an online nursery? he wants to ask Neeraj, but he prefers the conversation to die a quick death.

'Dhiren—'

'Fuck off.' Dhiren pushes the bowl away and leans back in his chair.

Neeraj places his hand on Dhiren's to get his attention. 'Bhai.'

'I'm going to saw off that hand and shove it inside you. *Peechhe kar* [Move back],' says Dhiren.

'It wasn't our fault.'

Dhiren wants to get up and slap him right across the face.

Neeraj continues. 'That's what my therapist says. Did you see one, bhai?'

'Neeraj, stop talking.'

'But bhai, talking is what helps,' says Neeraj. '*Suno naa* [Listen], bhai. See those guys, they didn't read the fine print. They tapped on the 'Agree' button. If they lose their money, it's their fault. It was a legal document.'

Dhiren's head is pounding. He's going to hit Neeraj. He doesn't want to, but he's going to do it. He's going to hold him by the collar and slam his head against the wall. When he goes down, he's going to stomp on his fingers and crush them.

'You want to hit me, bhai, I can see it on your face.'

'And I'm going to do it.'

'If you were seeing a therapist, you could have resolved it by now. All this machoism is useless, bhai.'

'*Chup baith, madarchod* [Keep your mouth shut, motherfucker],' snarls Dhiren. 'Enough.'

'Bhai . . .'

'*Maa chuda le* [Fuck your mother]!' roars Dhiren.

'My therapist—'

'Fuck your therapist.'

Dhiren feels his heartbeat quicken. His fingers clench into a fist. The memories come rushing back to him. All the noise. All the articles against them. People in their DMs wishing them death. All those rape and murder threats in their mail. Even TV news anchors screamed for their arrest. They were trending, there was no escape. All doors seemed to be closing.

Neeraj had had enough. He had staged a suicide attempt. He shut himself in a garage, inside a car with the exhaust pouring fumes—he put out a Facebook post telling everyone he didn't have any money and the game wasn't his. The police found him unconscious.

'You could have been dead.'

'Bhai, I had planned it well. If I really wanted to die, I wouldn't have posted that on Facebook, would I?'

The seemingly earnest suicide attempt tempered the anger against them. Everyone believes the words of a dying man. Sort of.

Neeraj continues. 'Bhai, the bell curve of our customers shows most of them invested less than two thousand rupees. What is two thousand rupees? Why would I be guilty about that?'

'Should I send you the links to the articles?'

'Bhai, online magazines will write anything for clicks. If they can turn a movie star's suicide into an international conspiracy, they can do anything.'

'Seventeen-year-olds lost their college fee because of us. A forty-year-old lost his house. That is real, not clickbait.'

'Bhai, you tell me, how could we have returned their money? Our company didn't exist,' says Neeraj. 'It's not our fault.'

'Is that what you keep telling yourself?'

'Yes, because it's not our fault.'

There was no way they could have returned the money. After the servers crashed, no one could redeem their money from the game. The game itself was outlawed, so the users couldn't transfer it to any exchanges. It was their money to keep. Unless they converted all of the cryptocurrency to cash in Dubai, transferred it to India, thereby avoiding taxes, and then distributed it individually to the millions of users, while admitting that they were responsible for it all.

'We wouldn't have to return it if you hadn't stolen it,' says Dhiren.

It was true that soon after the ban, the load on the servers had skyrocketed. But the servers could have handled it. It was much later that Dhiren came to know that Neeraj had tripped them. He had actively sabotaged the servers so they could keep the money for themselves. Neeraj had told Dhiren nothing about it. Neeraj stole the money. He told Dhiren about it when he was recovering at the hospital from the fake suicide attempt.

'You kept me in the dark,' says Dhiren.

'Because I thought you would have stopped me. Maybe. But I know, a part of you would have wanted to do what I did.'

That's the *truth*. Most likely, Dhiren, too, would have stolen like Neeraj did. But he would have been okay with that. What fucked him up was that Neeraj stole it, instead of him.

When they first met, Dhiren saw Neeraj as a little brother. Over time, Neeraj slowly cured Dhiren of the loneliness he had felt before. Neeraj was the sibling, the family Dhiren never had. He was no longer alone in the world. But slowly Dhiren had screwed Neeraj up, made him into a little Dhiren—incorrigible, selfish, hateful, rotten.

Neeraj's theft proved Dhiren's parents right. They often said to Dhiren—after he did something terrible—that even if they hadn't aborted the child, Dhiren would have spoilt the child and turned it into a hateful, ungrateful person. It's exactly what Dhiren did with Neeraj. He corrupted his little brother.

'Then why come to me? Go, live your life.'

'Because you're my bhai, bhai. You will always be my bhai.'

Dhiren gets up.

'C'mon, bhai. We work great together, that won't change. You only told me people don't change.'

'You did, madarchod,' spits Dhiren. 'And that is my fault.'

20.

Smriti Gupta

Smriti knows from experience that people who try to hide their money are often wealthy. The young, mid-twenties guy who introduces himself as Neeraj is one of them. In the CCTV footage, she watches Neeraj park his Volvo in the free parking across the road before walking to her office. He doesn't come from a moneyed family, Smriti assesses. His knowledge of money is far too nuanced for him to be a spoilt brat with inherited money.

'Are you sure you don't want us to do your taxes? The portfolios we manage—'

Neeraj shakes his head and repeats what he wants—to invest in fledgeling new businesses that are resistant to market changes and cycles.

'I will send you a list by the evening. I can set up a meeting if you like something, and we can take it from there,' says Smriti.

'Is there something that's top-of-mind? Some client you're working with who's starting something promising?'

'As I said, I will send you a list by the evening,' answers Smriti sternly, reminding herself to keep some power in the equation no matter how rich her prospective client is.

'That sounds great,' says Neeraj and gets up.

'Raju will show you out,' says Smriti, shaking his hand.

As Neeraj leaves, Smriti opens the Excel sheet of Cute Buttons's finances. She has reworked and juggled the numbers around—and she comes to the same conclusion every time.

If Cute Buttons sticks with just one branch and doesn't expand, it's dead in the water.

She saves the Excel sheet, packs her bag and gets into her car to see Aishwarya. She reminds herself to be stern with her—just as Aishwarya was throughout her college life. Thinking about it now, she wonders how she could have ever lived without Aishwarya always ready to provide assurance and relief.

She remembers it as though it was yesterday—the day she walked into Aishwarya and Vinny's PG. Though Aishwarya and Vinny had been living there for a week, she could have sworn they knew each other for years. She was envious of how Aishwarya doted on Vinny, like a helicopter mother fussing over her every need. She maintained her distance from the two of them.

It didn't last long.

It had been two weeks since she moved when Smriti's boyfriend, Amit, came knocking on their door at 2 a.m. Smriti was fast asleep. Aishwarya went to get the door and heard the portly, ugly, crying, screaming Amit banging on the door.

Waving Vinny's hockey stick, Aishwarya opened the door and thundered, 'Leave right now, or I will bash your head in and call the police to put together the jigsaw of your skull.'

Amit slunk away.

Next morning, Aishwarya was waiting with a tray of poha and steaming hot tea in her room.

'Eat up. Today is a long day. We need to tell the police exactly since when he has been harassing you. You need to remember all the details,' said Aishwarya.

'Behen, you don't have to worry. I have connections,' added Vinny, standing at the door.

'Maybe it's my fault . . .'

'Take a bite,' ordered Aishwarya and fed her a spoonful of poha. 'And tell me, why do you think it's your fault? Boys often gaslight girls into believing it's their fault. So I would need know everything.'

'I—'

'Finish what's in your mouth first.'

Smriti gulped. 'We have been dating for eight years.'

'And?' asks Aishwarya.

'Amit's parents thought it was enough and wanted us to do a *roka* ceremony to make it official. But my parents don't know about us. If I tell them, they will make me drop out of college.'

'You have been lying for eight years?!' gasped Vinny.

Smriti nodded. 'Instead of asking his parents to give him more time, he's asking me to tell my parents about us.' Tears sprang up in her eyes. 'Now his parents are looking for girls for him.' She breaks down in ugly sobs. 'You should see the girls his parents are making him meet. Some of them don't even have a job!'

'Why was he here?' asked Aishwarya.

Smriti wiped her tears. She wanted to hide the truth, but when she looked at Aishwarya, it bubbled out of her unchecked. 'I messaged the girls he was meeting. That he's . . . an abuser.'

Smriti noticed Vinny judge her. But when she looked at Aishwarya, she saw kindness, acceptance.

'You, too, think I'm wrong? Amit must think I'm so cruel,' sobbed Smriti.

'It doesn't matter what I think, Smriti,' said Aishwarya, holding her hand and caressing it. 'We are all correct in where we stand. From our perspective, things are seldom our fault. And we are all cruel. Nature has programmed cruelty into our code for our survival. Babies scratch, teenagers gossip, women poison, men rape—everything is self-taught. Our cruelties seem necessary to us.'

'This is why I think love is bullshit, behen,' Vinny butted in. 'That's why arranged marriage is the best.'

Aishwarya ignored Vinny. 'Smriti, suno meri baat, next time you feel like messaging any girl, you text me. There's nothing in the world that can't be saved by a) rajma chawal, b) a good dosa and c) butter chicken. We can assess what you need at the moment.'

'I can't eat myself out of this,' cried Smriti.

That's exactly what she did. Aishwarya healed Smriti through love, acceptance and generous amounts of butter chicken. It has been years, and Smriti still hasn't paid her back.

But now she can.

Smriti parks her car. The thought—and now the sight— of Cute Buttons always makes her feel conflicted. She admires Aishwarya's bravery, but she also knows there's a small difference between bravery and foolishness.

She remembers the arguments Aishwarya and she used to have back in college when Aishwarya had first proposed Cute Buttons's wonky business model.

'Parents pay a percentage of their salary to the nursery as fees,' Aishwarya had said excitedly. 'So, if parents earn 10 lakh rupees a year, they pay Cute Buttons say, 5 per cent, which is 50,000. If they earn 10,000, they pay me 500 rupees.'

'That's the most horrible business plan of all time,' Smriti had pointed out. 'Listen to me, Aishwarya. I won't send my kid to your nursery if I'm rich. Why would I spend so much on you? Why would I pay 50,000 rupees when someone's paying 500?'

'You would if you knew we were the best,' argued Aishwarya.

'Think about it. Poor people will flock to you. They will pay you almost nothing. This is charity, not a business!'

'Are you saying people shouldn't have access to my nursery because they are poor?'

'I take my words back, but I don't get where you will get your money from.'

'From the interview process,' explained Aishwarya. 'My profit-making target group is young women at the cusp of success, like entrepreneurs or women on the fast track to upper management. They might not have a lot of money right now, but they will. If a child enrols for three years, they will make Cute Buttons progressively more money as the mother gets richer.'

'What if they change schools?' asked Vinny.

'Will you ever move out of this PG, Smriti?' shot back Aishwarya.

Living with Aishwarya was addictive—she was a friend, therapist, cook and the love of their lives rolled into one. She would never move out.

'The idea's romantic, but what if you get no rich parents? Or no one becomes successful in your group of new mothers? This is a gamble, a bet.'

'Why would I bet on anyone else but new mothers?'

'Even then, you need to have a bunch of branches, not one. You will have to spread your risk and hope that a few women see skyrocketing success.'

'No one works as hard as a new mom, Smriti,' said Aishwarya. 'But it's not just that. Cute Buttons will be like a network. Imagine all these mothers from different economic backgrounds, industries and workspaces coming here to drop their children off before going to work. What do you think will happen?'

'What?'

'They will network, buddhu. They will talk about work, employ each other, make big career moves. The *poor* mothers you're talking about—they will find more work, more opportunities.'

Smriti butted in again, 'Again, for that, you need a lot more than just one branch.'

'I will work on that,' said Aishwarya impatiently. Smriti watched Aishwarya's eyes glaze over as she continued, 'Imagine a girl sending us her child while working on a start-up. What if that start-up gets a billion-dollar valuation? Imagine every woman employee of that start-up sending their kids to Cute Buttons. That itself would make Cute Buttons float.'

'You have counted a billion eggs that haven't hatched,' mumbled Smriti.

She knew even then that scaling Cute Buttons would be a problem: not financial but emotional. Aishwarya couldn't be at two places at once. That would be relinquishing control of the children, something Aishwarya couldn't do. She would trust *no one* with children. Back in college, Aishwarya didn't even let go of Smriti and Vinny, two eighteen-year-olds. She would always keep them in sight if it were up to her, like a hawk.

How was Aishwarya ever going to run a branch of Cute Buttons without being there at all times? She's paranoid about the things and people she loves. She installed CCTV cameras the first day she moved in, for heaven's sake!

And now, not only had she sidestepped the conversation about the second branch, but she was also going nowhere with her hiring. Every time Smriti asked her if she had thought about hiring, she responded with either stone-cold silence or the broken-record reply, 'No one's good enough.'

Smriti pushes open the gate of Cute Buttons. She spots a worker in the garden. A young man is bent over, mopping paint from a bucket with a large rolling brush. He has headphones as big as earmuffs clapped on. He's built like an ox, so she knows that he is not hired labour. And then it strikes her. It is the cricket-obsessed, vegetable-garden-hating, mutton-cooking guy from the first floor. But what's he doing here?

'Smriti!'

Smriti turns and sees Aishwarya running towards her. The squeak in her voice is unmistakable. She's trying to hide something.

Aishwarya catches hold of Smriti's hand. 'Let's go inside.' Aishwarya drags her inside and makes her sit on the sofa. 'Stay here and don't come out.'

Smriti watches as Aishwarya walks to the boy and tells him to take a break. The boy picks up the large buckets of paint without straining and puts them aside. As asked, he obediently climbs up the wall and hops on to what Smriti assumes is his balcony. Smriti's heart starts to race. 'That boy has been helping you from the very start?' she asks Aishwarya as soon as she comes back.

'His name's Dhiren. He saw me struggle and offered to help.'

'Do you like him?'

'He's a friend. That's it.'

Smriti watches Aishwarya's face flush. She knows he's not just a friend. She's possessive about Aishwarya, but more than that, she wants Aishwarya to be loved, to have a *proper* family. Wouldn't it be the luckiest thing in the world if the boy turned up in the same house as hers? Smriti decides she won't poke. She doesn't want to make Aishwarya nervous about whatever is going on between the two of them.

'I'm glad you have help,' says Smriti and takes out her laptop from her bag.

'Why am I always scared when you take out your laptop?'

'We need to discuss the second branch, the hiring, and how you need to take everything that I say seriously, or Cute Buttons will shut down before it opens. Once we are done, we will circle back to this guy Dhiren,' warns Smriti. 'First, tell me if you found someone to hire.'

Aishwarya shakes her head.

'So, no one except this piece of meat who hangs around in his Under Armour tank top in your garden.'

'No one's good enough,' says Aishwarya.

'Good enough? Or as good as you?'

'They should be at least as good as I am.'

Smriti knows that will be impossible. And, as an effect, the second branch of Cute Buttons will be impossible.

21.

Dhiren Das

Dhiren wakes up slowly. Then he lazes for another fifteen minutes before he extracts himself from the warmth of his bed and walks to the kitchen. He makes his coffee and takes it to the balcony where he sips it slowly. Just a few weeks ago, mornings were hellscape. He would wake up with shallow breaths, his heart already in overdrive. He would reach for his phone, fearing the worst. Then he would google his new name and the old name to check if anyone had connected the two. Before making his coffee, he would go to the balcony and scan the neighbourhood for boys with iron rods.

Now, he wakes up thinking of Aishwarya. The thoughts of her have replaced his morning anxiety. It reminds him of what they say about addicts. You replace one addiction with another.

He finishes his coffee and makes his way down to Aishwarya's apartment. The door is open as she said it would be till they wrap up working together. Sometimes, Dhiren wonders what if he walks in one day and finds her in a state of undress. The thought both embarrasses and excites him.

He finds her just as he finds her on most days, sleeping on a mattress on the floor, bunched up in a ball, one leg outside the blanket, the other inside. Her mouth's slightly open. Her hair's covering half of her face, she's snoring like a chainsaw. He records the snores to embarrass her about it later. When he checks the video, the volume's on mute, yet he watches the full minute of her sleeping.

Then, Dhiren cooks a light breakfast of poached eggs, butter and jam sandwich, and vermicelli. He serves it on two plates but realizes he has done it too well. He doesn't want her to think making her breakfast is his highest priority these days—which it is—and so he makes it look shoddy. He gobbles down his breakfast.

He places her plate right in front of her nose. Like a puppy, she wakes up sniffing and crinkling her nose. Then, like a medieval mercenary, she doesn't brush, picks up the sandwich and throws it straight into her mouth. For a nursery teacher, much of her behaviour isn't worth emulating. Like her wiping her sweat off with her sleeves that turn brown at the end of the day. Or how she doesn't charge her phone till it's almost dead. And how loud she puts on the women's India versus Australia series commentary on the radio. Also, how sad she gets when India keeps losing, and her favourite, Sonali Raj, keeps failing. Or how she touches him to explain something and keeps her hand there for a long, long time. And sometimes, how provocative she looks in her running shorts. But he knows that's on him, not her.

'What's that paper?' she asks, squinting through one open eye.

Dhiren wonders if he's overstepping a boundary. 'I ran some rough calculations on Cute Buttons and—'

'We need more branches,' cuts in Aishwarya.

'So you know?'

Aishwarya now sits up straight. 'I'm not stupid. Smriti keeps reminding me every day. More branches, more branches, more branches—that's what she keeps on repeating like a broken record.'

'And what are you going to do about it?'

He sees Aishwarya flinch. The discomfort is apparent, and he doesn't want to have this conversation. But he knows he has to.

'Have you hired anyone for this place?' asks Dhiren, knowing she hasn't. He knows she will pull double shifts and look after every child walking through the doors. When they are out hardware shopping, he has seen how she looks at children and their parents. She wants to snatch the crying children, the children on iPads, the screaming children, and take care of them. If she doesn't trust a parent, how's she ever going to trust a teacher?

Aishwarya gets up from the bed, visibly irritated. She's wide awake now, yellow yolk is dripping down the side of her mouth. She wipes it on her sleeve. He fixates on the corner of her lips.

'Aishwarya, you can't put it off for too long,' he says. 'You've got to start hiring people.'

'Why? Have we finished?' She points to the walls, the empty spaces, the plywood. 'We are still many months away.' She now puts on a smile. 'I know you and Vinny and Smriti; everyone thinks I'm too much of a control freak to like anyone, but it's not like that.'

'Are you sure about that?'

Aishwarya's face lights up. 'You're working with me, aren't you? So clearly, I know how to let others share responsibilities.'

'Paints and flooring aren't the same as children,' argues Dhiren.

'I have a list on my computer, and I'm looking at applicants right now,' she says. 'Can we put this to rest and start working? I'm *really* excited about the walls!'

Dhiren lets it go. 'What are we thinking? Peppa Pig? Mickey Mouse?'

Aishwarya shakes her head. 'A study at the University of Toronto found that kids learn more from stories with humans than human-like animals.'

'What about Noddy? He's human. I have a few illustrations of him that we can paint on the walls. You know, nice guy, builder, polite, people's person. Though his best friend is a dinosaur, his town's mayor is a mouse. A cute mouse, but a mouse nonetheless.'

'You know a lot.'

'Papa would buy me anything to keep me quiet and in a corner. I grew up watching TV, then tablets and iPhones. Ask me anything.'

'I'm sorry.'

'Don't be. At the time, I thought this was how every family worked. Funny how families work. You will believe everything they say. They used to tell me I was so lucky to have all these toys and screens, and I thought it to be true.'

'Families are brainwashing kids like communist governments,' says Aishwarya. 'They hide what they do under the sacred secrecy: what happens in the family stays in the family.'

Dhiren watches Aishwarya reach for the scar on her right hand.

Aishwarya continues. 'You don't survive because of your family, you survive despite it,' she says. 'You can rot on the inside, but when your neighbours see your faces in the window, you must have smiles painted on like clowns.'

It's not the first time Dhiren has wanted to ask Aishwarya about her mother.

'Anyway,' says Aishwarya, snapping out of it. 'So, we can't put characters that they see on TV here. It will only drive the kids back to TV when they get home. We have to create our own characters.'

Aishwarya fetches a sketchbook from a large box and hands it over to him. 'Look, these are a few I made. I'm still fine-tuning the backstories of these characters.'

'What's this boy's story?' asks Dhiren, pointing to a boy who looks like Harry Potter.

'So he wears prescription glasses. But one day, a few mean children break his spectacles, so he goes to get new ones. And guess what, when he wears these, he can see into the future. So the mean kids can't bother him any more.'

'The plot of the story is that he becomes a trader, earns a lot of money, calls the mean kids to his lair and feeds them to crocodiles?'

Aishwarya chuckles. Her eyes widen and light up the entire room.

'Anything else would suck.'

'Should we start the sketches with this?' asks Aishwarya. 'We should get the paints tomorrow to save time.'

Dhiren's flipping through the sketches and the stories when he notices a pattern. 'These are all positive, underdog stories.'

'Of course.'

'This is not how the real world is—it's dark, scary. It's setting false expectations.'

'These are children, Dhiren,' explains Aishwarya. 'They need to see the good in the world.'

What about the bad, wonders Dhiren.

She continues. 'And no one's *really* bad, Dhiren.'

Dhiren would love to differ and give her a list of truly bad people.

'I know you're going to say Hitler,' says Aishwarya. 'We need more characters. Think of someone. But positive, okay? Someone with an uplifting, nice story!'

'Is there a character who brushes first thing in the morning, because I think that's an important habit to teach people?'

'I don't smell . . .' Aishwarya brings her palm to her mouth and blows in it.

'See.'

22.

Aishwarya Mohan

Aishwarya wakes up to the soft clanging of utensils in the kitchen. Ever since Dhiren's pointed out her bad breath, she sleeps lightly during the mornings. Now, when she hears him in the kitchen, she sneaks off to the bathroom, brushes her teeth and slips back into bed.

Today, like other days, she slips out of bed and tiptoes to the washroom. She throws a bunch of tissues into the commode and pees stealthily. Then she brushes her teeth and does the quietest gargle of all time. When she looks into the mirror, she's stunned by how groggy she looks. Has she spent all her life's early mornings looking like a character out of *The Conjuring*? Puffy eyes, droopy cheeks, dead skin—it's like staring at a meth addict's mugshot. That's not how Dhiren should see her! She washes her face with cold water and it slowly breathes life into her skin. But she's still not satisfied, so she combs out the knots in her hair. She checks herself as her hand reaches out for the lipstick. *What am I doing? Is this the age for a crush?* She is shocked at how much she cares. So she messes up her hair and rubs her eyes, but it doesn't do much. She looks presentable, and this irritates her. All the lessons she had taught herself, such as *dress up for yourself, not the boys*, have come to naught.

She's plodding back to her bed when she notices Dhiren in the kitchen. He's working with headphones slapped on to his ears, a searing intensity in his eyes. His hands are a blur—moving with the efficiency and hypnotic surety of an automaton. There's a slick rhythm to how he stirs the pan with one hand and washes the fruits with the other. His grip's sure, tight; his fingers deft and skilful. Before cutting the fruit, he twirls and lobs the knife dangerously from one hand to the other. It's something only serial killers and butchers should be confident enough to do. When the blade touches the cutting board with the frequency and sound of a machine gun, she's worried about him. She wants him to stop, but she also wants him to go on. His arms pulse with effort, his jaw tightens. When he cooks, his measure of spices is entirely by hand, and he tosses around the bhaji like it's a circus trick. The heat from the stove sends rivulets of sweat down his thick neck. Every few minutes, he lifts his T-shirt and wipes them off, baring his carved abdomen. Mid-cooking, he dips his finger in the food and licks it; once, twice, and smiles wryly.

He looks gorgeous.

She watches him plate the pao bhaji, arrange the fruit and pour a glass of milk. But his own breakfast he wolfs down, stuffing in mouthfuls as if it's a hot-dog eating contest—all that effort for nothing. Unlike her, he double-washes the plate and keeps it back.

That's Aishwarya's cue to go back to bed. She makes a big show of waking up when he brings her breakfast. She wonders if she has overdone it. Does she look sleepy enough? When she feels his eyes on her, she regrets not having put on a hint of lipstick. *Stop it*, she screams inside her head.

'This is great,' she tells him as she eats.

'We will leave in fifteen? I will get my helmet and see you outside,' says Dhiren.

She sifts through everything she has and eventually settles on workout clothes—a high-waisted lower paired with a black T-shirt in which she ties a knot on one side. Cute, she thinks. She hears a horn. When she goes outside, Dhiren's sitting on the driver's seat of a scooter he has hired. She clambers on and holds the rear grip.

Dhiren turns on the ignition. Suddenly, she's aware of how close she is to him, mindful of every atom of dust that separates his body from hers. She bends over and whispers in his ear, 'Let's go.' As he drives, his cologne wafts to her. It's sharp, but it soon settles. At the Dwarka Mor speed breaker, Dhiren takes a sharp left and her hand flies off the grip. She touches his arm to steady herself before quickly pulling back. Her hand's warm from all the blood that has rushed in. She wants to feel the firmness of his arm again. Her heart races.

She wants to not think of him so she closes her eyes for a few moments of peace. But now, she's thinking of her clasping one hand around his chest, the other resting on his thigh, slowly creeping up. She jerks open her eyes and chastises herself for this sudden desire for his body.

Stop thinking about it!

Nothing helps. Her desire for him burns like a bright flame inside of her.

When they cross Moti Nagar, she leans forward to tell him which right turn to take. Her lips hover around his ear, and when he leans in to listen, it grazes against her chin and her lips. It leaves her breathless. When he brakes, she feels her body against his, and she wants to melt into him.

Her heart settles only when they reach Lajpat Nagar. She can't remember the last time she felt so turned on.

It's 8.45 a.m. and Lajpat Nagar is still coming to life. Showroom owners are pulling open rusted shutters, scaring away pigeons with their screeching and clanging. They start their hunt for the cheapest deal on paints. With every passing shop, Aishwarya realizes Dhiren's even stingier than she is.

It's late evening when they find Das Paints and Electrical Supplies, a small shop tucked away in a dark lane. The shopkeeper gives them a reasonable rate on the paints.

'I will withdraw money from the ATM,' says Aishwarya.

She crosses the road. While she's waiting in line, she watches Dhiren walk to the other side of the road to help the loaders with the paint. He's rolled his sleeves right up to his shoulders. His grey T-shirt is now drenched black and clings to his body. The sweat makes every muscle in his shoulders pop. It looks to her as if someone's knifed away the fat from his arms, leaving behind only muscle tissue, like an anatomical specimen in a laboratory. Every time he lifts a bucket of paint, there's a network of bulging veins criss-crossing his forearms that come throbbing to life. Every time he jumps on to the truck, his beefy calves get striated, leaving her wondering when did she start caring about calf muscles of all the things in the world. Once done, Dhiren and the other men walk to the chai *tapri* [stall]. He splashes his face with water from the little *matka* [pot], then washes his arms and his shoulders. Then he promptly stops the man and insists on making the chai himself. He tosses and pours the tea into the blackened utensils, handling the hot surfaces with his bare hands like it's nothing.

A man taps her shoulder from behind. It's her turn at the ATM. She has to physically shake herself to stop thinking of his body and his presence. When she leaves the ATM clutching the money, she can't spot him.

'Where's Dhiren?' she asks the shopkeeper, her pulse rising. 'The boy I came with?'

The shopkeeper shrugs and gets back to counting the money. She calls his number, but his phone is switched off. 'Did he say where he was going?'

'*Tension kyun le rahe ho* [Why are you getting worried]?' says the shopkeeper when he sees her panic. He gets back to his counting and adds, 'He'll be back.'

It's what her father used to say—she will be back—when her mother had been gone for years on end. She's older, and she doesn't fall for it any more. Grown-ups, unlike children, don't cling to you like you're the only thing in the world. They leave without explanation.

Ten nervous minutes pass before she sees him walking towards her. He spots Aishwarya and waves to her. Her heart settles, and she feels stupid and weak. He smiles and adrenaline rushes through her body.

On the way back home, Aishwarya repeatedly goes over the scenario in her head till it hurts. *How did he have so much power over her? How can she get attached to him so quickly? Stop it, stop it, stop it,* she keeps telling herself. And yet all she wants is to lean her head against his strong back and rest.

Back home and at her desk, she sifts through the CVs for the position she had advertised on job websites. Some candidates are well-qualified, experienced, significantly more suited than her, but there's something not right about each one of them. Shouldn't hiring be based on one's gut? Her gut's screaming these women aren't right for the job, for the children, despite their qualifications. What would be the use of hiring someone if she has to overlook everything? Wouldn't she do it all on her own then? Young children need presence and consistency, not change. And she would be the constant in their lives, not some random young woman with degrees in education who was just doing a job. And what would these kids go through when they didn't see her and found someone else for half of the days? Why let the children be disappointed?

She will have to do everything herself. And why not? She can. She shuts down her laptop and goes off to sleep.

23.

Aishwarya Mohan

Dhiren straddles two stools as he repaints the hair on one of the characters on the entry wall of Cute Buttons. The stools are risky, tottering death traps, yet Dhiren frequently climbs on them, which Aishwarya thinks is foolish and brave, but mostly foolish.

'Looks great, much better than Noddy,' says Dhiren.

She's not looking at the painting. She's watching him, thinking how great, how perfect he looks.

Dhiren jumps down from the stools and rubs the paint off his hands. His white T-shirt is drenched and clinging to him. Aishwarya sees the point of wet T-shirt contests. Right now, as

Dhiren stands in front of the fan, Aishwarya wants to hose him down. Her mind—churning ideas for pornographic movies—only settles when his T-shirt dries off, obscuring his muscles.

'When Cute Buttons shuts down, this is going to be one creepy place, with all these huge characters staring right at you with their big heads and pervy smiles.'

Aishwarya turns and finds her younger brother staring at the illustrations, shaking his head.

He continues. 'Didi, imagine these illustrations staring at you in the night. Goosebumps.'

Yatin turn to Dhiren. 'Hi! I'm Yatin, her brother. She really likes me.'

'Dhiren.'

'Did Bangalore kick you out?' asks Aishwarya. 'Or did you miss your Mumma and want to crawl back into her lap?'

'You're funny, Didi, very, very funny. Lol, lol, lol. Office is shifting, they gave us an off.' Yatin limps around the place, opening doors and checking out the space. 'You're really doing this, wow. I thought someday you will realize how dumb all of this is.'

Yatin's her height, 5'4", and a lot of people have told them they look alike. He's a lot fairer though—Maa never let him out in the sun lest he hurt himself playing or something.

Yatin turns to Dhiren. 'Why don't you knock some sense into her? People her age are building edtech start-ups, and she wants to change nappies.'

Aishwarya's heart fills up with hate as it always does. She turns to Dhiren and points at Yatin. 'This is why couples should stop at one child.'

'Why do you care what couples do? Aren't family structures outdated something something for you?'

She watches Yatin hobble, wincing ever so slightly from the pain in his leg. Her anger melts and guilt washes over her entire body. Her throat closes up. Everyone's told her that there's nothing to feel sorry about—Yatin leads a charmed life—and yet her heart shrinks. Yatin would have been living a different life had it not been for her. Some memories burn into you, and that day's memory is something Aishwarya has tried and failed to cauterize.

Aishwarya was six. Yatin was one. Maa never left Baby Yatin alone—not even for a single moment. She would hover over him every moment of the day, as if just looking away would result in him dying. Every time Aishwarya held the little Yatin, Maa would bristle with anger. That day, Yatin had turned 393 days old. Aishwarya remembered this because that's what Maa used to whisper into her father's ear every morning with a smile. '345 days old', '346 days old.'

That day, Papa convinced Maa to go to his brother's wedding. The wedding was close by, and it would hardly take an hour. They discussed whether they would take the kids. But they knew how chilly it could get at Delhi's outdoor December weddings.

Before leaving, her anxious mother instructed Aishwarya, which sounded like a threat, 'Guard Yatin with your life.'

As soon as they left, Yatin woke up screaming and shouting. This was Aishwarya's moment—to prove to Maa that she loved Yatin and was a worthy sister. She picked him up and sang to him the songs Maa did. Yatin screamed louder and fought in Aishwarya's arms. She put him down with the toys and did everything she had seen Maa do to soothe and engage him. Nothing helped. He was screaming so loudly, it seemed he would pass out from the effort. Every few minutes, she would wipe his tears, worried that her parents would walk in and see him covered in snot and tears. She wanted desperately to show Maa that she could take care of Yatin, that she loved him. If only she could do that, Maa would love her back.

As a last resort, she did what her mother used to do—give him warm milk.

'Stay here, my cutu button, I will be back,' she said to Yatin and went to the kitchen.

She put the milk on the stove to boil and came back to the room to find Yatin chewing on a small screw he had extracted from a toy, seconds away from swallowing it. She ran, pulled it out and threw it away. Yatin let out a full-mouthed wail. His mind was set on swallowing the screw. Aishwarya picked up a screaming and flailing Yatin and carried him to the kitchen. He quietened down when she put him on the slab. He started to lick the cool kitchen counter. For the first time that hour, Aishwarya breathed easy. The milk was on the boil now. She switched off the burner and poured the milk into a pan to cool it down. And that's when, out of nowhere, Yatin lunged at the pan. Hot, scalding milk splashed all over Aishwarya and Yatin. Aishwarya went into shock. Yatin's ugly, inhuman screaming overwhelmed everything. It erased Aishwarya's memory from here on. Sometime later, it could have been ten minutes or twenty or an hour, her parents came home to find both kids on the floor. Yatin was still crying, Aishwarya was holding him in her arms. At the hospital, Yatin lost a chunk of flesh from his calf. The skin of Aishwarya's right arm had burned off, leaving a huge scar.

Aishwarya didn't see Yatin or Maa for an entire year—her mother moved back to her parents' house in Mumbai. She and Papa were alone again. 'It's my fault, it's my fault,' she would keep repeating, her words barely audible behind the tears.

Yatin walked eight months later than a child his age should have walked. The limp never went away. It was pronounced through his formative years. Over the years, physiotherapy and the gym strengthened Yatin's leg so much that sometimes, you didn't even notice the limp. What had lasted was the mental damage. All the years he spent with the pronounced limp, he hated Aishwarya with the fury of a thousand suns. He channelled the anger as sarcasm and verbal bullying.

'There's nothing in the fridge?' remarks Yatin. 'Is that why the two of you are fit? Or is it all the sex you're having?'

'You need to shut up, bhai,' gripes Aishwarya.

'Your sister's a nice person. She doesn't deserve this,' Dhiren says.

Aishwarya looks at Dhiren and finds in him an anger she hasn't seen before; the muscles on his forearm are straining, as if preparing for a brawl. She's scared for Yatin. She wants to hold Dhiren's hand and tell him to calm down. She wants to make Dhiren understand that Yatin's and her hatred for each other was the tip of the iceberg, dangerous and capable of sinking an unsinkable ship. But what's below the surface is love, which far outweighs the hate.

She addresses Dhiren softly, 'I will talk to you later.'

Dhiren stands down. His tense muscles relax. He throws Yatin a murderous look and then leaves.

'Is he going to give you your baby? He looks genetically sound,' mocks Yatin. 'By the way, that scar on your hand has become uglier.'

'So has your limp.'

'By the way, did I tell you that Maa doesn't like both ideas? The IVF and this Cute Buttons thing.'

'I'm surprised both of you are suddenly so interested in my life,' says Aishwarya. 'Even my rakhi brothers at school were more involved than you.'

'Ouch, that's a new insult,' laughs Yatin. 'Have you tried tying a rakhi to a woman and asking her to be your Maa?'

'I did, actually,' answers Aishwarya. 'Those women told me the only way to be a mother is to push a baby out of your vagina and then disappear out of the child's life. Do you know someone like that? Oh, I know, it's our Maa!'

This, Aishwarya knows, is the sweet spot. This has got to hurt. Every time Aishwarya lets loose something about Maa, it's a hot knife through Yatin's heart. She *likes* it.

'Maa wasn't well after she had me,' defends Yatin. 'You of all people should know that. She was depressed and—'

'So she abandoned me?'

'You had Papa,' counters Yatin.

'She left him too. How did you think he fared? Or should I feel that I'm the luckiest girl in the world that my father didn't abandon me too? Staying is always an option, Yatin. She chose herself. She was selfish.'

'You can't understand what she went through.'

'What about later? What about when she had you and came back? I was still waiting in the corner alone, watching her dote on you like you were a fucking delicate flower that would wither if she didn't spend every second with you! She didn't even bother to hate me. Then at least she would have felt something for me. She just ignored my entire existence. I can't think of a worse mother, Yatin.'

Yatin squirms because he knows she's speaking the truth. He got all the love from their mother, while she got nothing.

'Can we talk once without bringing this up? The same things, over and over and over again?' he says irritably. 'Don't you get tired of the same old bullshit? Every time I see you, you start with this.'

'What I don't get is, why did they choose to have you when they couldn't even raise me?'

Yatin stays silent.

She walks to the couch and flops down. As the anger settles and the blood retreats from her face, annoyance rushes in. *Why does she bring this up every time? What's Yatin fault in this? She regrets shouting at him. Maa–Papa screwed up, and Yatin was at the receiving*

*end, just as she was. She should really let it go. It was a long, long time
ago.*

'You want to eat butter chicken? I will order some,' offers
Yatin.

The two of them wait for the food and all the bad blood to
be forgotten before they can be brother and sister again.

'You let some random boy help you with Cute Buttons but
not me?' asks Yatin.

'You're broke, have literally zero skills with children and you
can't draw a straight line with a ruler. You're useless to me.'

'Moral support, mental strength, etc., etc. I moved to
Bangalore, and you didn't even call me.'

'Just talking to you gives me a hangover. My brain right now
is in splinters.'

Despite everything, she knows that if everything went belly-
up, he would be there. He wouldn't be of much help, but he
would be there with her. That's often what one wants. To be
present for someone is the most significant gift one can share. Not
solve their problems and offer solutions, but just be there.

'When's your IVF date?'

'Soon,' she answers.

'How soon?'

'Next week.' She catches Yatin's gaze and declares, 'And I
will be the best mother of all time. You just wait and watch.'

'It's not a competition, Didi. I don't care as long as I am just
the cool *mamu* [uncle] who buys them Lego. Does Dhiren, that's
his name, right, know about the IVF thing?'

She doesn't tell him about the drunk night where she told
Dhiren about Akshay's rejection and her plan to have a baby
alone. 'What does he have to do with anything?'

'The way he jumped in for you, it's clear he likes you, and
you like him.'

'No,' she says.

'Fine,' replies Yatin, not believing her. 'He's creepy anyway. That Akshay guy was much better for you. By the way, I read about him in the newspaper. His start-up is *really* taking off.'

'And what about Bangalore girls?' she asks, to change the topic.

They spend the rest of the evening talking about Yatin's college shenanigans.

'You didn't have to move so far. There are colleges here too,' says Aishwarya.

'Stay here and have Maa breathing down my neck all the time? No, thank you. I don't want to report to Maa all the time.'

Aishwarya's eyes flit towards his bad leg. 'Does it hurt?'

'Sometimes it feels like it hurts you more than it hurts me,' answers Yatin with a smile.

'It was still my fault,' says Aishwarya, trying to keep the memory away from her mind.

Yatin raises his hands, exasperated. One small incident, and he finds that his sister is still paying for it. He says, 'Will you be able to blink when this place is full of kids? Will you allow yourself to look away from them for one moment? You won't be able to breathe, Didi.'

'I won't look away from them for even one moment.'

'You hate Maa, but you're just like her. Every child here will be a Yatin, and you will be Maa, constantly there.'

'I'm the exact opposite of her.'

'Call her.'

'No.'

They eat silently. As the memories flood back, she wonders where she would be if that day had ended differently. What if Maa had come back and seen Aishwarya and her brother sleeping next to each other, with Yatin's soft, chubby hand on Aishwarya's cheek? Would she have loved her then?

24.

Dhiren Das

Every time Aishwarya looks at Dhiren at the other side of the room, scratching his head while staring at the furniture diagrams, her heart does a little somersault. Despite the struggle, Dhiren works tirelessly, his tongue hanging from one side of his lips like a schoolboy. It had never occurred to Aishwarya before that a boy built like a bull could look so cute. Beneath that rough surface, he's still a little boy in want of attention. She has noticed how he perks up after he's told how good a job he's done. When he does that, she wants to wrap her arms around his head and kiss him on the forehead.

Aishwarya walks up to Dhiren to tell him that he's forgotten to keep the margin to sand the wood for the second time today.

'You're supposed to be good at woodwork, with all that muscle. You should be good at breaking, sawing, violent stuff.'

When he sees her looking at his arms, it's embarrassing for both of them.

Thank God he speaks to break the awkwardness. 'We all used to love violence. We still do, in different forms—boxing rings, Formula 1 car crashes, Mortal Kombat deaths?'

'*Saw* and *Final Destination* movies,' she adds.

He shrugs, his voice lowers. 'But we have modernized violence. We can now hurt people with a keyboard.'

He pauses for a little bit. It feels personal for him. *Is that the reason why he's not on social media any more? Because someone hurt him online?*

She changes the topic because the hurt in his eyes pains her. 'Fine, let's go over everything again.'

Aishwarya spends the next couple of hours teaching Dhiren carpentry as she would teach a child. He puts his head down and works as if his life depends on it. Little jolts of electricity course through her body every time his hand brushes against her.

She finds herself taking mental snapshots of him as she has been doing for the past few weeks. These snapshots creep into her mind every morning, in the shower, and her mind wanders and sometimes her fingers. Right now, she wants him to push her against the wall, peel her T-shirt off, hold her hair and take her.

Every day, she has to remind herself that this is not the time to indulge in a crush and cook up future scenarios. And yet she does it, time and again. She imagines them together even though that's an impossibility. She's trying to have a baby on her own for heaven's sake.

Her IVF appointment is in a few days, and she can't allow a passing crush to overwhelm her. What role can he play in her life? None. Keeping her motherhood plans shielded from the influence of any boy is not a decision she has taken lightly. She can't entertain these silly infatuations.

Once Dhiren gets the hang of things, Aishwarya returns to her workstation. Her heart settles. She looks around. Cute Buttons is starting to look close to how she imagined it; her childhood dream is slowly coming to fruition. Now she understands why bankrupt people in business cook up accounting books, embezzle and lie, to keep their business afloat for one more year, one more month, one more day—it's like abandoning a part of you. After all, who is she without Cute Buttons? No one.

After Dhiren leaves for the day, Aishwarya looks at her projections, the launch date, the nature of her finances. Without Dhiren's help, she wouldn't have been able to keep pace and stay within the budget. She's about to start mindlessly scrolling through Instagram, because that's the only way she doesn't sleep thinking about Dhiren, when her phone beeps.

It's a reminder from the clinic about her appointment.

Dr Nikhil Datar. Monday. 11 a.m.

It's finally happening. And, of course, Dhiren doesn't need to know. If he was interested, he would have asked.

25.

Smriti Gupta

Smriti, Aishwarya and Vinny are in the waiting room of the Nayi Shuruat Fertility Clinic, waiting Aishwarya's turn.

'This feels like an exam,' says Aishwarya, who's flushed with nervousness.

'There's still time to think about this,' says Smriti. 'Men like to say benevolent things, that the girl's past doesn't matter to them, but when the time comes, they use her past like little assault rifle bullets to rip apart the relationship. What if you fall in love later? When you have a child.'

'It will be a good filter, behen. Take care of both or get lost,' says Vinny.

None of the women in the waiting room are younger than thirty-five. Some are sitting with their husbands. The husbands look younger—though they are quite obviously not. Smriti senses a sadness she thought was only possible in a cancer ward. *Who knew the miracle of life could entail so much misery?* Smriti can't wait to be out of there. She asks a nurse who tells her they have to wait for an hour.

Vinny points at a guy who's playing a game on his phone while his wife is nervously fidgeting and says, 'Do you think men also have this all-consuming need to father a child? Like, do they look at a child and think "I want one of my own"? They don't, right?'

'Behen, we are conditioned this way. Men have turned us into child-producing and rearing machines,' says Vinny.

Smriti doesn't think so. 'Women are built this way. Amritanshu drives me absolutely crazy, yet I want another one. There's no sense in that.'

'It's the complete human experience,' says Aishwarya. 'To have children, create art, fall in love, eat a good meal and survive are the only five truly human and fundamental experiences.'

'We have enough children in the world,' argues Smriti. 'There's no point in having more.'

'There's *no point* in doing anything other than these five if you think about it. Is there any point to your job, your company, or your promotion in a world with 6 billion people? That's not counting the 94 billion people who are already dead. Every one of those 94 billion people thought they mattered.'

'So, we don't matter?' asks Smriti.

Aishwarya shakes her head. 'You're no better than a cockroach that lived and died. You're bigger, of course, but so were the mammoths. The point of life is *you*, yourself, living in a fulfilling way.'

Vinny rolls her eyes. 'And fulfilment comes from having a child?'

'Fulfilment comes from experiences, and to some, creating a child and caring for it is the best evolution has to offer. Imagine explaining to an alien what you do. What would be simpler to make it understand? Taxes? Or that you helped create life? What's more human?'

'Men *clearly* don't need the human experience,' says Vinny, pointing at another guy on the phone.

'AISHWARYA?' the nurse calls out. 'Follow me to the IUI room.'

Smriti and Vinny give Aishwarya a big, tearful hug, lead her to the IUI room like dutiful husbands and keep standing there till the nurse orders them to leave. They walk back to the waiting room and take their seats.

Smriti taps Vinny and says, 'Hey Vinny, you need to talk to her about Cute Buttons's expansion. I have tried and she keeps avoiding it. You know—'

'Is this the place to have this conversation?' asks Vinny.

'I just thought of it. You know, thinking about her stomach expanding—'

'Kuchh bhi?' cuts in Vinny. 'Achcha, tell me something. You met Dhiren, right? Is he good-looking?'

'I was too angry to notice.'

'Do you think he likes her? Or why would he work for her?'

'Does it matter? After what she's doing, every boy will run away.'

26.

Aishwarya Mohan

Aishwarya's green dress hangs in the corner. She shivers in the flimsy hospital robe that's meant to cover nothing. If it were not for the cold tiles of the IUI room, she would have felt like she was in a pornographic movie waiting for Johnny Sins.

The nurse is an older woman, probably in her fifties.

'Are you comfortable?' she asks in a croaky voice.

Aishwarya nods.

'Impotent husband? Or gay? We get a lot of those cases.'

'I'm not married.'

There's a glint of recognition in the nurse's eyes. 'Oh yes, you're the young one, yes, yes, right. The one who doesn't need a husband . . .' she says as though Aishwarya has been a topic of conversation at the clinic. She continues. 'But you have a good face, a firm body, nice breasts. You didn't find any boy?'

'There were too many. How to select one, sister?'

The nurse laughs. 'Good one! Wait here, I will go and check on the doctor.'

As the nurse is leaving the room, Aishwarya calls out to her. 'Can you dim the light?'

The nurse does so and Aishwarya closes her eyes and settles her breathing. It's suddenly very quiet in the room, and she can hear the dull but urgent thumping of her heart.

It's finally happening.

Her mind is a minefield of emotions. This is the biggest moment of her life. After today, a little life will start shaping itself inside her. It won't be just her any more—it will be her and a part of her.

Her own little family.

She feels a small ball of fear and happiness uncoil in her stomach—she's alone in this.

Just a month from today, she will miss her first period, which will indicate pregnancy. She will then get a doctor to confirm it. And so will start the most critical months of carrying a child—the first three. Most miscarriages happen in that time, when you're yet to hear the heartbeat of a child. She imagines herself in the doctor's room, watching her baby's little heart beating urgently and the doctor telling her that everything's going to be just fine.

She will then take that image of the sonogram and stick it in her file. Her baby will be Roll No. 1 at Cute Buttons.

She can see herself juggling work, doctor's appointments, prenatal yoga and buying new clothes. She's going to start to show, and she's sure she will get a bunch of clothes from Vinny and Smriti. She imagines the two of them doting over her, scolding her for working too much and being envious of her pregnancy-related glow.

The later months will be filled with excitement and impatience. She will be walking around like a penguin with a pumpkin-sized stomach, counting down the weeks, always keeping the baby's hospital bag ready just in case.

And then, one day, she will be wheeled to the hospital screaming in labour pain, flanked on either side by Smriti and Vinny. Fifteen hours of painful, earth-shattering labour, and the nurse will hand over the cutest baby of all time. Vinny and Smriti will suggest names and get into a little fight.

And just then, from behind the doctor will emerge a beaming Dhiren.

Come, look at it, look at my baby, she will offer. But Dhiren's smile will vanish. *Whose child is this*? he will ask.

Aishwarya opens her eyes with a start.

27.

Dhiren Das

'Seriously *nahi le rahe aap* [you are not being serious about it], Kamlesh ji,' says Dhiren, refusing to step out of the car. The property Kamlesh has driven them to is ramshackle and requires plenty of work. 'I need something I can move into tomorrow. *Ekdum* [Absolutely] perfect condition.'

Kamlesh Ahuja nods vigorously. He turns on the ignition.

'*Aur* [So] Dhiren ji, looks like the work is almost finished?'

'That's why we called you. We need to start planning the second branch, but you're disappointing us this time. Gupta ji from the next gully was telling—'

'*Chor* [Thief], number one chor. You wait, I will show you such *chumma* [beautiful] properties you will die.'

Dhiren is tempted to throw money at the problem and make it go away. But if he is to be a serious investor in Aishwarya's business, he needs to make it look legit. Aishwarya will not accept charity. Which, of course, is stupid because everyone should accept charity and demand for more. Wealth is not equally or deservingly distributed, so who cares where the money comes from? Self-respect is overrated and doing whatever the fuck you want is underrated.

'Do you have anything near Sector 14? Away from the red light area.'

Kamlesh thinks for a while. 'There's something. But I already got the token amount. If you can offer more . . .'

'You show me the property first and then we will talk,' says Dhiren.

Kamlesh takes a U-turn and drives towards the edges of Dwarka. Dhiren can sense from a distance which kothi he's driving towards. It's a corner property—three floors, new construction, no main roads nearby. It's *perfect*.

When Kamlesh parks the car, Dhiren declares, 'Talk to the guy. And we will give market rate.'

'*Dekh to lijiye* [See it at least].'

'It's final,' says Dhiren.

'That ladka is nice, shouldn't be a problem. I will tell you by the evening. This time also the payment will be all at once?'

'Monthly.'

Kamlesh smiles wryly, as if he knows Dhiren's money is ill-gotten.

'Kamlesh ji,' says Dhiren. '*Ek request hai* [I have a request]. Keep this a secret between the two of us. Aishwarya Madam shouldn't know about this.'

Kamlesh chuckles. 'Oho oho, surprise! Is there a scene between the two of you?'

'I find her a good property and she dances naked for me,' Dhiren confesses. 'I'm sure Bhabhi ji and you also have such adventures in your bedroom.'

'Dhiren ji . . .'

'You started it, Kamlesh ji. *Kyun ghuste ho itna andar* [Why do you get so much into it]?'

Kamlesh shakes it off.

Dhiren continues. 'If that guy doesn't agree to give up the property, give me his number.'

It is late afternoon by the time Dhiren gets home. Aishwarya is in the garden planting saplings. With all the paint tins and plywood out of the house, the garden is finally coming into its own. Nothing Aishwarya does is short of stunning.

Aishwarya doesn't notice him coming through the gate. She's bent over and her fingers are wrist-deep in the mud. She looks beautiful in her favourite faded Sonali Raj jersey. She's wearing shorts, but he can't see them, and even though he knows that she is, it explodes imagination-sized grenades in his mind. When he looks at her sculpted thighs, her toned arms, the sharp curve of her hips, he feels envious of everyone who has ever touched her, lover or not. *What must it be like to touch her, to run your fingers through her hair, touch her face, hold her tiny waist and pull her towards yourself.* Dhiren can stare at her for hours, as if she's a piece of art.

What does a guy have to do to deserve someone like her? Even if she hadn't made up her mind not to be with someone, she would have been alone. Her kindness is blinding. You can see it in her eyes. She's cute when she's laughing, and she's irresistible from afar, but when she's looking at you, you feel a sense of calm, of being heard and listened to, of being witnessed. It's hypnosis. This is why, he reckons, children love her. She's the truth, and they can see it in her.

Of late, he googles Akshay once in a while. It's isn't voluntary. He wants to know who she once *loved*. He knows Akshay is a decent guy, his app just raised money in two rounds of funding, and yet, he concludes that somehow Akshay doesn't deserve her. No one does.

These days, he's getting a trim every ten days, and shaves so close that he looks like an investment banker. Akshay keeps a close shave, so he guesses that can be one of the criteria. His own behaviour makes no sense to him at all. He's been working with Aishwarya for months for nothing when earlier he would want someone to pay him even if he breathed.

Aishwarya waves at Dhiren when she sees him at the door. She gets off her knees and rubs her hands clean.

'Hey? Smriti and Vinny are coming to drop their children with me.'

'So we aren't working today?'

'I'm not sure if they will be okay with you being here with their children,' explains Aishwarya with hesitation in her voice. 'It's nothing to do with you.'

'I get it.'

'I don't want to ask them also because then you know how girls are. They will ask me *hazaar* [a thousand] questions about you. Anyway, they keep asking why you are helping me. They will eat my head.'

He wants to ask her why does she think he's helping her. The reason's clear as day to him—she's the only person he would ever do this for, and he would do anything for her.

'I will be hiding upstairs,' says Dhiren. 'If they want any more convincing, give me a missed call and I will throw some garbage in your garden. Or spit on them.'

'That might be overkill,' chuckles Aishwarya. 'They know you're nice.'

Dhiren has a sinking feeling in his stomach, thinking of everything she doesn't know. It's not unfair that Aishwarya needs to hide him. Dhiren wonders, if he wasn't hiding his murky past, would he offer to meet Vinny and Smriti? Maybe they would have liked him. But he can't do that, can he? Because he's an asshole. Aishwarya might not have seen it because she sees the good in everyone but surely they would. They would take one look at him and know what he's made of. Worse still, what if they recognized him?

Dhiren enters his apartment and prepares to hole up there for the rest of the day.

His head hurts and his palms are clammy. He closes his eyes and tries to breathe. It doesn't help. He lies on his bed and watches the fan turn above him. In the distance, he can hear the gate open. There are giggles and excited voices from the floor below. He can hear the chirpy squeals of the kids. As he lays hiding, he wonders how long he will have to hide from the world. How long will he have to hide from Aishwarya? What will she do if and when she comes to know his true nature?

His phone beeps. It's Kamlesh messaging him.

Kamlesh: Nahi maan raha ladka [*The boy's not agreeing*].

Kamlesh: Here's his number. Neeraj +91-7045879271. He is asking you to call him.

28.

Aishwarya Mohan

Cute Buttons has made steady progress, but it's still a far way off from being completely baby-proof with stray pieces of wood, metal and paint everywhere.

For the last hour and a half, Aishwarya has been running around like a headless chicken trying to keep Amritanshu and Vihaan from hurting themselves, which little kids are quite adept at doing. It's taking everything Aishwarya's got to reign them in. After a couple of hours, she wants to put on nursery rhymes on ChuChu TV or CoComelon and enjoy a few moments of peace. She even feels like taking performance-enhancing drugs to tide over a low point. Parents can do it—they aren't professionally trained for childcare; they do it with gut feel and love—but there's no excuse for people like her.

She makes herself a triple-shot espresso—a bitter bomb that annihilates her taste buds. She's telling the kids the story of the three little pigs. The two-year-olds don't understand the words, so they just react to her expressions. She acts out every word, exaggerating her expressions. She feels like she's running on fumes. She just wants to sleep for a little bit.

There's a tap at the door. It's Dhiren.

'I brought food,' says Dhiren and holds up the Tupperware. 'Idli for you, and there's vegetable puree for the children. If they don't like it, there's soup for them too. I don't know if you can microwave the food for them, so I put it in a thermos.'

'Can you stay?' asks Aishwarya.

Dhiren comes in. Just him being there calms Aishwarya's frayed nerves.

'Do we put in our mouth things that aren't food?' Aishwarya asks the boys who are now trying to bite through a wooden toy.

The boys laugh and continue chewing.

'MONSTER!' grumbles Dhiren.

The boys step back from him. Aishwarya is about to tell Dhiren off—she doesn't want to raise the boys by striking fear in their hearts. She wants to tell him that fear-based parenting is convenient but unhelpful in the long run.

But Aishwarya stops when the two boys stumble back, laughing at Dhiren's monster impression. When they stop, Dhiren repeats, 'MONSTER MAX.'

The boys laugh again and close their eyes.

'MONSTER PRO MAX!'

The boys laugh harder.

Dhiren looks to Aishwarya and says, 'They are dumber than stray dogs.'

'Don't say that.'

'YOUR LIFE IS DOOMED! WE HAVE DESTROYED THE PLANET WITH PLASTICS AND EXHAUST FUMES!' Dhiren growls.

The boys roll over in laughter. Vihaan shouts out, 'AGAIN!'

Dhiren steps closer to them, walking like a Sumo wrestler. 'YOUR LITTLE CHICKEN STUFFED TOY? YOUR PARENTS ARE GOING TO COOK AND FEED IT TO YOU NEXT YEAR.'

Vihaan runs away laughing.

Dhiren bends over, brings his pupils to the centre making Amritanshu laugh, and says, 'DEMOCRACY IS UNDER THREAT!'

Amritanshu runs away.

'Great, just no abuses, don't want them to learn cusses,' says Aishwarya. She finds a place to sit.

For the next fifteen minutes, she watches Dhiren run after the two boys. Whenever Vihaan or Amritanshu are near a wall corner or an unprotected area, he picks them up, distracts them and places them where they can't hurt themselves. It's not often that Aishwarya gives any attention to adults when children are around, but she can't look away from the beaming smile on Dhiren's face. Many parents, caretakers and almost every teacher pretends to be happy when dealing with children. It's a necessity, but Dhiren at the moment seems to be genuinely enjoying himself.

She's looking at him, and it tempers the tension, the tiredness. She doesn't notice when she puts her head down on the table and dozes off.

When she wakes up three hours later, she's in her bed, ensconced in her blanket so snugly that she panics and struggles to get out of it.

Fuck, fuck, fuck, fuck, fuck, fuck.

She jumps out of bed and rushes to the living room. The lights are dim. She wants to shout but manages only a whisper. And that's when she notices the two cribs. She finds Vihaan and Amritanshu sleeping, tucked in perfectly, two baby monitors switched on near the heads of the cribs. A wave of guilt washes over her. She makes her way to the kitchen where Dhiren's washing the plates the boys ate out of. As a matter of habit, her eyes dart to the Tupperware box.

'Don't worry, they finished their food. No TV, nothing. I might have told them that the soup was made out of the crushed souls of the farmers of our country,' says Dhiren with a laugh. 'The boys are fun. The fat one laughs so cutely.'

Her heart's still beating hard in her chest. *How could she have left them alone? Unattended? With a man they didn't know? With a man she didn't know well either.* She wants to hit someone—her, him, the wall. *Why didn't he wake her up? What did he do? What if . . . he had hit them? Or worse . . .? He didn't even like children, so what ulterior motive could he have to take care of them? He's a fucking . . . asshole, isn't he?* She's burning up. She's sure that this monster touched them; had they cried, he would have slapped them into silence and then given them Maxtra to knock them out. She wants to pick up one of the kitchen knives, drive it through his heart and twist it till she sees the light go out of his eyes.

'Are you okay?' he asks.

'They are babies, don't call them fat,' she grumbles.

Dhiren smiles. 'Fine, the one with the big forehead.'

'Vihaan!'

'Fine, Vihaan. Vihaan laughs cutely. Happy? Man, both of them are a riot. Fucking irritating assholes, but so cute.'

Aishwarya rolls up her sleeves. She picks up the empty Tupperware box to wash it.

'I'm handling this. Warm up the food and eat some. You've had a long day,' says Dhiren.

Aishwarya nods and turns away from him. She feels the anger retreating. She no longer wants to ask Dhiren to fuck off from her line of sight. He's no longer a reminder of . . . her failure today.

She puts the sambhar to boil. 'I will be back.'

'Susu?' jokes Dhiren.

'Shut up, yaar,' she says and walks away. On the way to the washroom, she picks up the laptop.

She locks the washroom and swiftly navigates to the recordings of the CCTV cameras she had installed weeks ago. She plays today's video. Her fingers are numb and she feels like she's dying little by little.

She fast-forwards the video to where Dhiren's running after the children. She presses play.

The video shows her dozing off. For the next fifteen minutes, it's more of the same. Now comes the moment: Dhiren notices she has gone to sleep.

She pauses the video, closes her eyes and starts to pray furiously. She presses play, her mind already in overdrive, thinking of how Dhiren will end up behind bars, raped by fellow criminals because murder is pardonable, but exploiting children!

Dhiren walks up to her, the boys follow him like he's the Pied Piper. He stands there, just looking at her. It's creepy, thinks Aishwarya. He's making sure she's asleep. And then, in one swoop, he picks her up and takes her to her room.

She switches to the other camera.

Dhiren puts her in bed. He enlists the boys to help him with the blanket. They are doing a lot of nothing, but Dhiren is clapping for them. When they start clapping too, Dhiren puts a finger on his lips to quieten them. He ushers them out of the room. But before leaving, he walks back to Aishwarya, bends over and tucks in her hair behind her ear. He goes back out. The boys are running around, too close to the edges of the table. Dhiren gives them an instruction and they stop. He picks out a book and sits on the carpet. They lie down in front of him and listen to him. Ten minutes pass by, then twenty and then half an hour. The boys are listening to him in rapt attention. He closes the book with a slam and snaps his fingers. He fetches stationery, some paints, a few pieces of vegetables and a blunt knife. He cuts the vegetables into little shapes and helps them paint. A little later, he gets their food ready in the kitchen while popping in to check on them every couple of minutes. When he's done, he sits them both down on the baby chairs she had bought and feeds them. Even in the grainy video, Aishwarya can see his animated face, his lips curving into a song, him prancing around like a monkey, an elephant and all sorts of animals to make the children eat. He cleans them up after and puts them to bed.

For the rest of the video, he's in the kitchen, cleaning up.

She pauses the video. Her body calms down. She can breathe again. From the archive of the videos, she opens multiple files and hastily clicks through them. She watches Dhiren's morning routine—entering the house, preparing breakfast meticulously but making it look careless, him standing over her and staring at her. In the work videos, she catches him staring at her. Her heart pounds.

'AISHWARYA!'

She slaps down the laptop in a hurry and jogs to the kitchen. The sambhar's boiling over. She lowers the flame and puts the idlis into the microwave. As she waits for the food to heat up, she tries to calm her beating heart. She wants Dhiren. She wants to hold his hand and lead him to her bed—to thank him. She would thank him in so many different ways. *Shut up, just shut up*, she tells her errant mind. She reminds herself of the two boys sleeping within earshot. With two bowls of idli and sambhar, Aishwarya and Dhiren sit in front of her laptop, watching the highlights of India's 2007 World Cup win on mute.

They have just finished eating when Vihaan wakes up crying. Aishwarya walks up to the crib and lulls him back to sleep. By the time she's back, the utensils are washed and stacked up for drying. A couple of hours later, when Varun comes to pick them up, Dhiren's gone.

'Were they tough?' asks Varun.

'Easiest they have ever been,' answers Aishwarya.

She straps the boys into the car seats.

Varun watches Aishwarya nervously in the rear-view mirror. Aishwarya knows what he wants to ask. When she is done, Varun finally finds the words. 'Vinny was asking if you're . . . you know . . .' His eyes wander to her belly.

'It hasn't even been a month,' says Aishwarya. 'And your eyes aren't ultrasound so . . .'

'Sorry, I don't know why I was staring there,' mumbles Varun.

She watches the car turn around the corner. When she looks up to the balcony, she sees the lights in Dhiren's room go off.

As she walks back inside, she feels a lightness she hasn't felt before. She has spent years caring for her father, then her brother, her friends, then Smriti and Vinny, and though she enjoys the responsibility, it always left her with a heaviness. What are the people she guarded with her life doing when she's not around them? The thought usually made her anxious. But not today. She doesn't feel guilty for having left the children with Dhiren— something that would have otherwise given her nightmares.

She's alone in Cute Buttons, fixing the cribs, putting the bedding to wash, when she realizes that maybe she doesn't have to be alone in her journeys. Of neither Cute Buttons, nor her own. She can, once in a while, take a nap. She gets into bed and opens the applications of nursery school teachers. At the time of the interview, no one had seemed deserving of a second look. Now, it seems otherwise. She marks out a few people she can call for a second interview. She shuts the files and falls asleep quicker than she has in the longest time.

As she sleeps, her phone beeps with a message from Kamlesh Ahuja. He has sent her pictures with options of where she can open the second branch of Cute Buttons. Kamlesh Ahuja would have deleted those pictures had he known the functionality existed on WhatsApp. Since he didn't, he texted her that he meant to send them to Dhiren, and it would be helpful if she didn't tell Dhiren about his mistake.

When Aishwarya wakes up the next day, she reads the message and doesn't ask Dhiren about it. Instead, she takes a small jaunt hunting for the properties he had selected and rates them on her feasibility scale. And while she's doing that, she convinces herself that Dhiren's interest is in Cute Buttons, not her. Definitely not her.

23.

Dhiren Das

Dhiren can easily run away. He can pack in a matter of hours and disappear. Out of this house, out of Aishwarya's life, out of having to do anything with Cute Buttons. He has got more than he bargained for, a friendship he didn't think was possible, a purpose and acceptance. He has felt peace and relief from crushing, overwhelming anxiety after a long time. He should cut his losses and go into hiding again. Aishwarya won't miss him— not for long anyway. She has a school, a possible pregnancy to manage, and he would be forgotten. This would be the sensible option. She might google him occasionally, but she won't find Dhiren Das anywhere. He will save her from the hurt.

And yet, he has spent the entire morning doing three things: a) building a makeshift sprinkler for the garden, b) googling solutions for the growing seepage on his roof, and c) trying not be a coward. Running away is always the easier option. Not any more. Thinking of a life where he doesn't get to see Aishwarya crushes his spirit. The thought of waking up without her near paralyses him.

But staying and continuing this lie is also no longer possible. Sooner or later, she will get to know the truth about him, and he will lose everything. If he wants to give this a shot, a drastic step is needed.

So now, he sits in his car outside Neeraj's house, bracing himself for what's about to come.

'I knew it!' grins Neeraj as soon as he sees Dhiren at the door.

Dhiren knows Neeraj is feeling proud and smug about picking the house from Kamlesh before Dhiren. He can see it on his damn face.

'Let's go inside.'

'Is it weird that I knew exactly which house you would pick, bhai? So it's happening. You and me, in this together. Don't make that face, bhai. It's going to be brilliant. Both of us owning the second branch of Cute Buttons! With Aishwarya, of course.'

'I'm not here to talk about the house,' says Dhiren. 'That comes later.'

Six months ago, he wouldn't have considered doing what he was about to do. Even this can end very badly, but it's his only option. If he has to sacrifice everything he has, it will be for her. He takes a deep breath, trying to muster up all his courage. As the words come up at the back of his throat, he knows exactly what he feels for Aishwarya.

'I want to give up all we stole, everything,' says Dhiren. 'Make an official statement, take the punishment, close the case, get the name struck off records. You will be an innocent bystander in all of this. I will run you through my statement, so there are no holes in what we tell the police.'

'What . . .'

Dhiren notices the fear on Neeraj's face. He would have felt the same, too, had he heard it from Neeraj. 'I can't run any more. This has to end.'

Neeraj's face flushes red. 'Have you talked to Uncle–Aunty about this, bro? This can go down very badly. They will be gutted . . .'

'I know,' says Dhiren.

'And you don't care?'

'If it makes them unhappy, even more reason to do it.'

Neeraj leans forward and looks at Dhiren. He wonders if it's a prank, a silly joke. He finds Dhiren's eyes as serious as death. 'Are you sure about this?'

'I have never been more sure about anything else. This is how I'm going to—'

'Shut up, bhai. You need to tell me why. Why are you doing this? And why now?'

'I told you. I can't run any more.'

'No one cares about us any more. What happened in the café that day was a freak incident. I haven't been recognized anywhere in ages,' argues Neeraj.

'It's not about that day.'

Neeraj shakes his head impatiently. 'They will soon forget us. The boys whose money was in our app have grown up. No one gives a shit any more. Why bring this up now? It's suicide.'

'We need to move on, and we can't with this thing hanging over us. We need to get this over with.'

Neeraj doesn't fall for it. Dhiren hadn't expected him to. He knew Neeraj would dig deeper and eventually Dhiren would have to tell him the truth. 'Bhai, bhai. Don't give me this bullshit. I'm asking again, why are you doing this?'

Neeraj's question is met with silence.

'It's about Aishwarya, isn't it?'

Dhiren nods. 'I can't have Vishwas or his lackeys kicking down the door of Cute Buttons.'

'Bhai, *main chutiya nahi hoon* [I am not an idiot],' Neeraj frowns. 'You can call them anywhere and they will crawl on all fours to come and collect their bribes. You have enough money to keep a thousand Cute Buttons insulated from *thulla*s [cops].'

'People richer than us have been screwed over,' Dhiren reminds him. 'Right now, it's still in our hands. We can make a deal that's suitable for us and get this over with.'

'I have nothing to gain out of this. Just because you're jumping into a *khai* [ditch] doesn't mean I have to as well,' argues Neeraj. 'I won't be a part of any investigation.'

'I'm offering you your freedom. After it's done, no one's going to bother you any more. No bribes, no more hiding, nothing. As I said, you will be an innocent bystander in all of this, I will take all the blame.'

'You're looking out for yourself, bhai. Like you always do. I respect you for that,' says Neeraj. 'And I know why you're doing this. You're in love, and you're ready to give up everything for that. Which I think is a boring cliché. But I'm out. People have forgotten about me and doing this will only remind them.'

'You have no choice.'

Neeraj frowns. 'What do you mean I have no choice?'

'I'm going to Vishwas. And once I confess that I stole the money, they are going to come for you. Then you can tell them whatever you want to. Your discomfort will be less if you stick to what I tell you.'

Neeraj nods, trying to absorb what it would mean for him. 'So I say I'm innocent, I didn't steal any of the money, but you did. But if you're guilty, you will have to pay back the money that you stole. And you don't have that. So you want my share of the money to give back to the police, don't you? That's the catch here, isn't it?'

Dhiren shakes his head. 'All my investment in cryptocurrencies has pumped. I have enough to cover the full money, plus interest. I'm not touching your money.'

'How much return did you manage?'

'Seriously, Neeraj? The point is, I have enough.'

Neeraj falls silent. He rubs his palms, confused as if trying to turn Dhiren's sentences over in his mind to check if he has missed something. 'Bhai, this is a trick, isn't it? You're recording this conversation to make me say I did it. Then you will turn me over to the police.'

'This isn't a movie, bhosdi ke.'

'Then why would you take the blame?'

'Because you have nothing to gain out of it.'

'And what do you have to gain out of it? You're willing to lose all your money?'

Dhiren doesn't answer his question.

Neeraj continues. 'Let's assume Aishwarya gets to know of this tomorrow. She will think you are a haraami, which you were. Fair. But bhai, if you take the blame and surrender, she will still know that you were a haraami.'

'What if she looks past it?'

Neeraj has a sad smile on his face, as if he's looking at a terminally ill patient and telling him it's going to be okay. 'She will look past the fact that you stole from thousands, have a legit criminal record, and let you be part of a playschool business? That will be quite shady of her, no?' chuckles Neeraj. 'Any other business I could understand, but her business, no way. Do you know her business model, bhai?'

'I do.'

'Of course you do. You know everything about her because you're stupidly in love with her.'

'No.'

'She's going to target new mothers who are entrepreneurs.'

'How do you know that?'

Neeraj sighed, exasperated. 'How did I know which property you're going to select? How do I know Cute Buttons will have a second branch? Because you might not consider me as a friend, but *tu mera bhai hain,* and a brother is always a brother. Anyway, no matter how much you give up, no new mother is going to send their kids to a school with your name attached to it.'

'I have to try.'

'If you don't confess, you're not a criminal. Simple. You're a start-up founder who's mistakenly believed to have stolen funds. Just tell her that. When girls like boys, they tend to believe all their lies.'

'I'm not lying to her, Neeraj. My decision is final.'

Neeraj leans back in his chair, exhausted and out of options. A few moments of silence pass before he says, 'Cool. But I have a condition.'

'You're not changing my mind about this, Neeraj,' says Dhiren.

'This is non-negotiable. After all this is done, you and I work together again, be it Cute Buttons or whatever. That's my final offer. You want Aishwarya in your life, and I—'

'Don't say it.'

'You're my best friend. I know you fucked me up, but I wanted to get fucked up. So it's not on you. It's as much on me. Anyway, tell me about this girl.'

'We aren't talking about her.'

Neeraj picks up Dhiren's car keys from the table and throws them at him. 'We are going to Saravana Bhavan. We are going to take one of those big endless thalis. Then you're going to tell me everything there is to know about Bhabhi ji.'

30.

Neeraj Kothari

On the way to Saravana Bhavan, Neeraj hassles Dhiren with questions about his trading and is met with stony silence. Sooner than later, he will pull it out of Dhiren. A 2X return is possible, but it's no joke.

He holds out on his first question until the thalis come and Dhiren has had something to eat. He's got even thinner from what Neeraj remembers. *And why not? The girl has been making him sweat. Nah. What's he thinking? You can't make Dhiren do anything he doesn't want to.*

'But why do you want to do this now?' asks Neeraj.

'I'm running out of time. She knows.'

'She knows that you love her?'

'I don't love her,' rebuts Dhiren. 'Kamlesh sent her a text. She knows I went looking at properties for the second branch of Cute Buttons. And then, she also hired a couple of teachers for the first branch. Which means she's open to the idea of opening a second branch. And then, out of the blue, without asking me about Kamlesh, she asks me if I want to meet her friends.'

'So?'

'If she didn't want to open another branch, or didn't want me to be a part of it, she would have said so. She didn't react to Kamlesh's text, and then she asks me to meet her friends?'

'She wants to open the second branch with her friends and you,' Neeraj connects the dots. 'Of course, now her friends, you and me.'

'She wants to work with me.'

'She likes you. Of course she likes you.' For an intelligent person, Dhiren can be incredibly stupid at times. 'I can't believe you don't see this! Why would she invest in her childhood passion with a person she hardly knows? Only love makes you do stuff like that.'

'And talent. We spent less than a year at Gamer's Inc., and you worked with me,' says Dhiren.

'Not for your talent, but because of our romance, our bromance!'

'Don't call it that.'

'Fine, she doesn't like you,' says Neeraj. 'But say you come out of this clean, will you tell her how you feel?'

'There's nothing to tell.'

Neeraj waves at the waiter. 'Sambhar.' The waiter ladles hot sambhar into both their plates. 'What do you mean there's nothing to tell?'

Dhiren licks the rice clean from his fingers. 'She has a full life—the nursery, friends, there could be a baby on the way.'

'Did you say "baby on the way"?'

Dhiren nods. 'She wants to raise a child on her own. No husbands or boys in the picture. She earlier thought of using her ex-boyfriend as a donor, but he backed out, so it's IVF now.'

'And you knew it from the start?'

'She told me, yes.'

'And all this time you were working together, you knew she was going to get this IVF thing done?'

'I did, yes.'

'So the procedure is done?'

'In all likelihood.'

Neeraj frowns. 'What do you mean "in all likelihood"? That's a yes or no question. Either she got it done, or she did not.'

'She didn't tell me,' answers Dhiren. 'But she went out a few days ago without giving me a reason. And, of late, she excuses herself whenever she has to pick up something heavy. I have seen her hover her hands over her stomach, so I'm guessing it's done.'

'How long ago was this?'

'Been more than a couple of weeks.'

'And she didn't tell you this? About the procedure? Or what happened after?'

'Why would she?'

'Don't be a saint. The two of you work together, practically live together, and she missed out on this detail? That's fucked up. No, I'm serious. Don't act cool about it.'

'So what, according to you, must she have done?'

'It's obvious that you like her,' says Neeraj. 'If I can sense that about you, how can she not? If I can tell that about you, of course she can too.'

'So, she should have asked me to impregnate her?' mocks Dhiren.

'There's no need to be defensive.'

'I am talking rationally.'

'This is not right,' says Neeraj. 'This is a shit move from her. You're talking about possibly going to jail, or at least judicial custody and she's walking around with someone's semen dripping down her thighs.'

'I'm going to punch you.'

'I'm sorry I said that,' accepts Neeraj. 'But you seriously need to reassess this. I never thought I would say this, but you're taking a pretty fucking chutiya deal for the first time. This girl is— '

'You don't know her. Finish your rice. I need to leave.'

'You weren't hurt she didn't tell you?'

Dhiren stops eating. 'Compared to what I haven't told her, it's nothing.'

'That's not the question.'

'What if she did tell me? What would I have said? She wants to have a child and that's that. I wouldn't have told her not to have one. And would I want her to have my child? First of all, can you hear this? It sounds fucking strange. That's the oddest thing.'

'It's odd, I agree.'

'But do I feel left out? Yes. It's not logical but yeah, I do.'

'Heart beats logic every time,' says Neeraj.

'I will be all right,' says Dhiren.

When they finish eating, Dhiren calls Vishwas Bothra for a meeting. Neeraj still feels nervous about it. The police can be all-powerful assholes if they need to be. Even though the money on the table should make Dhiren untouchable, you never know. The police can be vengeful.

'Be careful, Dhiren,' warns Neeraj. 'You have humiliated these police guys a lot. All that swearing and . . .'

Dhiren smiles.

'I am worried about you, bhai. All they need is one day in jail with you. And you treated them like shit.'

Dhiren takes out his phone from his pocket. He swipes through to a folder. 'Look.'

In the folder, there are labelled voice recordings of Dhiren with various law enforcement officers. In each of the recordings, he's detailing the money he has given them, but more important than that, he has treated them like roadside whores who will do anything for money.

'This is what will keep you out of jail,' Neeraj remarks.

If the policemen act fresh, the videos of them taking bribes—acceptable—but more importantly them allowing themselves to be humiliated for cash—unacceptable—will be Dhiren's get-out-of-jail-free card.

'Haraami ho ekdum, Dhiren bhai,' says Neeraj.

Dhiren agrees.

31.

Aishwarya Mohan

There's nothing to lose, Aishwarya reminds herself. None of the guys Aishwarya has made her friends meet have ever been accepted by them. Rejection is a certainty, so what's the worst that can happen? She checks the time on her phone. It's been ten minutes since Vinny and Smriti have been sitting stone-faced in Costa Coffee's Sector 10 branch. Dhiren's due to arrive any moment to face his inquisitors.

'Behen, a young, ripped Nelson Mandela can walk in and I'm still going to hate him,' warns Vinny. 'Is he good-looking?'

'Does it matter?' asks Aishwarya. She looks away from them to hide what she truly feels about him. Her friends have always managed to find the truth in her eyes.

'I still think we should keep Cute Buttons within us. You can keep him as labour if you want to, but that's it,' warns Smriti. 'Does he have any idea that you're going to ask him to be part of Cute Buttons?'

Dhiren has no idea, but it doesn't matter. What matters is that he wants to be a part of this, and more importantly, he's meant to be a part of this. In that little time he spent with the two boys, he showed what even parents fail to show in the entirety of a child's early years—patience, love and total surrender to their whims. Raising a child requires selflessness. Dhiren showed he had that aplenty. Dhiren did more that day to convince her she could open another branch than Smriti and Vinny have been able to do in years. Aishwarya was not about to let an asset like him go. He had to stay, he will have to stay. And Dhiren wants to stay. No one else but he went to scout for properties. Dhiren will be a part of Cute Buttons, come what may.

Earlier this morning, when Aishwarya told Dhiren that her friends needed to talk to him about Cute Buttons, he had nodded. It felt like a foregone conclusion that he was going to be a part of this. No dilly-dallying about '*How did you get to know about the property?*', '*Do you want to be a part of this?*' It's like a quiet understanding passed between them. She knew he wanted a part in the next Cute Buttons and she accepted.

Vinny sighs. 'My answer is already no. Cute Buttons will stay between the three of us.'

'Good to see both of you are keeping a positive and open attitude towards this,' says Aishwarya. 'This is just a nominal meeting. He will be a part of this. Cute Buttons needs him. It's non-negotiable.'

Aishwarya spots Dhiren in the distance, parking his car.

'He's here. Please behave yourselves.'

As Dhiren walks towards them, Vinny and Smriti's faces are set in a deep scowl.

'Hi,' says Dhiren and waves at them.

Both of them have their arms crossed in front of them like bouncers on a Friday night.

'Sit,' orders Vinny.

Aishwarya wonders if other people's friends are as dramatic as these two.

Aishwarya can tell Dhiren has made an effort today. His hair looks well-set and it feels like her fingers will glide if she runs them through it. He smells like a rainy Sunday morning. Aishwarya wants to nuzzle his shoulder and stay there for the entire day. He has just shaved and his jawline is sharply in focus. She turns to look at her friends. Dhiren's beauty is blinding. It's an objective fact, a universal truth that Dhiren is godlike.

'Thank you for helping her out with Cute Buttons,' says Smriti in an uncharacteristically soft tone. Dhiren can have that effect on anyone.

'I have seen you somewhere,' says Vinny, bending forwards and squinting. 'Where have I seen you?'

'Can we talk about Cute Buttons?' butts in Aishwarya.

Vinny catches Dhiren's gaze. 'Look, Dhiren. We know you were looking for a house for the second Cute Buttons. But you can't be a part of it unless you invest in it, dude. You will not be salaried or anything. As Taleb says, "Skin in the game."'

Dhiren smirks. 'Does that mean I was salaried for the first branch?'

A small silence descends.

'I'm joking,' he says and then adds enthusiastically. 'Of course I'm in.'

'That's quick,' says Smriti.

'You don't need to think about it?' asks Aishwarya.

Dhiren catches her gaze and says, 'No.' He pauses and looks at Smriti and Vinny with an intensity Aishwarya has never seen any other boy muster in front of her friends. 'I want to say that I'm almost as careful with money as you are, Smriti, and as ambitious about money as you are, Vinny. I will be a great addition to this already brilliant team.'

Aishwarya can feel the temperature rise. His voice is like a warm blanket, one of calm assurance. The glacial intensity of the meeting seems to be thawing.

'Welcome to Cute Buttons! You're now a part of the team!' says Aishwarya, beaming. Her heart's exploding with joy. Just the thought of seeing him every day sends swarms of butterflies fluttering inside of her.

'I always was, wasn't I? I laid the flooring down,' jokes Dhiren.

'*Zyada smart mat bano* [Don't try to act smart],' says Vinny and then asks, 'But where have I seen you? Have you done a print ad somewhere?'

'Are you saying I'm good-looking enough to be in a print ad?'

'She didn't say that,' butts in Smriti, 'but you could be.'

'Yes, he could be,' reiterates Vinny. 'Spend a little more and get a contractor for the next branch. I can get you one at a cheaper rate.'

'It won't be the same if we don't do it ourselves,' says Dhiren. 'But we get your point. We will outsource the less creative bits to a thekedar to speed up the process.'

Aishwarya's heart melts into a tiny puddle. He's using the word '*we*'.

Aishwarya nods. 'We have to do it ourselves. That's the only way.'

Smriti shoots a murderous look at Aishwarya. 'You have always wanted to be pregnant, right? And yet you don't know what not to do in the first trimester?'

'No lifting weights,' warns Vinny. 'How many times do I have to remind you that you could be pregnant this very moment?'

'She won't,' says Dhiren.

Aishwarya's heart thumps with nervousness. For literally decades, she knew this was what she was going to do: have a child on her terms. To birth an entire person who would be just hers, her family. It would be something she wouldn't have to share with another guy. And yet, as her friends tell Dhiren she might be pregnant, a string of anxiety uncoils in the pit of her stomach. She hadn't found the words to tell Dhiren about the visit to the IVF centre. After that day in the clinic, she kept telling herself she would tell Dhiren once she took the final test and the pregnancy became a certainty. *What's the point of telling him about it prematurely?* she kept telling herself. *What will he do with the information?* She repeated this to herself like a mantra. *He has nothing to do with it*, she chanted.

Telling him would have been so simple. She could have just said, *Hey Dhiren! I'm going to the clinic today, so no work, and I might be starting my motherhood journey.*

But the nausea, the pain in the stomach had kept her from doing so.

Even after she was back from the IVF centre, she could have said, *Hey Dhiren! Remember the day I went to the clinic? I think I might be pregnant. Nothing's sure as of now, but I feel the pain and the morning nausea kick in.*

And yet she didn't say anything.

But now that her friends just broke the news to him, she realizes there was something else at play. She knows why she didn't tell him.

She wants a child, still wants it badly, but . . . now her heart wants something else too. *What if the child could be Dhiren's? What if he could be a part of the journey too? What if she had someone to share this miraculous journey with? What if her family also included Dhiren?*

This is why she didn't tell him. She was scared. What if Dhiren felt the same about her, as she did for him? What if he was attracted to her? She was terrified that telling him could derail her plan. What if he told her that he didn't want her to get pregnant on her own? She would look into his dreamy eyes and postpone the appointment. She would start wishing Dhiren to be a part of the process too. What if Dhiren promised her that if she decided to wait a little longer, he would commit to it? What if Dhiren backed out later like Akshay did? Aishwarya couldn't have taken that chance.

'You're pregnant?' asks Dhiren.

Dhiren's tone doesn't change. Aishwarya wonders if he even cares. She wonders if she was overthinking Dhiren's liking for her. Maybe she's just a friend to him. All that's between the two of them—the spark, the happiness—is it just in her head?

'There's still a few days to go before I can do the test,' she says.

An uncomfortable silence starts to take over.

'Congratulations, then,' says Dhiren with a smile. 'I thought you would tell me. Was it on the day you wore the green dress?'

Aishwarya can't tell what Dhiren feels about this. She can't decipher his smile. *Is that genuine? Is he putting up an act of being okay with this?*

'Why would she tell you?' says Vinny and holds Aishwarya's hand. 'It was between the three of us. You're not that good a friend, okay? You're an acquaintance. The three of us have only husbands and acquaintances. *Theek hai?*'

'Just saying . . . because had I known, I would have been more careful about what we were eating,' says Dhiren.

Maybe Dhiren's unaffected. But then, why does she feel weighed down?

This was what *she* wanted. What does Dhiren have to do with it? Her decision has nothing—and should have nothing— to do with him, or what he feels. So what if she likes him? She measures the words in her mind. What kind of a word is 'like'? It's light, like candyfloss. It doesn't mean anything. You can also *like* the paint on the wall, a piece of furniture. What do you call it when a person becomes another word for a smile, for happiness, for calm? That's what Dhiren is to her. But does he like her? Yes, Dhiren likes her. But 'like', again, is flimsy. What am I to him? Why am I even thinking about this? Especially with a possible baby, what does this even mean? Her life is not hers any more. And this question of liking seems silly. It's fluff.

She's overthinking this. Dhiren doesn't care whether or not Aishwarya has a baby.

'Aishwarya?' says Dhiren.

'Yes?'

'I have a small surprise,' he says with a smile. 'We may know where the next branch of Cute Buttons might be, but they don't. Should we show it to them?'

See, he doesn't care, Aishwarya notices.

32.

Aishwarya Mohan

It's Sunday morning, and so the spectacle of two contractors fighting over which diesel generator would be able to cope up is being watched by a neighbour who's on the adjacent roof, putting clothes out to dry.

'Hey!' says Aishwarya and taps Dhiren's shoulder. 'Who knew diesel generators would be so complex, no? Been an hour already and they can't decide where to install it.'

She has missed Dhiren these past couple of days that he has been busy. Why is he doing other things when he's now working with her at Cute Buttons? There's no reason for him to spend one waking minute away from her. He should be with her all the time, looking at her, brushing his hand casually against hers, making her food, taking care of her. *Stop thinking like that!*

Dhiren looks at her. 'As long as they don't overcharge us, they can fight among themselves all morning.'

'You okay? You seem a little . . .'

'Just work on the other fronts,' explains Dhiren. 'Some things need wrapping up. It's almost done. And then you're the top priority.'

He said *you*, not Cute Buttons. Aishwarya reminds herself to not read too deeply into his words.

'Sorry, sometimes I forget you also have other work.'

'We need to institute a penalty for your constant apologizing,' says Dhiren and laughs. 'And I'm here, am I not, listening to the most interesting conversation about generators?'

And yes, he's here. Vinny has always said that Aishwarya has an expressive face, a clear French window to her soul—like an anime girl—and so now she worries what Dhiren's reading on her face. Does he read that in a short time he has climbed up the chart of the most important people in her life? Does he know what he truly means to her? Does her face tell him that she's nervous about bringing a child to the world that's not his and that makes her hate herself a little bit? Does he know that she has procrastinated telling him about her feelings because that's surely going to mess everything up? After battling with these thoughts for the past few days, she has come up with a foolproof plan. She's never going to tell Dhiren what she feels about him. She's going to drill a hole in her soul and bury her feelings for him down there.

Sooner or later, she will have a baby, and babies overwhelm everything. Her crush, her liking, her attachment, her obsession with Dhiren will surely take a backseat. Dhiren might be the handsomest amongst men and gods, but he can't be more important than a child.

The butterflies, the desire will pass. Like a season.

The contractors seem to have reached a conclusion. They walk up to them and one says, 'The garden has to go. The generator is heavy and needs to be placed in the centre where the strong beam is. We can't keep it on the side where you want it.'

'We need the garden,' murmurs Aishwarya, hoping her anime eyes are working and can go against the laws of physics.

Dhiren looks at her, and Aishwarya knows she has driven the point across. Dhiren nods like he understands. When he does that, Aishwarya feels like he's wrapping his arms around her and kissing her on the forehead.

'The garden stays,' says Dhiren sternly. 'Put a cantilever on the wall and suspend it from there.'

'We will have to ask the owner of the house.'

'Arre, sir ji, let's keep it to ourselves. Just tell us what will be the extra charge,' says Dhiren.

The contractors walk away again to have a long conversation between themselves.

Dhiren turns to Aishwarya. 'If you want the garden, the garden stays. I will try to get someone else if they don't agree.'

Aishwarya nods. 'Is the seepage in your room under control?'

For the past few days, the walls in his bedroom have been dripping water from the edges. But every time Dhiren has told her about this, she has only thought about what it would be like to be in his bed, below that cracking wall.

'It's something I have to live with. We need the sprinklers on the roof for the garden, so those can't go. It's not a big issue,' says Dhiren. 'By the way, Vinny has sent a list of contractors for the second branch. I can call them and you can talk to them. Speaking of Vinny, did she say something about me?'

'Dhiren.'

'I'm interested.'

'They don't hate you. That's a very good assessment, I'm telling you. If they didn't like you, they would be here all the time trying to poison me against you. Take that as a sign,' she says, relishing the fact that her friends' opinion matters to him.

Just then, a sharp pain rises in her stomach. She sees this as a reminder to not read too much into what Dhiren says or does. Whatever liking or adoration he might have for her will swiftly evaporate once she puffs up like a balloon. She will be fat, unlikeable with all the hormone-fuelled mood changes, and she will be busy. That's not any boy's dream. Whereas he is . . . what he is.

Dhiren walks up to the contractors who have decided to make the adjustment. He turns and gives her a thumbs up and a smile that makes Aishwarya lose sensation in all her fingertips. She wants Dhiren—perfect, perfect Dhiren—to stride towards her and kiss her while the whole world is watching. She wants to freeze that frame and live in it for as long as possible.

'They are going to install it in a couple of days. They need some extra material for the cantilever, but it's going to be okay. The garden stays,' he says with a smile. 'Kamlesh is not going to know.'

She can't make out the words he says. Her eyes keep straying to his lips. She has to physically restrain herself from not lunging at him. She has heard pregnancies make women horny, but that is in the later months. Why now?

'Hey? Do you want pakoras?' he asks. 'Come.'

And just like that, he holds her hand and leads her downstairs to his apartment. He chops up onions and potatoes and dips them into a bowl of gram flour paste, He adds salt and red chilli powder and a generous hand of freshly chopped coriander leaves. He lights the gas and starts to deep-fry the onions and potatoes. All this while, she wants to stop him and say it's not healthy, it has too many calories, and yet she finds it sensual as well as ridiculous that she finds it sensual.

'Why did you not tell me about the fertility clinic?'

'Huh?'

'You called your friends and made a big deal out of it, and didn't tell me. Why?' he asks.

Aishwarya notices an intensity in him that she hasn't ever noticed before.

'I . . . I . . . didn't want . . . Vinny and Smriti have been there with me since, you know, and I felt comfortable with them.' She takes a deep breath and prepares to lie as little as she can. 'It's not something a lot of people react positively to—questions and judgements. I wasn't ready for it.'

He strains the pakoras and plates them on a tissue paper. Then he places a bowl of green chutney next to it.

'You already told me this is what you wanted. I wouldn't have judged you. It's your decision, your dream,' says Dhiren. 'It would have been nice to be included. But I'm happy for you. When will you know that you are pregnant?'

'There are still a few days to go. But . . . I can feel it . . .'

'It must be irritating for you to wait.'

Aishwarya nods. 'If only it were an ATM machine. Insert some sperm and get a baby. I'm glad it isn't, or I would have had like ten by now!'

Dhiren laughs. He passes on one pakora dipped in chutney to her. 'Could it be that the first thing your child tastes is this pakora?'

'Technically, it's just a bunch of tissues till a few months into the pregnancy. No consciousness, no life, just organic matter and that's why abortions are okay till—'

'Just eat it and we will remember this as the first thing he or she tasted,' says Dhiren.

The pakora warms up the inside of her mouth and everything it touches on the way down.

'Dhiren?'

'Yes?'

'I enjoyed it.'

'Deep-fry anything and it tastes like heaven. It's one of the easiest things to make.'

'I enjoyed working with you.'

'We are still working together,' he says.

'Just the two of us working in silence, making mistakes, figuring out things on our own. Things will change now, won't they? In a few days, there will be contractors and labourers running around, we will be splitting into two branches . . . you know, it won't be the same.'

After an uncharacteristic long pause, in which she notices a certain sadness in his eyes, he says, 'I will always be around.'

'Will you?'

Dhiren says after a pause, 'Yes.'

And though she feels in her bones that he's hiding something, she doesn't quiz him. She feels as if she will lose him, like he's already moving away.

33.

Vinny Shahi

'Oh!'

Vinny gets up with a start. It comes flooding back to her. She hadn't seen Dhiren in a print ad.

She tries waking up Varun; he stirs and, like always, pretends to be asleep. How has she been so stupid? She could have done this days ago rather than torturing herself about where she had seen Dhiren.

She pulls her phone away from charging and goes to the picture they had clicked with Dhiren the other day. She crops the rest of them and feeds the picture into Google's reverse image search.

'Fuck.'

She tries waking up Varun again.

'Fuck, fuck, fuck, fuck, fuck, fuck.'

*

Vinny, like everyone else, loves being right. In the pre-Google days, she would hold on to a disagreement over a fact long after everyone else had forgotten about it. And when the information presented itself, she would confront the person to tell them *I told you so*. But today, she doesn't like being right.

By the time Vinny reaches the McDonald's near Vishwavidyalaya metro station, Smriti's already waiting for her, fuming, having read through all the articles about *Dhiren Das*.

'Sit and calm down,' says Smriti to Vinny, even though it's Smriti who's sweating and trembling.

'This is—'

'It's your fault. You asked me to leave her alone with the boy. "Give love a chance, blah-blah, nonsense!" This is happening because of you. We should have met him earlier, but no, you wanted to give her space. *Ghanta* [Nonsense] space!'

'How could I have known?'

'Don't you know how guys are, behen? *Gadhi hai kya* [Are you an idiot]?'

'Have you ever seen her happier? What were we supposed to do? After years she found . . .'

Vinny can't believe Smriti. She wants to slap the shit out of her friend. 'What the fuck are you talking about? The guy is a criminal. *Samajh aa raha hai tujhe* [Do you understand]? He literally stole money from people and then said it was the people's fault. *Sar phod dungi uska main bata rahi hoon* [I'm going to break his head].'

'Look, you were right, okay? But what has happened has happened! What do we say to her now? She's going to be here any—'

'What do you mean by "what do we say to her"? We will ask her to leave. She's not going back to that house! And then we can tell Varun and Amit to deal with that guy. They will make him leave the house.'

'And what about Cute Buttons?'

'I don't know about all that, but she's coming home with me.'

'Who's coming home with you?'

Vinny and Smriti turn to see Aishwarya. She sits down and says, 'We need to hurry up. I've got to rush back and check in on the generator. Dhiren is getting it installed today.'

'We need to tell you something,' says Smriti and looks at Vinny as she always does, that coward. 'Vinny, tell her.'

Why does she have to tell Aishwarya anything? That too, when it is clearly Smriti's fault.

Vinny's anger is now replaced with sadness and a heavy sense of anxiety. A part of her doesn't want Aishwarya to know. She's now thinking of the scenarios under which Dhiren can just disappear. Died. Kidnapped. Had a heart attack. Anything that would save her friend the heartbreak.

Grief is easier to deal with. You can put the blame on god, or destiny. With heartbreak, the blame always slowly shifts to you. Your partner can be wrong without a shadow of doubt, but you have grown up believing it takes two to build or break a relationship. You start dissecting the relationship, and before you know it, you start dissecting yourself to see where you went wrong, what you lacked, what you could have done. You hate the person who left you, but you hate yourself more for having been the person who can be left. Vinny doesn't want Aishwarya to go through it.

Smriti pushes her phone towards Aishwarya.

'What's going on . . .'

Aishwarya looks at Dhiren's picture in the article, but the report calls him by a different name. Dhiren looks younger in the picture. Vinny shows Aishwarya more tabs, more images, more damning evidence. The boy living on the first floor is not Dhiren Das. He was once called by a different name. It makes sense now why his name threw up no search results. Dhiren's older name—Dushyant—throws up hundreds of articles accusing him of wrongdoing, criminality, theft and tampering of evidence.

'This is why he looked familiar, Aishwarya. He stole people's money. He's a fraud,' says Vinny.

Aishwarya speed-reads the article. At first, it seems to her that it's an elaborate prank. She wishes it were a prank and she looks up at Vinny and Smriti. This is not a joke. Then she reads the second article, and the third. Her eyes well up. Her lips start to tremble. Vinny and Smriti reach out for her hands. Tears stream down Aishwarya's eyes, but she doesn't sob. She keeps staring at the phone as if that alone will change the truth.

Vinny wants to hold her and tell her that everything's going to be fine. But Aishwarya looks past that. Grief has clouded her entire body. Vinny's worst suspicions have come true. She had begun to think that Dhiren was not just someone who was helping Aishwarya. She knew that Aishwarya also felt strongly for him. It's not Dhiren's fraud that's hurting Aishwarya. It's the pain of her heart breaking.

'It can't be him,' Aishwarya mumbles.

Vinny's heart breaks looking at Aishwarya. It seems as though she has aged a decade in the last few minutes.

'There must be some mistake,' says Aishwarya desperately.

'There's no mistake,' says Smriti. 'I checked and rechecked. Dhiren is not who he says he is. He's on the run.'

Complete silence descends around them. In that moment, Vinny feels as if there is nothing else in the world except Aishwarya and her broken heart. Aishwarya pushes the phone back towards them.

'I need to see him.' Aishwarya's voice barely escapes her lips.

Vinny musters up the courage and says, 'You can't go back there. He's a—'

'He will never hurt me,' says Aishwarya, her voice cracking.

She takes out her phone and dials Dhiren's number. Vinny wants to stop her, but she's frozen in her place. Aishwarya is breaking apart in front of her and all she can do is stare. Dhiren doesn't answer the phone. Once, twice. Every second seems like an aeon.

Vinny manages a whisper. 'Come home with me.'

The words don't reach Aishwarya. She looks at Smriti, but Smriti is crying too.

Aishwarya scrolls down and calls the guard of her residential community instead.

'Don't call him,' says Vinny, but she is ignored again.

The phone line connects.

'Hello!' says Aishwarya, her voice a silent scream. Tears sting her eyes and she wipes them away. It seems as though she has been crying for hours. There's no answer from the other side. 'Hello!' repeats Aishwarya and increases the call volume.

Vinny can now hear sirens from the other side of the phone. She wonders if it's the police.

'What?!' screams Aishwarya. She can barely form the words. 'I can't hear you . . . where's Dhiren? Hello?'

Smriti takes the phone from Aishwarya and switches it to speaker mode. '*Bhaisahab, Dhiren hai kya wahan* [Brother, is Dhiren there]?'

'*Sab toot gaya* [Everything is destroyed]!' a scream comes through the phone over the blaring sirens.

'What?' shouts Smriti.

'*Gir gaya sab* [Everything has fallen]!' the man on the other side screams.

'Bhaisahab, can you go to a quieter place and talk?' asks Smriti.

There's muffled silence from the other side.

'Hello? Hello?'

'Hello?' says another voice. '*Main* Kamlesh Uncle. Beti, where are you?'

'Kam—'

'Beti, the generator caused the roof to collapse! Building *gir gayi!*'

'Where is Dhiren?' asks Smriti.

'. . .'

'Hello?' says Kamlesh.

'. . .'

'. . . he was in the building, beti. Firemen are trying to find him.'

34.

Dhiren Das

One month later

We don't know pain till we experience it. We think we do, but we don't have the slightest idea. Some ignorant people fantasize about having cancer—not fatal cancer, but cancer that stays with you for six months, makes you shave your head and then leaves you—a story ripe for instant fame, motivational talks and a thriving Instagram profile. They don't realize that when the doctor asks you, on a scale of zero to ten, how much is the pain, the scale ends at ten. Anything above is still a ten. A thousand is also a ten. Pain, for those in the bang centre of it, can't be quantified. So while Dhiren was on the hospital bed, he couldn't tell how bad the pain was. All he knew was that the entire world was made of pain and he was drowning in it. He didn't remember a time before pain, and he didn't believe there would be a time after it. In the worst moments, only an astronomical amount of injected morphine and the thought of Aishwarya's face helped.

Death was so close. He held on to her smile in the most abject of times. His body felt so shattered, so desperate to get rid of his soul, it was as if he was holding on to a tenuous thread. He could let go like a spacewalking astronaut holding on to a thin wire and drift off into the darkness. It was her face, the need to look at it one more time, that kept him from thinking of dying. Of all the times he wanted to die, this seemed like the moment which was easy to grasp. Just close your eyes, think about how little you have left to live for and die. Clean. Simple. And yet, every time the morphine kicked in and his brain muddled, he wanted to wake up again.

For her.

'. . . the building collapsed,' he hears Neeraj say. 'It's been a month.'

He knows this to be true—he can still hear the roof crack. He remembers getting pinned down beneath the crumbling concrete. After that, his memory fails him. The next thing he remembers are snatches of a voice screaming his name, then the stern voice of the firefighter telling him he's still alive, then his voice asking where Aishwarya was and then the sobs of his parents much later.

Time's a jumbled, cracked mess. Days are a haze of doctor's faces, instructions, parts of overheard conversation. Pain and sedatives cloud everything. When he tries to move his arm, the pain and effort cause him to pass out.

'. . . and if he comes near Aishwarya, Neeraj, I'm telling you I will kill him myself,' he hears Vinny warn Neeraj at the hospital.

Dhiren wants to get up, but he can barely move his neck. He knows his jaw is shattered because they've bandaged it in countless layers. He thinks if he looks like a freak right now, it is a deserved fate for someone like him.

'Look, Vinny, he's here because of her. The generator she asked—'

Vinny cuts off an angry Neeraj. 'This madarchod is the reason she lost her child . . . she had a miscarriage, Neeraj. Tell this to the bastard when he wakes up.'

'Is she . . .'

'She hasn't eaten in days, she's depressed, and your friend is the reason,' snaps Vinny. 'So please tell him and unplug him. When you're done, kill yourself too. No one will miss two criminals.'

Dhiren's eyes don't open much, but even in the blurriness, he can make out the revulsion writ large on Vinny's face. It's as if he's made of glass, and she can see everything he's hiding inside— his stained heart, the murkiness of his soul, the dirt he carries.

And then one day, he hears Kamlesh talking to his parents and Neeraj.

'. . . they need to pay for the damage, bhaisahab. The two of them tried to put a five-ton generator on the roof. Destroyed the house.'

'I will manage,' he hears Neeraj say impatiently.

'The girl's contract is for three years,' says Kamlesh who has spent more time discussing with Neeraj how the roof collapsed than about Dhiren's recovery.

'Sir, it was a mistake. You know how young boys are,' says Dhiren's father.

'He was just careless. Can we talk about this later?' Dhiren's mother says.

'*Dekhiye* [See] bhaisahab,' says Neeraj, 'my friend is lying there, in pain, and you are . . . I will give you all the money. Don't come back here again. Now just turn around and leave.'

Dhiren's father is about to interrupt, but Neeraj snaps at them, 'Please, Uncle.' And then he shouts at Kamlesh. 'You're still here? *Thappad khakar maanoge kya* [Will you listen only after a slap]?'

Dhiren wants to go down under, sleep for a hundred years, or just be dead.

And then he wakes up to the sweet cacophony of shouting children. He gets up from the bed. He's back home. He takes the stairs and finds twenty little kids running amok in Cute Buttons. Aishwarya's running around like a headless chicken. She comes to him, gives him a bunch of papers to be dealt with by the end of the day. He's about to complain, but there's an ugly cracking sound in the air. Aishwarya, Dhiren and the kids turn to look at the ceiling. A big fissure appears there. Dhiren sees Aishwarya throw herself atop the large group of children.

The pain wakes him up.

'The deal with Vishwas is through . . . it's good. We are taking it,' Neeraj murmurs into his ear.

Neeraj places his hand on Dhiren's. The pain hits him with the fury of a thousand suns and burns him from the inside. He slips back into sleep.

Neeraj and Dhiren's parents are arguing. He senses it's about him. He perceives possessiveness in Neeraj's voice and abandonment in his parents'. When it all quietens down, Neeraj walks up to him.

'You're going to stay with me,' says Neeraj. 'You won't be able to tolerate them for long. Both of us know that.'

Dhiren tries to say something but realizes he still can't get his face to move.

A few days later, the doctor allows Dhiren to be shifted to the house. On the way home, he can feel every movement in his body. Everything hurts like a bitch.

The house is new. It's not his parents' house, but they are there, and so is Neeraj.

'Aishwarya . . .' he finally murmurs one day.

'She's gone,' says Neeraj. 'Get better. I'm working on a few ideas, all medical industry-based. We should work on them stat. See what I did there? I used the word "stat". That's medical lingo.'

'Do—'

'She knows. They know about . . . *us*.'

In the nights, he can hear his parents talk in disapproving tones. They talk about how Dhiren has always made questionable choices. He can tell by the inflection in their voices that they believed this was a long time coming. Why not? If it were up to them, he should have died. At least that's what his parents wished for once.

Dhiren's life has fallen apart twice.

The second time is now—when the roof crumbled down on him and Aishwarya abandoned him. Not without reason.

But the first time was when Crypto Cricket was shut down and his parents abandoned him.

20 October.

That was the date, the date it all fell apart, the date Dhiren became a criminal and went on the run. It's been a couple of years since then, but Dhiren remembers it like it was just yesterday. All five major newspapers in the country reported simultaneously about the biggest scam in the technology world. The money stolen was mind-boggling, beyond comprehension. Since the money in question was in cryptocurrency, it didn't run in the traditional news cycles for a long time. But online magazines kept writing about it. To escape the hounding of the rabid newspaper reporters, Neeraj rushed to his house. Dhiren ran to his. Reporters tracked Dhiren to his parents' house. They banged on the door and left lewd and threatening messages on his parents' phone number. Outside the apartment gate, a mob of young college guys exhorted him to step out of the house. By evening, the crowd had burnt both of his parents' cars. Twice, his father had charged at Dhiren with his old cricket bat. Dhiren's mother had looked at him with disgust and said, 'We are so thankful we didn't have another child. We should never have had you either. Look what you've done.' Dhiren's father had added, 'We should have adopted a dog instead.' By the following day, the cyber cell had arrested Dhiren and Neeraj on money-laundering and fraud charges.

He truly lost his parents that day.

Today, he mourns the loss of Aishwarya.

Slowly, over the next few weeks, he feels the pain retreat. The dosage of his sedatives is tapered. He spends more time in his senses. Now, there are times he wakes up and is lucid. He hears the drips, the beeps, but there's nothing else to do. His jaw is snapped shut. He can't move his neck, and all he does is stare at the ceiling.

He realizes the road to recovery is long. A full-time nurse hovers around along with his parents and Neeraj. He can manage a few smiles and a few words, but mostly he's too exhausted or dazed to speak coherent sentences.

When he can finally move his hands, he waits for both his parents to look at him. When they do, he raises a middle finger at both of them.

'He's not well,' says Neeraj.

Dhiren smiles in return. His parents walk out of the room, cursing god, cursing their luck for giving them the child they have. Dhiren doesn't give a fuck. And yet, it pains him. He lets it go because there's no sedative for the pain your family gives you.

Over the next few days, the nurse starts to loosen the bandage around his jaw. He's shifted to lighter sedatives. His mind clears slowly and he's able to think for longer periods of time. He knows he's in Dwarka. This is a new house. Neeraj and the nurse stay with him full-time while his parents visit once in a while.

He is also aware that Aishwarya knows everything. That he will never see her again. And that makes him want to not survive the collapse of his broken dreams and what he once called home.

He notices the GPS anklet on one of the long nights he spends awake, swimming in shallow pools of pain. He has pieced together what transpired. Neeraj has made good on the deal he has been offered by Vishwas—of money to be returned and house arrest instead of jail time. That's why the anklet. Neeraj had probably convinced his parents that it would be better and emotionally less scarring if he didn't carry out the sentence locked up in his childhood home. That's where the new house had come into the picture. He hadn't recognized it at first, but then it came to him. It was the property supposed to be the second branch of Cute Buttons. House number 46A, Sector 23, Dwarka. Neeraj has already paid the token amount. Now, lying in the same house that could have meant a new beginning, he rots and thinks how it's an end instead.

Sometimes he wishes he hadn't survived the collapse of Cute Buttons.

35.

Neeraj Kothari

Neeraj can never forget the greyscale X-rays the doctors showed him. Dhiren's bones were so shattered, it looked like a 1000-piece puzzle. His joints were mush and had to be put back together with grafted tendons, screws and plates. The doctors told Neeraj and Dhiren's parents that it would be a long time before he would walk properly.

Neeraj would sometimes lean over Dhiren's bed and joke, '*Aur banao body* [Do more body-building]!'

Dhiren would be too knocked out to react. He spent three months in the hospital. Every few days, the doctors would operate on a little part of his arm, leg or jaw. After each surgery, they would say it was successful. And yet he remained in bed, groaning in pain and mumbling in his sleep.

'He has a high threshold for pain. Anyone else would have cracked,' the doctors told Neeraj.

Of course he does, he's a bad motherfucker, Neeraj thought to himself.

And then someone asked, 'Who's this Aishwarya he keeps mumbling about?'

For the first couple of months, neither the doctors nor the nurses paid them any special attention. Dhiren was just another trauma victim.

Things changed swiftly when Vishwas and some senior IPS officers started visiting the hospital to iron out the deal between Dhiren, Neeraj and the state. Soon, everyone at the hospital knew about Crypto Cricket and the amount of money Dhiren and Neeraj had *allegedly* run away with. The police then asked Neeraj to cough up the cash since Dhiren was incapacitated.

'Since the money will be routed through you, you will take part of the blame too,' explained Vishwas.

The deal was struck—all the money was to be returned over six months, one year of house arrest for both Neeraj and Dhiren. Things moved swiftly after the money reached the government authorities: Dhiren was named the main culprit in the charge sheet; Neeraj was charged with negligence. Crypto Cricket was back in the papers, so were Neeraj and Dhiren. News outlets claimed a big win for the authorities.

Big win for Cyber Cell, finally trap the founders of Crypto Cricket! Crypto Cricket to return all the money

Founders to return money after RBI makes it impossible to spend their laundered money

Some print news outlets were still kind. The others painted a darker picture. They published pictures provided by Vishwas and the hospital staff—of Dhiren lying unconscious on the hospital bed with headlines like:

Once a millionaire, now penniless and dying

Karma hits back, crypto scammer loses everything

Accidental collapse of roof brings scammer under the hammer of the law

'They make you look like fools,' Dhiren's father told Neeraj. 'You should never have done it, squandered your life away.'

'What does it matter what they make us look like?' Neeraj answered.

Their son was lying in pieces and they cared more about how the newspapers made him look. Neeraj always believed that Dhiren painted a one-dimensional picture of his parents, but he realized they were surprisingly calm—sad but not devastated.

While Dhiren recovered, Neeraj got the new property in Dwarka fixed. When they moved in, Vishwas got his technicians to secure anklets on their legs.

'Where's he running away?' Neeraj had pointed to a supine Dhiren.

It's after a month of recuperating that Dhiren can finally sit up. That meant he was ready for more pain—physiotherapy. Dhiren didn't talk at all. He would spend hours every day with the physiotherapist, trying to get movement back into his limbs. And then he would go straight back to sleep. For two months, Neeraj hoped Dhiren would say something, yet he could never be drawn into a conversation.

But for the past few days, Dhiren has been doing a few more things—read the newspaper, try to flip through the pages of a book, play chess. And also talk.

Today, Neeraj hears him long before Dhiren shuffles into the kitchen in a slow, robotic walk.

'Dosa?' asks Neeraj.

Dhiren shakes his head. 'Sweet corn soup, chilli chicken and hakka noodles. Make fried rice too.'

'Cool, we will have dosas. You will love them.'

'Everything tastes like paper to me,' says Dhiren and settles down in the chair. 'Are they downstairs?'

Neeraj tells him they aren't. Dhiren's parents have gone back to work.

'How's it?' asks Neeraj as Dhiren bites into a dosa. 'Don't compare it to yours. In general, how's it? I'm getting better, bro.'

'If before extracting me from the rubble they'd told me that I would have to eat your food for six months, I would have refused to come out.'

'Seven months,' says Neeraj, reminding him of the duration of their house arrest.

Vishwas Bothra had run a challenging negotiation. A year of the strictest form of house arrest—no food deliveries, no guests apart from parents, no alcohol, no cell phones and no access to the Internet. The three constables outside the house would rummage through every grocery order. This was above and beyond the fine they paid to the government.

'In a day or two, the constables might be able to give us a phone and block the network jammer. We would have the Internet for that short time in-between,' says Neeraj.

'Okay.'

'You can message Aishwarya.'

Neeraj watches Dhiren's eyes cloud over.

'I don't want to,' says Dhiren, his voice betraying his emotion. He gets up and starts to walk towards his room. Neeraj reaches out to help, but Dhiren waves him down. 'I can walk.'

Later that night, the constable trips the power supply, knocking out the network jammer. He leaves a cell phone on the doorstep and says, 'Fifteen minutes.'

'We only need two,' answers Neeraj.

Neeraj searches for Aishwarya's whereabouts. The Cute Buttons nursery page, along with her own Facebook pages, are gone. So is every other trace on social media. The only clue is her LinkedIn profile. There remains a gap from when her last job ended to now. He drops in a few messages to Vinny and Smriti to ask about Aishwarya. It is late so he doesn't expect a reply. But he gets two.

A synchronized reply from both of them: *Fuck off*.

36.

Aishwarya Mohan

Hari Om International, the bookstore chain, started out as an enormous three-storey outlet in the centre of Connaught Place. The old-timers would say it was the crown jewel of the block. But in the past decade, the top two floors have been taken over— one by a coffee shop, the other by an authorized mobile repair outlet. The floor that's remaining now sells toys, bottles, diaries, gifts . . . and a few books.

The owners knew that even if older people don't read and just scroll endlessly on their phones, they want their children to read books. And so, just in time, they started a publishing wing where they produced brightly illustrated, poorly written children's books. The margins were high, the critics none and the production costs low; the illustrators reluctantly doubled up as writers. The cavernous room at the back—which was once a godown—now serves as an office for the publishing wing.

There are four rows of long tables where everyone—illustrators, accountants, salespersons—sits with nothing but noise-cancelling headphones between them. In the corner of one table sits Aishwarya, staring unblinkingly at the large 26-inch screen while scribbling on her drawing pad.

'Make the tortoise greener. How many times do I have to tell you that? Make it pop, Aishwarya, make it pop!'

Aishwarya turns to see Smita Kapoor, the second-generation owner of Hari Om International, standing over her shoulder, squinting at her illustration of 'The Tortoise and the Hare'.

'We will pay the printer full price, so why use muted colours?' asks Smita. She pulls up a chair and sits next to Aishwarya. Smita continues, treating Aishwarya like a brainless child, 'And look, Aishwarya, the children don't care about art, they care about the colours. Just give them bright stuff so they don't look up from the book and bother the parents. Okay? It's been three months and I keep saying the same thing over and over again.'

With Smita looking at the screen, Aishwarya turns up the green till it hurts her eyes.

'See? Was that so hard?'

The tortoise is now unnaturally green. That Hari Om International doesn't credit the writers-cum-illustrators is a double-edged sword. She doesn't want her name to be on these books anyway.

When Smita walks away, she turns down the saturation by a small margin. She adds a few warts to the tortoise, a few stray hairs, draws a small middle-finger sign on the bunny, a fish choking on plastic on the riverbank and a tiny dead rat in the grass. The team is small so Aishwarya oversees the production as well, and that's how she makes sure at least a few of the twisted books are published. It keeps things interesting, and real, for her. She wonders if any of the parents will find these quirks in the books. What will they do then? Complain to the consumer court? Or maybe, finally, pick up the books to find the other morbid, dead, maimed creatures she has sneaked into them? Or maybe they will be happy that the books are realistic? They are a more realistic version of life—imperfect, dark, shitty even. And life's not a fairy tale.

All of Hari Om International's employees huddle into the little pantry to have quick lunches. Aishwarya wolfs down her parantha in three quick bites and then takes a small walk around the bookstore. She walks past three new racks with Elsa and Anna dolls, a large-scale cut-out of Tom and Jerry, and a big screen playing Paw Patrol just above a stack of Chase and Marshall toys. There are three texts from Akshay. She replies to them and wonders how he still has time for her despite his nineteen-hour workday.

Aishwarya is rearranging the books in the fiction section when she hears Vinny.

'Behen, I found a couple,' says Vinny, holding out the Hari Om International version of *Cinderella*, illustrated and written by Aishwarya.

'Don't you have work?'

Vinny shows Aishwarya the pride flag popping from the prince's pocket and the fine slit marks on Cinderella's sisters' wrists. Then there are blisters on Cinderella's feet in one of the illustrations.

'It's not your age to read these books,' says Aishwarya.

'Vihaan found them.'

Aishwarya rolls her eyes. 'Of course, another slow day at the shop? People not buying saris or what?'

'You know how it is.'

They don't even bother to lie.

Vinny comes every second day to the shop to check on Aishwarya. For weeks after Cute Buttons was reduced to a heap of rubble, they put Aishwarya on suicide watch. After a month passed, they offered her money to start over—money they didn't have—and she turned it down. She didn't want anything to do with Cute Buttons. She was done. There would never be any Cute Buttons.

'We told Neeraj to fuck off. He messaged both of us, that chutiya,' says Vinny.

'I thought they weren't allowed cell phones.'

'They are criminals. What else would you expect from them? They will be free in a few months. Don't talk to him if he tries to.'

'Got it.'

'I'm serious, Aishwarya. This is all that boy's fault.'

'I won't,' says Aishwarya. 'I should get back to work.'

'What are the things I missed in the book?' asks Vinny.

'On the last page, Cinderella's sisters' toes are cut off.'

'Gross.'

Aishwarya shrugs. 'It's how far they were ready to go to realize their dream of marrying a prince. What are a few toes for that?'

Aishwarya returns to her seat. When she's sure no one's peering into her computer, she types Dhiren's name into the search bar. The latest news is from a few days after the roof collapsed. The article lays out Dhiren's arrest details and the deal struck with the lawmakers. The news outlets have wrung the news for maximum clicks. There are old pictures of Dhiren, when he used to look like a movie star, and then there are pictures of him on the hospital bed, bandaged, lying half-dead. There are more articles. The ones from tabloids scream: **Millionaire Crypto Scammer Lies Half-dead and Penniless in the Hospital**. She feels angry at the tabloid even though it shouts the truth that Dhiren never shared. Her stomach churns, looking at the picture. She wants to reach out and touch him. The words on the side that detail his crimes don't mean anything at the moment. She reads them over and over again, trying to force herself to be angry for the lies, for the hurt. And yet, the embers of betrayal don't flare. He was strapped to a bed, bones in a mush; and she was at home, unhurt. He had chosen to lie, but she had hurt him too.

He could have *died*. He could have been just one of the many who could have died. Kids could have died. Amritanshu and Vihaan could have died.

She snaps out of it and closes the tabs.

She reminds herself of what she had promised that day: to have nothing to do with Dhiren or Cute Buttons.

37.

Dhiren Das

Three weeks after Dhiren begins to walk at a half-decent speed, he drags a stool from the living room to his bedroom and places it in the centre.

Desperate times call for desperate measures.

He pulls down a curtain, makes a strong noose and passes the other end of the bunched-up curtain over the hook on the ceiling. He drafts a short mail telling Neeraj and his parents, and cc's Vishwas Bothra, that he's done with this life. He's tired; he wants it to end. To fuck Vishwas up a bit, he also adds that his condition has been exacerbated because of the police's misbehaviour during the house arrest. He alleges in his mail that a senior officer encourages the constables to piss on their vegetables before they are delivered to them. He tests the strength of the stool. It's creaky, but it will do.

Half an hour later, Neeraj finds Dhiren, limp and lifeless. He unwraps the noose and sees a deep bruise around his neck. Dhiren is unresponsive to Neeraj's frantic screams and frenzied slapping. A crying and desperate Neeraj loses precious time when he has to argue with the constables to let Dhiren be taken to the hospital. The blare of the parked ambulance, Dhiren's body lying lifeless outside the house, the shouting constables—all seems surreal. *This is not happening*, Neeraj keeps telling himself as he goes through the motions. The permissions take half an hour to come.

At the hospital, Neeraj is locked in a waiting room as if he isn't a white-collar criminal but a serial rapist and a murderer, and that he will go around plunging knives into the patients' abdomens. He waits for an hour before he's led in handcuffs to see Dhiren.

Dhiren has survived his fake, well-planned suicide attempt.

'It was scary, I will admit that,' says Dhiren. 'But it had to be done. And I learnt from the best.'

'My fake suicide was easier to execute than yours,' says Neeraj.

'We are the worst people in the world, aren't we?' says Dhiren. But he doesn't feel horrible. What's the need of being nice any more? What will he stand to gain? Aishwarya's long gone.

Dhiren continues. 'Vishwas Bothra is shitting his pants right now. Can you imagine his face? He will be fucked if there's a suicide on his watch.'

Neeraj nods. 'Let's hope the doctor who's assigned to you finds you suicidal. Once that's done, we are set. Bhai, I wish there was some other way of doing this.'

'No amount of grovelling or bribing would have got us a laptop and Internet in the house. Now, we will have both.'

Dhiren had no choice but to stage his suicide. He was going mad with grief and anxiety. He had to keep his mind busy. His empty mind was a minefield of memories. Quietness tortured him. Every time he let his mind wander, it would show him a future that didn't exist. He would see Aishwarya and himself in Cute Buttons. There were children painting, doing puzzles, sleeping in cribs, happy and loved. He would steal glances at Aishwarya—pregnant and beaming. And then, the image would shatter.

He had to make his mind stop.

It's his fault. Everything he touched turned to dust, every decision he has made has led to this disaster. He stole, then he hid his true self from her, then he let his feelings take over and put that generator there; he ignored the seepage, he hid the added weight from Kamlesh and he snatched from Aishwarya what she had been waiting for all her life . . . a child. If only Cute Buttons was still standing, she would have powered through, carried her pregnancy to term. He had destroyed the person he loved more than anything in the world.

As Vinny had said, he was the reason she lost her child.

The only true way of battling heartbreak is to work yourself to death. There was no other way out. He was desperate and choking. He felt as though he was short of breath the entire day. His mind would work non-stop. Sometimes it would be stuck beneath the debris; at other times, it would obsessively tell him how much Aishwarya hated him now.

With Neeraj around, he felt like getting into the grind again. They had enough money to play the VC game, get into the thick of things and stay busy enough to numb any uncomfortable feelings. But without the Internet and contact with the outside world, it was a dead end. Dhiren was surprised at how the supposedly complex plan came so simply to him.

'I will do what you did,' Dhiren had said to Neeraj.

Neeraj had agreed and they had planned it to perfection. The attempt was fake. But even then, standing on the stool, he could only think of *her*. Would he fall even further in her eyes if she got to know?

As expected, a frantic, sweating Vishwas Bothra marches into the hospital room, screaming.

'MADARCHOD, you pull something like this again, you're going to jail on a murder charge!' he says and turns to Neeraj. 'And what the fuck were you doing? Your roommate's about to kill himself and you don't sense it? *Andha hai kya, behenchod* [Are you blind, sister fucker]?'

'Depression often doesn't present signs, sir,' answers Neeraj.

'*Abey, tujhe kaunsa depression* [What depression do you have]?' says Vishwas. 'Next time you try killing yourself, I'm going to come and make sure you're actually dead.'

He tells them that as they are speaking, the police is installing cameras in the room, plastic spoons are replacing all cutlery and all bedsheets are being taken away.

'What if I left the gas on for a few hours?' asks Dhiren.

Vishwas lets it slide. 'There will be daily sessions by the court-appointed psychiatrist, and you better not die, madarchod,' he grunts. He pulls a chair close and sits down. 'And if you still feel like doing it and fucking me over, let me know where the rest of the money is. Because I don't believe for a second that you gave up all the money.'

'Wow.'

'What?'

'Look at you, Vishwas, you still want more,' says Dhiren. 'I will tell you what. Your chutiya constables are not going to be able to stop me from killing myself. But sure, I can give you the money before I go. Money's dirt where I'm going. Suck my cock, make me cum and I will give you everything.'

'*Behen ke laude* [Sister fucker]!'

'Unlike politicians, you won't have to lift up the paunch to find my dick. But you got to swallow, man. That's my condition.'

Vishwas has had enough by now. He asks Neeraj to follow him outside the room. They are still within earshot, so Dhiren can hear the rest of the deal: the Internet and a tablet for an hour every day for the psychiatrist's evaluation. Neeraj nods like a child who has erred. He promises Vishwas he will assess and report any suicidal behaviour.

'The court wants video call details to be submitted every day. While what happens on the call is protected by patient–doctor confidentiality, the doctor will show us the length of the call duration. If you guys fuck up, he will have to be committed to a facility,' says Vishwas.

Dhiren is discharged from the hospital after two days. Once back home, they are introduced to Dr Kalpesh Noorani, a dispirited, middle-aged psychiatrist. When Dhiren offers him Rs 1.5 lakh per session to do exactly nothing, he thinks it is a joke.

'What do you mean?' he asks.

'We are just going to use the Internet, doctor,' says Neeraj.

It wasn't until the first payment hit the doctor's account that he knew the deal was real. Starting then, they would log on to a call, switch off the camera, mute the call, and then Dhiren and Neeraj would get down to work.

After the first week, Dr Kalpesh submits a desperate and dire report to Vishwas Bothra, telling him that Dhiren was in need for more hours or he would certainly end his life. The session length was first increased to two hours and then two and a half hours. This gives Neeraj and Dhiren enough time to reach out to cash-strapped founders with fledgeling start-up ideas. They have enough money to fund at least a dozen start-ups. Much to Dhiren's surprise, no one in the entire ecosystem cares where the money is coming from. Dhiren and Neeraj's new project takes up a lot of time, eats up a lot of hours. For every half-baked idea, there are hundreds of founders pitching apps to VCs.

Dhiren and Neeraj are finalizing their investment in a fintech app when the speaker of the laptop blares. Dr Kalpesh's two sons, Rohan and Nauman, are screaming. It happens every once in a while. Rohan, the older one, put the mute button off and they can hear everything. Today, his tyrant boys are tapping random buttons on his laptop and shouting right into the microphone.

'I'm so sorry!' says Dr Kalpesh. 'I will just put him to sleep.' He picks up the younger one and leaves the room.

The camera and the speaker are still on. The older boy is now making faces and licking the camera. Neeraj throws up his hands in exasperation. 'I'm going to put my hand in a blender rather than keep looking at this,' he says and goes to the kitchen to make himself a sandwich.

Rohan is now spitting on the camera. Dhiren shakes his head.

'What?' asks Rohan.

'I enjoy doing that a lot, too, but you need to work on the range because this right now is no good,' points out Dhiren. 'Take a few steps back and try to hit it again. I'm sure you can do it.'

'Spit on the screen?'

'Yes, spit on the screen. Isn't that the game we are playing here?'

'I SPIT!' Rohan screams. 'I SPIT SO HARD!'

Rohan steps back, tries and fails.

'Almost there!' says Dhiren. 'Try again!'

'Should I?'

'You were so close. C'mon! Try again.'

Rohan tries and fails again.

'Take a deep breath, hold it in, make that spit and then, as you breathe out, spit with all the strength in your little body!' says Dhiren.

Rohan tries and fails.

'Again! You can do it, don't give up so soon. Try again, c'mon.'

Rohan fails again.

'Again!'

Rohan tries. And fails again!

'You're improving. Wow, your spit strength is amazing. You're a natural, not a lot of people can do that so easily. Try again, I see a spit king in you.'

'Thank you.'

'Don't thank me! This is your talent.'

Soon, Rohan exhausts both saliva and tongue strength to keep going. Dhiren smiles at Rohan. 'You did well. We will try again.'

'I like you,' says Rohan.

'And I like you, the spit warrior,' says Dhiren.

'Let's play another game, another game, another game. I will come running from . . . from . . . from that end and jump towards the iPad. You do the same, same time!' says Rohan.

'That's . . . that's an amazing game!' squeals Dhiren. 'But you know what? My leg doesn't work. You know what happened? I was buried under an entire building. AN. ENTIRE. BUILDING.'

'Whoa.'

'I was buried, for like, an hour.'

'AN HOUR?!'

'Like totally. Then the firefighters came and they shouted my name and couldn't find me. Can you believe that?'

'Show me your leg! Is it disgusting?'

'Totally. The bone came out of the leg, there was blood everywhere. LIKE. EVERYWHERE. Even my arm was broken in three different places, bent backwards,' says Dhiren and shows Rohan the scar.

'SO. COOL.'

'Are you guys done?' asks Neeraj, munching on his jam–butter sandwich.

'One minute, I'm showing him my scars,' says Dhiren.

38.

Aishwarya Mohan

Akshay and Aishwarya, that sounds good.

Her Hari Om International colleagues remind her of that every time Akshay comes visiting. Some of them point out that she should be more enthusiastic about her boyfriend, seeing that he's on the precipice of success. She never explains to them the transitory nature of the wealth of start-up founders like him. He could be ultra-rich or lose almost everything in a matter of months. But for now, he sits in a prime location, in a brightly coloured office, burning investors' money at a ludicrous rate. His start-up has gained momentum and funding at an astonishing pace. It could become one of the behemoths or be reduced to a cautionary tale.

And despite his nineteen-hour workdays, he finds time to visit Aishwarya. They tell her that he's always going to stick around—seeing that his ex-girlfriend cheated on him. He will cling and love and be perfect.

'He's trying to find an anchor in you. Give men a lot of money and they tend to go crazy. He wants something normal,' Smriti said to Aishwarya when Akshay's drop-ins started to become more frequent.

'Aishwarya is not normal, she's amazing,' countered Vinny, '. . . and she's loyal.'

Maybe Aishwarya is Akshay's link to the uncomplicated past. Which is strange because Aishwarya doesn't think she's the same person any more. This morning on the metro she saw a slightly pregnant woman reading a book, listening to music, carrying a laptop bag—all of her favourite things—and yet she didn't get up and offer her a seat. She waited and hoped someone else would and felt slightly relieved when she didn't have to give up her seat.

The old Aishwarya would not only have given her the seat but also thrown in a foot massage and conversed creepily with the foetus.

*

Today, Akshay and Aishwarya sit in the United Coffee House. Akshay is on the phone, simultaneously issuing instructions to his team and writing apologies on tissues for being occupied. Aishwarya doesn't mind this. She works on a new set of gory illustrations that she might sneak into a book, sketching them in her diary. Akshay's tea grows cold. She's now thinking of how Dhiren used to put everything aside for food, tea and coffee. It's not the first time she feels horrible for drawing comparisons between them. Between their hands, between the way they smell, how they look at her. Akshay's eyes are always flitting, always searching for something, always urgent and restless. But when Dhiren looked at her, it was like standing in the spotlight. It's only she who mattered, she was the central character of his movie. Everything she did was meaningful. She swiftly reminds herself that while Akshay was an honest person, Dhiren hid an entire life from her.

Akshay stepped in when he really didn't have to. The first few days after Cute Buttons's collapse were the hardest. She moved back to her home and for days, she could sense what her mother wanted to say to her. She knew her mother was dying to say it. Sometimes she wished Maa would just say it so she could fight with her.

'We told you not to do it,' Maa finally said in the second week.

Finally! thought Aishwarya. She looked at her mother and said, 'I am sure you wished this would happen. Oh no! You would have wished for it to collapse with me inside it!'

She watched Maa's face burn. Her mother said, 'It's no use talking to you. You will just turn it around and make me—'

'That's true, why did you start?' she said.

Later that night, Yatin called her to pick a fight. 'Why do you talk to Maa like this? And she did tell you not to do anything like this.'

'That's what you have called to talk about? Not one word about how I could have been—'

'Nothing happened, no. That's what matters, Didi. Was I scared? Yes. But it's gone now,' said Yatin in a cavalier tone as he always did.

'I don't want to talk to you,' she snapped.

'Didi, you're staying at home. Take this time to hash your issues out with Maa. It will be good for—'

She hung up.

A week later, Akshay helped Aishwarya move out. He found a studio apartment and got it furnished. All Aishwarya had to do was dip into the last of her savings and make the payment. He didn't have to help her, but he did.

In the restaurant, when Aishwarya looks up from her diary, she finds Akshay staring at her.

'There should be a market for this,' says Akshay as he moves next to Aishwarya. 'We have focus groups in office every day. Do you want me to run this past them?'

Aishwarya shakes her head.

'I would have remembered fairy tales better if there were a few cut-off limbs in them,' points out Akshay and smiles his perfect smile, his eyes twinkling.

Akshay lets his hand slip under the table, resting it on Aishwarya's thigh. He keeps it there, waiting for encouragement from her. She wants to take this forward. He has been everything you could want from a boyfriend. But her body revolts. The battle between what she wants her future to be like and what her heart needs brings tears to her eyes. She wants to kiss him, but her body doesn't allow her to. He's the only guy she has ever kissed. And yet it seems to her that she has never kissed him. Akshay's hand on her feels alien. And so, the hand stays there. Despite their history, Akshay is decent and patient, and he doesn't try to nudge her into intimacy.

'We are doing an office party thing tonight. Do you want to come?'

'When did you start going to parties?'

'HR tells me the boys and girls work too hard to find anyone to date. Parties, I'm told, are fertile grounds for finding people to love. And being in relationships makes people happy and more productive. They gave me a whole lecture.'

'Am I supposed to get people to this party? I know two girls who might be interested, but I'm not sure they are open to cheating on their husbands.'

Akshay laughs. 'I will get bored. I don't know what to talk to these people about apart from work.'

'I will try,' lies Aishwarya. There's no way she will prioritize a party over her Friday night plan of watching the Indian women's cricket team lose badly to the West Indies team, as it has been doing for the last three test matches.

Back at the store, she finds a six-year-old girl huddled in a corner with a book. It's the only copy of Aishwarya's grisly version of *Rapunzel* where the prince gets Rapunzel pregnant, is thrown off a roof and ends up blind, and Rapunzel is reduced to begging on the street. It ends with the prince and Rapunzel finding each other and living in a small hut on the outskirts of the village.

The girl's pregnant mother is in another section looking for stationery. What rotten luck! Aishwarya thinks. She never noticed pregnant women before, but ever since she came close to becoming one, she sees them everywhere.

The girl's smiling at the book's pictures. That's not quite the reaction she had expected from a child when she was drawing the gory images. When she printed it out, bound it and hid it in the library section, she wanted to evoke fear, ugliness, tears. Because sooner or later, every child will have to grow up and realize that life will throw curveballs at you no matter what you do. Unfairness, disappointment, sadness are inescapable truths in life. Believing in fairy tales, and trying to make your own, is idiotic. She had tried and failed. If it were up to her, she would scream that truth in every child's ears. Like an army sergeant training troops, she would command everyone to pull up their socks and expect disappointment.

Aishwarya instinctively starts to walk towards the girl. And then the girl begins to cry. Aishwarya does nothing to comfort her. The girl throws the book and runs to her mother. *Good*, thinks Aishwarya, *she's crying today, but it's preparing her for tomorrow because she will brush it off the next time she reads a gory book. The next time she reads a fairy tale promising her life could be like that, she will know it to be false.*

The mother takes the girl in her arms as the tears flow unabated. She points to the library section where the book is now lying upturned. Aishwarya scampers towards the book, picks it up and stuffs it into her jacket. When the girl's mother reaches the aisle, they don't find the book. The mother kisses and consoles the girl. She seems to be a good mother, a deserving mother, who can keep her daughter safe.

Aishwarya trudges back to her seat with a heavy heart. Just as she sits, her phone rings. It's a group call from Vinny and Smriti; one she has now begun to hate. They think she's depressed. They do everything to get her back to the way they were before.

'What are you doing tonight, behen?' asks Vinny.

'We need you to take care of Vihaan and Amritanshu,' says Smriti. 'We will drop them at eight, pick them around . . . three?'

'No,' says Aishwarya.

'What do you mean "no"? Of course, you will keep them,' says Vinny. 'It's either that or we slip into middle age and never go clubbing again. Aishwarya, we are just a few years away from the time when twenty-year-olds will look at us and wonder what we are doing in a club. Smriti and I need to go out tonight.'

'I'm going to a party.'

'You?' asks Smriti, confused but excited.

'It's Akshay's office party. I need to be there being his girlfriend.'

'Are you going to have sex later?' asks Vinny. 'If the answer is yes, I'm ready to stay at home and waste another Friday on a boy who will drop me to an old-age home at the first chance he gets.'

'Amritanshu hit me in the eye today because I took away his car,' says Smriti. 'They say gender is a social construct . . . it's not. Boys are horrible.'

'We don't believe you're going to a party,' says Vinny. 'Smriti, add Akshay to the call.'

'Guys . . .'

Before Aishwarya could say more, Akshay is added to the call.

'Oye, you're taking her out?' asks Vinny.

'Hi, Vinny.'

'Is there a party at your office?' fires Smriti, as if it's an interrogation.

'Yes, Smriti, there is, and she's invited,' says Akshay, trying his best to be cordial even though Vinny and Smriti have treated him like a petty criminal who's out to make their friend unhappier.

'Drop him,' says Vinny and Smriti drops Akshay out of the call.

'You can be a little kinder to him,' says Aishwarya.

'We will be kind when he seduces you out of your sadness,' says Vinny.

'We are happy you're going out,' adds Smriti.

Aishwarya tells them that she needs to go because she can't bear to be on the call any more. She cuts the call. Tears spring into her eyes as the hurt washes over her in full force. She can see the faces of Amritanshu and Vihaan—the two cutest boys of all time. She misses them so much, every part of her hurts.

But she can't be with them any more. Not after what she did. For the past few months, Smriti and Vinny have been trying to get the boys to meet their Maasi. She can't bear to see them. Her heart explodes. Not seeing them hurts, but seeing them hurts a little bit more.

She logs in to Facebook and goes straight to the Grieving Moms group. It's a group for women who have lost a child or suffered a miscarriage. It's the only place she feels a little like herself. She doesn't use her name. She starts to type a post.

Anam: I miss my nephews. My sisters wanted to drop them over and I couldn't take that. I miss them, but this is what I deserve. I can't be allowed around children. I can't keep them safe.

The comments start to pour:

Kareena: We are sorry.

Smita: Things will get better.

Jonita: New member here. Sorry if I'm intruding. What happened?

Aishwarya replies.

Anam: They could have died because of me. Not only them but more children.

Jonita: Was someone hurt?

Anam: Their father.

Another user asks.

Kiran: How?

Aishwarya should log out, but she doesn't. Continuously repeating what she did keeps her in her place. It reminds her of what she did, the blunder. She punishes herself by thinking about it.

She doesn't tell the group about the garden, about her idiotic decision to keep the generator on the roof for purely vain reasons. She had prioritized a vegetable garden over the lives of children. That's who she was.

Anam: I was driving. I was responsible for the lives of these kids. I looked away to admire something shiny on the side of the road. They could have died. All of them. I gambled with their lives.

And then she logs out.

Eighty-six days.

That's all that separated Aishwarya from ending up as a murderer. If the generator stayed on the roof for eighty-six more days, the roof would have collapsed with children inside the building. In eighty-six days, Vihaan and Amritanshu would have been two out of many children and babies in the building. The roof would have collapsed over those little kids. She had almost killed her best friends' children. How could she ever take responsibility for them any more? How could she ever take responsibility for anyone?

She lets her mind drift. Soon, she can hear the cries for help from the children buried under the rubble and the anguished screams of their parents. She shakes it off. She opens her laptop and starts working on another set of illustrations.

And then she receives a call from Akshay to ask if she's really coming to the party. She tells him she's not. Just like the last few Fridays, she makes a four-pack Maggi, uses eight packets of Maggi masala and tops it off with chilli sauce. She settles in front of the laptop to spend the night watching her hero, Sonali Raj, and the rest of the Indian team's batting order collapse. If Sonali Raj can fail, Aishwarya is a mere mortal.

Time and again, she is tempted to search for Dhiren. And as she has trained herself to do, she instead goes to the Reddit thread named /FraudDhirenBitcoin. Under the thread is a long list of people who have written in excruciating detail about how much money they lost. Of what they could have done with the money instead. At first, she wants to shift the blame on them.

It's *their* fault they gambled their money.

But with every account she reads, she feels an aversion bubbling inside her. Slowly it overtakes her desire for him. *Do we all get what we deserve?* she asks herself. For what Dhiren did, he was given a near-death painful experience. For what she did, she was to spend the rest of her life away from children, her calling, what she was born to do.

Later that night, Akshay comes home. She tells him she's sleepy. And though he puts her to bed, he's unable to seduce her out of sadness. She lies awake in her bed while he works outside.

She's just glad he's there.

39.

Dhiren Das

Dhiren wakes up in a cold sweat. It's the same nightmare again. He's trapped under the debris. He can hear Aishwarya's faint screams; she's looking everywhere for him. Aishwarya finally finds him, tells him she will save him, but then starts to laugh and leaves him to die. But this time, the noise isn't inside his head, it's *real*. And it's coming from downstairs.

He gets off the bed and he's reminded instantly that his body is not what it used to be. It takes time, quite a bit of effort and a tremendous amount of pain to do the littlest of things.

He shuffles down the stairs and sees Neeraj handcuffed to a window grill. There are three workers who are moving in pieces of furniture, wood, paint. Four constables check everything before it's placed in the corner of the room.

'We are making an office,' announces a bright-eyed Neeraj. 'Vishwas knows if you're not busy, you're going to put your head in the oven and die. I told him we need an office to work out of.'

'And who's going to build it?'

'We are.'

'Fuck off.'

'So you're saying you can make it with Aishwarya but not with me? This is what happens when you're thinking with your dick.'

Dhiren turns away and trudges up the stairs, flipping the finger at Neeraj. He's winded by the time he reaches the kitchen.

The memories of Aishwarya and Cute Buttons come swiftly and they hit hard. That time he spent building Cute Buttons seems as if it was from another life. He doesn't think he can ever be happy again. Grief does that. Grief robs you of the ability to imagine a future where you're happy. You think the best of your days are behind you. You're changed, and you won't ever feel the same again. There's a permanence about grief. Dhiren makes himself a plate of idli and joins the call with Dr Kalpesh, as mandated by the court order.

'Should we talk?' asks Dr Kalpesh.

'Weekends are a problem, aren't they?' says Dhiren.

No meetings are lined up on the weekends, but the call with the psychiatrist still has to happen.

'Where's Rohan?' asks Dhiren.

'He's outside.'

'Did he make the Lego set I sent him?'

'It was for 15+, he's just six.'

'I know how old he is. Why didn't he make it? Call him. We are going to do it together,' says Dhiren. 'ROHAN!'

A few moments later, Rohan comes running in, his hands slick with mud.

'Wash your hands and get the Lego, we are going to finish it. The record time is one hour twenty minutes. We are going to aim for two hours today,' instructs Dhiren.

It takes them three hours. The delay is mostly because the younger of Dr Kalpesh's sons wanders into the frame. To distract him, Dhiren starts to sing 'Five Little Monkeys Jumping on the Bed'. But then he wants to hear the song twenty more times. Dhiren sings the song over and over again, while Rohan assembles the less–complex parts. Dr Kalpesh has to remind them that the time's over and that he needs his tablet to work.

'Tomorrow?' asks Rohan.

'Ask your Papa to do it.'

'He can't.'

'Tomorrow then,' says Dhiren, knowing Rohan will be in school and he won't have to follow up on the promise.

The protocol requires Dr Kalpesh to tell Vishwas's lackey about the end of the session so they can suspend the Internet services, but today he forgets. Dhiren's waiting for the Internet to go off, which it usually does with a small beep. It's the small sound of impending nothingness, and the impending task of spending time with his thoughts.

'So you would rather sit here and get bored than help me?' asks Neeraj. 'Do you know boredom is worse than torture?'

'I'm guessing you're about to tell me how.'

Neeraj nods. 'An experiment locked participants in a room with a device that delivered small shocks. The participants preferred giving themselves little shocks rather than sitting and doing nothing for fifteen minutes.'

'Still not helping you.'

'Fine, then let's get bored together,' says Neeraj and pulls a chair next to Dhiren.

Today, Dhiren absent-mindedly googles things. Things he has been cut off from. F1 driver standings, ICC cricket rankings,

Shah Rukh Khan, new movie trailers. It's surprising how little he cares about these things ever since he had not followed them for a while.

And then, despite knowing better, Dhiren googles Aishwarya Mohan.

There's no recent online activity. The last Instagram post is of Cute Buttons being a 'Work in Progress'. There are seventy likes on the picture. He swipes through the names of those who have liked the picture: some of the names he recognizes, some he doesn't.

He stumbles on to Akshay's name. Akshay, the ex-boyfriend, the perfect boy. They had unfollowed each other after Akshay refused to impregnate Aishwarya. But he notices that Aishwarya's following him again.

He digs in to prolong his suffering.

On his Instagram timeline, Akshay looks busy and well-placed in what looks like a new office. It's so new that he can almost smell the fresh polish on the furniture in the pictures. All his Instagram feed is now pictures of the different corners of his office. And then, in one of the pictures, he recognizes a faint reflection on a glass.

Aishwarya.

He zooms in. It's unmistakable. He starts to scrutinize other pictures, other shiny surfaces that might have caught Aishwarya. There are none.

Just then, the Internet disconnects. He's about to spiral into anger. *What did you think would happen?* he asks himself. This is what he asked for. This is how things should always have been. And despite this obvious realization, it's painful how much every fibre of his being misses her. Luckily, Neeraj walks in and he snaps out it.

'What are we cooking today?' asks Dhiren.

After an intense, well-argued, hour-long discussion, they settle on dal-chawal, papad, a sabji each of paneer and carrots with peas, and a low-sugar helping of kheer. It takes them a couple of hours to put everything together. They are just about to sit down to eat when there's a loud thud on their reinforced glass window. They think nothing of it till it happens again, and again, and then again.

They get to the window and open it.

Next to the pavement, a car is parked. On the roof of the car, there's an angry woman waving like an air traffic controller.

'Vinny,' says Dhiren, surprised.

'WHO THE FUCK DO YOU THINK YOU GUYS ARE?' she screams and throws another stone, which narrowly misses him. 'CUTE BUTTONS IS OURS! It's hers! How dare you buy it?'

'What are you saying?' asks Dhiren.

'*Joota maarungi, saale. Bhola mat ban* [I will hit you with a shoe, bastard, don't act innocent]. You scum. You bought the domain name of the website. It was hers and you bought it before . . .'

'What? We did what . . .' Dhiren looks at Neeraj. 'Did you?'

Neeraj shouts back at Vinny. 'It was free for anyone to take. Too bad you're too slow. It's a good name. It would have been a waste with you guys. GET LOST, *PAGAL AURAT* [MADWOMAN]!'

'It's HERS! IT WILL ALWAYS BE HERS!' says Vinny in a screech that can shatter wine glasses.

'That's cute, but nothing's forever, behen,' laughs Neeraj. 'We are going to go now and have our dinner. It's getting cold.'

Neeraj turns away from the window and walks back to the dining table.

Vinny resumes her shouting. 'THIS IS THE MOST FUCKED-UP THING YOU COULD HAVE DONE. YOU'RE TRULY AN EVIL PERSON, AREN'T YOU, DHIREN?'

'I had nothing to do with it, trust me.'

'WHAT MORE DO YOU WANT FROM HER? YOU TOOK EVERYTHING FROM HER, DHIREN! EVERYTHING!'

The words pierce Dhiren's heart. He can't take it any more. 'Go home, Vinny. I will reverse it to you.'

Vinny gets down from the roof of the car. 'If you don't, I will slit both of your throats the day you're out of house arrest.'

Vinny flips her middle finger, gets into the car and drives away.

Dhiren closes the window. He finds Neeraj half-way through his dinner. 'We need to give it back,' he tells him.

'Why would we give up the name of our brand? Leave the business part to me, bhai. I have it all figured out.'

'Our brand?'

'What do you think we are building downstairs? The first branch of Cute Buttons, of course.'

Dhiren's confused. 'We? What?'

'We build businesses around the core competency of the founders. Don't you realize what you're good at? All that VC thing is great, keeps you from throwing yourself out of the window. But kids, that's what you're great at! You're like a kid whisperer. So that's what you're going to do once we are released. It's decided. I decided that for you.'

Dhiren can't believe it. How can Neeraj not know that without Aishwarya, Cute Buttons doesn't have any meaning. He wants to shake Neeraj up, tell him that even his own life doesn't seem to have any meaning without Aishwarya. 'Have you lost your mind, Neeraj?'

'Rohan would kill for you to adopt him. And so would his younger brother. Are you kidding me? This is what you should do. It's your calling, bhai.'

'Raising children is my calling?!'

'Don't be sexist, bhai. For a lot of women, it's their calling, so I'm guessing callings are distributed equally on both sides.'

'This is fucking nuts.'

'It's the only thing you can do now, Dhiren. You build stuff. Yes, of course, I understand it was something both of you wanted to do together, but she's not here any more, so why do you care? You have to do it.'

'Give her back the domain name,' says Dhiren and starts to walk away from Neeraj, wondering at what age dementia sets in, and if solitary confinement of sorts does speed up the process because Neeraj was slowly going mad.

'You're going to come around, Dhiren. And who knows, some day when Aishwarya thinks she wants to get back into this business, she can join you. That day you're going to hug me and call me a fucking genius.'

40.

Aishwarya Mohan

Like she did every day, Aishwarya wakes up to Akshay's calls. It's sweet that he calls to wake her up for work every day, but it's convenient, too, on his part. The people in her office are always impressed by this detail. Oh, he wakes you up at six? That's true love. They don't know that Aishwarya is fast asleep at eleven and Akshay goes to sleep at six in the morning. Waking her up is not sweet, it's a coincidence.

'But Akshay's still making an effort, isn't he?' Smriti had once said.

Aishwarya shrugged. 'Any effort in a relationship that comes without pain doesn't count. The amount of pain behind a gesture of love is what decides its sweetness,' Aishwarya had answered.

'C'mon, Aishwarya, you're romanticizing pain,' said the ever-so-practical Smriti. She hates those Instagram poets who equate love with pain and extol it as though it is a virtue.

'Look at your engagement ring. It cost Amit six months' salary. That's the only reason why it's so valuable to you.'

'It's valuable because he thought of me,' argued Smriti.

'If an engagement ring doesn't destroy finances, does it even count?' asks Aishwarya. 'Would you feel the same had Amit given you a five-rupee ring? Or a ring worth twice the cost, but paid for by a friend of his? Nope, it's valuable *only* because he spent his own hard-earned money and thus caused pain to himself.'

Aishwarya and Akshay's lopsided sleeping schedule has also made avoiding the question of intimacy easier. Their logistics don't match.

'Yes, yes, I'm up, not going to sleep again, I promise,' mumbles Aishwarya into the phone.

'Pukka?'

Aishwarya stifles a yawn and the urge to bury herself in the warm, safe confines of her blanket. 'Pukka.'

'I love you.'

'Me too.'

'That's a movement, not a declaration of love, but I will accept it. I will text you when I get up.'

Click.

Aishwarya stumbles to the kitchen with one groggy eye open. She microwaves water and empties three sachets of instant coffee powder. '**Are you up**', texts Akshay. She responds with a smiley and wishes he were a bad person. As the founder of a start-up with a high burn rate, he texts a lot and spends an awful lot of time talking to her.

When the coffee doesn't do the trick, she puts on yesterday's highlights of the India versus England Women's T20, India's last series before the World Cup. The story of the last few series repeats. India gets hammered, Sonali goes cheaply and England takes a 1–0 lead in a series of six matches. The critics have all predicted a 6–0 whitewash.

Michael Vaughan tweets, **Worse than ballgirls sitting out the field**

Isa Guha has said, **Brainless cricket from a bunch of overrated players**

And Sunil Gavaskar said, **Worst team in a decade**

Most people are blaming Sonali Raj for the rot in the team.

Aishwarya has no one with whom she can discuss the match. Just a few short months ago, she could rant about the game in front of Dhiren, she could abuse the commentators who have been asking for Sonali Raj's resignation. And he would know everything about the game, the players, the match—everything. She smiles sadly. How blind had she been? She had known nothing about him.

She takes a quick shower, changes, wolfs down a banana, leaves her studio apartment and lightly jogs towards the metro station. She prefers the normal compartment to the ladies'— where there are far too many pregnant women and toddlers. It's a disease, an epidemic: children and unborn children are everywhere. It reminds her of what she doesn't have. A phantom pain cripples her, as if someone has sawn off one of her limbs.

She reaches office fifteen minutes late and finds Smita staring at her from her cabin. To make up, for the next three hours, she works tirelessly on the bright and neurotically happy version of *Sleeping Beauty*. Smita drops in twice to check if the princess is thin enough and the prince has a strong jawline.

During the break, Aishwarya loiters around the bookstore. She watches parents come in, buy toys, leave the books untouched and then leave. Some parents flip through the books and ask their children if they want them; the children shake their heads and the books are returned to their place on the shelves. She's about to get back to work, dreading how long *Sleeping Beauty* is going to take when she spots a girl rummaging through the shelves. She's in a Sonali Raj jersey. Aishwarya's own jerseys were all . . . lost in the collapse. Since then, she has been meaning to replace them. But everywhere she has checked, the newer version—the World Cup jersey—is not available.

But this girl is wearing one. Aishwarya wonders if this is a knock-off. She has seen the fake jerseys on Janpath. She would rather be dead than buy a fake jersey. She wouldn't rip off the sponsors of the team by buying fake merchandise.

'Hey, hi, I wanted to ask . . .' Aishwarya taps the girl's shoulder.

The girl turns around. Only, she's not a girl. She's the short woman who's known the world over for her mighty, unbelievable sixes. Built like an ox, some have wondered if she has arms of steel. The woman, Sonali Raj, the captain of the Indian women's cricket team, looks at Aishwarya and asks, 'A picture?'

'Ummm . . . yes, of course, a picture, if you don't mind,' mumbles Aishwarya, her heart in her mouth. She takes out her phone. 'I'm a big fan. Yesterday's match . . . I was just watching it actually . . .'

'It was torture, wasn't it?' the woman asks with a laugh.

Aishwarya tries to click a selfie, but her fingers are shivering. The picture's hazy.

'Give me that.' Sonali takes the phone from Aishwarya's trembling hand and clicks a picture. 'That's a good one. No, wait.' She clicks another one. Sonali shakes her head. 'I don't like it.' She turns to Aishwarya and says, 'Smile.'

Aishwarya gives her the biggest smile. Sonali matches the smile, clicks a picture and gives the phone back to Aishwarya, which she receives with a bow.

'Thank you so much,' she squeals. 'Actually, I work here. Are you looking for something? I can help you out.'

'I'm actually . . . so, what I wanted was a book. Kriti, my daughter, came here and read a book which . . .' her voice trails off. '. . . it had a, let's say, different ending of *Snow White*.'

Aishwarya's face loses colour.

Sonali Raj continues. 'Three pages of the evil queen dying, that's what she told me. She didn't have money then, so now I'm here and can't find it.'

Last week, Aishwarya had put out her version of *Snow White* with three extra pages at the end. Unlike the sanitary version, where the evil queen tumbles off the cliff and dies, in her version, the queen is made to dance to her death at Snow White's wedding. She's made to wear iron shoes and forced to dance on hot coals till her feet burn to the bone and she crashes on to the fiery bed, slowly roasting to death.

Aishwarya wonders if she has been responsible for damaging the daughter of the captain of the Indian cricket team.

'I'm not sure which book you're referring to,' says Aishwarya.

Sonali Raj's face falls. 'My daughter loved it and she told her friend, and now both of them are eating my head to get it for them, but I can't find it here.'

'Are you sure . . .'

Just then, the other employees, who have noticed the selfie-taking and have recognized Sonali Raj, come up and mob her. When the news reaches Smita, she comes rushing out and harangues Sonali to click pictures at various places in the bookstore. All the while she's pitching Sonali a book about her career, about parenting as a working woman and a tell-all, explosive biography with match-fixing, sex and exploitation in cricket. Sonali waits for her incessant bile to stop and tells Smita she needs to go.

Aishwarya is waiting for Sonali in front of her car.

'Another picture?' asks Sonali.

Aishwarya musters up all the courage she has and says in her softest voice. 'I can give you the book, but it's not for sale.'

In her hands is a gift-wrapped version of the only copy of *Snow White* where Snow White is clapping as the evil queen's skin is burning off her body. When Sonali reaches out for the book, Aishwarya doesn't let go.

Sonali grins. 'What's it going to take?'

'A signed bat and a jersey,' says Aishwarya. She adds as an afterthought, 'Please?'

'This is extortion,' says Sonali with a laugh. She takes the book from Aishwarya. 'You wrote it, didn't you?'

'It's the only copy,' says Aishwarya, her voice down to a whisper, as if Smita can hear her from a mile away.

Sonali opens the boot of her car. She takes out a bat and a couple of jerseys. 'Do you have a marker?'

Aishwarya nods so hard it seems her head will fall off. Sonali signs the bat. Aishwarya can hardly believe it. Is she really holding Sonali's bat? Aishwarya wants to run away from there just in case Sonali changes her mind. The exchange is done. Sonali rips off the wrapping paper from the book and goes straight to the last three pages. The brutality catches her off-guard. But slowly, the smile returns to her face.

'It's just the sort of thing my daughter will like,' admits Sonali. 'So I'm guessing this is like a guerrilla project that your boss doesn't approve of?'

Aishwarya nods.

'This is the first time my daughter has asked me to get her a book. Do you have more?'

Aishwarya nods. She finds it impossible to string together a sentence. Her mind's exploding.

'Give me your phone,' says Sonali. She puts her phone number on Aishwarya's contact list. 'I will WhatsApp you the address. Send me everything you have and your bank account details.'

'I can't take money from you. It's . . .'

Sonali waves her off. 'My daughter's screen time is thirteen hours plus. She has played more games on her phone than I have on the field. At this point, I can sign off half my property to you, so shut up and send me everything.' She hugs Aishwarya. 'I will see you around.'

Sonali gets into her car and drives away.

Did Sonali Raj just hug me? What! She finds that there are tears streaking down her cheek. *How long has she been crying for?* Aishwarya looks at the bat and the jerseys in her hands. *This just happened*. She can't believe she just met her hero. After all these years of just seeing her on the television, she had been right in front of her! And she had said her daughter liked the book! She's walking back in a daze when her phone beeps.

Sonali: Send everything over.

Aishwarya spends the rest of the day in office in a blur. She can't wipe the smile off her face. She has spent more time wearing Sonali Raj jerseys than even Sonali Raj has. And she met her! Once back home, Aishwarya dusts off all the books she has illustrated and written, gory versions of fairy tales, her own stories from the past that she has since rewritten to make them scarier, and wraps them in newspaper. She books a courier and sends them off with a prayer on her lips.

Late at night, her phone beeps.

Sonali has sent her a picture over WhatsApp.

It's a picture of a bunch of children huddled together in a big hall. In their laps isn't a Nintendo Switch, an iPhone or the PS4 controller, but books—her books, her gory, bloody, damaging retelling of fairy tales with extra characters she made up herself!

Sonali: Thanks. They love the blood. I read some. Some of it is hardcore.

Aishwarya: They should keep kids away from me.

For the rest of the night, she opens the picture and Sonali's chat window numerous times. She had imagined a future where she would be surrounded by children; she hadn't thought it would be like this—where children are staring at her illustrations with morbid fascination and disgust.

And then, just like that, she googles Cute Buttons.

Under Construction, the screen flashes at her.

The domain name's taken. She deserves losing the name to someone else. Someone will do better with the name than her.

11.

Neeraj Kothari

Vinny's threats were not empty. She *really* wanted the Cute Buttons domain name back.

In the first couple of weeks, she cuts off the electricity. Not just switches it off, but rips apart the entire line. It takes a couple of days to lay down new wiring. Another time, she gets some shady guys to break the sewage pipes, making the entire neighbourhood smell. And then, a carefully scanned Amazon delivery reveals a dead bird. And then, at odd hours, she throws stones at the window. Neeraj refused to give up the domain name even in the face of these odds and a screaming Dhiren.

'You need this, trust me,' he would keep telling Dhiren. 'Someday you will thank me that I protected your passion.'

According to Neeraj, Dhiren is being a total dick. Why couldn't he see that everything Neeraj has been doing is for him? Instead of going after his calling, which is obvious, Dhiren still spends hours looking for the business he wants to invest in, projects he can take over, start-ups that they can consult on. It's a fool's dream, it's like willingly closing one's eyes and not seeing the reality.

Neeraj thinks it's laughable that Dhiren thinks of himself as a bad person. Neeraj knows he's a decent person. Dhiren often tells Neeraj his struggles with anxiety arose after they were caught and were hiding from people. He self-diagnosed fear as the root cause of his anxiety.

That's a fucking lie.

Neeraj knows Dhiren has been suffering from anxiety since a long time. At Gamers Inc., Dhiren would be anxious if the engineers were not paid well, if the managers behaved rudely and if the corporate guys tried to cut funding. Dhiren had been deathly anxious when they first stole the game, and had been anxious during the entire lifetime of Crypto Cricket. Had he truly been a haraami, he would have taken it in his stride. Not fear, but the feeling of doing something wrong is what made Dhiren anxious. And that can only happen to a decent person.

'I will find something for us. We just have to home in on an area of interest,' Dhiren keeps telling Neeraj. Even though Neeraj is as certain as death that the only business they should invest in is Cute Buttons.

Dhiren's letting Neeraj down, who knows it is a master stroke to buy the domain and construct the first branch of Cute Buttons. He thought this would breathe life back into Dhiren and lead him straight to happiness. And in time, who knows, even Aishwarya. She might look at it some day and think of Dhiren as a modern-day Gatsby, or the guy from *The Notebook,* and they would be together and have a bunch of kids who would laud Neeraj for bringing their parents together. But Dhiren has been disappointingly unmoved.

If Dhiren's indifference to his plan isn't enough, there is Vinny. He thought Vinny would tire of it. *Which adult has so much time on their hands to spend a significant amount of it trying to wreck someone else's peace?*

Finally, getting no support from the thankless Dhiren, Neeraj gives up the domain name, and instead, buys SweetButtons.

'I only did it because you were getting uncomfortable,' says Neeraj to Dhiren that day.

That evening, they receive a cake from Vinny and Smriti. It's a dick-shaped cake. Curiously, the balls are missing. Dhiren cuts himself a piece and starts eating. Neeraj notices that he is in a good mood. Those are words he never thought he would use for Dhiren again.

'You're smiling. Why?' asks Neeraj.

'I might have found something for us to do,' says Dhiren. 'As I told you I would.'

'Bhai, we could be given Tesla to manage and it wouldn't matter. You are born for Cute Buttons. No matter what you do, you will always feel something's lacking,' insists Neeraj.

'Are you sure little children are my calling?' scoffs Dhiren.

'That makes you sound like a paedophile. But yes, managing and building a business that looks after the welfare of children, that's your calling. As strange as it might sound to you,' says Neeraj.

'Think harder. What else could be my calling?'

Neeraj thinks for a while and then blurts out. 'Aishwarya.' He watches Dhiren's face fall. He course-corrects. 'Cooking? Don't tell me you're building a foodtech-related app. That market is boring and saturated, bhai. We—'

'Cricket,' says Dhiren.

'You're too old for it. You weren't any good at it either.'

Dhiren laughs and answers, 'Now, listen to me. We have to help create a fantasy game for the T20 World Cup. The sponsors want it to be a side gig. Nothing too complex, basic and PR-heavy. No gambling, of course. Half gameplay, half fantasy league,' explains Dhiren.

Neeraj feels as if his breath has been kicked out of him again—the first was when he became a dollar millionaire, the second when he heard about Cute Buttons's collapse, and this was the third.

Dhiren continues. 'We would need to meet the team managers, coaches, support staff, that sort of stuff. It needs to be done quickly. The English and the Indian teams are here, so we've got to start from there and slowly move on to the other teams,' says Dhiren.

'You're fucking with me, bhai. *Chutiya bana rahe ho* [Don't take me for an idiot]. This is not real. Is this real?'

Dhiren shrugs. 'Why would I lie to you? It's quite an elaborate lie for very minimal return on amusement. There's no reason why I would fuck with you.'

'You mean there's a chance Rahul Dravid and I will be sitting in the same room? Maybe even Virat? And Lord Shardul?'

'No.'

'Then who? Batting coach? Sanjay Bangar? Yeah, I can do that. Still good, still good. Still promising. Do we get box seats too?'

'It's the women's team,' says Dhiren.

'What?'

'Women's World Cup team. Sonali Raj, Anjali Kumar . . .'

'I know the team, but yeah,' says Neeraj and, after a pause, adds, 'I want to say I'm less excited now, but I won't because that would be sexist. I like them, just not as much. No, it's great, what am I saying? It's fucking cricket! We will do this!'

'I told you I would find something.'

'You got lucky,' says Neeraj and lunges at him.

Dhiren wiggles out of Neeraj's embrace. 'That's one thing I'm not.'

42.

Aishwarya Mohan

Despite Smita Kapoor's long and unprofessional voice notes, the stinker emails she has read and ignored, Aishwarya refuses to report to office for the entire week. She tells Smita she is sick and feels that she will endanger the health of others. Smita sees no reason why potential sickness should supersede money.

'Can we come over? I have some leftover biryani,' Vinny asks during a group voice call.

'Only if you can help me illustrate. Otherwise you are of no use to me right now,' answers Aishwarya.

'Amritanshu draws better than me. I can get him,' says Smriti.

'My house is too dirty for your kid,' Aishwarya shuts down the request immediately.

'We haven't seen you in a week! We will just sit and watch, behen. We won't say a word,' adds Vinny.

'You two will only give me performance anxiety if you're here, so absolutely not. Sonali's giving me enough nervousness, trying to hurry me along. She keeps telling me it's for the kids so I can draw anything.'

'What is she like? Does she, like, look ripped?' asks Smriti.

'Hey, I'm getting a call from Sonali.'

'Hello . . .'

Aishwarya switches the call.

'Come over,' says Sonali Raj.

'Come over?'

'Yes, come over to the team hotel. You're home only, no? So come over quickly, okay? You have one hour before the match begins,' says Sonali. She turns away from the phone and talks to someone. 'Should we call her to the stadium or the team hotel? Stadium? Okay. You're coming to the stadium for our match today.'

Aishwarya checks the number again. Of course, it's Sonali Raj. It's not a prank. She *really* wants her to come over.

'But . . . the books aren't ready yet.'

'Stop being such a writer and get whatever's ready. We have your other books anyway. Read them out for my daughter and the other kids here.'

'Are you sure?' mumbles Aishwarya, her heart thumping. She wants to say no, she wants to switch off her phone and hide, but she freezes.

'When I go out to bat today, I don't want to think that my daughter is playing on the phone for three straight hours. Anjali's son is asking for you too.'

'Anjali Kumar?'

There's a different voice on the phone. Someone's shouting from a distance. 'HI, AISHWARYA! MY SON LOVES YOUR BOOKS!'

'Did Anjali . . . the bowler . . . take my name?'

'That's the only Anjali I know,' says Sonali with a laugh. 'She's going to open the bowling for us and I want her to be thinking about cracking skulls open, not worrying if her ten-year-old has found porn on the Internet yet.'

Aishwarya can't believe she's on a first-name basis with the Indian cricket team.

'The car will be there to pick you up in one hour. Whatever illustrations you have made, send it to the number I'm sending you. He's the one who takes care of all the printing for the team. He will get the books ready just like that,' instructs Sonali.

She cuts the call, leaving Aishwarya trembling with anxiety. She's still dealing with that when, within the next minute, a savvy, quick-talking Adil calls and asks her to mail all the files to him.

'The illustrations aren't in order, there's no cover, nothing. It's all quite bad,' says Aishwarya, trying to delay the process, wanting to go over the books one last time.

'That's what we are for,' says Adil. 'I published the biographies of three of our former captains, including Kapil Dev. There's also one by Azharuddin, but it was too controversial to be published. I'll tell you all about it when you get here. Now, send. Quick, quick.'

'Hey?'

'Tell me quickly,' says Adil.

'Does Sonali want me to read to the children?'

'I don't know,' says Adil. 'But you're great, or I'm sure she wouldn't have called you. She's like a hawk when it comes to Kriti. She can literally claw people's eyes out for looking at her daughter. Now, will you send me everything or should I come over and take it from you?'

'I can only write. I'm not very good with kids.'

'I can smell the lie from here,' says Adil. 'Should I switch to an unlimited calling plan between you and I because this conversation is stretching out?'

He disconnects the call.

Aishwarya feels as if she's being swept away by this current. She doesn't give herself too much time to think about it. She dresses up in a white Lucknowi chikan kurta, wears a bright orange dupatta and puts on green eyeshadow. Too much? She thinks for a moment and then reminds herself that some fans paint their entire bodies.

The car's there in an hour. The BCCI logo is emblazoned on the side of the BMW 7-series they have sent for her.

'Who's the most famous person you have driven in this car?' asks Aishwarya, only trying to make conversation because she thinks she will pass out from the nervousness.

'Sourav Ganguly,' the driver answers. 'And also Narendra Modi. In that order.'

'In that order?'

'Madam ji, we bleed blue, so that order is correct.'

During the half-hour drive to the Feroz Shah Kotla Ground, many people peer into the car, trying to see if it's someone famous. The car's not stopped at the gates of the stadium. Aishwarya's heart thumps. Her face feels like it's on fire. They come to a stop in the VIP parking. Someone is waiting for her.

'I'm Adil.'

'You published Kapil Dev's biography? You're a child!' says Aishwarya, surprised at the short, thin boy shaking her hand, who still has soft facial hair and the skin of a newborn.

'I'm 2000-born, so I'm pretty old,' says Adil. 'We should walk, the toss is about to happen. I don't want to miss it. If Sonali wins, it's going to be the tenth straight win and I will have to get memes around it.'

'If you're old, I'm a rotting corpse, Adil,' says Aishwarya, trying to keep up with Adil's rapid pace.

How was he walking so quickly with his spindly legs?

'The books are ready,' says Adil. 'They are in the box. I read *Red Riding Hood* and it's fucking . . . sorry, it's amazing. The kids are going to be scarred for life.'

'How many are there?'

'Five, right? *Red Riding Hood, Cinderella—*'

'The kids. How many kids? The kids I am reading to?'

'Twenty,' says Adil. 'You will be fine.'

Twenty.

Aishwarya's breath becomes ragged. They are now in the corridor where the VIP boxes are.

'Can I go to the washroom?'

'Do you have to?' asks Adil.

'I think I will hold it in and get kidney stones.'

'You're so dramatic. Of course you are. You're a writer. Go, go. Straight and left.'

Aishwarya is panting by the time she reaches the washroom. She can hear her own heartbeat. She leans against a wall as her head spins. Every breath becomes an effort. There's an ocean of tears waiting just behind her eyes, but even trying to cry doesn't let them free. She had promised herself she would never be around kids again. *But should she say no to Sonali? Would Sonali have allowed her to be in the same room as her daughter had she known how she almost led little children to their potential deaths? Would Sonali* even talk to her if she knew Aishwarya had endangered the lives of so many? *Should she tell Sonali? No, of course not. That would be crazy.* And then a sharp realization strikes her. *She's not very different from Dhiren who hid his past from her. It's exactly what she's doing now.* She looks at herself in the mirror and mutters silently to herself, 'You can do this, stop being such a loser. It's just a couple of hours, stop, please stop, please stop feeling this way. I beg you, please bhagwan, just today. Look at where you are. You won't get this chance again.'

'Are you done?' Adil is banging on the door. Aishwarya washes her face and emerges as good as new.

Adil has his hands on his waist. 'You took a long time.'

Aishwarya takes a deep breath. 'Didn't know you were timing me,' she says.

Adil leads Aishwarya to the VIP box, which is labelled TEAM. The VIP box is more than a lounge from where you can watch a match. It's a huge, luxurious hall complete with leather sofas, sparkling chandeliers, cricket memorabilia, and is neatly divided into two parts. On one side are drinks and food, where most of the adults are—the husbands of the cricketers, commentators, former cricketers, drinking, eating, talking. There are a few faces Aishwarya recognizes. The other side is for children. There are beanbags, TVs with cartoons playing on them, PS4s and, as Adil said, about twenty children.

There are the children's nannies in another corner, keeping an eye on them from afar. Some of the nannies are rocking infants in their arms. It's like a small school with kids of all shapes and sizes.

'Come. Let me show you where the action happens, babu. The best seats in town. Come, come, you don't want to miss this,' says Adil.

Aishwarya follows Adil out of the box and into the balcony with descending seating that looks out to the ground. It's frighteningly close to the field. It feels as if she could almost step on to the ground where the cricketers are doing final-minute practices. She spots Sonali and Anjali in the distance. She still can't wrap her head around the last few hours of her life.

'And let's get back to the kids,' says Adil and taps Aishwarya's shoulder. 'While the mothers are on the field, these hooligans spend their entire time in front of their screens. It pisses off the players.'

'What about the fathers? They can read to the kids, or play games or paint while the mothers are . . .'

Adil smiles and looks at Aishwarya. 'Really? Are you *really* asking me that? They are the ones who are buying them screens, so they don't have to entertain the little brutes. The mothers play, the men drink and enjoy, the kids are . . . here.'

Except for a couple of fathers who are running behind their children, the rest have looked the other way while their kids cradle iPads in their laps.

Once inside, Adil gathers the attention of all the children. The older ones are still on their phones. 'Hi, guys! This is Aishwarya. She's the favourite writer of some of you! I will pass around the books she has written. She's going to read a few out to you. Are you guys excited?!' A couple of girls squeal; others look on bored. Adil pushes a big carton into the centre and rips it open. 'Here! Take one!'

Kriti, Sonali's five-year-old daughter, rushes forth and takes her copy. The others stay put.

Adil turns to Aishwarya. 'You want to give it a shot?'

Aishwarya's feet are bolted to the ground, her face paralysed. She shakes her head.

'This is what you're here for. Snap out of it. You can do this.'

'I can't,' mumbles Aishwarya.

She looks at the children running around, and all she can think of is the number of ways she can screw up. The small boy in the red shirt can swallow a little piece of his toy. The older boys who are fighting can trip and smash their heads against the table. The girl in the cutest dress can brush against an exposed nail in the furniture.

'Sonali's counting on you,' says Adil.

Aishwarya takes a deep breath and blocks her thoughts out. She steps forward, puts the brightest, most expressive smile on her face, and says, 'What if I told you that these are the original fairy tales just the way they were told? That these stories were banned because children used to cry reading them? Because the children were scared! I'm not sure if you guys are the brave ones or the scared ones!'

That gets everyone's attention.

'It's true. Fairy tales were used to scare children like you guys here. There was a lot of horror, blood, cut noses!' says Aishwarya.

She sees a flash of him right in front of her eyes as she makes scary faces at the children. *MONSTER. MONSTER MAX,* she hears the words. How naïve was she, trying to make lives perfect for kids? But today is not going to be the day she will let thoughts of Dhiren overwhelm her. There are times she feels a physical ache not being around him. Even after all that's passed between them—the secrets, the lies, the anger—she can't forget all the good she saw in him. Dhiren used to say that about her—she can only see the good in people. And sometimes, that's all she remembers of him. To her, he was the kindest, sweetest guy of all time. How can it all be a lie? She blocks Dhiren out of her mind. She snaps out of it and starts talking again.

'The children used to cry at the mere sight of the books! So, should we read the books, or do you want to stick to your baby games?! You guys aren't ready for the books, are you?'

The children squirm in their places hearing Aishwarya, but they are no longer looking at their phones. Slowly, they file towards the carton and pick up the books.

'Freaks,' mumbles Adil.

Aishwarya picks up the last copy.

Adil's got everything printed in stitched hardback. The books look haunting. The covers are in weathered black leather binding with gold lettering and bare-minimum line illustrations, and her name etched in bold. The mysterious books give the feeling that they are centuries-old grimoires that witches and *tantriks* [godmen] carried rather than children's books. She cracks open *Red Riding Hood*. She's shocked at how well-produced the book is—the illustrations are vividly printed, some of them are pop-out artwork.

'You're welcome,' says Adil. 'Now, get them to be quiet for the next three hours.'

The kids huddle around Aishwarya. She looks at them. 'Are you sure you want to read the real story of Red Riding Hood?'

No one bats an eyelid.

'Goosebumps,' says Adil.

'Go away,' says Aishwarya.

No one opens the book. They are terrified, but no one asks her to stop.

Aishwarya continues. 'Once you open the book, there's no going back. Shall we open it?' She waits for a beat. 'Red Riding Hood is the story of a young child, could be a boy or a girl, who talks to strangers. It's about eating your own grandmother, being trapped by someone with a bad touch and about murder.'

Aishwarya scans the children. The youngest is five. They can take it, she tells herself.

'Shall we start?'

The children nod and slowly open their books.

For the next three hours, Aishwarya does three tellings of the story where Red Riding Hood, a girl who doesn't listen to her doting mother, leaves the house without permission to meet her grandmother. On the way to her grandmother's, she meets a creepy wolf who comments on her hood. The wolf then fools the grandmother, eats a bit of her, slices the rest of her, drains her blood into a bottle and waits for Red Riding Hood. When she gets there, the wolf offers the young girl wine and meat, which are actually pieces cut from her grandmother. Once she's drunk, the wolf tells her to take off her hood and climb into bed with him. And then he devours her. The story ends with the mother slicing open the wolf's stomach and filling it up with stones, so the next time the wolf goes to drink water, it drowns.

Little does Aishwarya know that meanwhile, on the ground, England has smacked the living daylights out of India in the match. Only when she stops does she realize that the other adults in the room are drunk and sad. India has lost by a considerable margin and England now leads the series 2–0.

'You were good,' says Adil when Aishwarya takes a break.

Aishwarya nods.

'That's dark though,' says Adil.

'The world's dark,' mumbles Aishwarya, her heart a strange mix of adrenaline and fear.

'Whatever keeps the little shits busy,' he says, pointing at the children who are still flipping through the pages of the books. 'I'm going to send the kids away with their nannies. Team meeting's happening.'

'Okay.'

'Sonali asked me to tell you to wait. You can eat now.'

'Thank you for letting me eat.'

'We are going to be great friends,' says Adil before leaving.

The VIP box is suddenly empty. The husbands are gone, the nannies have left, and so have the children. All except for one nanny who's cradling an infant in the corner, a bottle in her mouth.

Aishwarya scoops one of everything from the buffet on to her plate. She asks the sole nanny, 'You don't have to go, Aunty? Have you eaten?'

The woman nods. 'Her brother has just gone to sleep in the other room. If the baby starts to cry, he won't sleep, so Anjali Ma'am asked me to wait.'

Aishwarya sits next to the woman and starts to eat. 'Is that breast milk?' asks Aishwarya, noticing the consistency.

'Anjali Ma'am insists on it,' says the woman.

'Good, good,' says Aishwarya. 'She's so cute. Where's the father?'

'With the boy,' says the woman. 'But the father is nice. He's not like the others.'

Aishwarya assesses whether she should gossip about the husbands of the cricketers she looks up to, but then decides against it.

The woman though is eager to share.

'Most fathers don't have the patience. You know, women like us, we are good with children.'

Aishwarya wants to disagree. The woman doesn't know.

'The husbands just don't have it,' says the woman. 'They think it's enough they are letting the women play and travel. On top of it, they don't want to take care of the children all the time.'

'So most of the players travel with nannies and children?'

'Most of the team's players quit after they have children. For the rest who still fight and play, BCCI pays us. It's a good salary. The ma'ams themselves can't take care of the children. They are tired all the time.'

Aishwarya nods.

'The men's team doesn't have that problem,' continues the woman. 'They leave their children behind with their wives.'

Aishwarya doesn't react. The woman stops talking once she notices that Aishwarya is not interested in the conversation.

Then suddenly she shoves the little baby towards Aishwarya. 'Can you take care of her for a minute? I will go the toilet.'

Before Aishwarya can react, the woman drops the child into Aishwarya's lap and hobbles away.

As if on cue, the little girl starts to cry. In a moment, she's back in her old house and the little girl in her hands is Yatin, screaming for his mother. Aishwarya waits for the woman to show up. The girl's cries become more urgent. Aishwarya, with trembling hands, lifts her little body up, like she has done a million times before with great success. But the baby bursts out crying louder. She tries to mumble to the child and sing, but her mind fails. None of the hundreds of nursery rhymes she knows come to her. The baby squirms in her hands, and she feels she will drop her. She can see it vividly. The baby will fall to the ground; her soft head will open up. The little girl will die on the floor.

Aishwarya's grip becomes loose and her chest thumps urgently. Now the child is crying so hoarsely that she's croaking, her face all red. Aishwarya thinks she's going to pass out. She tries calling out 'Aunty!' but she's too far away. *Shut up, please, shut up*, Aishwarya tries to say, but she can't form words. *Please, please, please*, Aishwarya struggles to mouth the words. Panic invades every part of her body. She stumbles and almost falls trying to sit. She wants to place the baby somewhere and run.

Just then, the woman comes back. She doesn't notice Aishwarya's streaked cheeks or her twitching face. She takes the baby and says, as though it's obvious, 'She probably needs a diaper change.'

Aishwarya slumps to the ground, her body shaking.

An hour later, she's at home. She has no memory of how and when she sneaked out, what pretext she gave Sonali, or how she will ever be happy knowing that her lifelong dream has swiftly turned to ashes.

43.

Dhiren Das

When the news of Dhiren and Neeraj being recruited by Pan Bahar, the gutkha empire sponsoring the World Cup, to develop a game reaches Vishwas, he loses his shit. It is clear that there has been a glaring breach of security. He screams for so long at the constables, that he loses his voice. And despite his calls and protestations, he cannot change a thing. There are only a few doors in India that cricket doesn't open. After Dhiren and Neeraj are selected for the project, they are allowed six hours of high-speed Internet starting that day.

'Should we wear our jerseys?' asks Neeraj on the first day of the meeting with the game developers, BCCI and the representatives from the team.

'Just in case they don't know which team we support?' asks Dhiren, setting up the laptop for the first Zoom call with the game developers, the investors and the captain of the Indian team, Sonali Raj.

'Bhai, I can't believe Sonali's going to be there. Shouldn't she be concentrating on the World Cup? It's irresponsible,' says Neeraj.

'Says the criminal locked up for a legitimate crime,' points out Dhiren.

'I only had the weight of my own greed on my shoulders, while she has the expectations of the entire country on hers. There's a difference.'

'Please don't say stuff like that in the meeting, okay?' says Dhiren. 'Try shutting up for the next five minutes and maintain that for the rest of the meeting.'

Dhiren knows Neeraj has recognized how important this meeting is. He has noticed Neeraj's nervous tics—the shaking of the knees, the rubbing of the fingers, the sweaty palms, his stupid words. This could be a way of legitimizing their lives again. For the next five minutes, they sit in silence facing the laptop, waiting to be let into the meeting, their hearts thumping in anticipation. The meeting starts and the black screen changes into the image of what looks like a hotel conference room.

'Sonali's not there?' asks Neeraj right off the bat.

'I'm Adil, the guy who's going to be your point of contact. And as you have quite intelligently noticed, Sonali's not here, but I will surely tell her you asked about her,' says Adil. 'This person,' he says, pointing to the girl next to him, 'is heading game development and will be working with the two of you.'

'I'm Aditi,' says the girl. Dhiren and Neeraj have heard of her before. She's the person behind many high-grossing games on Google Play and the App Store, most notably of Pink Penguins, a game where penguins have to catch flying fish—addictive, cute and with a million downloads. There are many genius game designers; you throw a stone in Bangalore and you will hit one, but only a few of them are lucky enough to turn their talent into money.

'Dhiren.'

'Neeraj.'

'I know you guys,' says Aditi. She's not happy to see them. There's a deep frown on her forehead.

'We have publicly apologized,' says Neeraj. 'We are deeply sorry about the hurt we have caused people through our nefarious—'

'Shut up,' says Aditi.

'Yeah, shut up, Neeraj,' says Adil.

'I lost money because of you guys and Crypto Cricket,' groans Aditi.

'Me too. A couple of lakhs,' adds Adil.

Dhiren shakes his head. 'Aren't you guys working for a gutkha company right now? And why was a BCCI employee playing Crypto Cricket?'

Neeraj laughs. 'As he said, and as our lawyers have indicated, we are sorry. But has any gutkha company apologized for the cancer deaths?'

'This is going to be fun,' says Adil. 'We will keep it quick for this meeting. Guys, the only aim of this project is to finish it. It has to be simple, non-buggy, very crickety, and even housewives and house husbands should be able to get it, with no offence to either of the two.'

'We have a few ideas,' says Neeraj.

'Of course you do, that's why you're here,' says Adil.

'I will need you to leave, Adil,' cuts in Aditi.

'Sure,' says Adil, shrugs and gets up to leave. 'Send me the meeting recording.'

'What have you got?' asks Aditi, opening a little notebook to take notes.

Dhiren turns the laptop towards himself. He starts to rattle off game ideas that he and Neeraj have outlined. Aditi shoots all of them down—too complex, too easy, too much luck, too much skill, no stickiness, no reason to come back, and the like.

After a long time, Dhiren doesn't feel like a piece of shit living on borrowed time. But every few moments, his eyes flit towards the corner of the room where Aditi's assistant is taking notes. The assistant is a short, petite girl wearing the jersey of the Indian cricket team. Every time she comes into the frame, Dhiren has to quieten his mind. It's not Aishwarya.

On some days, Dhiren fantasizes what it would be like to see Aishwarya. *What would he do? Would he fall at her feet and ask for forgiveness? Would he ignore her and save himself more pain? Would he tell that he loves her, that he could and would do anything for her?* And then he wonders, *how is she now?* Neeraj told him a few days ago that she was working for a children's publisher. Dhiren was happy about that. *At least she's doing something that's still about kids. She had always been a good storyteller.* He wonders if she still thinks of him. *She has to know that not everything they shared was false. She has to, right? Those days they spent with no one for company but each other, those meals they shared—that experience was true, lovely. Tainted by his past, but true nonetheless. Does she ever think like this? Are there moments when she wants to forgive him? Would she have forgiven him had he died? Does she know that he loves her no matter how bad a person he might be?*

Finally, they hit on a straightforward idea. A one-player match-up between two teams—an arcade-type game. A bowler bowls six balls to a batsman, and then they switch roles, the one with the most runs wins. Aditi thinks for a while. The pause is so long that Dhiren believes the video has paused. Aditi, her eyes unmoving, chewing her nails intently, looks like Dr Strange going through future possibilities with the game.

'Very rudimentary, quite stupid, but not that bad,' admits Aditi. 'Though this would require biomechanical imaging of all the players if we want to make the game stick. The game's too simple for the imagery to be simple as well. And we will need you guys to be here for the shot selection. We can't do this online, it's stupid.'

'We can't leave our house,' says Dhiren.

'I know that, Sherlock,' says Aditi. 'We've got to make it happen.'

'What does that mean?' asks Neeraj.

44.

Aishwarya Mohan

'What did you think, Aishwarya? The CCTV cameras are dummies?' thunders Smita, her face barely moving from all the Botox and fillers she has done recently.

'Your skin looks amazing,' points out Aishwarya.

Aishwarya has seen those cameras—there are far too many at Hari Om International—but she thought they didn't work.

'Also, I didn't see any security person, so I assumed the cameras were there just to scare people,' says Aishwarya.

'I check them every night,' says Smita. 'I have let this go on for too long, Aishwarya. Frankly, I didn't expect this from you.'

She pushes a laptop in front of Aishwarya. On it, there's a stitched video of Aishwarya's experiments with the books: she's hiding the book, the children are crying, the mothers are looking for the book, and it culminates in the Sonali Raj episode. She also has photographic evidence of the reading session in the VIP box. Adil had uploaded a picture on the cricket team's Instagram handle.

Smita continues. 'This is a crime. You can go to jail for this. This is an intellectual property theft.'

'This is a serious thing then, isn't it?' asks Aishwarya, amused at Smita's attempt to blow this out of proportion. 'By the way, the books I was reading at the stadium weren't printed at your printer.'

Smita glares at her. 'It doesn't matter. You conceptualized the books here, sitting in this office, taking my salary. How naïve can you be, Aishwarya? I took you to be a sensible girl.'

Sooner or later, Smita's going to ask for something. Maybe it will be Sonali Raj's endorsement for the bookstore, a ticket to the VIP box at the stadium, a meeting with some of the players. It could be anything.

'It's illegal and dangerous,' warns Smita. She leans back in her chair. 'What will I do with you, Aishwarya? You have jeopardized the brand name of Hari Om International.'

Yeah, right. Aishwarya tries her best to not roll her eyes at Smita.

'I'm sorry to disappoint you, Smita. But I promise I won't lie again. So if you want to call the police, you can,' says Aishwarya.

'But because I want to be truthful to the police, I will have to tell them that you're selling books without bills and trying to cut corners with the GST. The government is pretty serious about GST.'

Smita's unmoved. She leans forward. 'I want to help you, Aishwarya. You came here when you had nothing. Your nursery collapsed because of *your* fault. You had no money and nowhere to go . . .'

Aishwarya brushes it off. 'Vinny, Smriti, my father, my old school, I could have turned to multiple people.'

'And yet, you took this job. Let's be real for a moment, Aishwarya. There was no way you were going to your old school,' says Smita. 'Let's not forget that I gave you a job despite your lack of experience in writing books.'

Aishwarya's patience is wearing thin.

Smita continues. 'We can put this behind us if you continue to write these stories. A small print run, nothing big, just to test the water.'

There it comes. Finally, to the part where Smita puts forward what she wants.

'These stories?'

'These twisted stories,' says Smita.

'Why?'

'The children seem to like them, don't they? Who knows what these children want, anyway?' Smita shrugs. 'You're going to write them for Hari Om International. You have a knack for them. I can't ask the others to write these books; they are too soft, they haven't seen anything. You, on the other hand—'

'You're weaponizing my grief,' interrupts Aishwarya.

'I don't know what that means, but I want to repeat here that you're in no position to negotiate,' says Smita. 'Everything you did here while being on my payroll is my property. I own the intellectual property.'

'You own the intellectual property rights to fairy tales that go back centuries? Nothing I wrote or drew is original. I just went back to the scarier versions of the past.'

'You can have your name on the book. But in the acknowledgements, you're going to thank me for the idea,' concedes Smita, her voice still stern. 'And you have to make these cricketers post stories on social media about it.'

'Do you think these cricketers and I share burgers at night? They aren't my friends. I can't ask them to do anything.'

'Then be friends with them,' brayed Smita. 'You will get 5 per cent royalties because I'm taking a risk with you. It's the best I can do, and honestly, I think this is a LOT for someone who tried to steal from me. So, is this a deal?'

'Does this mean I can work from home?'

Smita bristles. 'Fine, you can work from home.'

The more Aishwarya stays silent, the more agitated Smita becomes. 'What are you still thinking about?'

She's thinking about the responsibility it comes with and whether she should be allowed to take it. Back at Cute Buttons, she had thought she would try to avoid reading to the children the writers who had made mistakes—racist writers like Roald Dahl, Enid Blyton, Kipling, and the like. She, too, had made a mistake, but it was different. She defends herself against the thought. She was not taking care of the children, she was just writing for them. She would have turned Smita down if she had asked her to run a crèche. This is just writing for children.

'This is the only chance you will get to be a children's writer.'

Aishwarya doesn't want to be a children's writer. But isn't she already one? At least she will get to do it on her terms. She nods.

'Now, get out,' says Smita. 'And congratulations! I just turned your life around. This is what we do at Hari Om International. Change lives!'

She walks out.

At her desk, Aishwarya is trying to make sense of what this would mean when someone taps her shoulder. She turns around to see Adil standing over her.

'Nice bookstore. Too bad it's going to die soon,' says Adil.

'How did you—'

'You are needed at the team hotel.'

'What? Why?'

'You look like someone who stole something,' Adil chuckles. 'Did you steal something, Aishwarya? Sonali told me you have a thing for jerseys.'

'No.'

'Then why are you scared? Just get up and follow me.'

'Did someone complain about the books?'

'Will you please get up, Aishwarya? This office is claustrophobic, man. There's a team meeting happening with all the coaches and support staff. You have been asked to join.'

'Why?'

Adil throws his head back in frustration. 'Babu, I don't work for you, so stop asking these questions and just come.'

'Why do they need me?'

'That's what I asked. The team management looked at me as if to say I cannot ask these questions. That's the same look I'm giving you right now. Can we please leave? I don't want to get stuck in office traffic.'

'I need to tell Smita . . .'

'Sonali called her. You're free to go,' says Adil and moves towards the door. Aishwarya follows him. He turns towards her and adds, 'Congratulations on your book deal. How long do you think your career will be?'

'Excuse me?'

'There are only a few fairy tales. Once those are done, you're done. Your original characters need a lot of work.'

'You're such a positive light, Adil.'

'I have been told that. I'm practising being positive,' says Adil while leading the way out. 'This store, by the way, is a fire hazard and should be shut down immediately.'

In the drive down to The Leela, the team's hotel, Adil's equally tough to myriad people on the phone. Realizing there wouldn't be any conversation, she plugs in her earphones. She takes the notebook from her bag and, fuelled by Adil's harsh but correct assessment of her work, starts to write.

But soon, her mind is drifting.

She daydreams about the success of her unwritten books. She can see herself sitting among hundreds of children, narrating stories from the books she has written. They don't want to go home even when she's finished. But she whispers to them that she can't be responsible for them. Because she *almost* murdered a bunch of kids earlier.

'Go back to your mothers,' she tells them. 'Stay with someone who will keep you safe.'

At the hotel, the staff has cleared an entire floor for the cricket team. As she walks through the corridor, people turn to look at her and give her nods of recognition. She doesn't recognize anyone, except for a few children running around playing hide-and-seek in the corridors.

'In here,' says Adil and points to the conference room.

'You're not coming?'

'I'm not your babysitter,' says Adil.

Aishwarya knocks and then opens the door. Everyone who's talking stops and turns to look at her. The entire team is there. Sonali. Anjali. Lara. She has only seen them on television. They all look bigger and stronger, like they could strangle a bull. Most of them are taping their shoulders and legs; some are bandaging old wounds. They all look battle-weary. Some nod at her. Others wave.

Sonali comes running from the other side of the room.

'Girls, girls, girls,' she addresses everyone. 'This is Aishwarya. And this is everyone.'

'Komal,' a player says and waves at her.

'Sameer's mother,' says Aishwarya and waves back.

Komal frowns. 'Didn't know I am only recognizable by my son's name. I'm offended. All these years of service for the nation and I get this?'

'No, no . . .'

'I'm kidding,' chuckles Komal.

'Who's my daughter?' asks Lara.

'Aranya.'

'And mine?' asks Sonia.

'Yash.'

'Okay, guys, enough,' cuts in Sonali. 'I told you she was great.' She turns to Prarthna. 'Throw me a jersey. Quick, quick.'

A jersey comes flying at Aishwarya. She snaps it mid-air.

'Not bad,' says Sonali.

'U19 team,' explains Aishwarya shyly.

'Guys, so this is Aishwarya. You all know her. She's an amazing storyteller and my daughter wants her more than an iPad, so that's saying something,' she addresses everyone. 'Starting today, she is part of the Indian cricket squad.'

'What . . .'

Her voice is drowned out in the hooting and clapping of the players. Everyone shouts 'Congratulations' and gets back to dressing up.

'Congratulations!' says Sonali and hugs Aishwarya. 'You're to join the support staff starting today. We are thankful for what you did that day. We would like you to keep doing that for the upcoming World Cup.'

'Sonali . . .'

'Wait,' says Sonali. She turns to the players and claps thrice. 'Time to go, people, time to go!'

Her team members perk up and start filing out of the room. Some pat Aishwarya on the back, welcome her and tell her they will see her around. After everyone leaves, Sonali sits Aishwarya down and tells her. 'You can't say no, Aishwarya. This is my last World Cup and I want my players to give their—'

'Why is this your last World Cup?' interjects Aishwarya. 'Listen, ma'am, don't listen—'

'Call me Sonali.'

'Sonali, don't listen to social media. You just turned thirty.'

'I know how old I am.'

'I'm sorry, Sonali, but you have plenty of years left. Please don't leave,' pleads Aishwarya. This is worse than even Dhoni retiring. 'You're my favourite player; you're everyone's favourite player. This is just a bad patch, that's it.'

Sonali smiles. 'It's been four years since I scored runs. It's time to go. As captain, I can't keep failing. There's a Batman quote about this, isn't there?'

'You either die a hero or you live long enough to see yourself become the villain,' says Aishwarya, fighting back her tears. 'How can you be a villain? You are the team!'

'Don't say that to Lara,' chuckles Sonali. 'This team needs you, Aishwarya. After this series, the team has one month of training to get everything right.'

'But . . . '

Sonali waves her down. 'The kids' summer vacations are starting. The senior members of the team need to be on the field knowing that their kids are all right and not running around getting into trouble.'

Aishwarya tries to say something.

'Stop,' says Sonali. 'You're making me want to manipulate you. You said I'm your hero, right? So will you *really* say no to me? Or do you want Kriti to keep spending time on her iPad?'

Aishwarya shakes her head like a little child.

'See you around.'

'Are you really retiring?'

Sonali nods and leaves the room.

For the next few minutes, Aishwarya stands there, feet bolted to the ground, cradling the jersey in her hands. It says 'Aishwarya 9'. As she leaves the hotel, she finds the team training on the small ground. The players are falling, jumping, diving, giving it their everything. It's hard for Aishwarya to believe these women are losing.

Later that night, Vinny and Smriti connect for their scheduled check-up-on-Aishwarya video call.

'I'm still alive,' she tells them as soon as she picks up the call.

And then she tells them about Sonali's offer. For the first time in months, she sees the worry on their faces ease off. When she shows them the jersey, they lose their minds.

'This is the best thing that's happened to us!' squeals Vinny.

'I can't believe this is happening,' adds Smriti. 'When are you taking us to meet them?'

'It's the best you can ask for, behen,' says Vinny excitedly.

'Cricket and children!' adds Smriti.

'Can you get us jerseys too?' asks Vinny.

'I want the number 5,' says Smriti.

'3 for me,' adds Vinny.

And though she's happy, she has to fake a smile for them. Of late, she has become good at lying. An hour after she disconnects the call, a courier guy rings the bell. Smriti and Vinny have sent her a cake. She clicks a picture and sends it to them and writes 'Thank you!' followed by dancing smileys. And she eats the entire cake hoping she would feel as happy as they were feeling for her.

45.

Dhiren Das

Dhiren doesn't hear back from Aditi and Adil for an entire week. He and Neeraj go through a whole gamut of ideas for the game, but it will all be for naught if they decide to drop it. It wouldn't be the first time someone junks the idea of a cricket game. It seems likely now, especially after India's disastrous performance against England.

'2–0? Can you believe it? No fight,' says Neeraj. 'It's like the England team is playing with toddlers. I'm telling you, India's going to lose 6–0 and then no one's going to make this game.'

'Don't say that in the meeting,' says Dhiren.

'Sonali should step down.'

'Okay, Harsha Bhogle.'

'She hasn't hit a single century in three years!' points out Neeraj. 'She has a daughter, she should take care of her instead of the team. Enough. How many more chances should she get?'

'She has earned them. Ten years, fifty-four international centuries,' argues Dhiren.

Dhiren's fingers hover over the keyboard. They don't have any meetings. But they do have the Internet for six straight hours. And Dhiren wants to spend all of it searching for Aishwarya. Today he's angry thinking about her and how things turned out. He's not feeling sorry or guilty, just furious at how things turned out between them. Everything can't be his fault.

'Your fingers are shaking,' points out Neeraj. 'Like an addict.'

'I'm over her,' counters Dhiren. 'It's fine, whatever happened. I'm not going to mope over it any longer. I'm just fucking angry with her. I made a mistake and tried to correct it. She should have just got over it. If I knew this is how it would end, I would have never thought about coming clean.'

'Look at the bright side, bhai. Had we not come clean and put this behind us, the Pan Bahar guys would probably have chosen someone else. I'm sure they read some of the reports and thought, yeah, we should hire these guys. *Jo hota hai, achche ke liye hota hai* [Whatever happens, happens for the best].'

'Whatever happens doesn't always happen for good. Nothing good is coming out of childhood cancer, wars, epidemics, bad Marvel movies, the ageing of Shah Rukh Khan and Dhoni, and starvation deaths,' grumbles Dhiren. He adds after a pause, 'You know what? It's not all my fault.'

'I see what's happening here. You're in the anger stage of grief.'

Dhiren ignores what Neeraj has to say. 'Neeraj, you tell me, what's friendship? How do you define it?'

'I think you have an answer ready for that, that's why you're asking me.'

'Friends accept each other's flaws with enthusiasm. I was young and stupid. Big deal. Didn't she lie to me when she went to the IVF facility?'

'She did, bhai. She did lie to you.'

'We are all paying for what we did, didn't we? So after it's done, we should get a clean slate. We should be as pure as anyone walking the streets right now.'

'*Ekdum.*'

'If not, why not give life imprisonment to everyone?'

'Bhai, you're in a mood.'

'Don't I deserve to be?' grumbles Dhiren. 'I know I'm not the best guy in the world. But I'm also not the worst. I'm sure there are people way worse. And what was I trying to do? I was trying to be better, nahi? I built that nursery with her, touched death and came back, gave up everything. What more can I do? I can't go back and change the past, can I?'

Neeraj starts to laugh.

'Why are you laughing, behenchod?'

'You're healing, that's why,' says Neeraj. 'The therapist would say you are past denial, and now you are angry. Just two more steps—bargaining and depression—and then you will accept your break up.' He rubs his hands in delight.

'You're looking forward to me being depressed? Fucking great,' says Dhiren. He adds after a pause. 'Bad people have love in their lives too. So it wasn't like I was expecting too much.'

'You said "*love*", bhai.'

'Eva Braun was crazy about Hitler,' says Dhiren.

'And are you serious when you're comparing yourself to Hitler, bro? You're smart, *theek hai,* but Hitler had some other level charisma.'

'Okay, Nazi.'

'Give me the laptop.'

'Why?' snaps Dhiren.

'I need to show you people who are more in your league,' says Neeraj. Neeraj types into Google: *Biggest Money Laundering Banks.* 'Look at this. HSBC, 8 billion; Standard Chartered, 265 billion; Goldman Sachs, 600 million. *Sab ke sab chor.* These are *real* crimes. Bro, compared to them, you are a pickpocket. These guys in suits got away with small fines. And they laundered money for drug barons, dictators, warlords and shit.'

'My point is, Aishwarya can forgive me. We are on the same page here.'

Neeraj nods. 'Which is what I've been saying from the beginning. You know what? If she cared about you, she would look past it. Who abandons someone in the hospital? You could have died, bhai.'

'Exactly. She could have come and seen me once, you know?'

'Finally, you see the light, bhai. So this is what we are going to do. We are going to close this Aishwarya chapter and move on. People make mistakes, they are punished, and then they are clean. So we are clean now. We deserve to have girlfriends and have fun. We are going to do that.'

Dhiren wants to find Aishwarya, grab her and ask her if it was so easy to forget him and move on. The anger is burning him from within. It literally feels like she left him for dead.

'She left me in a wreck. All the love I had for her, it's churning into poison.'

'You said "love" again, bhai.'

'I hate her,' he says. 'Every fibre of my being regrets having met her, helped her, let her into my life. She's the worst thing that has ever happened to me. And I have been hated by thousands, almost sent to jail, and got my body bent and broken.'

'Bhai . . .'

'I wish for her to be unhappy, unsuccessful, unloved.'

'Are you sure about that, bhai?'

Dhiren shakes his head. Tears spring to his eyes. After a long silence, he mumbles, 'Is this what happens when it sours? None of the "*I hope they are happy*" bullshit, but "*I hope they lead a miserable life*" without us? If you love something, why would you set it free? Why would you take that chance? Why wouldn't you hold on to it for dear life?'

'You love her, bhai.'

'I lost everything. But what did she lose?'

And it comes to him in a flash. Vinny's words in the hospital. And when she came to this house. Had it not been for him, Aishwarya would have been weeks away from realizing her dream of being a mother. All the anger Dhiren felt for her changes course. He directs it to himself.

This is, truly, his fault.

'Oh.'

'What?'

'They are calling. Aditi,' says Neeraj.

Dhiren picks up.

Adil and Vishwas Bothra are on a conference call. Vishwas is already frowning. Dhiren feels like punching his face through the screen.

'You guys look horrible,' says Adil.

'I want to say the same, but your skin looks deeply moisturized,' says Dhiren.

'I like people who flatter their seniors,' says Adil. 'Guys, I talked to this police person over here. He's ready to let you come for a few hours on weekdays to set the entire thing up. He's concerned that you guys are hardened criminals. Will you behave?'

'They shouldn't be on this call,' grouses Vishwas.

'Well, they are now. I have permission from the BCCI president, the minister and the commissioner of police. Who else do you want to go against, Jaikant Shikre?' asks Adil, rolling his eyes.

'They *are* criminals,' protests Vishwas.

'Vishwas, there are active bomb-blast accused sitting in the Parliament and you're calling us criminals?' asks Neeraj.

'Neeraj yaar, don't blame Vishwas. Look at his face, just look at it. It's slowly turning blue. Do you know why that is?' asks Dhiren. 'When someone's balls are in a tight clamp, the capillaries in the face bruise. Vishwas can tell you more about it since he has been in this position for a really long time.'

'See what I mean?' complains Vishwas.

'What I can see is that you can't take eighth-grade insults from two immature guys,' answers Adil.

'It was a good insult,' says Dhiren.

'Definitely not eighth grade, first-year college maybe,' agrees Neeraj.

'Four hours every day,' says Adil.

'One hour,' answers Vishwas firmly.

'Four.'

'Two.'

'Four.'

'Three.'

'Four and let's call this deal done,' says Adil with finality.

Vishwas's shoulders droop. 'Four,' he agrees, 'but there will be two guards, and they will be handcuffed.'

'As long as it's consensual, I don't care, Vishwas,' says Adil. 'You can do whatever with these two.'

'He likes light pegging and dominatrix stuff,' says Dhiren.

'Eighth-grade insults,' says Adil, dismissing Dhiren. 'See you tomorrow.'

The call cuts unceremoniously. For a few seconds, Dhiren and Neeraj are in a trance. Freedom, or at least part freedom, is just a few hours away. They will be out of this house. Dhiren looks at Neeraj in disbelief.

'Bhai!' squeals Neeraj. 'Did this just happen? Did they call us to tell us we can be out of here every day?'

Dhiren nods.

'I want to pluck flowers from the gardens, smell that fresh gutter smell, run around and jump in puddles, be like Alia Bhatt in that movie, or like Bambi,' says Neeraj. 'We did it, bhai. World-class criminals always do beat the system.'

And though Dhiren's happy, it's short-lived. A small, thorny thought punctuates his happiness. Tomorrow, he will be out in the world. And in that world lives Aishwarya. And she hates him.

46.

Aishwarya Mohan

'*Koi baat nahi* [It's okay], we will win the World Cup,' Aishwarya says to the driver who's not in his usual cheery mood.

'They will.'

Neither of them believe it can actually happen.

Yesterday, England humiliated India in the third match of the series. She had been in the VIP box with the kids and could hear the silence as England thrashed them. She put on a cheery smile and entertained the children nonetheless. She can't even imagine what Sonali and her team must be going through. To put in their blood and sweat only to be humiliated in defeat.

'Call me when you need to be picked up,' says the driver.

The mood at the Leela is sombre. There's deathly silence on the Indian cricket team's floor. From a distance, she sees Adil running towards her.

'Practice is cancelled. They are taking a day off to recuperate. You can go home. They are with the kids,' says Adil.

'I will stay.'

'Do whatever the fuck you want,' says Adil and almost turns away. He stops. 'I'm sorry, shouldn't have sworn, the loss . . .'

'I should stay. If they need a break from the kids, they can drop them off with me. They could use some thinking time.'

Adil continues. 'Are you sure?'

A swift, brutal wave of anxiety washes over Aishwarya. *Why would he ask her if she was sure? Did he have doubts about her ability to keep them safe?*

'I'm sure,' says Aishwarya in a voice that doesn't sound sure at all.

'I will drop in a message to them,' says Adil. 'Be in the kids' room and don't call or text me, or exchange pleasantries with me. Done? Done. See you later.'

Adil strides away from her. He doesn't tell her where the kids' room is. She has to go through a bunch of rooms till she finds it. It's a banquet room that has been repurposed to look like a children's play area. Adil has had someone spruce it up. Apart from Aishwarya's books, there are now books from other writers, art supplies, little models of jungles, sets of Lego. Everything Adil's bought is in a big dump, so for the next hour, Aishwarya rearranges the room. The more time she spends in it, the more it starts to look like a preschool.

Another hour goes by and not a single child turns up. She locks the room and wanders out into the corridor. It still bears a deserted look, though there are faint noises of giggles and laughs coming from the rooms the players are staying in.

She's at the café when she's joined by Kiran Chopra, the nineteen-year-old wicketkeeper.

'No children duty today, Didi?' she asks.

Aishwarya shakes her head.

Kiran continues. 'Makes sense. They are not going to give up the only day they have to themselves.'

'You look like you're going on a date,' says Aishwarya, who has come to like Kiran a lot.

She doesn't bear the serious look the older cricketers have. Through even the most tense situations, when half the side is back in the pavilion, she's on a recliner playing games on her Nintendo Switch.

'I can't leave the hotel today,' she says, her shoulders drooping. 'There's a game being developed for the World Cup, so they need me to test out the system for them.'

'A date would be better,' jokes Aishwarya. She wants to hold back, but the words come out anyway. 'I heard someone saying our captain's quitting after the World Cup? Is that true?'

After a moment's hesitation, Kiran says, 'Didi's my hero. She's everyone's hero.'

Aishwarya can't even imagine what it must be like for her and the others in the team. 'She was my wallpaper for a while.'

'The board is making her quit. Didi's not been in form since, you know . . .' Kiran's voice trails off. '. . . since she came back after Kriti was born.'

Aishwarya's heart sinks. Cricket for her was synonymous with Sonali.

'I know how you feel, Aishwarya,' says Kiran. 'Nothing prepares you for the fall of your heroes. For us, not having Didi in the dressing room is unimaginable. Anyway, what can one do? I will see you around.'

Aishwarya settles in the coffee shop with her laptop and starts work on her next batch of stories. Hardly fifteen minutes have passed when her phone beeps:

It's Kiran.

Kiran: Game room, quick.

Aishwarya: Where's that?

Aishwarya: ?

It doesn't take her a lot of time to find the game room. It's packed with people—a few lightmen, a couple of people testing out several cameras perched on tripods, a group of three people hunched over heavy-duty desktops.

'Aditi,' a tall, skinny girl introduces herself. 'Where's Kiran?'

'I don't know. She texted me to come here.'

Aditi moans and throws her head back. 'I should have known this would happen. This girl, I tell you, is a pain in the ass.' She turns towards her team. 'WHO WAS RESPONSIBLE FOR GETTING KIRAN HERE?'

'Can I help?' asks Aishwarya.

'How will you help?' snaps Aditi. 'We need to test our system with Kiran before the senior cricketers come in. We need someone who can mimic their movements.'

Aishwarya's eyes light up. 'Ummm . . . I can do it.'

'What?'

'I have played college cricket. I love cricket. I know how these players play,' explains Aishwarya.

Aditi now looks at her as if trying to assess her. 'You wear a suit with sensors and move around, do some cricket shots, run, etc. These cameras you see,' she points to the twenty-odd cameras arranged in a square around a huge black mat, 'will capture your movements. This is what we do to replicate player movement. We need to check for bugs. You think you can do it?'

'Yes, yes!' says Aishwarya like a little child.

'Okay, let's give this a shot,' says Aditi and points to the guy in charge of suiting people up. 'The suit is a little tight and difficult to get out of, so pee right now.'

'I'm twenty-five; I'm always dehydrated. I'm good.'

'Suit her up!' says Aditi and claps her hands twice before running off like a drill sergeant.

Aishwarya has to force herself into a skintight head-to-toe suit, which looks like a scuba diver's suit. Then, three women attach little white bulbs on the suit to capture her movements.

'Take this,' says Aditi, passing a bat to her. 'Just do whatever you want with it.'

Aishwarya walks to the middle of the black mat. She starts to shadow-bat some cover drives almost immediately.

'Not yet, not yet, we aren't recording data yet. We are yet to do some last-minute hooking up and are waiting for someone to join in,' says Aditi with a laugh.

Despite that, Aishwarya continues to shadow-bat because the bat feels good in her hands. When she turns it around, she sees it's signed by Sachin Tendulkar.

'Is it . . .'

The guy who's checking the wires nods. 'It's the gaming company's lucky bat, so they keep using it for these sessions.'

Just then, the door opens and two Delhi Police constables walk in. She wonders which celebrity cricketer is going to pop in. It's her lucky day after all! She's shadow-batting for the Indian cricket team using a bat signed by Sachin Tendulkar. The possibilities are endless.

And then two more policemen walk in with their hands behind them. They are holding a rope that's tied to the handcuffs worn by two men. The men are wearing caps so she doesn't get a good look past the constables. They are led to the tables facing the black mat. She loses the faces in the lights that are shining on her.

The two constables open the handcuffs and lock them on the legs of the table. She hears the two men talk to Aditi, but she can't make out the words.

'We can start now,' says Aditi with a clap. 'Police people, can you clear the field? Good, good. Can you leave the room, please? These two aren't going anywhere. This is national duty, guys. CAN WE ALL CLEAR THE FIELD?!'

The constables step back to the far edge of the room.

Aditi continues. 'Aishwarya, these are the guys who are a part of our team and they will help us to make the game authentic . . . and you're Aishwarya, helping us to test out our equipment.'

Aditi turns the dial down. The lights dim. She can now see who's chained to the table.

The faces become clear. It's *him*.

47.

Dhiren Das

'Can you stop moving like a tranquillized horse, please, Aishwarya?' barks Aditi. 'And Neeraj, get your partner to snap out of it and start working.'

Dhiren feels his heart being ripped apart in real time. *Is it her?* It wouldn't be the first time he imagines her to be there.

While for the past months, he has been wallowing in grief, missing her like a part of him has been amputated, Aishwarya has been doing fine it seems. Look at her. She looks even more beautiful than before, something he didn't think was possible. There are no telltale signs of grief, of depression, of anything that would suggest she missed him. Clearly, she didn't. On the contrary, she has been doing fine, doing the things she likes. Dhiren bristles with anger thinking of how he thought of multiple lifetimes with her while she was still living this one to the fullest. Dhiren remembers what Neeraj had said to him. He was in the anger stage of grief.

'Dhiren?' repeats Aditi impatiently.

'I would work if she were any good,' answers Dhiren, hate bubbling to the surface.

'Calm down, bhai,' says Neeraj.

Easy for Neeraj to say that. He wasn't the one who was abandoned and left to die in the rubble of her building. Dhiren's been unsuccessfully trying to read her eyes. He sees no anger, only indifference. Like he was nothing. Like the time they had spent together was nothing. *At least be furious with me*, he finds himself thinking. *Feel something for me*, he's pleading.

'She has played college cricket,' argues Aditi.

'We can't test and calibrate with her; she's too slow. Do you think the cricketers we shoot with are going to be walrus-slow?' snaps Dhiren.

He wants to ask if she wondered whether he would survive. *Did she ever think of visiting him in the hospital? Was all that they shared for nothing?*

'Behave, Dhiren. She doesn't work for you, she works for me,' snarled Aditi.

'Didn't you just call her a tranquillized horse?' says Neeraj.

'This is my room, Neeru.'

'Did you call me "Neeru"?'

'I can call anyone anything, and right now you're a wannabe coder in handcuffs whose best days are behind him,' snaps Aditi.

'I like Neeru. Call me Neeru again,' teases Neeraj.

Aditi turns to Aishwarya. 'They are right though. You're slowing us down. If you played college level, then show us that.'

'I'm try—' Aishwarya tries to speak, but Aditi raises her hand.

Dhiren's mind is a short-circuited mess. He wants to be angry, but he also wants to apologize and ask her how she's doing. He wants to run away, but he also wants to hold her hand and stay that way. But most of all, none of this seems real.

'She's here, isn't she?' he whispers at Neeraj.

'Of course she's here,' answers Neeraj. 'See, I will wave at her and she will wave back.'

Aishwarya doesn't wave back.

Aditi turns to another employee and seethes. 'Get me Kiran. Call her and ask her to get here asap. How can she go missing? Get me Adil too. Where the hell is he?'

Aishwarya smashes an imaginary ball to the fence. 'Was that quick enough for you guys?'

She looks at Dhiren, eyes boring into his. Dhiren's hurt, but it's good. He still has a place in her heart. Even though it's anger, he exists.

Aditi turns to Dhiren. 'Quick enough?'

Aishwarya shoots Aditi a murderous look. 'Am I seriously getting feedback from people who didn't even make it to their school teams?'

Dhiren shakes his head and moans. 'She's still slow. How are we supposed to use someone who failed at college level? This is the Indian team we are talking about. This is just a waste of time.'

A project manager comes running to Aditi with an iPad and says, 'Aditi? 20 per cent more bat speed than Kiran.'

Aditi turns to Dhiren, frowning, 'She's not slow, so what's the issue here, Dhiren?'

'She's not—'

'The handcuffs are on your wrists, not on your brain. Just get the work done.'

'She looks slow to me.'

'Just do your job,' hisses Aditi. 'Can we start recording shots that we are going to make the batsmen play in the game?' She scans the room and shouts, 'AND CAN SOMEONE TELL ME WHERE IS ADIL?'

Dhiren leans back in his chair. He looks straight at Aishwarya, his heart in pieces. The pain's more than he can handle.

He addresses Aishwarya, 'A straight drive. High backlift, full follow-through.'

She doesn't look at him.

And even though Aishwarya does well, he says, 'That's horrible. Can we get someone else in the suit, please?'

Aishwarya does it again, this time with more power and speed. Beads of sweat form on her forehead. And yet, she doesn't spare Dhiren a look. *Look at me*, Dhiren wants to shout.

'Not good enough. Again,' says Dhiren.

'No, not good enough. Again.'

'Again! Too slow.'

'TOO SLOW!'

'FASTER!'

Aishwarya is sweating profusely in the suit. She looks down at her bat. She takes her stance again.

'No. Again!'

'Terrible. Again!'

Neeraj leans over. 'Bhai, what are you doing . . .?'

'Move your feet. Again!'

Aishwarya grunts with the effort. She keeps going.

'Again!'

'Again!'

'Fuck you,' says Aishwarya. She locks her eyes with Dhiren. Her face is slick with sweat, her eyes are bloodshot. She swings the bat with so much force that it slips out of her hands and flies right at the camera, knocking it down.

'GUYS!' screams Aditi. 'What the fuck is happening here?'

Aditi's team rushes to fix the camera.

'This is what happens when you get frauds to work,' grumbles Aishwarya, still panting. 'I'm out.'

'Wait, wait, wait!' Aditi raises her hands in frustration. 'What's happening? You can't head out. We are not wasting a day here.'

'Listen to me, Aditi. I'm doing you and Adil a favour, so of course I can be out, and I am,' rages Aishwarya and walks off the black mat and into the changing room.

Aditi turns to look at Dhiren, 'What the hell just happened here?'

'You got an unprofessional to work with us,' shrugs Dhiren. 'What did you expect would happen?'

'Let's take five and regroup or I will hit someone, and by someone I mean you, Neeraj,' grumbles Aditi.

'My name's Neeru,' Neeraj corrects her.

'I will do the checks instead of her,' says Dhiren. 'I have played enough cricket to do this. I will suit up.'

'Sorry, madam, orders *hai upar se* [from the top],' says a constable who emerges from the shadows. 'We can't take off his handcuffs and give him a bat.'

'You two are carrying guns,' says Dhiren. 'What does this say about your balls?'

The constables squirm.

'Let us ask Vishwas Sir,' the other constable says.

'So extra-small?' says Neeraj.

Ten minutes later, Dhiren's in a suit and working on the calibration. As he's swinging the bat around, his mind's still firmly on Aishwarya, replaying the events. He feels stupid. *What was he thinking? What right did he have to be angry with her? What did this achieve? All this while he had wanted to see her just once, and now that he has, was this how he should have behaved?*

Dhiren trudges through the rest of the day punishing himself by recalling his behaviour.

On their way back, Dhiren says, 'I didn't have to treat her like that today.'

'It happens. You're angry. Then you feel like a fool that you were angry.'

'What do you know?'

'I have lost too,' says Neeraj.

'What did you lose, madarchod?'

'I didn't lose anything?' asks Neeraj sharply.

'No.'

'So I lost nothing?' Neeraj says and shakes his head. The lightness on his face disappears and he continues. 'I lost Crypto Cricket. I lost my best friend. Bhai, I was angry with you too.' Neeraj turns to look at him, trying to fight back the tears. He calms down and points out, 'Bhai, you abandoned me after calling me your family.'

'I never called you my family.'

'You didn't have to, bhai,' Neeraj shrugs. 'You picked your family. We all do as we grow up. We picked each other. I was your brother. I was the brother you never had. You spoilt it all.'

Dhiren doesn't want to cry. How sad would that be? Dhiren shrugs and says casually, 'I wanted a sister, not a brother.'

'Aditi did call me Neeru today,' says Neeraj with a small laugh. 'It's okay, bro. Families disappoint. That's the distinguishing factor of families. No one can break your heart like your family can.'

48.

Aishwarya Mohan

Aishwarya bristles with anger when she reaches the kids' room.

Back in the game room, she wanted to rip Dhiren's head off. The bat slipping out of her hands wasn't an accident. She had tried to hit him, and she still wanted him to be hurt. Why wouldn't she? He had shown her a lovely dream and then crushed it. He had no business playing with her feelings like that. She feels stupid to have not dug into his past.

But it wasn't her responsibility. He kept secrets.

These past few months, she has dreamed up countless scenarios where Dhiren comes clean. He cooks biryani and sits her down. With tears in his eyes, Dhiren tells her everything about his past life—the game, the scam, the money he stole. In every one of those scenarios, she forgives Dhiren. *What does that say about her? That she was rotten?*

'You had an episode in the game room I heard,' says Adil.

'When did you get here?' she asks when she turns and sees him right behind her.

He sits next to her. 'You guys have history, Dhiren and you. The nursery you were building with him, the accident, and I'm guessing you had a thing too. You were friends, or you were in love, one of those things.'

'How do you—'

'One has to be careful with all the betting stuff flying around. In the cricket business, you have to run background checks. You don't know how many different ways people find to get close to cricketers.'

'Why did you involve him when you knew I'd be here?' complains Aishwarya.

'Umm,' Adil hesitates. 'You came here after him.'

'But the game thing . . .'

'We have been planning the game for months. We knew Dhiren and Neeraj were the right people to build it. We were all fans of Crypto Cricket, but literally, god dropped a building on our plans.'

'Cute Buttons.'

'Yes,' says Adil. 'I knew you from the background checks before I met you. Imagine my surprise when Sonali dragged you here. Honestly, I didn't think you would just waltz into the game room and meet him. So it's your fault, Aishwarya. You had a kids' room, you had to stick there.'

'What else do you know?'

'We know that you had no idea who Dhiren was,' says Adil.

'How do you know that?'

'What part of background checks did you not understand?' asks Adil, his eyes glinting mischievously. 'We also know that sometimes you take the longer route home. The route takes you to the locality where he's under house arrest. You stop outside his house, wait for a little bit and then drive off.'

Aishwarya feels ashamed. She wanted to hide this secret so deep that even she wouldn't find it. But it was there for Adil to see. *What must he think of her? A girl who was dumb enough not to know who Dhiren was. A girl who still misses him despite all the lies and the secrets. Did Adil and Sonali talk about her, shake their heads and say, 'Look at the poor girl, still grieving for the boy who just lied and lied and lied to her?'* She promises herself not to take that route again. *What was she thinking anyway? What would happen if she ever saw him in the window? Could they ever put what happened behind them? Their story is poisoned forever. He's a reminder of her failure, of her naivety, of her thinking that she could create a perfect future for herself.*

Adil pours a glass of water and gives it to Aishwarya. 'Allah *kasam* [I swear on Allah], this is a coincidence.'

'Adil, but he's . . . he's . . .'

Look at me, just look at me. I can't even say the words.

'Everyone steals,' says Adil waving her off. 'They were just smart enough to fool a lot of people out of a lot of money.' And then, with some seriousness, he adds, 'They are good, decent boys, talented boys who made a mistake; sometimes that's all there is to it.'

'Decent boys don't steal.'

Adil chuckles. 'No one's job is truly honest, Aishwarya. My cricketers endorse gutkha, your favourite movie star sells alcohol and my college friends sell credit cards to vulnerable people and wipe them out.' He gets up. 'Anyway, I will make sure your paths don't cross. I don't want any drama in this team. Kiran's back, so she's handling it.' Just as he's leaving, he asks, 'Just curious though, do you still love him?'

'I hate him.'

Adil laughs. 'You're a horrible liar. No wonder you couldn't spot his lies,' he says and leaves the room.

'And I hate myself for what I did to him,' she mumbles to herself.

Despite her effort, she slips into a thought spiral.

The generator was her fault.

A couple of days after the men had installed the generator, Dhiren had pointed out, 'Could we look at putting the generator on the ground floor? Might make it easy for repairs in future.' She must have frowned because he had quickly added, 'It's good where it is.'

She would have never put the generator on the ground floor.

It was a vain choice—she knew the risks. And Dhiren paid for it. He could have died that day. The firefighters, the doctors said his survival was a miracle. His financial crimes might have been his fault, but getting pinned under the falling roof wasn't.

It was her fault.

There have been times like today when she has been furious with him. But there are times she wants to apologize to him, which her friends disagree with.

'Behen, it was a freak accident that could have happened to anyone,' they had said.

'What should I do then?' Aishwarya pleaded. 'Should I close my eyes to everything that could have happened? Should I pretend that I didn't almost kill dozens of children? That I almost didn't kill him? What if Vihaan and Amritanshu were in the building?'

They want her to move on, start over. They keep asking her to start Cute Buttons again. And she keeps telling them that Cute Buttons is now forever tainted. All because of her carelessness, all because she put herself before the children she was supposed to take care of.

'Shall I take the Dwarka route?' the driver asks.

'Not today,' she answers.

When Aishwarya gets home, the door to her apartment is slightly ajar. She knows Akshay is inside. Her first instinct is to run away. *But where will she go?* The door opens with some effort, hitting some obstruction. When she enters, she finds the room's floor decorated with balloons. There are petals strewn about and little candles everywhere.

'Surprise!' says Akshay, smiling his puppy-dog smile, arms outstretched.

This is hardly a surprise, Aishwarya thinks. This is going to be a nightmare to clean afterwards. She wants to tell Akshay she's not a teenager; instead, she squeals.

'Yay,' she responds, forcing a smile. 'What's all this for?'

Take that, Adil. I can lie if I want to.

'There's some news,' Akshay says and comes to her. He holds her hand, catches her gaze.

Her eyes shift. She notices that the petals have flown below the sofa. She will have to remove it to clean the floors. That's an extra hour of work.

'But you didn't have to do all this, Akshay. Very sweet though.'

'Come,' he says.

He leads her to the table where there's a small pastry on a plate. She thanks god he hasn't ordered a cake because her fridge has no space.

'So, Aishwarya. There's some *big* news. The VCs who funded the start-up are opening an office in the US, a big operation. They want me to step out of this company and join them instead.'

'Step out from your own company?'

'They believe I can do better in that role. They are saying I have done what I could for the start-up. They will install some other guy, and I will still have all the control.'

Aishwarya opens the food package. 'Is the food from Wok? They use too much colour.'

Dhiren would have never ordered from Wok. He would not have ordered from anywhere at all. But then again, he didn't spend hours working. He was too busy manipulating legal loopholes.

'It means I'm set for life, Aishwarya!' gushes Akshay.

'But your start-up? You're going to leave that?'

'In someone's able hands. This is leapfrogging into something amazing!' he beams. His eyes are glinting like a madman's. 'I will be a part of many companies at the nascent level. It's going to be super exciting! Why work at one start-up when you can have your fingers in many?!'

'You're going to take it?'

He nods.

'You're going to move to the US?'

'Not just me.'

'Your team?'

'Why will I take my team?'

'Then?'

Akshay shakes his head. 'You and me, of course. Our team.'

'What?'

'We are set for life. I will be in the start-up business, but with no risk. It's the dream!' he squeals. 'And you can do whatever you want there. Away from here. We know you can use some distance from that Cute Buttons episode.'

'Akshay . . .'

'It also means manageable working hours, a US visa, a citizenship soon, and a certain lifestyle. We can have children, like many, many children.'

'But you don't like children . . .'

He pulls her into an embrace.

'What if I do now?' he asks, holding her close. 'Do you see what I'm seeing?'

'I see it,' she lies.

Because all she sees when she closes her eyes is Dhiren.

49.

Aishwarya Mohan

Aishwarya hasn't received Adil's call yet.

But she can hear him screaming into her ear.

She should have been at the team hotel two hours ago. She has been up for all this while. She has made and had her coffee. She has had two little breakfasts. And yet she hasn't been able to get herself to leave.

In the few moments that she has been able to breathe, and seen the lighter of side of the shit she's in, she wants to make a pros-and-cons list. There's a) working with the Indian cricket team while Dhiren hovers nearby, and taking care of those children, and then there's b) run miles away. She knows how her friends will react. Vinny will tell her to stay, and threaten Dhiren with dire consequences if he comes near her. Smriti will goad her to move on, start a family when it's time and lead a happy, normal life without complications. As she has discovered, she can keep lying to them.

She gets up and makes herself another coffee. She wonders what pretext she can give for being unavailable. She waits for the phone to ring. And when Adil doesn't call for another half an hour, she is concerned. *What are the kids doing? And the players?*

Finally, she picks up her phone and calls Adil. 'I need to tell you something.'

'Tell me what? That you're running away from your ex-boyfriend? Oh, by the way, you didn't tell me he was good with kids too. Was that how you two bonded?'

'What are you saying?'

'Check your phone.'

Adil's sent her a picture of Dhiren. He's still chained to a desk—surrounded by kids who are looking at him with rapt attention. He's reading from a book.

'That's your book, by the way, he's reading. He knows them by heart. That's such a cute-ass move,' says Adil with a laugh.

'There's nothing cute about you leaving the children with a guy who has a police record.'

'I know people in the team management who have committed graver crimes than him, but suit yourself. Anyway, see if you can come; if you can't, it's okay because Dhiren's doing a bomb job.' He adds after a pause, 'I'm being sarcastic. If you care about the kids, get your ass here.'

Within ten minutes of the call, Aishwarya is on her way to the team hotel. She jumps out of the auto, runs to the floor and then to the game room. Her heart's thumping from all the nervousness and the running.

She stops short at the door when she hears voices and peeps in to see what's going on.

Sonali's daughter asks Dhiren. 'Rohan here says you killed someone and that's why you're chained to the table. Is that true?'

Dhiren laughs. 'I didn't murder anyone. I stole some money from some people and kept it for myself. I used to love money.

I could buy so many things with it: iPads, computers, games, that sort of thing,' he says and winks at the children.

The children giggle. Kritika's son says, 'That's not a good thing.'

'I know, I know,' confesses Dhiren and raises his free hand. 'And you should NEVER do that, okay? Never. Say it with me . . . I will never ever steal!'

A few kids murmur. 'I will never ever steal!'

Dhiren continues. 'If I steal, I will be punished with SMELLY FARTS AND LOOSE MOTIONS all day!'

The children start to laugh.

'Is that what happened to you?' asks Rohan.

Dhiren nods. 'I was on the toilet for months! Doing ughhhh . . . ughhhh . . .' Dhiren's face turns red and he keeps going, 'Ughhhh . . . ughhhh . . . ughhhh.'

The children double over with laughter.

He continues. 'You can laugh now, but if you don't say it, you will get double the amount of smelly farts. So repeat after me . . . If I ever steal . . .'

'IF I EVER STEAL!' the children repeat.

'. . . then I will be punished with smelly farts and loose motions all day!'

'I WILL BE PUNISHED WITH SMELLY FARTS AND LOOSE MOTIONS ALL DAY!'

The children laugh till their faces are slick with tears. They are now accusing each other of being fart bombs. Aishwarya wants to step in, take the children away, but she doesn't move. She's like a child, listening to Dhiren with rapt attention.

And just then, Adil taps Aishwarya's shoulder. Before she can react, Adil marches in, clapping his hands and announcing, 'Break time over, children! Let Dhiren Uncle work; your favourite teacher is in the house!'

The children turn towards the door. Aishwarya's heart thumps as her eyes lock with Dhiren's. Sonali's daughter, along with a few others, run towards her and lunge into a hug. 'I missed you!' she squeals.

Aishwarya wants to look away from Dhiren's sad eyes, but she can't.

'I missed you too,' Aishwarya whispers into Kriti's ear. 'Help me get everyone to the kids' room.'

Kriti nods, and like a dutiful shepherd dog, herds the children out of the room. Adil follows them out, and just as he's leaving, he stops near Aishwarya. 'As I said, don't talk to him. I don't need drama.'

'Please go,' says Aishwarya.

Adil leaves the room leaving behind Aishwarya, Neeraj and Dhiren.

'I would have left too, but I'm chained,' says Neeraj. 'But, Bhabhi, pretend as if I'm not here.'

Dhiren and Aishwarya throw him a murderous look.

Aishwarya takes a deep breath to calm her frayed nerves. She walks towards Dhiren slowly, checking her steps. Any faster, and her body will betray her and she will throw herself into his arms. When she comes close enough, she pulls a chair and sits in front of him. A moment passes in silence. There's nothing that she has to say to him. Nothing. She just wants to be here. Breathing in the air that he's breathing. She's waiting for some magic to happen. For this nightmare to end and just to wake up in the garden of Cute Buttons, planting a flower. She fights back tears.

He begins, 'I'm sorry . . .'

Aishwarya shakes her head. *He doesn't need to apologize for anything. What purpose can his apology serve? Will it turn back time? Will it heal the pain and the hurt? Can anything? Maybe running away with Akshay will.*

'What can you say that will make it better, Dhiren?'

'I was a coward,' he says.

Aishwarya notices the quiver in his voice, the tremble in his fingers. She's angry with him, but she also wants to hold him, heal him, be one with him.

'I thought I would lose everything,' he says.

'We did lose everything.'

'Aishwarya, if there's anything I can do . . . we can get past this,' he pleads.

She wants to reach out and wipe the tears off his cheek. But she keeps her hands to herself. *How can they ever get past this? What they had once is now dust.*

'And get where? Where do we go from here, Dhiren? You're sitting here in handcuffs serving time. And I'm lost. Everything I wanted to do, everything I dreamed of, was taken away from me.' Aishwarya shakes her head. 'We can keep saying sorry to each other, keep going around in circles and it would mean dirt. Both of us are facing the consequences of our actions. What we are led to this, where we are.'

'What do we do about us?'

Aishwarya looks away from him. 'I hid going to the IVF centre from you. I didn't want to tell you. That should tell you what I felt about you. There's nothing more that I have wanted than to be a mother and yet, when I met you, I had doubts. Can you believe that?'

Aishwarya can feel his heart break, as she can feel hers.

'What matters is that you and I are in this room, right now, talking, and as long as we can keep doing that . . .'

Tears spring to her eyes. 'Dhiren,' she says, her voice cracking. 'You're everywhere. I close my eyes and I see you, I sleep and I see you. You were there at the IVF centre when I closed my eyes. You know what I imagined then? I imagined myself in the hospital. You were holding my newborn. And then you told me you hated me, and you left. You abandoned me, you abandoned my child. It was the happiest moment of my life, but I was mourning your loss.'

'I would . . .'

'Dhiren, I have been abandoned before. By my mother, my brother, even my father, and it's okay. It hardly registers. But in what should have been one of the happiest moments of my life, I wasn't happy. I wanted you.'

'Why would it have mattered to me whose child you were carrying?' Dhiren asks impatiently. 'It would have been a part of you, and how could I ever hate something that's a part of you?'

Aishwarya scoffs. 'You're a great liar, Dhiren. See, my heart wants to believe every single word that you're saying. Look at your eyes. Truth and honesty, that's all I see. And that's my fault. Because I know that you're a liar. You have always been a liar. And I couldn't see it.'

Dhiren leans forward. His hand is jerked back by the handcuffs.

'I'm not lying,' says Dhiren. 'The truth is . . .'

'The truth is that we both did wrong. You lied about everything.'

'What we had was real, Aishwarya. It's the realest thing I have ever felt.'

'And I almost killed you.'

'Aishwarya . . .'

'You should hate me, Dhiren, and I should hate you. That's all there should be between the two of us.'

'I would pick death over hating you.'

Aishwarya smiles and says sadly, 'You always had a flair for the dramatic. Too bad it's over now, Dhiren. All the drama with us, with Cute Buttons. It's all done and dusted. We destroyed it.'

'It doesn't need to be, Bhabhi,' says Neeraj.

'I'm going.'

'Where?' asks Dhiren.

'With Akshay.'

'Are you saying that to hurt me?'

Aishwarya shakes her head. 'As I said, everything's finished here.' She gets up.

'It doesn't have to be, Aishwarya,' pleads Dhiren, his voice dire and desperate.

But Aishwarya is already walking towards the door. Every step's a fight, but she knows the longer she stays, the more she would want to forgive everything and go running into his arms.

50.

Neeraj Kothari

Neeraj has been in love more times than Dhiren has, but none of them had the same intensity that he just saw in the game room. They are back at their house when Neeraj says, 'That's the strangest admission of love I have ever seen.' Dhiren doesn't answer.

Neeraj continues. 'At least you can be happy about that, bhai. She finally admitted that she loved you.' Dhiren doesn't respond. Neeraj wishes there was a button he could press and factory-reset Dhiren to what he was. He asks, 'Do you want a coffee? I ordered a new machine. It works straight from the app.' When he gets no answer, he says, 'I'm going to make one anyway.'

The new coffee machine splutters and spits out two espressos. By the time he turns, Dhiren's back in his room.

To take his mind off things, Neeraj fires up his computer to work on the biomechanics of the few players they have recorded. Half an hour into the simulations he's developing, he notices something off with Sonali's recordings. As he superimposes data from Sonali's previous matches to what they recorded, he finds that Sonali's bat speed has slowed down, her pupils dilate more than they used to and there are twitches in her hands and her thighs. She's *scared*. Even with imaginary balls, her movements are severely limited. It's like him seeing a different player on the screen. No wonder her performance has dipped over the last few years. But in the game they are making, Sonali's still the highest-rated player. This is a problem. They can't have the best player of the game twitch and be unsure of her shots. Without Sonali's array of shots, the game would be incomplete. Every reviewer is bound to pick the highest-rated player and take her for a try-out. When they see the glitches in the shot-making, they will tear apart the game. And there's no way Adil's going to allow more time with Sonali.

As he keeps watching Sonali's old footage, he remembers.

He frantically goes back to the first reference movement they had shot. The file's named Player A. They were the shots Dhiren had put in the bin—these were Aishwarya's shots.

He opens two windows—one with Aishwarya's footage and one with Sonali's older videos. He leans in towards the screen. The resemblance is uncanny. Before Sonali became a mother, structurally, she was quite similar to Aishwarya. The foot movement on the screen, her little tics—they are all the same. And why not? Aishwarya's a fan, no wonder she has modelled her batting on Sonali. Neeraj gives himself an imaginary pat on the back.

The only thing he has to change is the arm lengths since Sonali has longer arms.

He changes the player's name to Aishwarya.

Neeraj alters Aishwarya's movements to fit Sonali's. It blends like a dream. He's in Aishwarya's medical file to change her arm length and proportions to suit Sonali's. He's about to put the numbers in when he notices something in the corner of the screen.

Any past surgeries?

No.

Any past pregnancies?

No.

Any joint issues?

No.

He scrolls up again.

No past pregnancies?

Fuck.

Neeraj leans back into his chair. He tries to recall the conversation about Aishwarya's pregnancy. And he connects the dots. *Fucking bitch.* Neeraj logs into an Internet calling service. He dials Vinny's number, *that cunning witch.*

'Hello?' says Vinny.

Neeraj takes a deep breath. He puts on his squeakiest voice possible and says, 'Hi! This is Soumen, and I'm calling from the IVF centre. We tried calling the patient, Aishwarya Mohan, but her phone's not working. You were the emergency contact so I'm getting in touch with you. I wanted to tell you that the centre has instituted a money-back policy for all our patients who didn't carry the pregnancy to term. Would you like your friend to apply for the money-back?'

'What?'

'The last date is today, ma'am. If she didn't carry her pregnancy to term, she can avail the money-back offer.'

'Is it applicable if the procedure didn't work?'

'Sorry, ma'am, despite being the best in the city, it's not very uncommon to believe the procedure didn't take. I will make a report internally. But for that, can you tell me what do you mean by saying the procedure didn't work? It's for the report.'

'She didn't get pregnant.'

'So you're saying, ma'am, that she didn't get pregnant?'

'Yes.'

'Never?'

'No.'

Neeraj clearly remembers the day Vinny had come seething to the hospital to let them know that it was because of Dhiren that Aishwarya was no longer pregnant. All that was a fucking lie. *Behenchod. Does Aishwarya know what Vinny said to them? Or did Aishwarya tell Vinny that to keep Dhiren away from her?*

'So, no pregnancy? Not even one?' asks Neeraj.

'That's what I mean, bhaisahab. What's so difficult to understand—'

Click.

Neeraj disconnects the call.

51.

Aishwarya Mohan

First shot, 30 ml, her bathroom.

The vodka burns everything on its way down. If she needs to do this, she's going to need a little Dutch courage. She brushes her teeth immediately. She doesn't want Akshay to know that her decision to go with him to the US took alcohol. In fact, she's surprised it's taken her just alcohol. Seeing Dhiren that day broke her in a way she didn't think was possible. How can someone miss someone so badly that it feels like their entire being is being burnt from the inside? When she comes out of the washroom, Akshay's booking them a cab to Safdarjung Enclave. Smriti and Vinny are going to meet them there. She wants them to be there because they thought it was a great idea to start seeing Akshay again. So if this relationship, the move to the US, all goes south from here on, she has someone to lay the blame on. Why should she take the responsibility for any decision?

Not tipsy yet, but she's definitely getting there. She's swiftly reminded of the last time she drank. She had spent the night with Dhiren talking incessantly. She wonders how a few months spent with someone could feel like a lifetime. She has more memories with Dhiren than she has with Akshay. *Don't compare the two, you fool*, she tells herself.

On the cab to Plum, she curses internally every time they hit a bad patch of traffic. She doesn't want the alcohol to wear off. They take fifteen minutes to reach the restaurant. When she gets down from the car, she can still feel the vodka glow on her skin.

'Vodka and coke,' she tells the waiter as soon as she takes her seat.

'Nothing for me,' says Akshay.

'Are you sure?' she asks Akshay, sensing an opportunity. 'Get the same for him or he's going to share mine.'

'You're in a good mood,' says Akshay once the waiter leaves. He reaches out for her hand and holds it.

His cold hand feels repulsive. She wants to brush it off. But then, he's the man she's going to live with in a foreign land, away from her friends, from her Papa, from even Yatin and Maa. She's going to have to learn to love it. So she puts her hand over his, clasps it tight and smiles at him.

'It's a big step for me, so I'm excited,' she says.

'You aren't nervous?' asks Akshay.

'Me? Not at all!'

Just then the waiter brings the drinks. She sips slowly at first and then takes it down in one gulp. Relief courses through her. She can even see the logic of her decision clearly. She won't be here any more. She would be thousands of miles away from the memories of Cute Buttons, of Dhiren, and of him wanting to do anything to make amends. She needs nothing out of those. Out of sight, out of mind, isn't that what they say? Staying in the US, Dhiren's pleading eyes will mean nothing. She will forget his sad eyes and his apologies. She will take him out of the equation and start afresh. She smiles thinking of her new beginning. It will be painful in the beginning, like ripping off a Band-Aid. But underneath, it will be a brand new her! New place, new her! As she keeps thinking, she realizes she wants to move to the US, live in one of those huge houses she sees on Instagram, develop a hint of an accent and live the rest of her life as a potentially rich person. That's what she needs—distance.

'Do you want more?' asks Akshay, tapping at her glass.

'In a little while,' answers Aishwarya, straining to make sure she doesn't slur.

Akshay leans forward and says, 'So they want us to move in the next two months. They have a house picked out already. I have asked for pictures, should get them in a day or two. Things are moving quite fast.'

A few minutes later, Smriti and Vinny walk in through the front door. She can read suspicion on their faces. There's no hiding from them that something's up.

'What's the occasion?' asks Smriti as soon as they sit down. 'Hi, Akshay,' she adds coldly.

'Are you drunk, behen?' asks Vinny.

'She's taking it slow actually. We both are,' says Akshay with a smile. He puts his arm around Aishwarya. 'We need to tell you guys something.'

'This is stressing me out. What is it?' asks Smriti.

Aishwarya sees no point in dragging this out. 'I'm moving to the US!' she squeals.

Aishwarya expects a deathly silence and that's what she gets. Vinny and Smriti look at her as if trying to discern if this is a prank.

'You're definitely drunk,' says Vinny, her voice shaking. 'Why would you move to the US?'

'Actually, we are moving to the US. I have a job . . .' says Akshay.

'Did we ask you?' questions Smriti sharply.

'This is what we wanted, right?' says Aishwarya, putting an arm around Akshay. 'Him and me! This is what we had talked about. Not only are we getting his sperm but all of it.'

Akshay's face goes red.

'I'm sorry,' she pats his hand.

Smriti and Vinny look at each other and then at Aishwarya.

Vinny says, 'Have you thought about it?'

'Of course, I have thought about it. This is what I want. The people from his office are going to send us pictures of our new house. I couldn't be more excited!' She turns to Smriti. 'Back me on this, isn't this what you wanted? You two were right all along! I can't raise a child alone. There, I will have him,' she says and turns to Akshay. 'And you will keep a nanny for us, I am hoping. Not that we are having a child right now. But whenever we do. I'm going to leave this life behind and build a new one and it's going to be amazing!'

Smriti and Vinny exchange a smile.

'Congratulations, guys,' says Smriti dryly.

'It doesn't look like it's coming from the depths of you. It's looking like empty words,' says Aishwarya. 'Why is that? Tell me.'

'Ummm . . . just that you're going to be away from us,' answers Vinny. 'This will be a first. We will miss you, that's all. Believe me, I am happy for you. When do you leave?'

'In a month or two,' answers Akshay. 'It's up to us, really. If she's not ready, we can delay it by a few weeks.'

The first tears come into Vinny's eyes. And then Smriti starts to cry. Akshay looks at all of them and says, 'I should excuse myself, give you guys some time to process this.'

When Akshay leaves, Aishwarya turns to the two of them. 'You need to be excited for me. I'm trying to put my life together.'

'By being a housewife in the US? No offence to housewives in the US, but I'm not sure this is called putting your life together,' says Vinny.

'Are you sure you're not just running away?' asks Smriti.

Aishwarya can't believe them. 'I remember you guys specifically telling me to run away with him! He's the dream boy, perfect for me and whatnot.'

'But this doesn't feel right. All of this feels too rushed. Especially now,' says Smriti.

'You have a good thing going, behen. You can't leave the series and the World Cup to go do nothing in the US. Stay here, at least till the tournament ends.'

Smriti continues urgently. 'You're writing books, you're working with children again. Maybe this is not the time to go. Wait for six months; if you still feel like going, we are not going to say anything.'

Aishwarya goes silent for a bit. And then she says, 'Dhiren's working for the Indian cricket team, too. He's making a game for them. If I keep working where I am, I will have to see him every day.'

Vinny and Smriti stop dead in their tracks. They look at her to ascertain if she's serious or just yanking their chain. She's not joking. They don't ask her how he got the job, or if he will be constantly around her. They don't say anything. Aishwarya waits for them to come up with an alternative, but they stay silent. That's what Aishwarya had thought. There's no way out of this.

52.

Dhiren Das

Dhiren turns over to the other side when he hears a disturbance.

He's now used to hearing the rattling sounds of windows and doors quite often. These are precursors to an oncoming nightmare. His subconscious has learnt to brush these away. But today, the sound is more urgent. Even though he knows it's not real, it feels real. He can't pull himself out of it. The pain in his knee returns in anticipation. He knows the course of this nightmare—the building will collapse on him and his breath will slowly leave his body.

He prepares himself for it.

But suddenly, he feels a soft, tender hand around his chest. This is new. He opens his eyes. This is *real*. This is not a nightmare. He looks at the wall in front of him. The hand lingers around his chest, clasping it tight. His first thought is Neeraj, a hooker, and a stupid plan from him. He turns around with a jerk. He's about to move away when he looks at her face. Framed by darkness and the yellow glow of the night lamp, she looks like a dream. How can it be his imagination when he can feel her warm breath on his face? It's real—the tears and the sadness in her eyes, the alcohol on her breath. Her hand on his chest feels as though it has bored through and is on his heart. She can reach out and crush his heart. He wouldn't mind. He has surrendered already.

'Hey,' she whispers in the softest voice he has ever heard.

'You're real,' he whispers back.

'Dhiren,' says Aishwarya softly. 'I'm here.'

He runs his fingers gently on her face, trailing down from her temple to her lips and down to her neck. Touching her feels like someone's breathing life back into him. 'You're here. This is real.'

She shakes her head. 'This is not real.'

'Is it not?' he asks.

'Kiss me,' she orders.

Dhiren slips his hand behind her neck and pulls her towards him. He can taste the sweat, the alcohol and the hunger. Her want feels urgent, ancient, necessary. She pulls him in and pushes herself on to him. Dhiren pulls away, cradling her little face in his hands as if she will melt away if he doesn't look at her. But Aishwarya pulls him back, puts her lips on his. She kisses him lightly, enveloping his mouth with her hand, and then ravenously, her tongue around his, her hands firmly pulling his head towards her. They pause for breath.

'Why are you here?' asks Dhiren.

He rests his hand firmly on the small of her back, slowly pulling up her dress. He fears this moment will end, that she will remind herself of their past and walk away.

'Don't talk,' she says and plants her lips on his neck.

Dhiren melts instantaneously. His body stiffens and loosens at the same time. He's at her mercy, her command. In this moment, he can kill for her, die for her.

'We should have done this before,' she says.

'We didn't know we wanted this,' he says.

'I did,' she whispers and looks into his eyes. 'I did the first time I saw you. I have always wanted this.'

He pulls off her dress in one fluid motion. He picks her up and rolls over on top of her. With one snap, her bra comes off. She lets him look for a moment. She's in total control, and he is in a state of total surrender. And then she pulls his face towards herself. She moans as he bites her.

'Yes,' she whispers, her voice cracking. Her grip on his head becomes more firm as he continues.

For a moment, he thinks of what time it is. *Is it going to be morning soon?* He wonders if she will leave after tonight, never to be seen again. Or if this, what they are doing right now, will make her stay. His trance is broken when she pushes him down. She lets him strip her naked.

'Now,' she says, pushing his head in between her legs.

She grabs his hair with both her hands, her thighs gripping his face in place as he eats her out. She lets his tongue explore her, take all of her.

'Stay there,' she mumbles.

When he looks up, her eyes are closed tight. *Why wouldn't she look at him?* he wonders. Look at me if you're thinking of me.

Even though she's here, he's jealous of everything she has shared with everyone. He wants it to be perfect. He wants to give this moment his everything, so that if she leaves, she can never be whole again. Every time she's in bed, she will remember this warmth. She unclenches her thighs. She holds his face and pulls him up. She turns towards his ear, kisses it and whispers, 'Get naked.'

With some awkwardness, he gets his shorts off, and then his T-shirt. He wonders if he should have taken his T-shirt off first. She pulls him towards the side while her hands slip down to his cock. He moans in anticipation.

'What are you going to do when I—'

She interrupts him when she licks the length of his cock. Whatever he is about to say comes out in a moan when she takes him in her mouth. His mind is mush. And yet some part of it is telling him this is not happening. So he opens his eyes and finds Aishwarya staring at him, rolling her tongue over from the tip to the base.

'I'm here,' she says and throats him.

His thighs tense up. She seems to notice that, because she runs her hands through them as if asking him to relax. And then it all happens too quickly. His eyes are closed when she slides up, and in one fluid motion, slips him inside of her. His hands grab her breasts as she rocks against him, her eyes open and locks with his. The warmth, the wetness, and her body knocks out anything else he has been thinking about. It's just her, him and this moment.

'This is what I imagined,' she mumbles.

He plunges harder, giving it everything, ploughing into her. She urges him on. And like a bull, he keeps thrusting maddeningly.

He feels the clenching. She digs in her nails and shudders. He feels himself at the brink too. And then, just as her body stops to tremble, she shudders again, and this time he comes with her. She lets her body go and slumps over him.

He kisses her, finally coming to his senses. She kisses him back. This time with less hunger, more tenderness, like a kiss that can go on forever, soft and smooth.

'I missed you, Dhiren,' she says.

'I missed you, too.'

53.

Aishwarya Mohan

Aishwarya wakes up with her body intertwined with Dhiren's in a way she didn't think was possible. The touch of his skin against her gives her goosebumps. With a shake of her head, she washes away any morning-after guilt. She turns to see Dhiren lying naked on his chest. His broad back now bears scars from the operations. Even now, while sleeping, his body's like granite, smooth and hard, inviting. Last night's images come sharply to her. The feeling of her hands on his chest. She can feel every striation, every muscle, each pulsating hungrily for her. When she had grabbed his ass, she could feel it harden with every thrust of his. Every time he plunged into her, she could feel her heart thump faster. No. She stops herself from thinking. She pulls the blanket over him. She doesn't want to look at him or . . .

That's when she watches her phone glow at the side of the bed. There are missed calls from Akshay, Smriti, Vinny. They are looking for her. She sends them the same text: **'Was too drunk. Came to Papa.'** And then she switches her phone off.

'I didn't hear you call me Daddy,' says Dhiren in his early morning croaky voice, looking into her phone.

The sexiness of his voice hits Aishwarya with all its unexpected force. Dhiren pulls her into his arms. She would have pushed him away, but he smiles that honest, dreamy smile. It makes her insides melt.

Aishwarya rests her head on his bare chest, still sweaty from a few hours ago when they finished in a heap of limbs and blinding sensations.

Aishwarya shakes her head.

'What happened, baby?' he asks.

She doesn't like it. He shouldn't call her 'baby'. She has grown up hating people who call each other 'baby'. And yet, when he says it, it feels all right. She wants to be his baby, in his arms, safe and warm.

'I'm the worst person in the world right now,' she says wryly. 'Two friends and a boyfriend I sort of agreed to move to the US and have kids with have been looking for me and I have been—'

Dhiren stops her with a kiss. 'It was amazing.'

Aishwarya shakes her head. Last night, when she slipped into his bed, a part of her felt that the next morning they would blame it on the alcohol, that she would be guilty and then they would put everything behind them. But this morning, she's not guilty. Her body wants more. Her body wants all of him, all the time. He's all she wants.

Aishwarya kisses his ear, letting her tongue wander inside. 'That's what makes me a worse person. For enjoying it too much, for wanting it again.'

'Do you want it now?'

'You should be inside me, right now,' she says.

Aishwarya feels him tense up beneath her. His body's a rock, his grip firm. She's reminded of a horse galloping, with all the muscles separating and contracting, and she smiles at the comparison. That's what he felt like last night—like a racehorse, every muscle bred to perform.

She shakes her head. 'There's too much light, I'm too sober and I'm in a pit of self-pity and hate.'

'Pull the curtains, drink a little,' offers Dhiren. 'But I don't share any of your concerns. I'm yours any time you want me. I was always yours, from the first day I saw you. From that day, there's nothing else that I have wanted. Just you.'

Aishwarya smiles sadly. 'This is the full circle. This is where it ends.'

'Full circle? What does that mean?' Dhiren runs circles around her nipples with his finger. 'It's a little difficult for me to solve your riddles when you're naked next to me.'

'My chasing perfection in my life, I thought would end here with you. But what happened last night was as far from perfect as I could get,' she says.

Dhiren doesn't seem to care. He's obsessed with her body right now. She likes him like this—kissing every part of her like he's deriving life force from it.

'That's understood. Sleeping with me is not something one should do, I know,' he says.

'This, right here, is the lowest I can get.'

Aishwarya nuzzles into his neck and starts to kiss him softly. She wants to capture the warmth she's feeling so she can unpack it, relive it whenever she wants. She continues. 'You know what's worse, Dhiren?'

'I can't think of anything worse, Aishwarya, than you telling me that the lowest point in your life is having sex with me. And yet, I don't care. This is the moment I have thought about a million times—you, in my arms, and it's better than I imagined.'

'I don't feel bad about this, that's worse,' she says. 'This feels as though it's me. Like I can be the person who cheats on her boyfriend.'

She looks at him. She knows she's hurting him. But she can't stop. She wants him to push her away because she can't. She wants him.

'What are you thinking, Aishwarya?' he asks, pulling her face into his.

Aishwarya lets his lips linger on hers. She licks them softly, not wanting to part with them.

'Dhiren? Did you feel guilty about what you did? You stole, you ran and you lived with it.'

Dhiren catches her gaze, and it feels to Aishwarya that all the pain in the world resides behind those eyes. He says, 'I felt more guilty about dragging my friend down with me. Neeraj was a nice guy, you know?'

'And you weren't?'

Dhiren shrugs. 'I was damaged, attention-seeking. Sooner or later, I had to screw up. But Neeraj, he didn't have to be a part of all that I did.' He adds after a pause, 'But nothing made me more guilty than having to hide everything from you.'

'Did you have a choice?' she asks.

She has debated this numerous times. There was no place for truth in their relationship. Had she known who he was, she would have never worked with him.

She continues. 'I feel guilty every moment of every waking day. That's all I feel. I am drowning in it every moment. It's so hard to breathe.'

'Baby.'

'Everyone knows it was my fault,' she says, fighting hard to keep her tears from flowing. This is not why she's here. In fact, she doesn't know why she's here. She continues in a soft voice, 'We were a few weeks away from opening that branch. Can you imagine if we had opened . . . so many children would have . . . '

Her voice trails off.

'But it wasn't open. We would have known if the roof was getting weaker by then. It would have never happened,' he says matter-of-factly. 'Is this what you're torturing yourself about?'

He pulls her closer into his embrace.

'There could have been—'

'But there weren't. There are a thousand things that could have happened, but not everything is in our control, Aishwarya.'

'This was in our control,' argues Aishwarya, tears streaming down her face.

Dhiren wipes her tears and runs a hand over her forehead. He kisses her on both cheeks. 'You always thought you could control everything.'

'But I changed,' she says. 'I changed when I met you. The teachers, the second branch. I changed and look what happened. Life taught me a lesson. One that you had been trying to teach me.'

'Me?'

'That life's scary, it's not a fairy tale,' she says. 'You ran after Vihaan and Amritanshu screaming "Monster, Monster." They enjoyed it, they laughed. That's how life is, isn't it? You're scared and yet you know it will pass, so you laugh.'

A sense of recognition flashes through Dhiren's eyes. 'This is why the twisted books. No more positive stories.'

Aishwarya nods.

'And yet, you still have children hanging on to every word of the stories you write. You're lovely, Aishwarya. The children see that. You can't hide that brilliance.'

Aishwarya shrugs. 'But no one has any expectations. How good can a girl be with children when she writes scary stories?'

'The captain of the Indian cricket team thinks otherwise,' says Dhiren.

Aishwarya gets up. She starts to look for her clothes. Sooner or later, her friends are going to call. She needs to get her lies in place.

'Don't go,' says Dhiren and reaches out for her hand. For a few moments, she lets her hand nestle in his. She wants time to stop, this moment to be, just be, to have him looking at her with love and regret, and her body being alive with emotions. She wants to spend the rest of the day naked in bed with him. And then she pulls herself out of it.

'You are going back to him?' asks Dhiren.

'His name's Akshay,' she says. 'And what would you have me do? Would you want me to be with you? The guy who lied and lied and lied? Not just to me but to hundreds before me?'

Dhiren gets up from the bed. He puts on his boxers and his shorts. He walks close to her, holds her hand and tells her, 'I was young, I was stupid. I hadn't met you. I hadn't met anyone for whom I wanted to be a better person, but now I have.'

Aishwarya shakes her head. She can't help him. 'I can't make you better. I can't be responsible for anyone, not you, not those kids.' She looks at him and lets her mind take over her heart. 'I can't. I can't trust you. I have read everything about you since then.'

Aishwarya sees Dhiren's face lose colour. He could have lied to her once, but not any more.

'Adil told me both of you were looking at start-ups to invest in. Whose money is that? If I were to take a guess, both of you would have made a lot of money from investing the money you stole.'

Dhiren doesn't answer her question.

Aishwarya slings her bag over her shoulder. She pulls Dhiren close and kisses him lightly on the cheek. 'It's okay, Dhiren. As I said, this is life.'

'I returned . . .'

'We try to be perfect and life spits back in our face. You, me, we are all the same. We are broken and we try all our lives to fix our fault lines, but we fall and break on the same lines.'

'So? Akshay's perfect?'

Aishwarya shrugs. 'I'm sure he's not, but I have plenty of time to find out.'

She leaves through the window, climbs down the parapet from where she came. But this time, the constables, the neighbours and Neeraj all see her.

54.

Dhiren Das

Neeraj walks straight in after he sees Aishwarya leave. He bombards Dhiren with leery questions about the night before, but Dhiren waves them away.

'Give me till the evening,' he says and closes the door on Neeraj's face.

'YOU THINK THERE'S SOMETHING MORE IMPORTANT THAN YOU HAVING SEX WITH AISHWARYA?!' Neeraj screams from the other side of the door.

Dhiren doesn't answer.

He fires up his laptop. He logs into his crypto wallet. There lies all of the money Dhiren has earned on the appreciation of bitcoin. It has remained untouched since half the payment to the government was made by Neeraj when he was recovering. It's the ill-gotten money Aishwarya was talking about, the money they were supposed to invest in start-ups.

Dhiren logs into his Donate.org account. He splits the money into a few dozen medical cases. It still doesn't put a large dent in the money. For the next hour, he searches and finds various medical crowdsourcing websites and completes the fund requirement. It's more fun than he thought it would be. When he runs out of crowdsourcing websites, he donates to medium-sized, non-politically affiliated, cash-strapped NGOs. Most of them will be shocked at their donations going up 100x in a day. Dhiren feels a rush of blood. Giving away money is exhilarating. Granted, it isn't his money to give away. It takes him six relentless hours to find, research and give away every last rupee that he owns. Once it's done, he leans back in his chair, feeling light and suffering from a mild case of saviour complex.

It happens sooner than Dhiren anticipates. Within an hour of completing the last transaction, Neeraj comes barging into the room.

'WHAT THE FUCK DID YOU JUST DO?!' shouts Neeraj.

Neeraj had taught Dhiren the stages of grief. So Neeraj guesses Dhiren has already been through the stage of denial. This isn't a mistake. Neeraj knows that the transfer of assets is wilful. Dhiren has done it—he has given away every last paisa they earned from Crypto Cricket.

'Something we should have done long ago, man. It was not our money anyway,' answers Dhiren, trying to underplay what he has done.

Neeraj looks like he's going to pass out from the shock and the anger. 'Madarchod, that wasn't your money, it was mine!' he bellows.

'We are brothers, aren't we? You needed us to work together and now we are. Do the other things matter? No. These are your words, not mine.'

'Have you . . .'

'We will make more money,' says Dhiren casually. 'Lots more. Once this game hits people's phones, we will be the hottest—'

'ARE YOU OUT OF YOUR MIND?! How can you sit like that after giving away ALL OF OUR FUCKING MONEY?'

Neeraj's face is flushed red. It looks like he's undergoing a small cardiac arrest. He has to really concentrate to put together a coherent sentence.

'Dhiren, here's what you're going to do. You're going to call these charities you have donated to and you're going ask for the money back. They are charities, so I'm assuming they aren't assholes. Sure, you want to make amends. Do some kind of *prayaschit* [penance] or god knows what you want to do, give them a percentage, but get the fucking money back, bhai!'

'I'm doing nothing of that sort. We don't need that money.'

Dhiren can see Neeraj's fists clenching. He's going to step forward and hit him. It has to happen, Dhiren knows that. He hopes Neeraj does it. Because the money's not coming back.

'*Bhai, bohot pitega, bol raha hoon* [Brother, you will get a good beating for this],' warns Neeraj. 'Do it now or I will kill you.'

'I don't want anything to do with that money.'

'Did she ask you do it?'

'She didn't ask me to do anything.'

'Girls never do. They fucking hint, the bitches,' grumbles Neeraj. 'She asked you do it, didn't she?'

'If you keep talking like that, I'm going to break your head open,' warns Dhiren.

'Talking like what? Calling her a self-righteous *kuttiya* [bitch]? It's the truth, madarchod. First she almost kills you and then makes you give up everything.'

'Neeraj.'

'No, Dhiren. Just because she gave you a blow job . . . that's a fucking expensive blow job, Dhiren. THAT'S THE MOST EXPENSIVE BLOW JOB IN THE WORLD! You . . .'

Before he can finish, Dhiren buries his fist into Neeraj's jaw. The crunch of his teeth against his fingers vibrates through his entire hand. Neeraj buckles away but steadies himself and drives his skull right into Dhiren's chest, knocking the breath out of him. Dhiren stumbles and charges at him, pinning him to the ground.

'RANDI!' Neeraj shouts even as Dhiren rains punches on his face.

Neeraj pulls away and delivers lusty kicks into Dhiren's stomach. The room soon fills with expletives, sprayed blood, saliva and sweat. Twice, they stumble to opposite corners of the room, catch their breath and go at it again. Numerous times both of them feel they have cracked a bone, splintered a rib, punctured a lung, but they still carry on. Dhiren has been in fights before, but this time the pain is significant. They don't stop till they both feel that going at it any longer will end in an accidental death.

'Why?' mumbles Neeraj through his bloodied mouth.

'I need to do anything I can to get her back. *Anything*.'

'Even if it means losing your best friend. You know what? Fuck you. You have always been like this. Your world, you at the centre of it, and whatever you do is right and everyone else can just fuck off.' Neeraj clambers up to his feet and limps towards the door, mumbling 'madarchod' under his breath. He turns towards him. 'Why did you choose her over me?'

'That's what friendship is, Neeraj,' answers Dhiren. 'We leave friends who would die for us for the one we love.'

'Well then, fuck you and fuck your friendship.'

'I don't have energy for another round,' says Dhiren, spitting out the blood from his mouth.

Neeraj wipes the blood dripping from his nose. 'Did she tell you that she didn't get pregnant from the IVF?'

'What?'

Neeraj shakes his head and chuckles sadly. 'She didn't. I called the IVF centre. So ask your self-righteous girl to shove it up her ass! We lost everything. She lost *nothing*.'

55.

Aishwarya Mohan

Aishwarya is in the passenger seat of Akshay's car, swiping through the pictures of their new house in the US. It's just as Akshay had described it—dreamy. And yet, she can't dream of herself in that house. She tries to, but she doesn't see herself there, only him. When Akshay tells her where they can sit and read books, where they can barbeque, have some friends over, the words and situations sound alien to her. *When has she ever barbequed? When has he? Why would they suddenly start doing barbeques on their front lawn? And lawn? Why are they moving to a house with such a huge lawn?*

'I'm speechless,' says Aishwarya, not wanting to lie more than she already has.

'I knew you would like it,' says Akshay and puts his hand on her thigh. If she hadn't known him better, she would have thought this was a move. The guy is literally taking her to his new house thousands of miles away. He can put his hand on her thigh.

'It looks like the kind of house you can live and work in,' adds Aishwarya.

'I will see you in the evening?' he asks, stopping the car near the drop-off. He leans in for a kiss and Aishwarya gives in.

When he drives off, she feels her body burn up with shame, guilt and desire. And yet she knows that at any opportunity she gets, she's going be in Dhiren's arms.

She's not going to fight it. It's what she wants for now.

She has debated this endlessly in her mind, turning the situation in many different ways, justifying it each time.

I'm not a good person.

She's okay with this assessment she has made of herself. She can live with it. What she can't live with is staying away from Dhiren at the moment. All the bad blood aside, she has discovered a desire she didn't think was in her before. For as long as she can remember, sex, though enjoyable, was the means to a goal. But now, she wants his body. And she wants to feel desired, loved, and she's craving to see Dhiren's eyes filled with love and want.

She has made a deal with herself.

She would give in to Dhiren for the next couple of months—and then she would snap all contact the second she left India for the US. She will love Akshay when their life starts in the US, but for now, she needs to be with Dhiren for a few weeks. And why shouldn't she look out for herself? She deserves it, surely. She has had two dreams violently snatched away from her. She deserves a sniff of one. A dream of love, passion and desire.

The more she thinks about it, the sounder the justification gets in her mind.

She gets to the hotel lobby—she is early by a couple of hours by design. She passes by Lara who waves at her. 'All set for the match?' she asks Lara.

Lara starts to limp. 'Out with injury.'

'Get well soon,' says Aishwarya.

'Don't go missing again, Aishwarya,' says Lara. 'Our captain starts to miss you.'

Aishwarya does a mock roll of her eyes.

Lara chuckles. 'No, really, you're an important part of the team now. Don't desert us, okay?'

She nods.

'See you around,' says Lara and walks away.

Aishwarya's going to miss this—being near the team, the stadium, the players waving to her. But it has no place in the bigger picture of her life.

She passes by the kids' room and walks straight towards the game room. She knows Dhiren is in the room by the presence of the constables outside. In the past few days, the constables have let Dhiren loose. Neeraj and he are no longer chained to the desk. There's already enough security in the hotel for them to keep tailing the pair.

She enters the room.

Dhiren immediately looks up from his screen and turns towards her. She doesn't say anything, but he understands.

Because fifteen minutes later when she's in the men's bathroom, hiding in the stall, Dhiren walks in and closes the door behind him.

'What does this mean?' asks Dhiren.

Aishwarya comes out of the stall. She walks to Dhiren and pulls him in for a kiss. She feels as though she has been thirsty for years. She feels like she can breathe again. She follows up by biting his ear. She can tell he likes it by his moans. She says, 'In about two months, I leave for the US and will never see you again. Till then, we are together.'

She first sees anger on his face.

'You're using me,' he says.

'Do you mind?'

It doesn't take him more than a few seconds. 'I love you.'

'It's not a question of love any more,' she says.

'Do I see you every day?'

'It depends on how slowly you work here, how many times you can sneak out and how many times I can sneak into your house. It's purely a logistical question. I want you, Dhiren.'

Dhiren nods dutifully. 'I can make time.'

'You better make time,' she says and runs her fingers across his stubbled face. 'Shave.'

'Anything else?'

She shakes her head.

Dhiren takes out a crumpled piece of paper from his pocket. 'What's that?'

'I'm dead broke,' he answers. 'This is a list of charities and the amounts I have allocated to them. You were right, there was money we made from the stolen money. But it's no longer with us.'

'The game guys have already paid you an advance, so you're not broke,' she says and takes the piece of paper from him.

'You're not wrong,' he says with a chuckle. 'But all that money, it's gone. Wiped clean, fresh start.'

Aishwarya takes the paper from him. She looks at the numbers. For a moment, they seem like a joke to her.

'That's a lot,' notes Aishwarya.

'What can I say? There are good returns in cryptocurrency,' says Dhiren. 'I will mail the document and the report to you. You can have them audited by Smriti. It's legit.'

Aishwarya catches her breath. The amount's not a joke. A city can live off it for years without starving. She folds the paper, looks at him and says, 'And then what? What if it's all true?' She points at the paper. 'We have just over a month. That's our truth, not this. We are beyond this. You could have kept the money.'

And she pulls him in to kiss him once again.

'We are fools, aren't we?' asks Aishwarya.

Dhiren doesn't answer the question because he's already taking her shirt off.

56.

Aishwarya Mohan

Vinny and Smriti look as if they have been slapped.

Lying in front of them is the crumpled piece of paper, the printouts of Dhiren's accounts and the truth of Aishwarya's rendezvous with him. At first they mumbled their questions, the reality not quite sinking in. And now they just look furiously at Aishwarya, as if it was not Dhiren in the bathroom, in his bedroom, but their husbands.

'It's a not a big deal, guys,' she tells them. Like every time someone says it's not a big deal, it almost always is.

'You're fucking him; how the hell is that not a big deal?' explodes Vinny.

'Don't say that,' cuts in Smriti.

'No, let her,' answers Aishwarya. 'Anything else would sound worse. Making love to him? Of course not. It's a secret, and not a pleasant one, so fucking is right.'

Vinny looks at her with what Aishwarya can only discern as disgust.

'I don't recognize who you are right now,' says Vinny. 'This is not you.'

She reaches out and clutches Aishwarya's hand as if she's drowning and only she can save her. Aishwarya smiles back at them as if there's nothing to worry about. She looks at both of them. 'Maybe this is me,' she says. 'Anyway, it's just for a month. In the long run, how does it even matter? When I'm forty, this will be like . . . I won't even remember it.'

Smriti, who's going through the files, remarks, 'This is . . . how can this be right? This is madness. Did he give all of his money away?'

'It wasn't his anyway,' corrects Aishwarya.

'But he didn't have to, that's my point,' argues Smriti.

'Is that the point you're stuck on, Smriti? Like, really?' says Aishwarya. 'Of everything we are talking about, this is what you pick on?'

Smriti says, 'Behen, you're not doing right by Akshay.'

'Says the girl who had wished hell on him when he refused to be the sperm donor. And let me tell you, there were a bunch of times you specifically asked me to dump him.'

'So what is this? Revenge?' asks Smriti.

Vinny throws her hands up in the air. 'Of course it's not revenge. She's horny and she's throwing her life away. That's what this is.'

'I'm not horny,' corrects Aishwarya. 'Not a lot, only a little.'

Vinny leans over and says forcefully, 'Listen, what has happened has happened. This is what you're going to do. We are not going to look at this audit because we don't care about

Dhiren. The decision of going to the US took us by surprise. We couldn't be supportive enough, but we know now it's the right thing. You're going to tell Dhiren it's over, you're not going to tell Akshay about this . . .'

'Vinny's right. What happened with Dhiren and you is going to stay between you and him,' adds Smriti.

Vinny continues. 'You're going to pack your bags and you're never seeing Dhiren, never thinking about him again. You're going to live till a hundred years and die a happy, saggy old woman with fifteen grandchildren. That's what Smriti and I have decided for you.'

'No.'

'What no?' says Smriti.

Aishwarya pushes the bunch of papers back in front of Smriti. 'You're going to tell me how true these transactions are. And you're going to do it soon,' says Aishwarya. 'Maybe he has changed.'

Vinny scoffs. 'So what if he has changed?'

'It will be something I achieved,' she says with a smile. 'With my love, I would have made a criminal give away all of his wealth. Is that not cool?'

'Are you listening to yourself?' asks Vinny.

Aishwarya doesn't answer the question because, from the door of the coffee shop, Akshay is waving to her.

'I need to go, guys,' she tells the two of them. 'Let me know about the audit. And, Vinny, that was a cheap shot. Telling him I lost a pregnancy because of all the stress from Cute Buttons collapsing and from knowing who Dhiren really was. All the time he thought I had a miscarriage because of all the stress.'

Vinny's goes hot in the face. 'It was the only way to keep him away from you, behen.'

'Well, it didn't work,' she says and gets up.

She leaves the coffee shop and goes straight into Akshay's arms.

57.

Dhiren Das

It's been two weeks since Dhiren gave away Neeraj's money. And for every single day of those two weeks, Neeraj has harassed him relentlessly.

It makes no difference to Dhiren.

For the last two weeks, Aishwarya and Dhiren have spent every free moment kissing and caressing and loving each other as if their lives depended on it. At work, Dhiren takes frequent water and bathroom breaks. They have found numerous risk-free rendezvous areas in the hotel, including Kiran's room, though she does insist they call housekeeping after they leave. They have had to change the mattress twice because of the busted springs.

Sometimes they meet at the hotel's three coffee shops and share a long, free cup of coffee billed to the BCCI. At times, she lets his hand rest on hers. And when people turn to look at them, he wants to tell them—like a schoolboy in his first relationship— she's my girlfriend.

Every day, Dhiren adds complexity to the game to stretch things out, which means he needs to stay out longer. And so, Aishwarya and he try out a new restaurant every night. Every once in a while, he carries a change, and so does she. Late evening, they change clothes, she puts on a hint of make-up, he douses himself in cologne, and they dine like a newly engaged couple. More than once, they have been told they look gorgeous together. And they agree. But whenever Dhiren has wanted to click a picture, she says, 'We aren't allowed that. Keep it in your mind and lock it away forever. Who knows, you might even forget it.'

Dhiren knows he's never going to forget her, or the time they are spending. Despite the circumstances, this is the happiest he has ever been. He doesn't wake up feeling choked, or with his heart thumping with anxiety. Some days he feels like he's back at Cute Buttons. Only this time, there are no lies.

And on some mornings, when the game set-up moves to the cricket nets, Dhiren and Aishwarya are the first ones on the field. Aishwarya, in her perfectly fitted jersey, bowls to Dhiren who has got worse at cricket after his accident. After a tiring net session, they share the shower back at the stadium's dressing room.

'Some famous players have been naked in this shower,' Aishwarya points out once.

Dhiren frowns. 'Thank you for putting the image of a naked Sachin Tendulkar in my mind.'

'I can do something to fix that,' she says and soaps his cock.

But of all the things they do, Dhiren likes it best when they are in the kids' room, working on projects together. The repurposed banquet hall looks nothing like it used to be. Aishwarya—with a little bit of help from him—has transformed the area into a children's paradise. There are paint and slime corners, games and bounce corners, there's a small stage for dance performances and even a tiny, wonky golf course.

'Won't you miss all of this when you're gone?' asks Dhiren, pointing to what Aishwarya has built in a few short weeks.

He doesn't ask her if she's going to miss him. Though that's the answer he's looking for. He wants her to tell him that she's going to be miserable for the rest of her life. Because Dhiren knows that's what he will feel.

'I will miss the kids,' she says. 'But I will be free of their responsibility.'

'You like it when you're responsible for them,' argues Dhiren.

Aishwarya shakes her head. 'I don't, not any more.'

'The players are going to miss you,' says Dhiren. *I'm going to miss you. It's going to feel like someone cut out my heart and gave it away.* 'Sonali's obsessed with you,' he adds.

'I'm sure she will find someone else.'

'I love you,' says Dhiren.

Aishwarya lets the moment pass. She never says it back, and Dhiren doesn't care. He loves her, there are no two ways about it. He doesn't want to regret it later that he didn't get to say it. He knows what they are sharing right now is love. What else could it be?

Neeraj knows what it is.

'This is emotional suicide,' says Neeraj one day.

It's that, too. Dhiren knows it's emotional hara-kiri. For both of them. Dhiren knows this month of spending time with each other, letting their hearts feel what they do will destroy them later. But does he care? No.

Neeraj continues. 'And secondly, you told me when you gave the fucking money away that this would bring her back into your life. Now you're saying you guys will fuck for a couple of weeks and that's it? Aren't you like the stupidest madarchod in all of history? How many times will you fuck her? Twenty? Thirty? Fifty? Let's just calculate how much money it is costing both of us per fuck. She will leave you a wreck. I will have to manage you and listen to you mope. I know you won't listen, but cut this thing clean off, cauterize and move the fuck on.'

Neeraj does have a point. It's going to hurt like a bitch when Aishwarya moves away and all he's left with are the memories. Every moment without Aishwarya is going to feel like death.

'So you're saying that the next time I see her, I should tell her that I won't ever see her again because she's going to leave soon and I will be alone and heartbroken?'

Neeraj nods. 'Haan, bhai.'

'That I need to protect myself and for that I'm going to let go of the opportunity to see her a few more times?' Dhiren continues.

'That's exactly I'm saying. Was that so hard to understand . . .'

Dhiren laughs and waves him off. 'If it's emotional suicide, then so be it. I am happy to sign up for a few hundred emotional suicides for a few moments with her.'

'You're useless.'

Just then, the bell rings.

'She's here,' says Dhiren.

The constables don't stop her any more. They know their story—and it helps that Aishwarya has big, wet eyes that can melt a stone, let alone cops. She walks into the room and finds the two of them looking silently at each other. She says with her hands on her waist, 'Is Neeraj asking you to put a stop to what we are doing?'

Both Aishwarya and Dhiren chuckle like kids.

'Fuck you, Aishwarya, and fuck you, Dhiren. You're going to be messed up, and I'm going to send you a text saying *I told you so* every day for the rest of your lives. Be my guests and fuck off,' says Neeraj, walking away to his room and slamming the door behind him.

'I missed you,' says Aishwarya and sashays up to Dhiren. She sits in his lap.

She plants a hungry kiss on his lips.

Dhiren picks her up with ease, takes her to his room and drops her on to the bed. He draws the curtains to his room. Her kurti and jeans are at the foot of the bed. Her arms are behind her, reaching for the hooks of her bra. Dhiren takes off his T-shirt. She throws the bra at him. 'Do you know how expensive bras have become?' she whispers.

'That's exactly what was on my mind,' he says and walks towards her.

Aishwarya reaches out, hooks her finger into his shorts and pulls him close, the shorts slipping down. Her eyes light up at how quickly he has stiffened up. He gets into the bed and she presses her nakedness against him.

'Hmm,' she says.

'By "hmm", do you mean "wow"?' he asks.

'I will have a closer look and let you know,' she says and turns him on his back. She slides down on him.

58.

Dhiren Das

Dhiren slips out of bed to make a cup of tea.

He knows that's what she's going to ask for once she wakes up. For years, he was misled. Movies and memes have led us to believe that pizza and cigarettes are the after-sex snack when it's actually chai and Parle-G. Chai restores the natural taste, Parle-G, your energy. This is hard science. It's a shame Aishwarya has started taking her chai with Sugar Free, which she carries around in her enormous handbag. It's the size of a backpack and carries grocery lists from the early 2000s. He wouldn't be surprised if he finds an anti-aircraft gun inside. He rummages inside it and starts stacking things aside when his hands hit a small container. *Finally*, he says to himself and takes it out. It's not Sugar Free.

It's a medicine: folic acid.

His head starts to thump. Dhiren knows what this medicine is for. He has seen the bottle lying around when he was living with her earlier. Folic acid is prescribed to women who want to get pregnant, and they are asked to start taking it a few months before they start trying.

Dhiren puts the water on to boil, but he's unable to do anything further. His head spins with anger. He can't see reason. He knew this was what he was getting into—to get his heart broken. *Why was he surprised now? Her life wasn't going to be with him. It was going to be with Akshay. And why wouldn't she plan for it?*

How quickly we get used to what life offers! Just a few short weeks ago, *he would have given everything to meet her just once.* Life's been kind. It has given Dhiren a month full of love, desire, tenderness and acceptance. And now he wants more?

He gets back to making the tea. He's not going to broach the topic with her. He leaves her handbag just as he found it. He's going to enjoy the present, be mindful and not rage against things he can't control. He tries to look for some kind of gratitude but finds none.

When she opens her eyes, he says in the calmest voice he can muster, 'You're trying to get pregnant.'

He pours the tea for her in a cup and keeps it on the side table. She doesn't look bothered. As if he wasn't sitting there, his heart bruised and broken.

'Why didn't you tell me?'

She rubs her eyes and answers him coolly, 'I didn't think there was anything to tell you.'

Her nonchalance irritates him. 'No? We are doing this . . . whatever this is . . . while you're trying to get pregnant? What . . . is this some kind of joke?'

Aishwarya takes a small sip. 'There's something off with the tea.'

'I asked you something.'

She looks at him. 'We weren't answerable to each other the last time I checked.' She keeps the cup on the side table. 'Our lives, what happened with us, yes, it's a cruel joke. And again, I don't need to tell you what's happening between Akshay and me. He and I were anyway going to start a family in the future. What part of that did you not get?'

'The part where you don't like him, where you're lying to him while you're naked in my bed.'

She sits up now. There's no longer sleep in her eyes. 'Give me my bra,' she orders.

Dhiren looks around. It's at the foot of the bed. 'Take it yourself.'

Aishwarya gets out of bed and starts to dress. 'Which part of our agreement did you not get?'

'Don't make me say it, Aishwarya,' groans Dhiren, trying to rein in his anger. He wants to punch something.

Aishwarya slips into her jeans and kurti. She ties her hair into a tight knot. 'Tell me, Dhiren. I thought I was quite clear. For any more clarity, I will have to draw a contract.'

'The part where you forgot to mention you would be fucking two guys and one of them gets to cum inside of you.'

'Wow,' scoffs Aishwarya.

'What "wow"? This is—'

'I mean, this is what you want to do? To cum inside me? Is that your overarching desire? To cum inside me because Akshay does so?'

'What if I'm fucking someone else?'

'I won't stop you. Please feel free to do whatever you want to, Dhiren,' she says.

The calmness of her voice is breaking his heart over and over again. *How can this be so normal for her? Does she not know that he loves her? That he would do anything for her?*

'Don't I have the right to know?'

'The last I checked, Dhiren, no, you don't. You don't have a right on me. This is specifically what we decided,' she reminds him.

Dhiren's head is bursting. 'This is fucked up.'

He feels like slamming his head into a wall.

'You're realizing it a bit too late,' says Aishwarya and laughs sadly. 'My friends told me you—'

'Fuck your friends! Just fuck them!' he screams, his spit flying everywhere.

'I'm not going to take that,' says Aishwarya and grabs her handbag. Dhiren reaches out for her hand, but she moves back. She warns him, 'You are not touching me.'

He takes a deep breath because otherwise he thinks his entire body will explode. 'You know what? I don't want to touch you, I don't want to see you, I don't want any fucking thing from you. Just get the fuck out of my house.'

'With pleasure.'

59.

Akshay Gambhir

Akshay has always felt that his boyish looks have gone against him. People think of him as dumb. Which he's absolutely fine with. He uses that to his advantage when the time is right.

And now he has proven it.

Within a few years, he has gone from struggling to keep his company afloat to turning it into one of the most heavily funded mid-range start-ups in India. He has managed to impress the VCs so much that they want him on their company's board rather than have him putting all his efforts into just one start-up.

So despite being that intelligent, does he not know what Aishwarya is doing with him? He does.

A few days ago, he found condoms and folic acid tablets in Aishwarya's bag.

The inference was obvious and yet it tore him apart. It was clear that Aishwarya had made up her mind—she wanted to start a family with Akshay despite her mental health issues at the moment. But at the same time, she had been going out with that guy she had no business being friends with in the first place.

Girls get predictable in love. Show them a hurt puppy on the side of the road and they will rush to help. That's what he—Dhiren—is, a hurt puppy. Boys who behave like hurt, wounded, angry puppies get rejected when the girls turn into women and realize they don't have time for a big, rabid dog.

Sooner or later, Dhiren is going to get rejected and she's going to come straight back to him.

To confirm his suspicions, he dug into Aishwarya's phone—she hasn't changed her password in years—and found texts that proved him right. Did he feel furious? Of course he did. He felt all the emotions of a jilted lover. But then, instead of taking it all out on her, he went to the office therapist and talked it out with him. That's what real men do. Men who are entrusted to build something.

The therapist reminded Akshay of what he felt for Aishwarya and what role she had to play in his life.

The only need for a partner for high-IQ, highly ambitious people like him is to maintain appearances, to network, to take to parties and indulge in small talk before the real talk starts. You need someone who is above-average in looks, good at having sex and raising children, who can host parties, and who should be just independent enough to entertain themselves.

He has been through enough relationships to know that Aishwarya will be good for him. He has hung out with enough venture capitalists to know that the start-up culture has enough drama to not have it at home too. Almost every forty-five-year-old ultra-rich venture capitalist has a conventional family to go back home to. Their wives hang out together, their children become friends and that's how networking works. And who better than Aishwarya, whose life's aim is to be the best mother there has ever been? She will fit in like a dream.

With that thought, he opens a bottle of prescribed Adderall, takes two and waits for the pills to hit. Once they do, he finds his laser-focused mind back again. All the nonsense about Aishwarya and the other guy is relegated to the background.'

60.

Dhiren Das

Dhiren and Neeraj sit in Adil's makeshift office at the Leela. At the centre of the desk lies a phone with a beta version of the game Dhiren and Neeraj have helped Aditi design. Dhiren knows what Adil's going to do. He will admit that the game has potential, but the market is unknown. He will sandwich the good between the bad. It's the golden rule of deal-making. He will do that to drive Dhiren and Neeraj's price down. Dhiren has always loved meetings like this, but not today. His mind is elsewhere. All he can think about is Aishwarya. For the past few days, all his apologies have met with a dead end. He blew the only chance he had. When he replays the fight in his mind, he feels idiotic. He doesn't care what she does when she's not with him. All that matters is her, them and that moment. And when he reaches this realization repeatedly, he feels lighter, like a changed person. Someone who can surrender, be allowed to be hurt, to feel, to empathize and to look beyond himself. He thinks for the first time that maybe he's nice, and that it might not be a foolish thing to be.

Adil minces no words and states quite bluntly, 'We love the game. It needs work, a lot of tweaking, marketing, but—'

'Cut to the chase, Adil,' interrupts Dhiren.

Adil nods. He leans forward and says, 'We need you on board for a year. The IPL, the World Cup, other tournaments, you have to do it all. And I don't know how you dealt with others, but don't negotiate with me. Whatever price you're thinking about, I will double it to save us both time.'

Adil looks at Dhiren for an answer.

'Adil. It might not be enough for us,' says Dhiren after a pause. 'See, both of us, we have nothing to lose. We have made cricket games before and we have proved that we can make them work.'

Dhiren watches Adil squirm in his seat.

'BCCI won't sell cricketer names and likenesses to you,' warns Adil. 'Your game is going to be with random player names.'

'BCCI won't, but the other cricket boards might. Custom players will face off against—'

'What do you want?' interrupts Adil.

'Do you know Aishwarya is leaving the country in a couple of weeks?' asks Dhiren.

Adil's face slowly goes into shock. 'What?'

'She is moving with her boyfriend to the US,' informs Dhiren.

'Isn't she . . .' Adil makes a fucking sign with his fingers.

'That's unprofessional,' points out Neeraj.

Adil waves Neeraj off. 'She can't go, of course, the team needs her here.'

'Everything's falling into place then,' says Neeraj and rubs his hands in delight.

'Drink some water and keep drinking, Neeraj, till we stop talking,' says Adil. He turns to Dhiren. 'The team's already in talks with the board to offer her a contract. She's leaving? Why wouldn't she tell me that?'

'You will try to stop her, maybe that's why,' says Dhiren. 'Anyway, here's what I'm thinking. You lock her into a contract, make her stay with the team and I will work with you for whatever price you pay.'

Neeraj frowns at the last part. He interjects, 'By "whatever" he means whatever price we want.'

'This is not a *sabzi mandi* [vegetable market], okay, babu,' says Adil. 'The team *loves* her, but that can't be a rider.'

'It is now,' says Dhiren.

'Let's talk about monies instead, yes?' offers Adil and reaches out for a pad.

'I don't need money,' says Dhiren.

'We need money, bhai,' argues Neeraj.

'Aren't both of you under house arrest because of it?' scoffs Adil. 'Why the fuck did you reform? Take the money. Look, I'm telling you I will pay her the world to make her stay. She has a great impact on the team, but . . .'

'Then make it happen, Adil,' says Dhiren and gets up.

'We will still take the money,' adds Neeraj.

'This is stupid,' says Adil. He gets up and comes across to face Dhiren. 'It's not in my hands, but this is a great opportunity for—'

'I don't care, Adil,' declares Dhiren.

He starts to walk towards the door.

'I will make him understand,' butts in Neeraj. 'You can try whatever you can, Adil bhai. Regardless, we will sign up with you.'

Adil throws his hands up in despair. As the two of them are walking out, he mocks, 'Anything else you want me to fucking do?'

Dhiren stops. 'Just one more thing . . .'

61.

Aishwarya Mohan

Adil: Two more minutes.
Adil: Another two.
Adil: Sorry, stuck somewhere. Give me ten minutes.

Aishwarya's patience is wearing thin. She wants to submit her resignation letter, end this pain once and for all and run away.

The more she stays in the office, the more she's inclined to go straight to Dhiren. Despite of what he said the other day. She needs to take the big step, cut off the gangrene that is Dhiren.

There's a knock on the door.

'You don't have to knock. It's your room,' says Aishwarya.

It's Adil's assistant.

'Adil Sir has sent this,' she says and gives her a cell phone. On the cell phone is a Post-it saying, 'For your eyes only.'

'When's he coming?' Aishwarya asks.

'Adil Sir has said this is still in beta, so don't show it to anyone who's not a part of the team,' says Adil's assistant and leaves.

Aishwarya unlocks the phone. There's only one app on the phone—it's named *Superover*. She fires it up and it takes her straight to the game—Dhiren's game. She's asked to choose a player, and she chooses Sonali Raj. The interface is a little glitchy and she has to restart the game to make it work. When it does work, the gameplay's beautiful. She loses the first game and the second and the third. But by the fourth game, she starts to get the hang of it. She knows what touches to make, how to change orientations of the batsmen and bowlers, and what shots to play. Before long, she's levelled up and is on her twentieth game. When she looks at the time, half an hour has passed by and she's neck-deep into the game, not wanting to stop. She exits the game. The exit credit starts to flash. In a small font in a corner she reads the words: Made by Dhiren Das and Neeraj Kothari.

'They know how to make a game, don't they?'

Aishwarya is startled.

She turns to see Adil looking over her shoulder.

'How long have you been here?'

'Long enough to know that you like the game,' he says. 'It's going to get better. You should have played Crypto Cricket, addictive as fuck. These guys are talented, man. Anyway, that's not what we are here for. Can I take the phone? Can't have it leaked.'

'I don't know anyone to leak this to.'

'So we are here for—'

'Because I wanted to talk to you about something,' she says.

'I don't care,' interjects Adil. 'You're here because I wanted to talk to you about something, or I would have turned down your request because, babu, I have a crazy, crazy day today.'

Just then, his phone rings.

'I need to take this,' he says. 'Hello? Listen, listen. I have talked to Sonali and she's not budging. She's going to announce that the World Cup is her last series after the next match . . . hmmm . . . I get it . . . I get it . . . it doesn't matter if we lose or win . . . I understand it's a bad look . . . no, she doesn't care . . . okay, bye.'

He turns to Aishwarya, 'So?'

'She's retiring for sure?'

'Don't tell anyone. We are trying to tell her to wait for us to win a match and then do it, but she wants to announce it after the next match.'

'Why?' asks Aishwarya. 'She told me she would, but I didn't think she would do it this soon.'

'She wants to get it out of the way and play the rest of the series and the World Cup with an open mind. We are trying to convince her, but let's see.'

Adil's voice doesn't have the zip it usually does. Sonali's absence will be a gaping hole. But what does Aishwarya care? She has a life to build, away from here.

Adil shakes the sadness from his eyes. 'So . . .' He smiles, stares at her and starts to nod. 'Do you know what's going to happen? I'm going to make your day, today, Aishwarya. I want you to remember this moment forever.'

'Adil, before you . . .'

Adil waves her down. 'So, I had to really push the board for this. We want to offer you a BCCI contract for the next two seasons. I know, it's exciting, but hold on for a second, because this is going to blow your mind to bits. So a women's IPL is starting just after the World Cup and it's going to be at the same time as the men's IPL. Same teams, same venues, back to back, it's going to be amazing! It's going to be FUCKING AMAZING!'

'What's that got to do with me?'

Adil laughs. 'You're so cute. I have no idea how you were going to do business on your own! Listen, we are going to have nine teams. Thirty players in both teams during a match, so we will need someone like you to herd the kids along. We need the teams' kid whisperer! And that's you! Of course, we know you can't be at nine places at once, so you will be a trainer who will recruit and train people like you.'

'I—'

'And that, by the way, is just the IPL.'

'Adil, you need to listen—'

'I'm not finished yet,' says Adil. 'After the IPL, you will also travel with the team overseas on tours. I feel like I'm a fairy godmother to you,' says Adil. 'You owe me like a million bucks. Damn. Just telling you this is giving me goosebumps. I can only imagine what you're going through.'

'I am going through a lot actually.'

'There's more good news,' says Adil. 'Not a godmother, I feel like a god to you. Like a literal god who can fulfil all your wishes. The guy you're fucking, Dhiren, he's getting a gaming contract with BCCI too.'

'So?'

'He's going to make games for every tournament and will travel with the team. Imagine your workplace romance or torrid affair, whatever you're calling it.'

'We are calling it nothing.'

'Nothing? Hmm. That works too. You're in a nothing with him. Nice, we should make that a thing,' says Adil. 'Because he's deeply in *nothing* with you.'

'I have nothing to do with him,' retorts Aishwarya.

Adil laughs. 'Sure.' He unlocks the phone, taps a few buttons and slips it in front of her. 'Then explain this.'

'What's this?'

'An extra feature of the game,' says Adil. 'You either play with established players, or you choose a rookie. Surprisingly, the rookie is named Aishwarya and looks *exactly* like you.'

Aishwarya picks up the phone. When she taps on *'Rookie'*, an animated version of her appears on the screen. *Aishwarya Mohan, Right-Handed Batsman, Leg Spin Chinaman, Team India.*

Aishwarya's heart jumps.

Adil continues. 'It was Sonali and Dhiren's idea. I opposed it, but it seems like you had both of them eating out of your palm.'

Adil gets up from his chair.

'I came here to quit.'

Adil starts to laugh. 'Yeah, right!' He takes the phone away from her. 'Of course.' Just then, his phone starts to ring. 'I will catch you later. If you ever want to touch my feet, please feel free to do so. Bye!'

And he walks out of the room.

62.

Dhiren Das

The doors at the Leela are heavy and soundproof. Dhiren can't make out what Adil has told Aishwarya, but he has a fair idea.

When Adil leaves the room, Dhiren is waiting for him.

'Did you convince her?' asks Dhiren impatiently.

'I'm a liaisons guy, not a hypnotist,' retorts Adil. 'And unlike you, I have work to do.'

Minutes after Adil walks away, Aishwarya opens the door and walks out. And just like that, Dhiren's breath becomes shallow and his heart feels like it's sunk to his knees. *How can he still have such irritant butterflies in his stomach after all this time?*

'I don't want to talk to you,' warns Aishwarya the moment she sees him.

Dhiren follows her as she walks away from him. 'Hey? Hey? I'm sorry. I just . . . I just lost it for a moment. It's wholly on me.'

Aishwarya stops. She looks at him with her big, sad eyes. 'It's on me as well,' she sighs.

'Dr Kalpesh is on a holiday and the kitchen is all mine to use. I can quickly make some pakoras and we can decide whose fault it is.' He watches Aishwarya waver. He ramps up his offer, 'And, of course, chai. I didn't see Adil's assistant offer you any.'

Twenty minutes later, they are in the kitchen. Dhiren's pouring everything into cooking the most perfect pakoras he can.

'It's not going to make me stay,' says Aishwarya, after noticing the effort. 'I have made up my mind. Akshay's my future. You're—'

'Taste this,' says Dhiren. He stretches out his hand with a small pyaaz pakora in it. 'Do you like it?'

Aishwarya shrugs but immediately reaches out for another one.

Dhiren continues. 'You are your future. The question isn't about me or Akshay. I understand he's the perfect guy. His skin's too smooth and he's irritatingly well-spoken, but that's not the point.'

'You stalked him?'

'Don't use the term loosely. I googled him. He's all over the place,' grumbles Dhiren. 'Anyway, you know this is the opportunity of a lifetime.'

'Is it? Is this the opportunity of a lifetime?' mocks Aishwarya.

Dhiren knows he misspoke. Nothing other than Cute Buttons is the opportunity of a lifetime for Aishwarya. Everything else is a pale second.

'It's not a bad second,' corrects Dhiren.

'You know what—'

'I know,' cuts in Dhiren sharply. 'What happened, happened. And you weren't the only one at fault. I was, too. And so was that asshole Kamlesh and the generator guys. There are plenty of fucking buildings with generators right where we kept it.'

The roof should have been strong enough to hold it. He knows that from the numerous calls he has made to the thekedars and builders.

Dhiren continues. 'Everyone makes a mistake. We are allowed to. That's what we are; we are imperfect, flawed people. And let me tell you, Aishwarya, you're the closest to being perfect as there could ever be.'

'Not close enough,' she says softly.

Dhiren wants to reach out and hold her face. He wants to hold her and tell her she's the most beautiful, loving, perfect person he has ever met. He wants to show her what he sees in her, what everyone else sees in her.

Aishwarya continues. 'We can't leave behind the things we did. They cling to us for life.'

'Maybe we should,' urges Dhiren. 'What if forgiveness was a legitimate option? Forgiving ourselves and forgiving others. Instagram poets keep harping on about its power. It can't all be for nothing. Maybe we don't have to carry the guilt and the anger for the rest of our lives. And god knows both you and I have lugged the weight around for a long time. Just try to imagine it. Have you never thought about what would happen if your mother talked to you? Or if you forgave her?'

Aishwarya laughs. 'Yes, right. Did you forgive your parents, Dhiren?'

'I'm trying to,' he says.

'You're a liar.'

Dhiren takes out his phone and holds it out to Aishwarya. Open on the phone is the WhatsApp chat group between his parents and him. Aishwarya takes the phone and swipes through their conversation.

Dhiren knows his parents and he are never going to be *fine*. They won't be like the others, but they can be their own thing with their own level of expectations, love and attachment. It would be a relationship they would decide on. A little cold, a little staid, but a relationship nonetheless. A relationship between imperfect parents and their imperfect son.

'How do you even forgive them?' she asks, looking at Dhiren.

'Mumma-Papa had me when they were the age I am now,' admits Dhiren. 'Look at me. Do you think I'm capable of having a child? I'm under house arrest for stealing, I'm talking to a girl who I love but she's leaving, and I have no idea what my future holds.'

'You're capable, Dhiren,' says Aishwarya.

Dhiren takes a deep breath. Hesitantly, he says, 'I have forgiven myself too. For all that I did.'

Aishwarya doesn't say anything. He wishes she would.

He continues. 'I had it all wrong. I was angry with everyone because I thought I had been dealt bad cards in life. I wanted everyone to love me and I wanted to reject their love. But I miscalculated. I rejected my own love. I hated myself.'

'And you don't now?'

'Not a lot. I'm an okay person, I think. I have the potential to be a good one too,' he answers. 'So imagine, if this is my assessment of myself, you're like a goddess.'

He moves close to her and holds her hands. She looks up at him, eyes brimming and fingers trembling. He holds her face and she lets it rest on his palms.

'Dhiren.'

'Aishwarya . . .'

'I can't do this.' She jerks away.

'Aishwarya? Listen to . . .'

Aishwarya has already turned away. She walks out of the door without once turning back. Dhiren's hands are frozen in mid-air, wet with Aishwarya's tears.

63.

Aishwarya Mohan

It's the third time Dhiren has called today, and it's the third time she has cut his call.

She's no longer angry with him. She's angry with herself. She allowed herself to get this deep. Taking care of the cricketers' kids and Dhiren—both were supposed to be a stopgap.

They were supposed to be like the last lines of cocaine, the last heroin hit for a drug addict. Just once and done. But now she's angry because she has found herself addicted again. Hooked to Dhiren's love, his want of her and the love of the children. When she's not playing the game Dhiren created, she's thinking of Sonali's daughter, about Lara's son, about Gitika's twins. She finds herself worrying about how these players will manage the World Cup and the IPL. Especially after Sonali retires and they find themselves grappling with the new team dynamics. As the time bears down for her to leave, she's torn. The choice was so simple just a wink of time ago. Either choose a life of uncertainty and anxiety or start afresh.

At times, she feels like she's cheating Adil and all the mothers who entrust her with their children. She shouldn't stay back, but she wants to. She shouldn't want to meet Dhiren, hold him and kiss him endlessly, but she wants to. She wants to break the promises she had made after the accident: stay away from children, from Dhiren, and stop being so naïve. And here she finds herself again, like a dumb person, wanting to stay away from a safe life, a safe love offered by Akshay.

'Are you okay, beti?' asks the driver.

Aishwarya nods.

But, of course, she's not. It's been a week and she's still dilly-dallying about her resignation. But today, she's going to do it. She has to find the courage to quit everything and go with the plan—Akshay and life in the US.

'Nervous about the match, beti?' asks the driver.

'A little.'

It's a tense day for everyone connected to the team. India is 3–0 down, and regardless of the result, Sonali Raj is going to announce her retirement from international cricket at the post-match conference. Everyone's hoping for a win, as it befits someone like her. But everyone knows India's poised for another drubbing.

Her phone rings just as she gets out of the car.

'Are you doing okay?' asks Akshay.

'As okay as I can be. Adil's going to flip when I tell him about the resignation,' she says.

'Do it after the match. Everyone's going to be too busy tackling the ripple effects of Sonali's resignation.'

That's probably the only silver lining in all of this. She had been worrying about disappointing her hero by running away. But does it matter when Sonali herself is leaving cricket behind?

When she reaches the VIP box, the children light up. She asks them how they are, and each of them breathlessly tells her what they did in the past week. The nannies and the fathers who were hovering over their children walk to the seating outside to watch the match, feeling relieved that she's here.

'What are we going to read today?' she asks.

'THE TORTOISE AND THE HARE!' says Kriti.

'Sure!' says Aishwarya. 'But before that, can we check what's happening in the match outside? We shall make a single file and then go outside and see, okay?'

They all nod and make a single file behind her. She leads them outside and makes them sit. England has chosen to bat and they are now in the eighth over. Aishwarya squints at the scoreboard.

Adil turns around from the row in front. He looks like someone has slapped him. 'We are fucked. We are so fucked.'

England is 160 for 0 after ten overs.

Adil continues. 'This is going to be the worst fucking loss in the history of T20.'

'Language,' says Aishwarya as she notices a few children turn to look at Adil. She turns towards the children and says, 'Should we go inside, guys? We will come back later.'

The children dutifully listen. As she walks inside, she feels a dull pain in her heart for the team, and for Sonali Raj who looks listless and haggard on the field.

Even though she tells the story of the tortoise and the hare the best she can, her heart's with the team. There's pin-drop silence in the stadium packed with 15,000 people. All she can hear is the cracking sound of the bat against the ball repeatedly over the TV screen at the other end of the lounge. The English batsmen have made mincemeat out of the Indian bowlers yet again. The older children who understand the game shake their heads in embarrassment. She tries her best to engage and distract them.

The innings end with a record total of 329 for India to chase.

It's 9 p.m. It's time for the children to go back to the hotel with their fathers and the nannies. Aishwarya forms a single file again and hands over every child to the respective caretakers. Kriti is the last to leave. She hugs Aishwarya.

'Mumma's going to lose today's match, isn't she?' Kriti whispers in Aishwarya's ear.

'She's going to do the best she can,' answers Aishwarya.

'She tells me she will announce today that she will stop playing this year.'

Aishwarya holds her hand. 'Your mother is the GOAT. You know what that means? Greatest Of All Time. If anyone can do it, it's her,' says Aishwarya. 'Now go along, you don't want to miss the bus.'

'Bye, ma'am,' she says.

Once the children have left, the box is enveloped in a funereal gloom. Aishwarya plops some food on to her plate, but she can't bear to eat it. She sits outside and watches the English team practise their fielding.

Adil comes and sits next to her. 'Sonali's going to be crushed.' He looks dejectedly at the field, as if someone has sucked the life force out of him. 'They used to call Chris Gayle the Sonali Raj of men's cricket. Just a couple of more years and she could have transformed the game, Aishwarya. If only that asshole . . .'

Of all the time Aishwarya has spent with the team, not once has anyone mentioned Sonali's ex-husband. He had abandoned her soon after their daughter was born.

'Ask her to stay on,' says Aishwarya. 'You can convince god himself to turn into an atheist.'

Adil shakes his head. 'And then what? Her game's become garbage after that nuisance was born.'

'Hey, behave.'

'She worries too much about Kriti—what's she eating, what's she doing, is she happy, is she taken care of. She's obsessed and constantly worried. How will she concentrate on the game when that keeps playing on her mind? We had three therapists talk to her, but it has not helped. Quitting is the only option she sees now. It's stupid. She can't hover around her daughter all her life.'

'Do you want kids, Adil?'

'Three at least,' answers Adil. 'But I don't want to take care of them. I want to have enough money to have help and then enjoy all the unconditional love they shower. That's my plan.'

'That's a good plan. We—'

'AISHWARYA!' she hears a scream.

'What—'

She has heard this scream in her dreams numerous times. Sometimes she has imagined it willingly. It's the sort of inhuman wail that signals the worst, most painful kind of occurrence— danger to a child. She jumps out of her seat and runs towards the scream. At the entrance of the box, a nanny is screaming and is in tears.

'KRITI!' she screams.

Before she can say anything, Aishwarya is sprinting to where the children board the bus to the hotel.

'CALL AN AMBULANCE!' she shouts to no one, but the shout is well-heard for everyone around to frenziedly take out their phones.

Adil runs after her, but he's left far behind. Aishwarya spots a line at the lift, so she turns left and jumps down the two flights of stairs.

At a distance, she sees the crowd gathering and shouts, 'GET OUT OF THE WAY!' The crowd separates and she sees Kriti bent over, choking, her nanny weakly tapping her back. Kriti's going blue in the face; her body's limp.

'*HATO* [MOVE]!' she shouts and pushes the nanny away, who stumbles to the ground.

'I'm here,' says Aishwarya and grabs Kriti from behind.

Holding her arms tight against the little girl's stomach, she pushes it inwards and upwards. Kriti's still choking, her face is turning cold. Her eyes have started to roll over. Aishwarya unclenches her hands and gives five sharp blows to the middle of Kriti's shoulders. Kriti's slowly losing consciousness. Aishwarya can hear the gasps, cries and pleas in the background. The women and children have started crying.

A man comes forward, 'Let me—'

'STAY THE FUCK AWAY.'

Aishwarya clasps Kriti again and holds her tighter and sharper, but it doesn't help. Without missing a beat, she gives five quick blows again.

'Stay with me, stay with me, stay with me,' she keeps muttering to Kriti who's far away now.

'Kriti, you can do this.' She holds her arms around the little girl again and pushes. She does the count again. 'One. Two. Three . . .'

And there it is.

A piece of candy pops out of Kriti's mouth. Kriti rolls over gasping. Rivulets of saliva drip from her face. Her eyes are bloodshot and she bursts out crying. Aishwarya takes Kriti in her arms and kisses her all over her face, 'It's fine, everything is fine, everything is fine. It's over, it's fine. I'm here.'

She doesn't notice it but tears are streaming down her face too. She holds Kriti and keeps rocking her till both Kriti and she stop crying. Then she kisses Kriti's face again and Kriti kisses her back. 'Don't ever do that,' Aishwarya mumbles into her ear and plants another kiss on her face. She keeps holding her close, feeling Kriti's heart against hers.

Just then, the ground vibrates with twenty pairs of cricket studs slamming against it.

'Kriti!'

Sonali Raj is running towards Aishwarya, her team behind her. Seeing her mother, Kriti squirms out of Aishwarya's arms and runs to her. Sonali, now wailing, kisses Kriti non-stop, even as Kriti breathlessly tells her how Aishwarya saved her.

'I couldn't breathe, Mumma, I couldn't breathe! She saved me! She held me from the back and she saved me!'

Adil comes running with a battery of security guards and clears the entire area. He shouts a warning that even if one ten-second video of the entire thing is released, he will personally come and destroy the person's entire family.

With military efficiency, Sonali, Kriti, Adil and Aishwarya are escorted to an empty conference room while the rest of the team heads back to the dressing room. The team's doctor checks on Kriti. The doctor tells Sonali, who hasn't stopped weeping, that Kriti is fine, and that it was a standard choking incident.

'Nothing about this is standard, doctor,' Adil snaps.

'Good work,' the doctor tells Aishwarya before leaving them alone.

There's a deathly silence in the room. Kriti is sitting on Sonali's lap. She has held her daughter tightly, as if she will fly away if her grip loosens.

Adil turns to Sonali and says in the softest tone Aishwarya has ever heard him use, 'I have delayed the innings start by half an hour citing security concerns. That's the best I can do.'

Sonali shakes her head. 'I'm not going out there,' she says hugging Kriti tighter, as if she would disintegrate. 'I'm done, Adil. Tell them I'm hurt.'

'We are going to lose,' warns Adil.

Sonali shoots him a murderous look. 'We are going to lose anyway.'

'But—'

Sonali stops him. 'I'm quitting today. I don't want to play the World Cup. Change the press release. I'm done with cricket. I can't stay away from her. It's final, don't argue with me on this.'

'What are you saying, Sonali? You can't—'

'I can!' Sonali thunders. 'Just tell them I am quitting today. Either you tell them or I will tweet right now that I'm done. How you want to do it is your call.'

Aishwarya has never seen Adil run out of words, but now she does. She looks at Sonali. If fear had a face, that would be how Sonali looks right now. Aishwarya walks up to the daughter and mother and sits near Sonali's feet. She reaches out for Kriti's face and caresses it.

'Let's think about it once,' says Aishwarya.

Sonali shakes her head. 'What if something happened today? I can't have Kriti grow up thinking I didn't have time for her. I don't want to be a bad mother.'

'She will not think that.'

'What if she does? What if she never forgives me for continuing to play cricket while she's growing up? She's too little to say anything now, but what if tomorrow she looks back at all of this and . . .'

Aishwarya doesn't answer.

'Have you forgiven your mother?' asks Sonali, her eyes welling up.

Aishwarya turns to look at Adil who raises his hands and mumbles, 'We just guessed during the background check.'

Aishwarya turns to Sonali, 'I will. Eventually.' She reaches out and holds Kriti's hand. 'Kriti, will you stay with me for a little bit?'

Kriti nods enthusiastically.

'No,' cuts in Sonali sharply.

Aishwarya holds Kriti's face and says conspiratorially, 'Am I asking your mother or am I asking you?'

'You're asking me!' giggles Kriti.

Aishwarya smiles and kisses Kriti's hand. She turns to Sonali and says, 'Sonali, I'm here for her. As someone who has looked up to you, I want you to be there on the field, for the girls, for the country. It's your legacy.'

'She's my legacy,' answers Sonali and holds Kriti tighter.

Adil rolls his eyes and blurts out, 'Everyone has a child, Sonali, almost every one. That's how this country got to a billion people.'

'Shut up, Adil,' growls Aishwarya.

Adil doesn't listen. 'But not everyone gets to where you are. You can't just quit right now. And she's there . . . look at her!' He points at Aishwarya. 'She will keep Kriti safer than you can! No offence, but this girl here is the Pied Piper.'

Aishwarya butts in, 'Adil's right. If I could, I would go in there and win this impossible match. I would change the history of the game by winning the World Cup too. But I can't. You know what I can do, Sonali?' Aishwarya holds Kriti's hand and loosens Sonali's grip around her. She pulls Kriti towards herself.

Aishwarya continues. 'I can do the second-best thing. I can help you create history. Kriti?'

'Yes, ma'am?'

'You know what we will do when your mother bats?'

Kriti's eyes light up. 'What?'

'We will play with slime. But you know how playing with slime gets better? It gets better when I tell the story of the dragon who melted down an entire mountain to give us the first slime in the world!'

Kriti squeals. 'Dragon slime?'

Aishwarya turns to Sonali. 'Can you tell her the story of the dragon?'

'Mumma is such a bad storyteller!' giggles Kriti.

'But she's the greatest batsman in the world.' Aishwarya picks up Kriti and tells Sonali, 'I'm here for her. Go out there and win that match. At the press conference, tell everyone you're going to play for another ten years because cricket defines you. When you walk off the field, I will give you your daughter, safe and sound. You can whisper your stats in her ear and she will remember every one of them as she grows up. Let's do things that we are good at, yes?'

Sonali wipes her tears. 'You're here today. What about tomorrow?'

Adil butts in, 'We will lock her in with a contract. Bonded labour. We will destroy her if she tries leaving the cricket board. Don't worry, I will take care of it. We will burn her passport or something.'

'Nice,' says Aishwarya.

Sonali gets up from the chair and looks at Adil and Aishwarya. She takes a deep breath. 'It seems that I will have to pad up?'

'FUCK YES!' says Adil and pumps his fists.

'Language,' warns Aishwarya.

'What's fuck?' asks Kriti.

For the next three hours, while Kriti listens to the story of the dragon that melted down an entire mountain, Sonali flips a switch on the ground. She picks apart and devours England's bowling attack. A record nineteen balls are hit out of the stadium, three are smashed into the press box and two hit the LED screens, causing them to short-circuit and shut down. There's pin-drop silence because in the ninety minutes that Sonali Raj bats, she burns and buries the careers of the entire English bowling attack. It's as if she is playing against schoolchildren.

India wins with three overs to spare.

When Sonali walks back to the pavilion, she raises the bat first at Aishwarya—who's in the stands, Kriti sleeping in her lap—and then the rest of her teammates. The team watches with bated breath as Sonali is called for the post-match conference. She tells the interviewer that the win was a team effort, that it's good to be back among runs, that the pitch responded well, and that she thanks her teammates, Aishwarya and the other support staff for this win. When the interviewer asks about her retirement, she answers, 'As you said, those are rumours. I have a few years under my belt, don't you think?'

A huge cry resounds from the stands and from her own teammates. She's carried off the field by the entire team. The celebrations are wild. It's as if they didn't win a match but the World Cup itself. When the celebration ends, Adil, in an uncharacteristically benevolent move, offers to drop Aishwarya home.

They have just left the stadium when Adil says, 'I'm going to lock you in an ironclad contract. I'm going to pay you so much that IT officials will plan to conduct raids. So much that you will be able to fix matches if you want. But don't do that, okay?'

'What I said in there was to get her to bat and keep playing. You can find many like me. Like you said with the IPL, you will need many. I'm immaterial.'

'No one's quite like you. What you did today was extraordinary. It should be obvious to you.'

Just then, Aishwarya's phone rings. It's Smriti.

'Hello?'

'It's as you suspected,' says Smriti.

'About what?'

'Dhiren. Who else? He has been funnelling funds out to another account. Small portions, but overall it's considerable. We were right . . . he's still—'

'A fraud,' completes Aishwarya. She can't hear her own voice over the sound of her heart breaking.

'No,' says Smriti.

'What? What do you mean?'

'The money . . . it's gone to an account I have seen before,' says Smriti. 'I checked my records. It's Kamlesh's.'

'Why would he . . .' Aishwarya's voice trails off as her stomach starts to churn. 'Hey? I will call you back.'

'Stop the car,' she tells Adil.

'What . . .'

'Stop the car!'

Adil swerves to the left and parks.

Aishwarya stumbles out. Her head's spinning. And just then, everything she had eaten bubbles at the back of her throat. She tries to keep it down and fails. She vomits all over the pavement.

Adil comes running out of the car. He pats her back and gives her water. 'Are you okay?'

Aishwarya washes her face. She takes a big swig from the bottle. Wiping her mouth, she says, 'No, I don't think so. I need you to take me somewhere.'

64.

Aishwarya Mohan

'What the fuck am I doing here?' says Adil from the other side of the curtain.

'Shut up, Adil,' mumbles Aishwarya.

The cold air of the doctor's room is making Aishwarya nervous. She doesn't want Adil to add to it.

'Doctor?' says Adil. 'When can we leave? I don't think Aishwarya has told you, but my time is . . .'

The doctor looks at Aishwarya and gives her a silent nod. 'See, do you see there?' she asks. Aishwarya nods, barely able to suppress her tears. The doctor swivels her probe. The images on the screen shift. The doctor has a small smile on her face. Aishwarya turns to look at the screen too. It looks exactly as she has seen in the YouTube videos bookmarked in her app.

The doctor points to the screen. 'That little dot you see there, that's the heart of your baby. It's about six and a half, seven weeks old. Our guess was correct. You're pregnant, Aishwarya.'

'Thank you, doctor,' mutters Aishwarya, barely able to speak. She feels stupid to be crying so openly. The doctor must see scores of women come here and find out they are pregnant. It's no big deal for her.

The doctor removes the probe and takes off her gloves. 'You can dress up now. I will be outside.' She pulls the curtain and walks out.

As Aishwarya dresses up, she hears the doctor talk to Adil. 'You're the father?'

'I would rather slit my wrists,' retorts Adil. 'She's pregnant? Like, really pregnant?'

'That's what we were testing,' says the doctor, a little surprised. 'And what does "really pregnant" mean?'

Aishwarya pulls back the curtain and sits on the chair in front of the doctor. 'He's just a friend, doctor. So, what do we have to do now?'

'I think I can go home,' says Adil. 'I don't know why she got me here.'

The doctor ignores Adil and addresses Aishwarya. 'Nothing for now. Go back home, keep taking folic acid. I will give you a list of dos and don'ts, just follow that. Come back in twelve weeks and we will do some tests then.'

'Thank you, doctor,' says Aishwarya, getting up.

Adil marches out of the doctor's room. Aishwarya is slower, her head spinning with possibilities. Once outside, she finds a chair, sits and buries her head in her hands. Adil, who has been itching to leave, spots her and comes back. He pulls up a chair and sits next to her.

'Look, Aishwarya. You don't have to cry. There are easy ways to terminate the pregnan—'

Aishwarya looks up and slaps Adil on the arm. 'Are you crazy? It's everything I ever wanted! These are tears of happiness!'

'Ew.'

'It's my child, don't say "*ew*",' she says, half laughing and half crying. She lunges at Adil and hugs him.

'I don't know what I'm doing here though,' remarks Adil. 'Don't you have any friends?'

Aishwarya wipes her tears. 'I can't tell them.'

'You will have to when you grow fat and ugly.'

Aishwarya smiles. Her hands slip to her stomach. *My child*, she whispers to herself. She looks at Adil and says, 'Not yet.'

'Then?'

'We need to tell the father first.'

Adil raises his hand. 'You used the word "we". *We* are doing nothing. *You* are going to do whatever you need to do, but I'm out of this.'

He gets up and walks towards the door.

Aishwarya keeps sitting there, deep in disbelief. She always knew her time would come. But now, it's here. She has her own little family. Her and her baby. She's . . . happy. She's just . . . happy. How long has it been since she felt that?

All the fear she felt in her mind evaporates instantly.

She searches inside herself and there's absolutely no fucking doubt in her mind that she will be the best mother possible. She's going to absolutely kill it. What was she even thinking all this while? She looks down and mumbles, 'I'm sorry, baby. I'm sorry I thought I wasn't good enough, but of course I am. I'm the best.'

'That's weird. You're talking to a foetus.'

'I will rip your throat out, Adil,' warns Aishwarya. 'Why are you back?'

'Ummm . . . I had a small question. Is it the guy who's going to the US? Or the gaming boy?'

65.

Aishwarya Mohan

Aishwarya can barely breathe as she sits in Adil's car, ready to drive all the way to Dwarka. As Adil floors the pedal, she becomes acutely aware of what's inside her—the beginnings of a baby, her own baby. Her little dream.

'Park here,' says Aishwarya.

'So it's Dhiren?' asks Adil.

She calls out his name.

'DHIREN!'

Adil jumps out of the car. 'It's Dhiren, right?'

There's no answer.

'DHIREN!'

Adil asks again, 'Or have you come here to end things?'

No answer yet again.

'NEERAJ!'

'Is it Akshay?'

'WILL YOU SHUT UP!' says Aishwarya.

Adil shrugs. 'Fine, I won't tell you that Neeraj and Dhiren got released today.'

Aishwarya frowns. 'What? What do you mean they got released today? Where are they?'

Adil takes out his phone.

'I asked you something.'

'Just wait, for fuck's sake!' snaps Adil. 'They signed a contract. There must be an address on it. Here . . .'

He gives the phone to Aishwarya. She reads the address and feels like her breath's stuck for a moment. She composes herself. What's he doing there? It was supposed to be her place—he has no business being there in the first place.

'Let's go,' she orders Adil.

Adil revs up the engine. 'So, is it him?'

The closer she gets to Sector 10, the more urgently her heart begins to thump. As Adil turns around the last corner, a building comes into view. For a moment she thinks she has come to the wrong sector, but how could she? It's the only place she has truly called home. This is where her new life had to start.

'How . . .'

Where once she had left rubble, there's now a three-storey building. She can read the board as they get closer. It says 'Cute Buttons'. For a moment, she thinks she's imagining it. Is she starting to lose it? No, it's really there. The board's huge, and in colour and lights, and is visible from two sectors out. It's straight out of what she had imagined it to be but never had the money for. What's in front of her is not the watered-down version she had made and what had crumbled down. But it was what she would have eventually built when Cute Buttons became a success. Her dream's alive and kicking.

Breathe, she tells herself.

'Stop,' she tells Adil.

She enters through the gate. And right in front of her is a generator. Where it should have always been. If only it would have been there . . .

The lawn is neatly trimmed and such a perfect green that it almost looks fake. When she barges in through the front door, it takes her breath away. Her heart's torn. She's furious, but she's also in awe. It's like she has decorated and designed the place. Every idea of hers has been replicated precisely and made better. The characters she had made then, and the characters from her books, are all there on the walls. It's Cute Buttons just as she had imagined it, if not better. It brings tears to her eyes. In the corner, Dhiren and Neeraj are bent over a table discussing something in animated voices.

'DHIREN!'

They both turn to look at her and are as surprised as she is.

'What . . . are you doing here?' asks Neeraj, raising his hands as if caught mid-crime. 'I should get out of here.' When he passes Aishwarya, he tells her, 'It's his doing, so don't come after me.'

She looks at Dhiren who straightens up and looks unfazed.

'Why?' she asks him.

She doesn't wait for an answer. Instead, she walks around, checking if it is a real school or a prank set. Walls made out of cardboard, printouts instead of real paintings. But it's not—it's a nursery built with the finest details. It's her dream.

'Why not? And what else if not this, Aishwarya?' asks Dhiren softly.

'Since when?'

'Been a few months,' he says. 'I had plenty of time on my hands.'

'But—'

'Neeraj said it was my calling. He can be wrong about a lot of things, but I figured he was right about this one. My calling was being around children. You made me see that.'

'This is not a joke.'

'Let me see,' says Dhiren. 'I have no money because obviously I gave the last of it away. And with the rest I had left, I played this really expensive joke. This is not a joke, Aishwarya. If there's anything I have truly wanted in my life, it's this. Of course, I wanted this with you, but I can't have you, so this is the next best thing.'

Aishwarya's eyes well up. 'Why didn't you tell me?'

'And then what? Spend the rest of my life trying to convince you that I have changed? I tried and you didn't believe me.'

'This is what you're going to do?' asks Aishwarya, realizing where the missing money went. 'You're going to run a nursery?'

'I am going to try. Being here gives me happiness. This is the place where I have found peace after the longest time. I found you, and for the first time, I felt like I had found my family. I don't plan to give this up. Cute Buttons and you are my peace. I intend to keep this with me.'

'And the gaming contract with the BCCI?'

'Neeraj is going to make the games, but he's going to hang around here. He always circles back to me.'

'Is that what everyone around you does?'

'Not everyone,' answers Dhiren. 'Not you.'

'I'm here.'

'Not for long. A new life awaits you overseas, doesn't it? The US? A big house, a family and whatnot. A life away from me.'

Tears stream down Aishwarya's face. Her heart feels full. 'Dhiren.'

'Aishwarya, thank you for—'

'I'm pregnant.'

'What?'

'You heard it.'

Aishwarya watches Dhiren's eyes burn. For all that he has done to her, she lets him burn up inside.

'Good for you. Congratulations! This is what you wanted, so good on you. The child is going to be extremely lucky to have you as her mother,' he says, barely able to muster up the words.

'Is it though? Is it good?'

'This was always your dream. Akshay and you having a baby together. Congratulations. You're going to be a great mother.'

Dhiren's trying, but Aishwarya can see the tears in his eyes.

'I also wanted this,' she looks around, '. . . from the very beginning. This is my dream, not yours.'

'Well, now I have it. Akshay has something of you, and I have something of you. *Hisaab barabar* [Now it's balanced on both sides].'

Aishwarya shakes her head. She walks up to Dhiren and locks her gaze with his. 'Dhiren, I am not to be divided. This child is my dream, this school is my dream and I ought to have them both. I can't give anything up. I have suffered enough and I want to put a stop to it. I want everything. I want love, I want my baby and I want my dream.'

'Why are you here?' he asks, trying his best not to crumble.

'Because this is where I always should have been,' she replies.

'But you are leaving now.'

'I just told you I'm pregnant.'

'So?' he says, his eyes burning embers, the nerve in his forehead pulsating.

'Akshay and I hadn't started trying.'

Dhiren takes a moment for it to settle in. 'What?'

Aishwarya takes a deep breath before she speaks again. 'We were supposed to start trying once we got to the US. We weren't having sex . . . it was only you,' she says.

Dhiren's face is clouded with confusion. 'What are you talking about?'

Aishwarya takes a deep breath. 'There was a very minuscule chance of the contraception failing, and it failed with us.'

'You're saying . . .'

Aishwarya nods. A lone tear streams down her cheek. 'Exactly that.'

'You're saying . . .'

'She's saying that you got her pregnant!' beams Adil who has sneaked in behind her. 'Strong sperm.'

'Fuck off,' says Aishwarya.

'I agree,' says Dhiren.

'I don't think you should be using that language here,' adds Neeraj.

Aishwarya reaches out to Dhiren and holds him. She lets him pull her close till she can feel his breath on her face. 'I'm going nowhere,' she says with a smile. 'Where would I go, Dhiren? I circle back and come to you. You're my family.'

Dhiren pulls her closer and plants his lips on hers. He grips her tight as if she will run away if he doesn't. With tears streaming down his cheeks, he mumbles softly, 'I love you, Aishwarya.'

'Thank you, Dhiren,' she says softly.

'Is that what you're going with?'

'For now,' says Aishwarya. 'That's what I'm going with. And also, I don't like the yellow paint. Do you think—'

Her sentence is cut off with a kiss.